Also by Desley Moore:

Such Morning Songs
The Apple Boughs

ONCE BELOW A TIME

by

DESLEY MOORE

BAHIA HOUSE PRESS
Brynfeinion, Dolwen, Llanidloes, Powys SY18 6LL

First published in Great Britain 2001 by
BAHIA HOUSE PRESS
Brynfeinion, Dolwen, Llanidloes, Powys, SY18 6LL, U.K.

British Library Cataloguing-in-Publication Data.
A catalogue record for this book is available
from the British Library.

ISBN: 0-9531502-1-6

Printed by Manuscript ReSearch Printing
P.O. Box 33, Bicester, Oxon, OX26 4ZZ, UKTel: 01869 323447/322552

And once below a time I lordly had the trees and leaves
Trail with daisies and barley
Down the rivers of the windfall light.

"Fern Hill"—Dylan Thomas

DEDICATION

This is for Newtown, my town,
the real central character of this Trilogy.
I love the old town, warts and all!

INTRODUCTION

In this the final part of *The Newtown Trilogy,* change comes to the little valley town in a most rapid and potentially cataclysmic form. The tendrils of one of the most malignant and evil events in the history of the world namely the Second World War reached out to families world-wide and not even the peace-loving Rees family could avoid their venomous touch.

It came in time for Mama and Dada, now failing but still the still centre of the family, to feel its initial effects: grandchildren in uniform, some more and some less enthusiastic, disappearing for long periods of time; air-raid warnings, gas masks, the home guard, bombs and ARP wardens, bringing insecurity and strange new concepts into the home.

On the positive side was the joyful, for some, return from the 'Diaspora' of Canada of part of the family, offset somewhat by the sorrows and hard times suffered by Reini and family. Times of war bring the most mixed and extreme of emotions.

Newtown itself, suffered its own invasions becoming a garrison town with various regiments stationed at various times, with none making more short and long term impact than the Irishmen of the 'Inniskillins'.

The local 'Dad's Army' made their mark with, at times, weird and wonderful exploits worthy of that fine TV series, and Newtown's eccentrics and eccentricities showed their heads well above the wartime parapets.

The stories in this book, as in the others, are the eternal ones of love and loss, of good and evil, happiness and tragedy, passion and hatred, in a Newtown marked deeply by the war but with the core of its identity still solid. The tale is told with warmth and humour in Desley Moore's usual acutely observed and humorous style, and with an affection that comes from her very real love of her Mid-Wales and its people.

CONTENTS

ACKNOWLEDGEMENTS

The author would like to thank David Higham Associates Limited and Dent publishers for granting permission to use the extract from 'Fern Hill' in *The Poems* by Dylan Thomas which is quoted at the beginning of this book and includes the title phrase *Once Below A Time*.

The author also wishes to thank Llyfrgell Genedlaethol Cymru/The National Library of Wales for permission to use the photograph of soldiers embarking at Newtown Railway Station from the Geoff Charles Collection which forms the cover illustration.

PART ONE

1

Franco and First Love

The birds were well into the dawn chorus in the old fir tree at Plas Gwyn when Edward woke on a Saturday morning in late April. He lay on his back for a while, savouring the fact that he was on holiday and could take his time in getting up. He stared out of the window of his bedroom and his gaze took in the cloudless blue sky of this first Saturday after Easter. He ruminated on his two years at Aberystwyth University, affectionately known as 'Aber Coll', two very happy years reading Economics and Law, hopefully preparatory to entering the office of Martin Phillips, his cousin Esther's husband. Martin had promised to give him a start in his solicitor's practice if Edward did well, and without being cocky, Edward felt pretty confident that the next two years would see him with the necessary qualifications. He yawned and raised himself up on an elbow to watch a dove which sat at the top of the fir tree uttering its mournful cry. Why did it have to sound so sad? After all, it was free - free to fly wherever it wanted. But perhaps it was hungry. Never mind, Mam always threw bread out on the lawn for the birds after breakfast. The dove could surely wait that long.

He lowered himself back onto his pillow and stretched his five-foot-eleven length luxuriously down the bed. He linked his hands behind his head and gave himself up to peaceful and contented thoughts. He might have known the peace wouldn't last! The door flew open and his younger brother, Huw, catapulted himself onto the bed, his dark curls standing on end, his eyes glinting with mischief. Edward groaned.

'Oh, no! Not you. What do you want, trouble?'

Edward drew his knees up as Huw bounced on his bed and cried

'Oh, don't be so stuffy, Ned,' then lowering his voice to a whisper, 'Got any fags?'

Edward winced at the weight on his feet. 'No. And If I had you wouldn't get any. You know what Mam says about you smoking. And don't call me Ned.'

'Mam needn't know. You don't have to tell her,' Huw wheedled, squeezing the hump of Edward's knees under the bedclothes.

'Ow! Stop that, or else!' Edward threatened. 'Get off my bed and leave me alone, will you?'

'Yep, I will, if you give me a fag.' Huw's eyes narrowed and he gave Edward's knees another thump.

'Look, why have you never got any fags of your own?' Edward pushed the younger lad away, exasperated. 'You get more money from Pryce Jones's than I get allowance. Why have you never got any fags of your own? You're always smoking OP's.'

'It's cheaper to smoke other people's!' Huw grinned.

'I don't know what you do with your money,' grumbled Edward. 'Anyway my fags are downstairs in my coat pocket. If you'll get off my bed I may get up and then we'll see. There'll be no more peace now anyway, will there?'

Huw got up and made for the door. He looked back at Edward. 'What do you want peace for, anyway? You talk like an old man. The last thing I want is peace!' He went out, banging the door behind him. Edward blew an exasperated raspberry after him and then gave a rueful grin. For all his irritating ways, the insouciant charm of his 18-year old brother usually found its way to Edward's soft heart, for he loved the rascal. It was the attraction of opposites, for Edward's character was in complete contrast to that of Huw.

Where Edward was steady, thoughtful and worked hard at his studies, Huw was mercurial and although he was bright and intelligent, he had never had the application to settle to his school work and had ended up in the tailoring department at Pryce Jones's, where he was apprentice to the chief cutter, Mr Jesse Pryce, whose efforts to keep Huw's nose to the grindstone were often undermined by the tailoresses, fair game for Huw's charm and high spirits. However, he was very popular in the department and did at least appear to be learning the trade. He was good-looking, with his dark curls inherited from his father, Davy, and his large dark eyes which he used to great advantage, especially where females were concerned! Edward was as fair as Huw was dark, taking after his mother. They were both tall and good-looking, and Davy and Nan, their parents were proud of them, despite the hot water that Huw got into, more frequently than was comfortable.

Edward rose and got dressed. When he had drawn on his flannel trousers and a well-darned blue jumper he leaned for a moment on the windowsill of his room. The dove still mourned on top of the fir tree, and to the left he could just see the tall trees of the Rectory drive. He watched the rooks coming and going from their nests with loud and raucous cries and smelled the sweetness of the morning. Below his window was a border of wallflowers and their perfume wafted up to delight his nostrils. He drew a deep breath then turned and left the room to go downstairs. His mother and father were in the kitchen which was warm and full of the smell of rising dough from the bowl placed near the fire for that purpose. All the Rees family declared that they could not eat shop bread, although there were a number of very good bakers in Newtown. But they had been brought up on Mama's home-made bread, three loaves of which had been freshly baked every morning until Mama had to finally admit that at seventy-seven she was getting too old to cope with that and with the weekly wash. Nan, Edward's mother, had taken over these tasks and Mama had nodded and placed the seal of approval on Nan's bread, to the relief of everyone. So an extra loaf was baked each morning to take down to Pool Road, where Mama and Dada now lived alone, since Esther's marriage to Martin Phillips and Owen's to Lena Owen. Dada was also seventy-seven and although he spent most of his day in the old wooden armchair beside the fire, his joints stiff with rheumatism, his blue eyes were still bright under beetling white brows and his thatch of fluffy white hair still stood erect like a halo, despite Mama's best efforts with a brush. At the moment both Dada and Mama had an extra excitement to make their old eyes sparkle and it was this that Nan and Davy were discussing when Edward entered the kitchen and took his place at the table.

'How many years is it now since Nell and Elwyn went to Canada?' Nan was asking. She nodded and smiled at Edward and reached for the big brown teapot which stood on the warm hob, to pour tea for him.

'More than I like to think,' Davy answered ruefully and his hand came up to stroke the wings of white in his dark hair. 'Anyway, as you know, they've got two children, a girl and a boy, and now that Elwyn has retired from the Canadian police they're going to settle back in Newtown. Good thing, too. They can look after Mama and Dada. There's plenty of room for them at Pool Road. From what Mama says, Nell is keen to take over Mrs Moses Owen's hat shop. Nell was a good milliner. Trained by old Madam Benyon, you had to be good! She was a proper old Madam, right enough.' Davy scraped the last of his porridge from the bowl in front of him, which he then pushed aside to take a slice of the good sweet bread, baked yesterday, and to spread it liberally with pale farm butter and a little of Nan's blackcurrant jam.

Nan ladled porridge into the bowl in front of Edward which he sprinkled thickly with sugar and onto which he poured creamy milk before attacking it with gusto. 'When are the Canadians coming?' he asked as soon as he had emptied his mouth.

'They should be here a fortnight today,' Davy answered. 'And don't call them Canadians, either. I don't know about the young ones but Elwyn and Nell still think of themselves as Welsh. Elwyn was Welsh-speaking anyway. The youngsters were given Welsh names, too. Rhiannon Mair and Gareth Rhys. Can't get much more Welsh than that can you?' He chuckled and took another bite of his bread and jam.

'Hmm,' Edward mused. 'Wonder what they'll be like? The girl's older than me, isn't' she?'

'About a year older, that's all. The boy is the same age as Huw. And where is that young rip, anyway? Time he was up. He promised to go down to Pool Road and chop morning sticks for them.

At that Huw came into the room and took his seat beside Edward. He beamed round the table and when his porridge was placed in front of him, set to and soon demolished it. He was soon cramming his mouth with bread and jam and his mother shook her head in mock despair.

'Take your time, Huw, will you? Why do you have to do everything in a hurry?'

'Well, Dad's on about the morning sticks for Pool Road, isn't he?' Huw protested through a mouthful of bread. 'Got to get on with it. Got a lot of things to do today.'

' Like what?' asked his father, with raised eyebrows. 'Oh, this and that,' said Huw, airily.

'I don't suppose 'this and that' includes giving me a hand to put in those cabbage plants today, does it?' Davy enquired mildly.

'Um, - don't know whether I'll have time today, Dad,' Huw rose from his seat hurriedly, stuffing the last mouthful of breakfast into his mouth. 'Going down to Pool Road now. See you at dinner-time. Daresay Ned here will give you a hand with the cabbage plants, won't you, Ned?' He grinned wickedly at his brother and disappeared in the direction of the back door.

Edward shook his head and smiled a little ruefully at his father. 'Funny we never seem to see much in the way of results from all his activity. Ah, well, that's Huw.' Nan and Davy sighed and nodded agreement. That, indeed, was Huw.

When Huw arrived at No.46 Pool Road, it was to find Dada, having finished his breakfast, seated in his chair by a roaring fire while Mama cleared away the breakfast dishes and carried them into the back kitchen. She moved much more slowly these days and her shoulders were a little bowed but the old indomitable spirit still showed in the sharpness of her tongue and the shrewdness of her dark eyes which were undimmed. When Huw bounced in she braced herself against the table and frowned at him.

'Boy, you are like an old whirlwind about the place. What are you in such a hurry about?'

'Come to chop your sticks, Mama. 'Morning Dada,' he raised his voice and smiled ingratiatingly.

Dada grunted. 'There are still a few cut sticks there, I do think. But you may as well chop a few more, seeing as how you've come. What is going on in the world this day? I see and hear nothing stuck in this old chair all day,' he added with an air of pathos.

Mama snorted, 'You do not miss much, my boy. You do know more of what is going on than I do, anyway. It is wonderful how long you can stand on that doorstep and gossip with all who do pass by. More than I have got time to do, that's a fact.' She picked up the last of the dishes and made her way out to the back.

'Half an hour at the most is all I can stand on the doorstep for,' Dada complained to Huw, indignantly, 'And who do I see passing, anyway? Jack Richards the Milk some days. He does pick up a bit of news from the women on his round, right enough, but he does not have much time to spare to tell it. He did tell me yesterday as Annie Bertha Lloyd has been sneaking down the Woolpack and pinching the mint that oul' Edwin Pugh grows in that bit of ground under his window. What the woman does not know is that Edwin Pugh throws his night slops onto that bit of ground.' Dada chuckled and blew into his whiskers. 'That is why that mint grows nice and strong, dessay.'

Huw pulled a face but he had to laugh at Dada, who went on,' The only other one I do see is Jumping Jesus and he is gone dafter than ever. You know what he asked me the other day?' Huw shook his head. 'Well,' said Dada, frowning fiercely, 'He asked me - me, mind you, a man who has been to church every Sunday of his life, and chapel before that, mind, every week indeed until just lately when I cannot walk that far. Yes, he had the cheek to ask me if I had been saved. 'Saved from what' says I. 'Saved from all your sins.' says he. I told him to mind his own business. My sins is my business, not his. Dessay he's got plenty of his own to worry about, from all I hear.' Dada went on darkly. 'Anyway, what chance have I to have sins with Mama breathing down my neck all day. Indeed, I told the man that I would welcome a few sins to call my own. Brighten things up a bit, like.'

'What old nonsense are you filling the boy up with now?' scolded Mama, appearing at that moment.

'Nothing, nothing,' Dada waved a hand dismissively. 'Just saying, I was. The day of judgement will be here any minute, according to that old fool. It is just as well that it did not come a few years ago. I might have had a few more sins to boast about then. There would have been more for the Lord to get his teeth into, isn't it?' He grinned as wolfishly as possible with only four teeth in his head. Mama was unimpressed. Shaking her head at Dada she turned to Huw. 'Come you and I will show you what I want chopped. Take no notice of that old man. If he has no sins of his own, he causes me to have enough.' She tossed her head and shed one or two hairpins from her thinning bun. Huw followed her out through the back door still laughing.

As they went out to the back, the front door opened and Llew and Owen came in. They had met up on the doorstep and were chuckling at a quip made by Llew. Owen was now taller than his Dad, but there was no mistaking the relationship, both had the same dark hair, flopping over their foreheads, although Llew's was well streaked with grey now whereas Owen's was still as dark and shiny as a blackbird's wing. The eyes of both were dark but there was a cynical light in Llew's which reflected his concern with all that was wrong in the world. Dada looked up at their entrance almost apprehensively. When these two got started on the old politics and socialism there was something disturbing in the air which Dada did not understand. But they greeted him happily now and he nodded and had his usual little grumble over his rheumatics and his worries over whether his garden was going to rack and ruin at the hands of Davy and his sons.

'Now, now, Dada. You know quite well that Davy puts in a lot of work on that old garden,' scolded Llew. 'I have been up to have a look round last week-end and it is looking right good. When Edward is home he puts in a good few hours there, too. I don't know about that rapscallion, Huw.'

'Shush!' warned Dada, with a finger to his lips. 'The boy is out the back chopping sticks for Mama. He is all right, mark you. Mind your tongue, Llew.'

'Aye well. Let's hope so. Not a patch on Edward though, whether you like it or not.'

'Edward is very quiet,' remarked Dada. 'A scholar is he. Sometimes I think I understand a rapscallion better than I do a scholar.' and he chuckled into his whiskers.

'I can think of a reason for that, Dada,' chuckled Llew back. 'Anyway, Nell will be back with us soon. It'll be good to see her. And Elwyn, too. We never really had a chance to get to know Elwyn before they went off to Canada. Nell kept quiet about her courtship. Must have been a steady sort of a chap, policeman and all. And the two young ones are Canadians, born there. Wonder how they'll fit in here? Be a big difference, daresay.'

'It will indeed be good to see our Nell again,' said Dada, taking out his red spotted handkerchief and blowing his nose loudly and wiping

23

his eyes. 'A sharp tongue she did have but she was a good girl and worked hard. Wants to start making hats again, so Mama says. Why for, I don't know. Surely they will have enough to live on with Elwyn getting a big pension from the Canadian police. The young ones will be old enough to work now, surely. No need for our Nell to go out working. She is getting no younger, anyway. I am not for these women going out to work if they have husbands to keep them and plenty to do at home. Your Mama never went out to work.'

'Out to work!' Mama came in at that moment and stared at Dada with raised eyebrows. 'I always had too much to do at home here. Bringing up my own four and then I had Owen and Esther to see to. Out to work indeed!' she said, indignantly.

'That is what I am saying, girl!' Dada defended himself. 'I was saying I do not hold with women going out to work when they have a husband to keep them and the children. That's why I don't see why our Nell wants to go out making hats.'

'I don't know that there is so much call for women's hats like there used to be,' mused Llew. 'Certainly not the big fussy things that Nell used to make at Madam Benyon's. Women's hats are mostly little things now, with only a feather or two for trimming. No bows and flowers and cherries and things, these days.'

Mama carried the teapot to the table and fetched in cups and saucers. 'You will take a cup of tea in your hands, you two? Dada and me will be having a cup now. I had better pour one for that young whippet, Huw. He has about finished chopping the sticks.'

On that Huw came in from the back, flushed and beaming. 'Done you enough for a week, Mama,' he announced. He sat down between Llew and Owen and blew on his tea to cool it. 'How d'you think this war in Spain is going, Uncle Llew? Think Franco is going to win?'

Llew sighed. 'I don't want to think so, but I'm very much afraid he will. Just read in the paper this morning about a place called Guernica. Hitler's air force have bombed it. Hitler is well prepared for war, any war. He's just flexing his muscles with this one. When he's finished in Spain, the rest of Europe had better look out. Him and old Mussolini, they're a bad lot. And there's too many people in our Government and among the aristocracy who are all for those two. They're going to be sorry some day, when it's too late.'

'Wouldn't mind having a go with the International Brigade myself,' Huw said, nodding. 'I'd go tomorrow, but Dad won't hear of it. Can't make him out. He's on the side of the Government troops in Spain, I know. He never lets you forget what a villain Franco is.'

'No point in going now, Huw, boy.' Llew sipped his tea thoughtfully. 'The cause is good but its lost, I'm afraid.'

Owen chipped in. 'I'm not willing to fight in any war unless its Wales that is threatened. I don't believe in fighting wars for somebody else.'

Llew laughed and clapped Owen on the back. 'Good you. Stick to that, my boy. I went to fight somebody else's war, but I vowed never again. We never even knew what we were fighting for.'

Huw gulped the remainder of his tea down. 'Well, if ever there is another war I am going to get into the Air Force. Flying sounds like fun.'

Dada had been listening in some bewilderment to the conversation, but the last remark of Huw's made him frown. 'What are you talking about, boy? If the good Lord had meant you to fly he would have put wings on your back. But he did only give them to the angels. I do not see you sprouting any yet.' His blue eyes twinkled at Huw who laughed and got up from his chair. 'No Dada, no fear of wings for me yet. At least not the feathered kind. But to fly in an aeroplane would be bozo. Must go now. Things to do. Ta-ra all.'

He lunged out, banging the door behind him and making Mama jump. 'Nemma dear,' she breathed. 'The boy is always in a hurry. Where he will end up, I don't know. He does wear me out just to look at him.'

'Never mind, Mama. You will soon have Nell to help you.'

'How will she help her Mama if she is going to go out to work making hats?' Dada asked, querulously. 'If she does that it will end up with your Mama looking after Nell's lot as well.'

Mama sighed wearily, 'Leave it now, boy. Anybody would think you won't be glad to see them come. Nell's children are well grown now. They will be able to help in the house, no doubt. The girl is twenty years old.'

Dada grunted. 'We are getting old, you and me. They must look to themselves and to us, too.'

'Quite right, Dada,' said Owen, passing up his cup for more tea. 'I don't remember Nell. She'd gone before I came on the scene. I was Meg's boy. I've always loved Meg.'

Dada's old eyes softened at the mention of his favourite. 'Meggie is good and always was. She settled down real happy with her German fellow. A good man that, tidy farmer too. I think that young Henry will take after him.'

Llew nodded. 'They've made a good go of the Walkmill. It's a very good farm. I like old Reini. He's a jannock bloke. Made our Meg a happy woman, anyway, and that's enough for me. She'd been through enough after that old fire. Funny how you never notice that old scar on her face nowadays. You're drawn to the shine in her eyes instead, perhaps.'

Mama nodded. 'She is right pretty again, now. She has a good man, thank the Lord, and a fine son. Enough to keep any tidy woman happy.' 'Indeed,' twinkled Dada, 'That's the way I kept you happy.' And for once Mama didn't argue with him!

In the meantime, Edward had decided to walk up to Bay House in Bryn Street to see Esther. He and his cousin had always been close, ever since the days when she nursed him as a baby and coveted him. Now she had two babies of her own, little blonde Mary, a five-year-old charmer who adored Edward and two-year- old Alun, a solemn little boy who followed his livelier sister around like a small shadow. Esther was a happy and fulfilled wife and mother, who at the moment suspected that she might be once again pregnant and was beginning to feel comfortably broody again. She had always wanted a large family and Martin, her husband, was so besotted with her that he was quite willing to indulge her. His business as a lawyer was thriving and they were comfortably off. They could even afford to have a woman to come in daily to help Esther to run her large house and look after the children.

Edward strolled through the town on this Saturday morning, enjoying the bustle as people went about their week-end shopping, fetched their bread from Pugh Humphreys's or Evan Evans's, and chose their meat from Maurice Powell's butcher's shop in High Street or from Dick Jones, Brimmon, in the Market Hall. The errand-boy from Mr Swain, the grocer was pedalling his bike along Short Bridge Street, with its big carrier in the front, getting ready to stand on the pedals for extra push as he came to hilly Kerry Road. The boy's hair stood up in spikes from the sweat he was working up and Edward remembered his days working as a delivery boy for Melia's in Market Street, in order to earn his pocket money while he was at the County School. He stopped to look over the Bridge Wall at the river below, running quietly over the stones, shining in the sunlight, with the black-headed gulls swooping and gliding over it. He leaned contentedly with his elbows on the wall and watched the piebald ponies on the Rackfield on the opposite side of the river. The spring was getting to them and they gambolled and frisked like large lambs, enjoying the sunlight. Edward was conscious of how much he loved the old town and was glad that there would be a job waiting here for him when he had, hopefully, finished his finals.

He strolled on, passing housewives with large baskets over their arms, sometimes with small children clinging to their skirts, or younger women pushing prams or pushchairs with round-faced, chubby-legged occupants. Here and there the women stopped to gossip with friends and older men meandered along with daily papers tucked under their arms. Edward enjoyed the leisurely Saturday morning bustle in Broad Street and was about to turn into Griffiths and Griffiths paper shop when he passed two old men standing outside the shop, gloomily regarding the cards in the window, which told of the latest deaths of Newtown's inhabitants.

'I see oul' Ivvy Plum 'as gone.' the one said. 'Well, 'e allus did say as 'is feet was killin' 'im.' He grinned toothlessly at his own wit. 'Will thee be goin' to 'is funeral?'

The other considered this solemnly. 'No, I dunna think so. Why should I? He wunna be comin' to mine, will 'e?' This was unanswerable and they moved on, while Edward stifled a chuckle and went inside to buy his 'Daily Despatch'. Possessed of this he wandered on up Broad Street, his eyes lifted to the Bryn Bank, which looked over the town, and which at this time of year was just beginning to display its golden cover of gorse, among which sheep could be seen grazing. He knew that over the brow of the hill stood the old Bryn farmhouse, a Tudor-style building with across its facade the enigmatic legend 'Not we from Kings, but Kings from us'. Many people took this to mean that the ubiquitous Charles 1st had stayed there, but this was not so. Edward's main interest in the farm was not its legend or its history, but the daughter,

Ruth, on whom he had had a schoolboy crush and who was still inclined to enter his dreams from time to time, with her tip-tilted nose, dark eyes and mop of unruly black curls. The very opposite of Edward both in looks and temperament, there had been an attraction of opposites and although it had never progressed further than a walk hand-in-hand up the Bryn Wood, Edward still looked on it as his first and only romance to date. He had been working too hard at Aberystwyth to have time for girls, although his tall, good looks meant he could have had his chances. He was friendly with many of the students, both male and female but as yet had not fallen very hard for anyone .

Now he crossed the Iron Bridge, looking over the side at the river flowing peacefully below, reflecting the tower and ruins of the old St Mary's church on the right bank, with its row of poplars standing to attention like guards beside the church wall. An optimistic man was fishing from the bank below the church and on the other side of the river Dick the Boats tended his punts and two canoes, from which he would earn a meagre living as the weather improved. He looked up as Edward drew opposite him on the bridge and raised his cap, giving a gap-toothed grin, which Edward returned with a cheerful wave. At the end of the bridge was Miss Andrews' small sweet-shop, once the Bridgend Inn, and Edward turned into the dim little shop to buy some sweets for Mary and Alun. The bell above the door summoned Miss Andrews from the nether regions and she twittered and fussed while he made up his mind between toasted teacakes and jelly babies, then decided to have a pennorth of each and let the children decide which they wanted.

Miss Andrew asked after each member of the Rees family in turn, remembering everyone by name, which took some time, but at last Edward edged his smiling way to the door and almost bumped into a girl who was entering.

'Hello, Edward! You home again? How's things?' The bright voice and even brighter gaze from the dark eyes brought a flush to his cheeks. It seemed as if she had just been conjured up by his thoughts and he stammered some reply as he pulled himself together. 'See you in a minute,' she said, smiling at him and he took this to mean he was to wait outside for her. He felt a rising excitement as he stood on the pavement outside the shop and found that he was still grinning foolishly when the bell clanged and she came out of the shop. She held out her hand to shake his and he hurriedly stuffed the sweets into his pocket, and reached out and took her small warm hand in his, experiencing a small tremor at the contact.

'Hello, Ruth. Long time no see!' His flush deepened as he realised the triteness of what he had said. He groped for something more original to say, but she grinned up at him unselfconsciously.

'You're still at Aber', yes?' she asked. 'Liking it ok?'

'Oh, yes. It's grand. Reading Law and Economics. Hope to go into Martin Phillips's office if I do all right.'

'Oh, of course, he married into your family, didn't he? Married Esther Rees. He's a nice chap and doing pretty well, I believe. So you're to be a lawyer, too, Edward?'

He found himself seemingly trapped in the sparkle from her dark eyes and answered almost automatically. 'Well, I hope so. Look, Ruth, I'm home for another two weeks. I'd like to see you again. What do you do these days? Are you working?'

'Me? No, well I don't go out to work. Have to help out at home. Mam's not to good these days and Dad doesn't like strangers coming in, so I've had to cope.' She shrugged and turned her head away for a moment. 'Its ok though. I don't mind, really,' but when she turned back to him he saw a shadow in her eyes.

'What about some evening? Can you come out to the pictures?' he asked, eagerly.

'I'd love that,' she answered earnestly. 'Why not? When?'

'How about Tuesday? I think there's a 'Thin Man' film on. D'you like William Powell in the 'Thin Man' films?'

'That would be lovely.' She dimpled and Edward caught his breath. 'Right then. First or second House?'

'Oh, first House, I think. Then I'll have plenty of time to get home before dark.'

Edward took her hand again and squeezed it. 'Don't worry, I'll see you home safely,' he assured her, before she withdrew her hand and with a smile and a little wave and a 'See you about six on Tuesday then.' she turned to walk briskly off down the bridge.

'Outside the Regent, all right?' he called after her and as she turned her head and nodded. 'I'll be waiting,' he added.

He watched her disappearing over the bridge and sticking his hands in his pockets teetered from heel to toe. That was quick work, he thought to himself and grinned. He felt sure she still liked him and his heart gave a flutter. He still liked her, didn't he? He thought of the dimple and the flashing eyes and turning on his heel and went on his way, whistling a tune and feeling no end of a gay dog.

2

Reunions and Wishing Wells

The train to Aberystwyth, reaching Newtown at four-thirty in the afternoon, had just left Shrewsbury. Elwyn and Nell Jones and their family were tired of travelling, but Elwyn and Nell were buoyed up by the longing to see their old home again, and Gareth, their son, was excited at the thought of seeing Wales for the first time, for his father had filled his head with Welsh folk-lore and pictures of his beautiful native land. However, Rhiannon sulked in the corner of the carriage, her lovely face spoiled by the resentful expression that marred her slanting dark eyes and caused the cupid's-bow lips to droop disagreeably. She hadn't wanted to leave Canada and all her friends and bitterly resented being dragged in the wake of her family to this back-of-beyond country, which was how she thought of Wales. Whereas Gareth had been keen to learn Welsh from his father and now had a good working knowledge of the language. Rhiannon had refused point-blank to even try to master what sounded to her like an outlandish language. She had happily learned French while in Canada, and spoke that fluently, partly because it seemed to her to be a 'sophisticated' sort of language, and she hoped above all some day to go to Paris, her Mecca.

She yawned and threw down the magazine which she had been leafing through with a bored air. 'For goodness sake, how much longer?' she grumbled to her mother.

'Not long now,' Nell assured her, 'And for heaven's sake, stop looking so disagreeable. If you keep on like this what on earth will the family in Newtown think of you?'

Rhiannon shrugged, 'To tell the truth, I don't really care what they think of me. I didn't want to come and I don't intend to stay. As soon as

I've saved enough money I'm off, either back to Canada or try my luck in Paris. I've been told I could earn my living as a model. Well I don't suppose there are many opportunities for that in Wales.'

She twisted a long dark curl silkily around her finger and turned to stare out of the window moodily.

'That's enough, Rhiannon!' Her father's voice was sharp with exasperation. 'We've listened to your moans and bad-temper from the time we left Canada and I for one am sick of it. Your mother and I are coming home at long last, something we've dreamed about for years You may make the best of it, my girl, and if you decide to go back then you can go. But first you'll buckle down and work, for I won't be paying your fare! Spoiled, you've been, with your Mam and I working hard to give you the best of everything, while never a hand's turn have you done for yourself. So you'd better brighten up and put a good face on it, for if you let us down with your sulks, Lady Jane, you'll be sorry!'

Rhiannon didn't answer, but her pretty lips tightened and with a lift of her shoulder she turned away from them. Nell frowned and shook her head, then her gaze softened as she took in the eager face of her son as he studied the changing landscape outside. The flat Shropshire plain was giving way to rolling hills and wooded slopes as the train ran over the border into Wales. Elwyn leaned forward with a sigh and stared out of the window as at a dream at long last coming true. He turned and smiled at Nell and she reached to squeeze his hand, her own eyes misty. They were really home at last after all the long years and their hearts were full.

'Is this Wales, Dad?' Gareth asked, 'Are we there?'

Elwyn nodded and grinned at his son, 'Yes, boy, we're there. Home at last. You know when you cross the border and come into the hills. Then you're in Wales, land of your fathers, lad, land of your fathers.'

Gareth's eyes shone as he caught his father's excitement but Rhiannon's lips curled as she looked over her shoulder at her brother.

'Huh! How can you be Welsh when you were born in Canada. You're Canadian, same as me. I'm not going to forget that, anyway.'

Eventually the train drew into Newtown Station and the newly returned Jones family gathered their luggage together and climbed down from the carriage. Elwyn went in search of the Guard to make arrangements for their trunks to be taken to 46 Pool Road and then they made their way over the bridge to the exit. Rhiannon looked round the small, sleepy station. 'What a dump!' she murmured. Nell shot her a warning glance as they descended the station steps to find Davy and Owen waiting to greet them.

Nell found herself in Davy's arms, unable to believe this middle-aged man with the gold-rimmed glasses and the white wings in his dark hair was the same Davy who was still a schoolboy when she had left. Owen she had to have explained to her and in turn she introduced the two younger ones. Davy and Owen shook hands with Rhiannon and Gareth, and Rhiannon's eyes brightened as she took in Owen's dark and handsome looks. Davy and Nell had much to catch up with as they all walked down Station Road, Davy and Owen taking some of the luggage and Elwyn following on, content to let Nell monopolise her younger brother. Owen walked between Rhiannon and Gareth, answering Rhiannon's questions as to what the large Pryce Jones buildings were while Gareth looked round, full of eager curiosity.

As they made their way down Kerry Road and turned into Pool Road, seeing the Bridge Wall and the river beyond, Gareth exclaimed as he recognised the landmarks which his parents had described to him. As they approached No.46, Mama and Dada could be seen standing on the doorstep and Nell began to run towards them, her travel bag banging against her legs as she forgot her middle-aged dignity. She flung herself into Mama's arms and they mingled their tears and incoherent murmurs, while Dada blew his nose and wiped his old eyes which suddenly developed mistiness. When all the greetings were over they were drawn into the house, where the old black kettle sang above a glowing fire and Mama had the old brown pot ready to make them a cup of tea in their hands, before they were shown to their rooms and Mama set about making them a meal, with the help of Nan, who had just arrived through the back door.

When they had settled their belongings in their respective bedrooms they descended the stairs and were soon seated round the table being served a tasty meal consisting of a piece of ham which Mama had boiled that day, accompanied by a selection of pickles and chutney and Nan's bread thickly buttered with fresh butter from the Walkmill, brought by Meg at the weekend. This was followed by an apple tart, made with apples, also from the Walkmill and stored in newspaper in the cellar There was thick yellow custard to top the tart and if anyone still had room there was a sticky lardy cake, thick with currants.

Nell sat back in her chair and wiped her lips with her handkerchief, 'That was good, Mama, Now I know I'm back home when I sit down to a meal like that.'

'Indeed,' agreed Elwyn, blowing his cheeks out and patting his stomach. 'Not but what Nell can put on a good feed when she likes.'

Dada beamed round the table, 'Aye, your Mama feeds us well, with the help of that good girl there,' nodding in the direction of Nan who was clearing away the dishes. 'We are neither of us able to do what we once did, but we do manage, with help from all. They are all very good to us.'

'Well, I am home again now,' said Nell, smiling, 'I can run this house from now on.'

Dada looked doubtfully at Mama, 'Well now, it is still your Mama's house, isn't it? She will be glad of your help, indeed, but you will find she is still the boss woman here.'

Nell laughed, 'Oh, indeed, She will give the orders and I will do what I am told.'

Mama frowned, 'Do not talk as if I am not here. We shall go along very well, I dessay, I am not finished yet, you will find. There is just one or two things I cannot do any longer, like kneading bread and lifting heavy bedclothes out of the wash. The strength is not there now, see.' She got up suddenly and turned to put hot water into the teapot, 'Another cup of tea, anybody?'

Gareth held his cup out and gave Mama a bright smile, ' I would like another cup, please, Nan, And I would like another piece of lardy cake.'

Mama looked pleased. She poured his tea and cut him another slice of the lardy cake. She turned to Rhiannon, 'What about you, girl? Would you like more of anything?' She bent a kindly smile on her grand-daughter, but Rhiannon merely shook her head. 'No thank you.' she said, coolly and looked down at her hands, folded in her lap. Nell's face tightened and she looked across at Elwyn. He shook his head slightly, but said nothing.

'The ferch i is tired after that long old journey, I am thinking. ' said Dada, 'She will get used to us and our ways in time, And you, young shaver,' he grinned at Gareth, who nodded and murmured something through a mouthful of cake, 'You will find plenty of butties with young Huw and Henry and Edward when he is home from Aber. There is a shortage of girls for this young 'oman for company, but Esther and Lena will take you in hand, no doubt. They are not that much older than you, anyway. Pity I do not have the pony and trap these days. Then we could go to Manafon to see our Meggie and her Reini and Henry at the Walkmill. We have had good times at the Walkmill, indeed,' he added, wistfully, 'I do miss my old pony and trap.'

'Whisht, boy,' Mama said, sharply, 'If you had that old pony now you would not be able to drive it with those rheumatics. What you miss is the mischief you got up to with it. That Beehive has missed a good customer since you could no longer manage the trap.'

'Not at all.' Dada's eyebrows beetled with indignation, 'Very seldom was I in the Beehive. Mostly when the old pony did need a drink, and while Mog did have his drink the 'ooman of the house did pull me a pint to tide me over while I waited. Duw, there was a good pint it was, too. They kept a drop of good ale at that Beehive.' His eyes lit up with the memory. 'Them days 'as gone now,' he went on, sadly, 'I do not go far these days.' He turned to Elwyn, full of pathos.

'Never mind, Dada,' Elwyn said, 'I have been thinking I might get myself a car now I am home, if I can drop on one cheap. I would like to see a bit more of Wales, You and me, Dada, we may yet have some good times to ourselves. What do you say?'

Mama snorted. 'He will be ripe for it, you mind. He was all against the old cars when they first came out. Could see no good in them at all. But give him a chance at anything new and he will be there like six men.'

Dada began to look excited, 'I was in a car once. That was to go to All Saints Church when our Esther was married. Bernard Phillips, Martin's Dada had a car and he called for us to go to the Church. I did enjoy that, indeed.'

He was quiet for a while, savouring the delights to come, while Mama and Nell caught up with all the news.

When the front door opened and Edward came in, smiling and eager

35

to meet the new arrivals, Rhiannon stared and her face immediately became animated. Her eyes sparkled at the sight of this tall and handsome young man and when he shook her hand with a firm and warm grip she felt a frisson of excitement through her whole body, 'Maybe this wouldn't be so awful, after all.' She gave a smile which caused Edward to blink, but as he was full of thoughts of the coming evening and his newly found interest in Ruth, unfortunately for Rhiannon, the smile left him cold. He passed on to shake Gareth's hand and immediately felt he was going to like this lad with the frank, open face and boyish smile. It wasn't long before they were joined by Esther, with her two children, and shortly afterwards, Lena. The latter made her way to Owen's side, mistrusting this new and beautiful young woman seated in Mama's front kitchen. Admittedly she seemed to have eyes only for Edward at the moment, but as that young man showed no interest, Lena wasn't going to have her making a set for her Owen. The room was crowded with Rees's as greetings were exchanged amid exclamations of pleasure and surprise. Under cover of this Rhiannon, moved over to the old horsehair sofa and looking at Edward, patted the seat beside her invitingly. To refuse would have looked pointed so Edward went to sit beside her.

Rhiannon looked up into his face and smiled sweetly, 'There are so many things I want to ask you about Newtown and the family. There are so many of you, it's all very confusing.' With her head an one side she adopted a little-girl air. 'Let's start with you.'

'Me?' replied Edward, feeling self-conscious, 'Well, I'm not very interesting. My parents are Davy and Nan, and that makes me a cousin to you, I've got a brother, Huw, two years younger than me. I'm at Aberystwth College - that's part of the University of Wales, you know-reading Law and Economics. Two more years to go and then with a bit of luck I should have a job waiting for me as a lawyer in Martin Phillips's office. That's Esther's husband. That's about all, really. I'm on holiday at the moment, going back next Monday.'

'Oh,' Rhiannon's face fell. 'I've only just met you and soon you're going away again.'

Edward shifted uncomfortably. There was something about this girl which he found disconcerting. No-one could deny that she was good-looking, lovely even, but there was something, yes, predatory in her face and in the intense gaze which Edward distrusted. If she was going to make a set for him, it was just as well he was going back to Coll on Monday. Although since he had met up with Ruth again he had not been so keen to return.

He meant to ask Ruth to write to him and hoped she would consent to wait until the summer hols, which wouldn't be so long. He'd be home again at the end of July. He became aware that Rhiannon had said something to him, and he blushed and said, 'Sorry?'

'I asked you, have you got a girl-friend?' she said, with a teasing light in her eyes.

'Yes, I have,' Edward replied, 'In fact I really must go now. I'm on my way to meet her, as a matter of fact. We're going to the first house of the pictures and I shall be late if I don't get a move on.' He rose with a feeling of relief and after murmuring to his mother and calling, 'See you again soon!' to the rest of the assembly, he went out and closed the door behind him, letting out a long breath, 'Whew!' He hoped he wasn't going to have trouble with that girl. She was altogether too forward for Edward's liking!

Back in the kitchen more tea was offered and drunk and so many voices were raised that Dada, sitting in his old wooden armchair, began to feel confused. Much as he loved his family he began to wish some of them would go. It was all a bit too much for one day. He was used to only himself and Mama nowadays, with visits from all the others at intervals. He looked around at the faces. It was good to see their Nell home again, but he hoped it wouldn't make too many changes. He was too old for changes, he told himself. He wouldn't mind a few rides with Elwyn if the boy did get one of them cars. As for the two young ones, he liked the look of young Gareth. A tidy boy. He would be looking for a job soon, dessay. He looked right bright. As for the girl, well, he wasn't so sure about her. She looked like she could be a handful, indeed. There was a bold look about her. Well, Nell could keep her in order, sure to. She had had a sharp enough way with her years ago, when she kept young Davy up to scratch, and him a tidy lad on the whole. It was to be hoped she would be the master of this young wench, time would tell, time would tell. The voices around him grew fainter and he dozed off as he was wont to do these days.

Rhiannon was also taking little notice of the voices around her. She was lost in her thoughts since Edward had gone. She had felt for the first time a really strong attraction to him. She wanted him and what Rhiannon wanted she set out to get, The fact that he had a current girl-friend she saw as no great obstacle. She knew herself to be beautiful and attractive to men. She had had ample signs of this back home, but none had stirred any answer in her. But this tall, fair boy, with the clear blue eyes which had looked at her with little interest intrigued her. It was unheard of for boys to look at her like that, and there and then she made up her mind that she would use every one of her wiles to attract Edward.

While she was thus musing, the front door flew open and Huw entered in his usual boisterous manner. He stepped in the kitchen doorway and with a smile looked around at the newcomers curiously. Then his bright gaze took in Rhiannon and he drew in a sharp breath. Why, she was the loveliest girl he had ever seen. From that moment poor Huw's normally wayward heart was captured and lost and he went through the other introductions as in a dream, until Rhiannon offered a cool hand which he took, while his heartbeat quickened and he was rendered speechless.

All this was not lost to Nan, who had watched with some anxiety Rhiannon setting her cap at Edward. She thanked heaven that Edward had seemed totally unmoved, for to her with two sons Rhiannon spelt trouble. She had to admit that she did not like what she had seen of the girl so far, but now she looked at her younger son and her heart contracted. His heart was in his eyes. She glanced at Rhiannon and saw her look calculatingly at Huw.

Rhiannon saw another good-looking boy, this time tall, dark and vivid, his black curls flopping over his forehead and his dark eyes gazing at her in a moonstruck way. She could obviously have this one for the asking, but he wasn't Edward and she had set her heart on Edward. However, she stored up the possibilities of Huw in her mind. He might have his uses. He would, at least, brighten up the weeks while Edward was away, if she didn't find anyone better. This fellow was good-looking and obviously smitten. Once again she patted the seat beside her and Huw, dazzled, hurried to accept the invitation. Nan's heart dropped to the pit of her stomach. Oh, no, that looked like trouble ahead. She just hoped that Huw's mercurial temperament would ensure a fast recovery.

The following evening when Edward set out for bell-ringing practice at the Church, Huw decided to appear casually at No 46 Pool Road and see if he could coax Rhiannon into going for a walk with him. However when he arrived there and enquired as to her whereabouts, he was informed that she had gone up to Bay House with Esther. Huw was about to leave but was stopped by Gareth.

'I'd like to go for a walk with you, Huw,' he said, eagerly.

'All right, come on then.' Huw invited with a grin, putting as good a face on it as he could. They set off towards Kerry Road, tall Huw and the slightly shorter Gareth, swinging along together and talking comfortably on the way. Huw wanted to know all about Canada, and whether Elwyn was in the Mounties. Gareth laughed, 'No, He was more or less an ordinary bobby like you have in this country. We didn't have Mounties where we lived in British Columbia. Oh, they were there, but not in our district.' Huw was disappointed, He thought the Mounties sounded very glamorous. Besides they always got their man, didn't they. He listened to the strange accent of Gareth telling of the Indian reservations in the North, which he had once visited with his father, and of the lovely gifts of bead-work and leather-work they had brought home for Nell and Rhiannon. Gareth related to Huw how uncomfortable he had really felt to see these proud people, who had once owned the whole of North America, now reduced to living on a reservation, selling things to tourists. 'The British and the French were mainly responsible for stealing their land and killing most of them,' Gareth went on indignantly, 'They were such a fine race, too, with a great philosophy of life and a wonderful relationship with nature.'

Huw's only idea of Indians was culled from cowboy and Indian films and he had always seen the cowboys as the goodies and the Indians as the baddies so he only grunted at this and began pointing out and naming the places they passed and then they began climbing the Vastre and they needed their breath for mounting the sharp slope. When they reached the top they paused and looked back over the valley, seeing the town nestling in the narrow hollow and nearer at hand the fields climbing on each side of the road. Huw named the fields and their owners:

Hamer's fields on one side, Watkins' fields on the other. Then, as they resumed their walk and they dropped into a hollow he pointed out the farm of Little Brimmon, owned by Dick Jones, who had the butcher's stall in the Market Hall from which Mama bought her meat. He pointed out the shed where the beasts were killed, Gareth shuddered. 'Times I wish I was a vegetarian,' he confessed. 'Aw, no,' Huw shook his head, 'I like my meat. I'd miss a bacon breakfast on a Sunday with the bread dipped in the fat, and a nice leg of lamb for dinner, with mint sauce and new potatoes, and then cold ham and pickles for tea.' He licked his lips and rubbed his flat young stomach, rolling his eyes. Gareth laughed, 'You win, I guess I like my meat too much, too. But I prefer not to think of where the meat comes from.'

They soon turned right to climb the Birches Lane, which would eventually bring them up to the Crows Lump, the highest point of the range of hills to the South of Newtown. Half way up the lane they came upon a small camp of gypsies in a clearing at the left hand side of the lane. One or two brown-skinned and barefoot children stood with fingers in their mouths watching the two youths passing and a full-breasted young woman appeared on the top step of the one caravan, a rope of thick black hair hanging over her shoulder, and regarded them impassively from mysterious dark eyes. Huw nodded and offered a civil 'Good evening' but there was no answer. An older woman squatted beside a fire which burned fitfully and a couple of mongrel dogs raised their heads from where they were lying in the ditch and issued a warning growl. This brought a large, swarthy man to the half-door of the caravan. He muttered something to the woman, shouted in Romany to the dogs and gave the two young men an ingratiating grin and touched his forelock respectfully. The boys responded in friendly manner and trudged on. When they were out of hearing Gareth asked, 'Are they the real gypsies? You know, romanies?'

'Yes, I think so,' Huw nodded, 'You can usually tell, Anyway, that was probably Romany that chap was speaking when he shouted at the dogs. They're quite different from the didicoys you get coming round here, the tinkers, you know. They can be a rough lot, but the Romanies have their own language and culture and they are basically pretty honest folk and very proud. Did you notice that beautiful caravan and the paintings on it, The tinkers would never have anything as nice as that.'

They carried on up the lane and skirted around the foot of the Lump. At the side of a rough path they came upon a square well with a wooden lid which could be lifted to reveal the clear, sparkling water within. They knelt and cupped their hands and drank deep of the pure, cold water. 'Make a wish,' Huw commanded. 'Why?' asked Gareth, 'Is it a wishing well?' 'Don't suppose so,' answered Huw, laughing. 'I never yet got any of my wishes from here. But then, I s'pose it was a bit much wishing for an aeroplane of my own. Even a wishing well couldn't provide that, I've wished for something possible this time.' and he winked. Gareth rolled his eyes and made a moue of his lips, 'Bet I can guess,' he said disgustedly, 'Got something to do with Rhiannon, has it?' Huw laughed, 'You could say that.'

'No accounting for taste,' Gareth replied, 'You don't know what you're taking on.'

'I'll risk that,' Huw grinned. 'Anyway,' Gareth rose to his feet and wiped his mouth with his handkerchief. 'It looked to me like she was making a play for your brother.' 'Edward?' Huw drew the back of his hand across his wet mouth, 'She'll soon get tired of that, if she thinks she can snare Edward. She wouldn't know what to do with him if she got him. He's a dry old stick. A great bloke, mind, though I wouldn't let him hear me say so. But a dry stick. Not Rhiannon's sort at all.' Gareth shrugged, 'Oh well, may the best man win. But I don't envy whoever is the best man. She's a handful, is our Rhiannon.' 'I'd risk it,' Huw answered, fervently.

They sat down among the bracken and gazed out over the valley. 'It's so peaceful,' breathed Gareth, 'I think I know already why Mam and Dad wanted to come back. Dad came out to Canada to better himself, he always said, but it was Wales he talked about, and especially Newtown, which he felt was special. I haven't seen much of it yet, but just looking down into the valley now I feel a little of what he must always have felt.'

Huw looked at him curiously, 'I suppose we take it for granted, living here all the time, like.' He returned his gaze to the valley below. Sheep dotted the hillside and below them was the Brimmon Wood which covered the lower slopes of the Brimmon Hills. On the opposite side

41

of the valley was the Bryn Bank, wearing a golden cover with the gorse in full bloom. The valley stretched out on either side, narrow to the west until it ran beyond the Dolfor Hills, but broadening to the East as it opened up a little towards Welshpool. As always there was a slight haze hanging over the Severn as it wound its way along the valley floor, bisecting the little town below. Huw was surprised to find the view clutching at his heart in the most unexpected way. He supposed it was because a stranger had made him look at it differently. He was embarrassed at the feeling and quickly changed the subject.

'I suppose you'll soon be looking for a job,' he looked questioningly at Gareth, 'If you like I'll keep my ears aflap at P.J.'s and see if there's anything going there.'

There was a moment's silence before Gareth answered, 'That's good of you, Huw, But I really want to work as a carpenter, I began my apprenticeship before I came over here. I did two years after I left school. I - well, I love working with wood. I love the feel of it, the beautiful grain and the way you can bring that out if you work it carefully. Its just something I feel for. I suppose it must be possible to get apprenticed to a really good carpenter here in Newtown, isn't it? Would you know of anybody?' He looked hopefully at Huw who pursed his lips judiciously.

' I don't think you could do much better than old Norman Oliver, if he would take you on. They say he's about the best in the business, Don't know much about it myself but the locals do speak pretty highly of him. I should go and see him, see what he's got to say. No harm in trying. There's one or two others, but I think they're mainly rough chippies. Not the real thing, like you seem to want.'

'I'll try him, anyway,' Gareth nodded, 'I really want to make beautiful things from the wood, not just work on a building site. I've done some stuff, mainly small animals and so on,' he added, and then, blushing a little, 'I could show you them sometime after we've unpacked. They're in the trunks somewhere. That's if you'd like to see them?'

'Yeah, I don't mind,' said Huw, chewing on a blade of grass, although he couldn't work up much enthusiasm over some wooden animals. Still they obviously meant a lot to the other lad. 'Yeah,' he repeated, trying to show interest, 'Soon as you've rooted them out I'll have a dekko at them. Anyway, we'd better be shifting, or it'll be dark by the time we get back down.' He rose to his feet and flicked at the bits of bracken which clung to the seat of his trousers.

'Are we going back the same way?' asked Gareth, thinking with some trepidation of passing the gypsies again.

'No, we'll go round by the Shwrwd and down past Brimmon farm. Won't take us long.'

'Will I ever get used to these Welsh names, do you think, Huw?' Gareth asked laughing.

' 'Course you will. Your Dad'll help you. You speak some Welsh now, don't you?'

'Yes, a little, But its a different matter, putting in into practice.'

They were soon running down the slopes and leaping over the small stream at the bottom. Eventually they reached Brimmon Lane which brought them out by Pryce Jones's. A further five minutes and they were back at No 46 Pool Road.

Huw was thrilled to find, when they entered the kitchen, that Rhiannon had returned and was sitting an the old horsehair sofa, leafing through a magazine that Esther had given her. After greeting Dada, seated by the fire in his wooden armchair, and Mama sitting at the table with a basket of darning in front of her, straining her eyes under the Aladdin lamp which was lit on the table, Huw went to sit beside Rhiannon. He had often been told he could charm the birds off the trees, and he was about to try this out on Rhiannon, but was a little taken aback when her first question was 'Where's Edward this evening?'

'Edward?' Huw blinked at the abruptness of the question, 'Well, it's Wednesday, isn't it? He'll be at bell-ringing practice.'

'Bell-ringing!' Rhiannon echoed, 'How dull.' She wrinkled her exquisite little nose and went back to her magazine.

'Yes, well, that's Edward, isn't it? He likes bell-ringing. Goes regularly when he's home from Coll.'

Dada coughed and stirred. 'I don't know as bell-ringing is all that dull, mind you. A bit dangerous it can be, indeed, I did try it myself once, when the organist did ask me once when he was short of ringers, if I would have a go. Well, I will try anything once, isn't it.' There was a sound from Mama at the table, but Dada carried on, 'I did do very well with the first pull, but then the rope did go up of its own accord and did take me up with it, My feet did leave the ground altogether. Diawl, it was a funny feeling, like I was going straight up to heaven.'

'Fat chance of that!' chimed in Mama and took the wind out of his sails.

3

Lamplighters and Sabre-Rattling

It was the following Saturday morning and Davy's family were at breakfast. Nan had finished dishing out the porridge and pouring out cups of tea, Davy himself was ensconced behind the Daily Despatch and Edward was reading the County Times.

'D'you think there'll really be a war, Dad?' asked Edward anxiously, lowering his paper and folding it away. 'I see by the County Times they're going to get the kids used to wearing gas masks. They're going to have Mickey Mouse faces to them, these masks. I should think they'd frighten the children to death!'

Davy peered over the top of his paper at Edward and shook his head, 'I really don't know what's going to happen. I don't trust Hitler. It seems to me Chamberlain is taking a lot for granted with his bit of paper he's brought back. Very bad things are happening in Germany itself. The opening of concentration camps, Nazi's picking on the Jews, though God knows what harm they do. I don't like the sound of it at all. They've over-run Austria already, but I don't think Hitler will be satisfied with that. He talks of 'Lebensraum - which I think. means 'living room' but I feel he wants more than that. Oh, I don't know, I just hope to God it doesn't come to war. I lived through one war and saw the filth and misery that caused. God knows, I wasn't at the front myself, but I know too many who were and it must have been like going down into hell.' He gave a short laugh, 'Talk to your Uncle Llew about it. Hear what he says about war. He came back a very bitter man from the last lot.'

'He wouldn't have to convince me,' Edward replied quietly, 'I wouldn't want to fight a war. There must be other ways of dealing with Hitler. What about the League of Nations?'

'Oh, yes, the League of Nations.' Davy folded his paper and put it down beside his bowl of porridge, which he tackled absent-mindedly. 'I must admit I haven't got much faith in the League of Nations. Oh the idea was good, but it doesn't seem to work in practice. Take the Versailles Treaty. Looking back it seems to me that was more about punishing Germany than trying to settle the issues that caused the war. It was thanks to the Treaty that Germany felt humiliated and lost her pride and when someone like Hitler comes along and appears to offer them a way of getting that pride back, then they are going to see him as a national saviour, which is what is happening now, I suppose.' Davy scraped the last of his porridge from the bowl and reached for a piece of toast, which he spread with butter and Nan's home-made marmalade.

Edward fidgeted with his spoon. 'If there is a war, d'you think I'd have to go?' he asked in a low voice. 'I don't want to, I don't think it's because I'm a coward although I don't fancy getting shot.' He gave his father a rueful grin, 'It's just that I don't believe in war as a means of solving disputes, Surely we've advanced in civilisation a bit more than that?'

'Obviously not.' Davy answered, dryly, 'The problem is that the people who decide to go to war are unlikely to have to go and fight it. The poor old chap in the street will have to do that. The statesmen rattle the sabres, but they don't have to use them or face them.'

'But surely after the last lot men won't rush to join up again?'

Davy shrugged. 'Some will. Some poor fools will see it as a chance at adventure. Others will see it as an outlet for natural aggression. And again some fools will see themselves with a chance to become heroes, And here's one of those coming now,' he added wryly, as Huw came into the room and pulled his chair out with a clatter before sitting down to his breakfast.

'One what?' he enquired as he poured milk generously onto his porridge.

'Fool,' supplied Edward, nodding at him. 'Ay-up, who're you calling a fool?' Huw asked truculently,

'We're just wondering whether there'll be a war.' Edward explained with a sigh, 'I suppose you would be one of the first fools to volunteer.'

'Too right.' Huw replied eagerly, 'I'd want to get in first so I could get a chance to join the Air Force. That's where the next lot's going to be fought, in the air. That'd be a change from Pryce Jones's, wouldn't it just.'

His father nodded. 'Quite a change. You can't get killed in the tailoring department very easily.'

'Poof!' scoffed Huw, 'That's a risk I can take. I like risks.' He grinned and swaggered with his shoulders.

Davy shook his head, 'You'll take one too many some day, boy. Anyway, talking of risks, it'd be as well if you don't get too involved with your cousin Rhiannon. He held up his hand as Huw flushed and made as if to speak, 'I've seen the way you've been looking at her and so has your Mam, and we're agreed that she's a bit forward for our liking. All right, she's very pretty and bright, but let her find her own level with other lads. You're likely to get hurt Huw, if you set your heart in that quarter.'

Huw pushed back his chair and stood up. 'You don't know anything about her,' he said indignantly, his face flushed.

'Neither do you.' Edward put in. 'So watch it.'

'I suppose you want to try for her yourself,' sneered Huw. 'Well, she'd soon get tired of a dry old stick like you, Ned Rees.'

'Thank the Lord for that, then,' Edward grinned, ''Cos I'm not interested. She frightens me. Anyway, I've got a girl, And even if I hadn't, I'd not go for Rhiannon.'

'Chance would be a fine thing,' Huw replied, hotly, and flung out of the room.

Edward shrugged and made a face, 'I hope he doesn't get serious about her. She'd eat him for breakfast!'

Davy looked surprised. 'Oh dear, you don't seem to have taken to your cousin.' he laughed.

'Well, perhaps I'm being unfair.' Edward admitted, frowning, 'I've only seen her the once, but I know she's not my sort. And I don't want old Huw getting hurt. He goes into things without thinking. Like he'd join up at the drop of a hat if war broke out. Don't know which is the most dangerous for him, Rhiannon or the war!'

Davy laughed and shortly afterwards Nan came in with a fat brown teapot and poured out tea for the three of them.

At 46 Pool Road, Owen wandered in at ten o'clock and first greeted

Dada who was in his usual place beside the fire. He brightened when he saw Owen enter the room and greeted him with some relief. The atmosphere had been a little tense in the kitchen owing to the fact that Rhiannon was still in bed and Mama was clucking her disapproval while Nell bustled around tight-lipped. Elwyn had buried his head in the Montgomeryshire Express and Gareth had returned to his room with his second load of wooden animals which had at last been rescued for him from the trunks.

'You are early this morning, my boy.' Dada remarked raising his bushy white eyebrows.

'Aye.' Owen responded, laughing. 'I beat a hasty retreat. Lena is heaving her heart up back at home, and blaming me! She was keen for this baby, but it is not improving her temper.'

'What do you men know about it.' Nell put in, hanging some washed teacloths on the string line above the fire. 'How would you like to feel as sick as a dog every morning? And indeed, sometimes when you look back you wonder whether it was worth it all.' With a dark look she went to the bottom of the stairs and yelled, 'Rhiannon! Are you getting up today or not? If you're not down here in five minutes you'll whistle for your breakfast and your dinner, my girl.' She marched with stiff neck into the back kitchen, while Mama rolled her eyes and shook her head.

'Lena is all right, is she?' she asked Owen, while she made a fresh pot of tea for Rhiannon and poured out a cup for Owen in the meantime.

'Oh yes, right as rain, really. A bit tetchy, especially in the mornings. I suppose I shall have to put up with that for the next eight months.'

'Oh she'll be better in another couple of months,' said Mama sagely, while she stirred the pot of porridge sitting on the hob keeping warm for Rhiannon.

'Hope so.' Owen said, making a face. 'Anything interesting in that old rag, Elwyn?'

Elwyn gave a chuckle. 'Just been reading an account of Newtown Urban District Council. They're wrangling over the street lighting. It seems they don't reckon to have the street lights on during the summer months. The clerk explained that no inconvenience was caused on moonlit nights. However some members protested that on dark nights it was dangerous. Councillor Dodd points out that people coming from the cinema have to use torches and he suggested that the lights should be kept on for all of May at a cost of £12. The Surveyor then suggests that only the darkest parts of town should have the lights lit and if that was done he could manage with only one lamplighter.' Elwyn shook his head in disbelief. 'I can't believe this! It's rich! Councillor Breeze says that people in the unlit parts of town will complain. The Surveyor says that if all lights were lit then one man wouldn't be enough as he would have to start extinguishing them as soon as he had finished lighting them, Isn't that rich?'

Owen laughed. 'Hasn't old Giles had anything to say?'

'Oh, yes. Councillor Giles said he had difficulty getting past telegraph poles, wireless poles and electricity poles and it was a wonder he was there at all. Laughter in the chamber!'

'I don't know what they're making all the old fuss about.' Dada chipped in. 'There is no lights out in the country and folk manage to get about their business all right. Indeed,' he added, chuckling slyly. 'There was times we was glad of the dark, isn't it? How would you do your courting else?'

Mama gave him a crushing look before returning to the porridge, as Rhiannon's step was heard on the stairs. Elwyn frowned at her over the top of the paper as she entered the room, but none of the men could remain unmoved at the pretty picture she made. She had on a Shantung silk dress with embroidery around the square neck. Her lovely legs were encased in flesh-coloured silk stockings and she wore high-heeled, champagne coloured shoes. Her dark, glossy curls hung to her shoulders and her attractive face was delicately made up. She paused in the doorway as though to give them time to take in the picture, but Mama, at least, was unimpressed.

'High time you was up, my lady. You'd better come to your breakfast. There's plenty to do around here, When you've finished your porridge you could wash up your dishes and then make a start on peeling the potatoes for dinner. It's a pity you put on all that finery, It'll only spoil.'

At the look of indignation on Rhiannon's face, Elwyn coughed and retreated behind his paper to hide a grin.

'I'm going out.' Rhiannon announced. 'And anyway I don't like porridge. I'll take a cup of tea and a piece of toast.' And she sat herself down at the table, her chin high.

Mama regarded her with raised eyebrows. 'Then you may cut yourself a piece of bread and toast it at the fire. I've got other things to do.' She removed the remains of the porridge and carried it out to the yard, where they could hear her scraping it out of the saucepan into the ash bin.

Rhiannon turned an outraged look on her father, but he had closed his paper with a snap and was regarding her coldly. 'You asked for that, young lady. Don't expect everyone to run to your bidding here. Until you get a job and earn your living you can turn to and give a bit of help around the house. Your Mam will have her work cut out helping Mama, who's getting too old to carry all the burden of this household. Think on!'

Rhiannon stood up, pushing her chair backwards and breathing hard. However, seeing the look on her father's face she forbore to reply and instead flounced out of the room and soon they heard the front door bang shut after her. Elwyn sighed and returned to his paper.

'Whew!' Owen let out a long breath. 'A young lady with a mind of her own, yes?'

'Yes!' Elwyn spoke through gritted teeth. 'She's a bit too old to have her behind paddled, but that's what she needs. But perhaps a bit of time with Mama will sort her out.' He added with a grin, 'Mama's not the sort to put up with tantrums. It might be quite interesting to see who comes off best!'

Owen laughed. 'My money's on Mama, I never yet saw anybody get the better of her, I've a feeling your young lady will come to her cake and milk eventually.'

'I hope so.' Elwyn replied, fervently, 'She badly needs taking down a peg or two. She's very strong-willed and she didn't want to leave Canada. She's tried to make our lives a misery ever since we left there. Different from Gareth. He couldn't wait to come to Wales. He'll soon settle down, He's gone to look for this character, Norman Oliver, the carpenter. He loves working with wood. Got a real feel for it, He hopes this chap will take him on as an apprentice. What's he like, Oliver?'

'A first-class carpenter. If Gareth can get in with him he'll do all right. I wish him luck.'

Rhiannon set off up Kerry Road, her shoulders back and her chin high. How she hated this boring backwater. Only the thought of Edward brought any consolation. She was going to go up to Plas Gwyn and see if he was there. He was going back to college on Monday, so she didn't have much time to work on him. She had no doubt that she could get him if she put her mind to it and he was the one she wanted. He was a challenge. She tossed her glossy dark curls off her shoulders and her high heels clicked on the pavement as she hurried towards Plas Gwyn. She reached the front door and beat a tattoo with the knocker. The door was opened by Huw whose startled face became lit with a delighted smile.

'Rhiannon! Come in!' He stood aside for her to enter. After she gave him a brief smile he followed her down the passage into the kitchen. Nan was just bending down to put a dish of home-made faggots into the oven to cook for the dinner, but turned with a welcoming smile when Huw cried, 'Look who's come to see us, Mam!'

'Rhiannon. This is nice, sit down girl, you'll have a cup of tea in your hand, yes?'

Rhiannon nodded and smiled sweetly. 'Yes please, I'd love a cup of tea.' Hoping she'd be offered something to eat as well. She was famished. While Nan made a pot of tea and asked her how she was settling down, and Huw sat gazing at her like a love-sick calf. She gazed around for signs of Edward. Nan poured a cup of tea for her and brought out a large sponge cake filled with home-made raspberry jam.

'You'll take a piece of cake with your tea?' she asked and Rhiannon assented eagerly.

'Where's Uncle Davy this morning?' she asked, while eating her cake in dainty bites, although it was so good she would like to have wolfed it down.

'Gone up to see Llew. Politics, I daresay. Its usually politics with them two. They're leading lights in the Labour Party round here.'

Rhiannon made a face, 'I don't know anything about politics.' She turned to Huw and smiled. 'Are you interested in politics, Huw?'

Huw, dazzled by the smile, shook his head, 'Not really, I leave all that stuff to Dad and Edward.'

Rhiannon seized the opening, 'And where is Edward this morning?'

she asked, striving for a casual air.

Huw grinned. 'Hoping to meet his dearly beloved, I expect. He'll want to see as much of her as he can before he goes on Monday, surely. He set off straight after breakfast. Must have it badly. Fancy old Ned falling like that. Never bothered much with girls before Ruth. Well, he was pally with her in school but this seems like the real thing now. She's all right, but nothing special. Not as pretty as you, Rhiannon!' His dark eyes sparkled at her but she only smiled and sipped her tea.

Nan offered more tea and cake and Rhiannon accepted both, complimenting Nan on her cake which she pronounced delicious. She was on her best behaviour and Huw was obviously smitten, but Nan was uncomfortable with her.

'Fancy a stroll round the town?' Huw turned to Rhiannon eagerly. 'There's not much to see, I know. I daresay there was plenty of life where you lived in Canada. Was it a big town?'

Rhiannon shrugged. 'Not really, but yes, there was plenty going on. I miss it and I miss all my friends.' she said wistfully. Nan also felt sorry for her.

'Yes, I'll come round the town with you, Huw.' With that she rose and dusted cake crumbs off her dress. 'Thank you for the tea and cake, Auntie Nan. It was lovely. I didn't have any breakfast, you see.'

'No breakfast!' Huw was indignant, 'Why didn't you get breakfast?'

'Well, I can't eat porridge, you see, and there was nothing else. Anyway, I'm full now, so let's go, Huw.' Nan watched them go down the passage and out of the door. That didn't sound like 46 Pool Road, where there was always plenty of bread for toasting and plenty of butter and jams or marmalade to go on it. She shrugged and returned to her preparations for dinner.

Huw and Rhiannon set off down Pool Road, Huw trying to shorten his stride to Rhiannon's quick light steps in her tapping high heels. They passed along Shortbridge Street and entered the Saturday morning bustle of the little town, the housewives with baskets over their arms, men out to fetch their daily papers and meet their friends to discuss football, to analyse Newtown's chances against Llanidloes. Delivery boys pedalled their bikes rapidly along the streets, with the big baskets filled with grocery orders in the front, dodging the milk carts and the beer drays.

Youths strolled about self-consciously in the nearest things to Oxford bags they could get, and with an assortment of jackets if they had no blazers, their hair slicked down with Brylcream, clean-shaven faces shining. There were not so many girls about at that time of day, since they were either working or helping at home.

Huw led Rhiannon into Taylor's, the tobacconists and sweetshop, and bought her a bar of chocolate for which she thanked him with a cool smile and dropped it into her small handbag. They then turned into Market Street and she stopped outside Mrs Reynolds' fashion shop. She stood there a while but soon moved on with a contemptuous sniff. Obviously nothing in the window would appeal to her. They strolled on but soon found their way blocked by Heron's stall which stood on the pavement outside his fruit and vegetable shop. Women milled around choosing their week-end vegetables so Huw and Rhiannon crossed over and entered the Market Hall. They passed Dick Jones Brimmon's butcher shop and moved on past the trestles where the farmers' wives sat patiently behind their wares, a few dozen eggs, both hen and duck, some sticks of fresh pink forced rhubarb or a bunch of herbs. Some had stored last seasons russet apples and offered a few of these for sale and there was the occasional small chicken or old boiling fowl. Some of them sat all day for a few shillings, since this was their own money to do as they liked with and was precious to them. At the last stall before the exit into High Street presided Mrs Giles, wife of the good Councillor Giles, and hers was a very popular stall, filled with delicious home-made jams and chutneys, marmalade and pickles and a mouth-watering display of her very good cakes and sponges, fairy cakes and jam tarts.

The two left the Market Hall and turned right, pausing to look in Osborne Edwards's photography shop. Wedding couples stood, stiff and beaming in their finery, babies sat on fur rugs obviously looking expectantly at the camera, and a few pretty girls, carefully posed with chins leaning on hands and eyes gazing into the distance.

'None of them are as pretty as you.' Huw murmured fervently, but Rhiannon turned away without answering. Out of the corner of her eye she had spotted a tall, fair figure standing patiently gazing into a butcher's shop on the other side of the Angel hotel.

'Look, isn't that Edward?' she cried, clutching Huw's sleeve and pulling him in that direction. As they drew near, Huw called out 'Wotcher, Ned!' and Edward turned, startled. He seemed less than enthusiastic when greeting his brother, but nodded to Rhiannon and said a guarded 'Hello'. She replied with a dazzling smile but before she could greet him, a girl emerged from the shop with a large shopping bag and Edward hastened to relieve her of it.

'Hello Ruth,' grinned Huw. 'How're things? I thought old Ned wouldn't be standing outside Maurice Powell's shop for nothing!' 'Hello, Huw.' Ruth smiled and dimpled and then turned her gaze to the glamorous girl at Huw's side.

Huw remembered his manners. 'Oh, this here is Rhiannon, our cousin from Canada. Rhiannon, this is Ruth.'

'Hello,' Ruth smiled and held out her hand. Rhiannon touched it briefly with cool fingers and let her gaze travel from Ruth's mop of short dark curls down to her brown leather sandals and back again. Ruth flushed and looked up at Edward who took her arm protectively. 'Come on, then Ruth, we'd better get going.' He nodded coolly to Huw and Rhiannon and guided Ruth across the road and in the direction of Broad Street. Rhiannon watched with tight lips as she saw his fair head incline towards Ruth as she looked up to say something to him.

'So that's Ruth!' she said, staring after the two figures. 'She's very plain, isn't she? Whatever does Edward see in her?'

'Oh, Ruth's all right.' Huw said, uncomfortably. 'She suits Ned anyway and that's the main thing.' But Rhiannon was thinking to herself that if she couldn't knock out that little nobody she'd eat her hat.

Meanwhile Edward and Ruth had crossed Broad Street and Ruth had gone into Griffiths and Griffiths paper shop for her father's Daily Mail and Montgomeryshire Express. She had become very quiet and when she came out of the shop Edward asked her what was wrong. 'Nothing,' she answered. But he wasn't satisfied. He put the shopping bag down and took both her arms in gentle hands. 'Come on, now. Tell Edward.' He gave her a little shake and she laughed and hung her head. He put a hand under her chin and lifted it.

'I was only thinking, your cousin is very beautiful, isn't she?' Ruth whispered.

Edward brushed his hand over his hair, 'Oh Lord, is that it? You think I might fall for her? Well, you can think again. I don't even like her very much. She's very spoilt and a heck of a lot too forward for my liking. If that's what's worrying you you can stop right now. Right?'

Ruth gave a shamefaced smile. 'I just wondered what you could see in me with somebody like her around.'

He leaned down and whispered, 'I love you, idiot.' Then he picked up the bag again and took her arm. 'Come on, I'll carry this home for you. I will see you tonight, won't I? D'you want to go to the pictures or just for a walk?'

'Just for a walk,' nodded Ruth and leaned closer to him as they made their way up Broad Street, needing to feel his nearness for reassurance.

It was Monday morning and Edward was standing on the platform on the far side of the lines at Newtown Station waiting for the twelve o'clock train to Aberystwyth. He had come up to the station early because Ruth had said she would try to come to see him off. He put his suitcase down and folded his arms, keeping an eager eye on the entrance of the other platform. Porters passed him trundling their heavy trucks and he passed a cheery word with them. He was dressed in flannels and his college blazer and his fair curls flopped over his forehead. Suddenly he saw a female figure emerge onto the platform and his heartbeats quickened.

All at once he stared in horror and frowned to see that the figure was Rhiannon, who waved gaily and hurried along the opposite platform and over the bridge. As she came up to him he shook his head in disbelief.

'What are you doing here?' he asked, sternly. Rhiannon pouted and stepped nearer, 'That's not a very nice way to greet me when I've taken the trouble to come up to see you off!'

'Look,' Edward backed away. 'You can't stay here. You'll have to go.' He looked at her angrily.

'Oh, Edward. You are cruel. Can't you see I've fallen for you?' She put her head on one side and turned the full force of her smile on him. Edward shied away like a frightened horse, but she stepped nearer. So intent was he in trying to think of ways to get rid of her that he didn't see what she had already spotted: Ruth coming through the entrance onto the opposite platform and stopping suddenly as she looked across and saw Edward and Rhiannon. Suddenly Rhiannon flung her arms round Edward's neck and pressed her body seductively against his. She planted a long and lingering kiss full on his mouth and it was then that he saw, out of the corner of his eye, Ruth standing there, frozen, her hand to her mouth. He pushed Rhiannon away with a strangled cry and called out Ruth's name, but the girl turned and fled back through the entrance and disappeared. Edward made as though to run towards the bridge, but just then the train steamed into the station and it was too late.

He turned back and picked up his case. He stood for a moment and stared at Rhiannon and the look on his face scared her for a moment and she took a step backward. Then the guard blew his whistle and Edward turned away and leapt into the nearest carriage, banging the door behind him and disappearing into a carriage. Rhiannon stared after the train as it steamed out of the station and wondered for a moment whether she'd made a mistake. Then she shrugged. That had probably got rid of Ruth and then the field would be open for her. She cheered up. She would get him eventually. With chin high and high heels tapping she crossed the bridge and left the station.

4

Rumours and War

'You goin' to 'ave any of these vacuums?' Edie Davies, Esther's charlady, paused with her hands in the bowl of suds in which she was washing the breakfast dishes.

Esther looked up from her seat at the kitchen table where she was completing her shopping list. 'Any what?' she asked, puzzled.

'You know. Them poor little kids what are coming from London and them places 'cos of the bombs. Poor little dabs.'

'Oh, evacuees.' Esther hid a smile with her hand. 'Well, I daresay I could manage one or two if I'm asked. I might even go to the Council Offices and offer.'

'Hm. Don't you think you've got enough to cope with now. Mary only seven and Alun five and that little 'un Johnny only toddlin'. Leave it to them with nowt else to do, I say.'

'Oh, no. Poor little things. We've got plenty of room for a couple more and enough food to feed them. I'm just thankful I haven't got to part with my three. I don't think I could. It would break my heart. Yet I suppose their Mams and Dads would rather that than see them killed by the bombs. It looks like war, and very soon too. God help us all. Martin won't have to go, but there's Huw and Edward and Little Jim, whose not so little now,' she added laughing, thinking of long lanky Jim, Mattie's boy, now twenty-years of age and just out of his apprenticeship at the Foundry. 'I don't think Meg's Henry would have to go because of the farm, but what about Nell's Gareth? Doing so well with Norman Oliver the carpenter, too. Oh dear, what an upheaval and worry it's all going to be. I wish there was still a chance it won't come to war.' She sighed and watched the baby, Johnny, as he walked round the sides of his playpen shaking the rails. He saw her watching him and gave his most ingratiating smile which showed his six teeth, shining like tiny pearls. 'Ma-ma.' he lisped and held out his arms, falling backward onto his well-padded behind and chuckling.

Esther lifted him out and went to strap him in his pushchair. It was a hot August day in 1939 and the very heat seemed ominous as the whole of Europe held its breath, waiting for what, at the moment, seemed inevitable, war. The older people who still remembered the Great War were worried and afraid. The younger people sensed some vague excitement, wondering what to expect if it should come. The Churches prayed for peace, the Generals plotted war and the people waited.

Mary and Alun had gone off to school with their Mickey-Mouse gas-masks in cardboard boxes over their shoulders. Mary had donned hers as soon as she had it, intrigued by the funny mask, causing the more timid Alun to scream with fright. He had refused all coaxing to put his on and Esther and Martin were forced to abandon the attempt for fear he would go into a fit. Esther hoped there would be no gas around Newtown. They had not even attempted to put Johnny's on, he had looked at it so suspiciously and with round frightened eyes. Surely the Germans wouldn't drop gas on Newtown. What good would that do them?

She set off now with her shopping bag hooked onto the back of the pushchair. It was only ten o'clock and she planned to drop in on Mama and Dada before going to the shops. After negotiating the seven steps down to the pavement she felt the heat of the sun as she pushed Johnny down Bryn Street, waving to Harry Harris, Martin Harris's son, as she passed the butcher's shop. She called through the door for him to keep her four pork chops for when she came back. She must remember to call at Heron's for onions on the way home.

She sauntered through the town, savouring the warm summer air. The children had only just gone back to school today after the summer holidays. She wondered why school always started on a Tuesday after a holiday, instead of on a Monday. Musing thus, she crossed the Iron Bridge. Only last week the children were still out of school. Boys were swimming in the river and diving off the bridge, and she had stopped with Mary and Alun clutching the sides of the pushchair, watching with fearsome glee the brown boys' bodies, shining wet, as they hung onto the railings of the bridge before launching themselves into the river. Down by the Old Church, boys had fished with home-made rods and bent pins, catching nothing, but contented in the sun, while the smaller ones were catching tiddlers with nets from Griffiths and Griffiths, and issuing blood-curdling threats to the girls who paddled in the shallows and drove away the swarms of minnows. As she walked through Broad Street the town was so quiet and peaceful under the late summer sun that it seemed that all the talk of war was just a nightmare and the world would wake up on the morrow with nothing changed. It was a Thursday, early closing day, and the last day of August, 1939.

She reached 46 Pool Road and walked backward up the steps, dragging the pushchair after her. She reached behind her and opened the door, pulling Johnny into the house. She called out a greeting then unstrapped the child and set him down on his two plump legs. He toddled through unsteadily and was promptly swept up into Nell's arms. She blew into his fat little neck and he crowed with joy.

'Look who's come to see us, Mama, Dada!' she cried and Mama came out of the back-kitchen, moving more slowly now, her hair white and her back a little bowed. She came forward and reached up to touch Johnny's rosy round cheek. 'Kiss Nan, then,' she commanded and Johnny bent down from his perch and planted a wet kiss on her wrinkled cheek. Then Nell set him down again and he toddled to where Dada sat in his armchair by the fire, extending plump arms to be lifted up.

'Do you lift this boy up on my knee, Nell,' Dada ordered, 'He is too heavy for me with my rheumatics.' Nell lifted Johnny onto Dada's knee and the little one wound his arms round Dada's neck and awarded him a wet kiss also. Dada grinned behind his whiskers and joggled him up and down on his knee, making him chuckle and hiccup.

'Do you be careful with that boy, now,' scolded Mama. 'You will have his breakfast up.'

Dada grunted and whispered some thing derogatory about women in Johnny's ear. As the whiskers tickled his ear, the boy chuckled again, then cuddled down against Dada's woollen waistcoat and Dada began to tell him a rambling tale in Welsh, which mattered not at all to Johnny, who listened to the rising and falling of Dada's whispers and was soothed and quietened.

Mama put tea leaves in the pot and tipped in water from the kettle singing above the fire. She poured tea out for Nell, Esther and herself and they sat down round the table sipping and talking in low voices.

'How does Rhiannon like her job at Pryce Jones's?' Esther asked.

'Oh, you know Rhiannon,' Neil sighed. 'When is she ever satisfied? Says its boring. But it's quite a good job in the office and there's not much else for her round here. She'll settle down eventually, I hope.'

'Martin would have given her a start in his office, being as his secretary is retiring soon, but he didn't think it would be a good idea with her and Edward not getting on.'

'Oh, Rhiannon would get on with Edward all right,' Nell said ruefully. 'But for some reason Edward took a dislike to her. I don't know what happened but whatever it was you can bet your bottom dollar it was Rhiannon's fault not his. He seems a reasonable sort of chap so she must have done something to ruffle his feathers. He only comes down here when he thinks she's out and yet she gets up to all manner of tricks to try and meet him here and there. Well, she can save her breath to cool her porridge now he's engaged to Ruth. They seemed to have patched up some bit of trouble they had a while back. I wonder if Rhiannon was at the back of that? How did we ever get that girl so different from Gareth. He's always been easy to manage.'

'He's a nice lad, is Gareth,' chimed in Mama. 'Doing well with Norman the carpenter. Couple more years and he'll finish his apprenticeship, isn't it?'

'Yes, if this old war doesn't come. He would surely have to go, if it does. It is these old men who make the wars. Left to us women there would be no wars to take our sons away from us.' Nell lifted the hem of her apron and dabbed at the corner of her eyes.

'There, there, girl,' Mama shook her head. 'Maybe there will not be a war. Maybe they will see sense, think you?'

'But Hitler must be stopped, Mama,' put in Esther, in a low voice. 'None of us want a war, but if that man is not stopped he will be over here soon. He has over-run Austria and Czechoslovakia. He's got his eyes on Poland next. Anyway, that's what Martin says.'

Mama sighed. 'I am getting too old for these old wars. I have lived through one. That is enough for any lifetime. My son came home to me last time. What of my grandsons this time?'

They heard the back door open and close and Nan came through with a basket full of clean linen and towels. Mama greeted her and fetched another cup from the cupboard. Nan sat to the table with them after smiling at the sight of Johnny, now asleep on Dada's knee. She seemed subdued and Esther asked her if there was anything wrong.

'Its Huw,' Nan replied. 'I'm sorry, Nell. But it's all on account of Rhiannon.'

'Rhiannon?' Nell looked worried. 'What's that girl been up to now?'

'Oh, well, I suppose its not really Rhiannon's fault. But Huw fell for her very hard right from the start. To be fair I don't think she ever gave him a thought, really, but he wouldn't have it. And they have been going round together from time to time. But it seems last weekend things came to a head. He wanted her to say she'd be his girl and she gave him her answer in no uncertain terms. Seems she told him the only man for her was Edward. When he reminded her that Edward was engaged to Ruth she told him she'd change that one of these days. He came home in a state. And now he's going to join the Air Force. Going the end of next week, war or no war. He says he hopes there'll be a war and doesn't care if the Jerry's get him.' Nell sniffed and buried her face in her teacup.

There was an uncertain silence round the table and then Mama patted Nan's arm. 'The boy is young. He doesn't mean that. Is he going to fly them aeroplanes?'

Nan nodded and sniffed again, 'That's what he wants. He's going to England to train to be a pilot if they'll let him. He's given in his notice at Pryce Jones's already. Davy and Edward tried to talk him out of it, but he won't listen to his Dad and as for Edward, he'll barely speak to him. Though, God Knows, it's not poor Edward's fault. As you know he's never encouraged Rhiannon. Quite the opposite.'

'It's not much comfort to you, Nan,' said Esther, ' but if the war comes they'll all have to go. I suppose he may as well get in early and get in the service that he wants to. Martin reckons the war is coming for sure. All the boys will have to go, Edward and Huw, Jim and Gareth.

Maybe not Henry, because of the farm. Oh dear. What's to become of us all?'

Nell had been plucking at the table cloth in silence, but now she looked up. 'I'm only sorry Rhiannon was the cause of Huw going off like that, Nan. Poor boy. I don't know where we went wrong with that girl, but she's always been determined to have her own way, ever since she was a small one. She seemed to set her heart on Edward right from the start and he, fair play, made it clear he had no time for her. I shall give her a right good talking to. I wouldn't like her to upset Ruth. She's a nice girl and her and Edward think the world of each other, don't they?'

'What is all this old talk of war?' came a voice from the armchair. 'There isn't a war on, is there?' Nobody does tell me anything.'

'No, no, Dada,' Nell reassured him. 'Not yet, anyway. Just talking, we are.'

'Well. Somebody did bring me some kind of a mask thing they say I am to put on in case of gas. The only gas I do know about is in the gas works. Harry Knock is in charge of that. What for would he let that loose?'

Esther hid a smile. 'Not that kind of gas, Dada. They're afraid if a war came the Germans might drop some gas on us. Then the gas masks would save us.'

Dada looked bewildered. 'Do these men not fight with guns any more? It used to be soldiers that fought the wars. What about these little ones?' He clutched Johnny to him more tightly, causing the child to stir and open a sleepy eye for a moment.

'Oh, they'll be fighting with guns all right,' Nell said bitterly. 'and with bombs and God knows what else they can drop on us from the aeroplanes. We can only pray that it doesn't come to war, is all.'

'Aye, that's all that's left to us now.' Nan rose from her chair. 'I will just put this washing away for you now Mama and I must go home to put the dinner on. The men will all be in for it soon.'

'I had better get going, too,' said Esther, rising also. 'Give me that big old boy, Dada, to put in the pushchair. I've got a bit of shopping to do before I start the dinner. Edie is very good at the cleaning and washing, but I'd rather get the meals myself.'

When Nan and Esther had gone, Nell cleared away the tea things and got on with the housework, still wearing a worried frown. Apart from the worry of Rhiannon she dreaded the thought of Gareth going off to war. He had always been such a good and pleasant boy and was doing so well with Norman the carpenter. From time to time she sighed and wondered what was to become of them all. Elwyn was too old to go now. He had a job as a doorman at Pryce Jones's which gave him something to do. He was a good, steady man and she thanked God for him.

Meanwhile Mama and Dada sat in subdued silence, both thinking of their grandsons and bewildered with the talk of a strange kind of warfare which might even put children at risk. At last, after chewing his whiskers and grunting, Dada said, ' They all do think there is an old war coming. I would not care for myself, but it is these boys who will have to go for to fight. Didn't these men in charge have enough the last time. Nearly all the young chaps either wiped out or crippled. Didn't they learn a lesson from that?'

Mama sighed. 'No, because the ones that make the wars don't go and fight them. We are getting old, boy. We do not understand these things. But I am just sorry for the Mams whose boys will have to go. Indeed, and the Dads. Our Davy will be worried to death about Huw and then if the war does come, there will be Edward to go as well. And young Gareth and Jim. Deary me. These are very bad times I am thinking.'

As she surreptitiously dried her eyes with her pinafore Dada blew his nose loudly. ' Maybe it's all just old talk, girl. We must hope so. Folks do like to talk even when they do have nothing to say.'

However, on the following Sunday morning it turned out that it was not 'just old talk'. At Plas Gwyn, Davy and his family were gathered in front of the big square wireless to hear the fateful words: 'Britain is at war with Germany.' Nan turned to Davy, tears spilling down her cheeks while he took her hand in silence. There was nothing to say. Edward turned pale and bit his lip but Huw tossed his dark curls with an air of bravado.

'Well, that's it! I've got in just in time. They'll want every pilot they can get now, so I'll soon be seeing some action.'

Edward turned to him angrily. 'Be quiet, Huw.' He nodded towards his mother and father. 'Think of other people's feelings beside your own, will you? You'll soon find it's not a game or some adventure from 'Boys Own Paper'. Have a bit of sense.'

Nan got up shakily and Davy rose too and with an arm around her waist led her from the room.

Edward turned to Huw again. 'Think on about what Mam and Dad are feeling, can't you. It'll break Mam's heart when you go next week.'

Huw gave a harsh laugh. ' Hers'll be the only heart that's broken, anyway. Nobody else'll care.'

' That's not true, Huw, and you know it. We'll all care, all the family.'

'All beside Rhiannon,' Huw answered bitterly. 'She'll be glad to see me go. Nobody to pester her while she sets about getting you from Ruth.'

Edward's face darkened, 'She's tried that before and got nowhere. She should have got it into her thick head that I'm not interested by now. Huw, why waste your feelings on her? She's not worth it.'

'You know nothing about it!' Huw got up off his chair and stood over Edward. 'You going to volunteer, or wait until they come looking for you?' he sneered.

'I'm going to do just that,' Edward replied, quietly. 'They can come and look for me, then if I've got to go I'll go, but not before. It's no good Kitchener or anybody else poking a finger at me with all that 'King and Country' business. The King's got plenty of people looking after him and as for Country, well Wales is my country. Nobody's declared war on Wales yet.'

'You're just lily-livered!' Huw hissed and turning on his heel flung himself out of the door.

Edward sighed and made his way slowly up to his room. He flopped onto his bed and lay with his arms behind his head and stared at the topmost branches of the old fir-tree outside, etched against a blue sky. It was so peaceful. Why did politicians and warlords have to spoil everything. His heart ached for Mam and Dad and he felt genuinely sorry for Huw and apprehensive about the future. He knew only too well how headstrong Huw was, blind to danger and always taking risks. He lay on his back, his thoughts sombre and had lost count of time when he heard the door of his bedroom open. He turned his head and when he saw Huw come in and close the door he sat up warily. His brother lowered himself onto the foot of the bed and was silent for a moment, his head lowered. Then he lifted his eyes to Edward who saw that they shone with unshed tears. 'Sorry, Ned,' he said hoarsely. 'I didn't mean what I said. Oh, Lord, why did I try to take it out on you. It's because of Rhiannon, as you can guess. She told me the other night that she wouldn't have me if I was the last man in the world. All she wanted was you.'

'Well,' said Edward, briskly, 'She's not likely to get me. I'm sorry, family or not, I've no time for her. Besides, I'm quite contented with Ruth.'

Huw brushed the back of his hand across his eyes, then got up and turning his back on Edward, stared out of the window. After a while he seemed to pull himself together. 'You're lucky, Ned. You've got a nice girl who thinks as much of you as you do of her. Me, well, I love Rhiannon. Fell for her the first time I saw her and I can't seem to put her out of my mind. But she's got no time for me. Oh, I'd do to take her around till somebody better turned up, but she doesn't care a rap for me or my feelings.' He turned and gave Edward a lop-sided smile. 'Well, I'll be gone at the end of next week. Up into the wild blue yonder, if they'll have me. Remember? I always did want to fly.'

Well, I'm going to now, with a bit of luck. Wish me luck, Ned. You know I didn't mean what I said, don't you?'

Edward got up, his throat aching, and put his arm round his brother's shoulders. 'Don't be daft, mun,' he said roughly, past the lump in his throat. 'As you say, you always wanted to fly. Well, now's your chance. There's no way you'd get to fly at Pryce Jones's. Anyway, you'll be too busy to think of Rhiannon and wherever you're stationed there's bound to be lots of girls. You'll wow 'em in that uniform!'

For a moment Huw turned his head into Edward's shoulder, then he straightened and gave Edward something of his old insouciant grin. 'I'll be one of the Brylcream Boys, right enough.'

'Yes,' said Edward, grinning back, 'And it won't be my Brylcream you'll be pinching. You'll have to buy your own from now on, and your own fags. Then you'll know what life is all about, my lad.'

Huw punched Edward gently on the arm. 'Thanks, Ned. I'll go and find Mam and Dad now. I've made a bit of a B.F. of myself, I see now, but if I survive I daresay I'll have grown up by the end of this lot.'

'I daresay you will,' said Edward. 'I'm going down to Pool Road now, see what Mama and Dada are making of the news. Want to come?'

Huw shook his head. 'I don't think so. Rhiannon is sure to be there and the less I see of her the sooner I'll get over her, I guess. I'll go down during the week when she's not there. Say goodbye to them, isn't it.'

'Friday you go, right? Well, we'll miss you, but I guess you'll have leaves and so on. I suppose I'll have to go myself, eventually. I don't want to but I daresay I'll be called up. They'll say that Martin can do without me and I suppose he can. I was getting on so well, too. Let's hope it won't last too long, that's all. I was hoping to ask Ruth to marry me as soon as I finished my training, but I can't really ask her till this little lot's over, can I?'

'Oh, I don't know. I daresay a lot of couples will rush to get married before the bloke is called up. But don't bank on it finishing soon. They said that about the last war and that lasted four years. What would you join, anyway?'

'I dunno. Haven't thought much about it, really. The Royal Welsh Fusiliers I daresay. Be a foot soldier. That'll suit me, don't you think? Plodding, you know.'

The brothers grinned at each other and while Huw ran down the stairs Edward shrugged on a jacket and left to go to Pool Road.

When he got there he found Llew and Owen sat round the table talking in low tones to Elwyn, while Mama and Nell were busy preparing the dinner and Dada was sitting by the fire. Edward took his place beside Owen in time to hear Llew say that Owen would be safe from call up.

' They won't call up teachers, I don't think.' he said. 'There'll still be kids needing schooling. What about you?' he asked, turning to Edward. 'Think you'll have to go?'

'Daresay,' replied Edward gloomily. 'Martin could manage without me at a pinch, although the work has increased quite a lot lately. I've no desire to go, though. It'll delay my passing out and getting qualified.'

'Damn that little housepainter, anyway. Upsetting everybody's lives!' growled Llew.

'Who is this housepainter, then?' asked Dada querulously, bringing his wiry white eyebrows together in a frown. 'The only housepainter I know is Sam Smout and he wouldn't upset people. Tidy man is Sam and quiet.'

'No, no, Dada. This Herr Hitler was only some housepainter.'

'You mean this old devil who is starting another war is only a housepainter!' said Dada, scandalised. 'Then why for is everybody taking notice of him? Good God, if Sam Smout tried to start a war they would lock him up, and quite right too. Are these Germans all daft?'

Nell came in from the back kitchen with a pot of potatoes which she put onto the trivet over the fire, followed by Mama. Both women were subdued. Mama carried a cloth and a large spoon. 'Mind to them legs, while I get to the oven,' she told Dada, but there was no edge to her voice. 'I want to baste this meat.'

Dada slowly moved his rheumaticky legs off the fender with something of an effort and much grunting. Edward watched the two women and felt a moment of great pity. Nell's Gareth would have to go to the war and as for Mama, she was getting too old for the worry and upset of seeing her grandsons going away. She still worried about all the family.

The front door opened while he was musing thus and Rhiannon came through into the kitchen. Her eyes sparkled when she saw Edward and she pulled up a chair close to his and sat down. Edward nodded coolly to her, then Elwyn said, 'There are plenty of jobs for you to do to help Mama and your Mam. Where've you been, anyway?'

'I've been up to Esther's house. I heard the wireless there.' Her voice rose with excitement. 'There's going to be a war after all! Isn't it exciting? This'll stir things up a bit. Don't you think so, Edward?'

Edward looked down at the bright eager face and had difficulty in concealing his distaste. 'Oh, it'll stir things up all right. A great deal more than any of us can picture. I tell you one thing, those who have lived through the last war won't be getting excited. They've seen all the horror before and its likely to be worse this time.' His voice trailed off, as he thought of Mama and Nell. 'Most of us will have to go. Huw will be going next Friday, into the Air Force.'

But Rhiannon's mind only registered what he had said first. 'But you won't have to go, Edward, will you?' she asked.

'Oh yes, I'll have to go, as well,' Edward replied, a touch of bitterness in his voice. 'Just when I was getting on well with Martin's firm. That's another thing with this war. Careers will be interrupted and studies go down the drain. No, I see nothing at all to get excited about.'

'Oh, I didn't think you'd have to go,' Rhiannon said, thoughtfully. 'I thought, you being a lawyer, you wouldn't be called up.'

'That's it,' Edward replied shortly, 'I'm not a lawyer yet.' He turned to Llew. 'I'm thinking of asking Ruth to marry me when they do send for me. D'you think I ought to? Would it be fair to her? I wanted to ask Dad what he thought, but just now they're pretty worried about Huw, and I don't want to give them anything else to worry about, although they know I'm going to marry her eventually. I was going to wait till I've qualified and I'd have more to offer her, but I don't know now. What do you think?'

'That's something only Ruth and you can decide, boy.' Llew said, shaking his head. 'I've no doubt there'll be a lot of folks wanting to get married before the men are marched off.'

'Where would you live?' asked Owen.

'Oh, I don't know. I haven't really gone into it all. I suppose I'll decide all that when the time comes. I suppose Ruth could stay with her folks while the war's on. I could go there when I come home on leave. I get on all right with her Mam and Dad.'

'Talk it over with Ruth.' counselled Llew. 'Anyway, I must get off home. I left Mattie cooking the dinner. She's a bit low after hearing the wireless, 'cos of Jim.' He sighed. 'I never thought we'd have to go through this again so soon. But there, men don't seem to learn from history. I am sorry for the young men who'll have to go through the mill, and I'm sorry for the women who are left behind to worry about them.' He sighed again, more deeply, 'God help us all, I say,' and he rose heavily, calling goodbye to Mama and Nell working in the back kitchen.

There was a thoughtful silence when he'd gone. Rhiannon had been dismayed when she heard Edward talking of marrying Ruth. She had been considering ways in which she could spike that romance, feeling confident that with Ruth out of the way she could win Edward over eventually. His very indifference to her intrigued her and fanned the flames of her infatuation with him. But if he was married it would be much harder. Not impossible, she mused, but certainly harder. When he too rose to go, followed by Owen, she repaired to her room, where she sat on the edge of the bed and contemplated, first of all Edward having to go to the war and the fact that he might marry Ruth before he went. She hadn't got much time left. She'd think of something. She always did.

5

Partings and Internment

Saturday morning was fine and sunny and at ten o'clock Nan had taken
the day's bread out of the oven and was wrapping two golden loaves in
a clean cloth prior to putting them in a large square basket to take over
her arm to Pool Road. Davy came in from the garden carrying a few
bronze chrysanthemums. Nan took them from him and fetching a vase
from the cupboard filled it with water and arranged the chrysanthemums
in it. Davy washed his hands at the sink, then, while he was drying them
with the coarse roller towel he turned to regard her thoughtfully as she
bent over the flowers. Then he went over and took her in his arms. She
buried her face in his shoulder and he patted her back without speaking.
He knew she had not got over the pain of parting from Huw the day
before and indeed he himself had been in a sombre mood ever since.
They had tried to hide their heartache from Edward but they couldn't
hide it from each other for they each knew the other's thoughts and
feelings too well. Davy pictured again the scene on Newtown station,
Nan putting on a brave face, Edward, who had begged an hour off to
see his brother off, ragging Huw a little half-heartedly. There was a
febrile look to Huw himself and his eyes slid away from their faces,
while he greeted Edward's jokes with a high, unnatural laugh. When the
train finally steamed into the station with all the accompanying noise
and bustle, Huw turned to them almost desperately, then swung on his
heel and leapt onto the train. He had closed the door then hung out of
the window, first clasping his father's hand, then Edward's and finally, as
Nan had stretched up on her toes, he had hugged her shoulders and
kissed her cheek. His eyes shone with unshed tears but he lifted his
head and with his usual devil-may-care grin he punched the air with his

fist, 'Look out, Adolph! Here I come!' Then, with a wink at Edward, 'Don't worry, Mam, Dad. It won't last long once I get up there,' pointing to the sky. 'It'll soon be Christmas and I'll be home. Get the turkey stuffed and the mince pies in the oven, Mam.' On that the train whistle shrilled and with a great puffing and bustle the train began to move and the three standing on the platform were left to wave to the disappearing figure as it was borne out of sight round the corner on its way to 'somewhere in England'.

Nan finally drew away from Davy's arms and wiped her eyes. ' I'll just go down to Pool Road to take this bread. I shan't be long. We're just having sausage and mash with a tin of peas for our dinner. That won't take much making.' She got her coat down from its peg in the hall, fastened it up and took the basket of bread over her arm. She reached for the door knob and then turned. 'He will be all right, won't he, Davy?'

Davy moved to take her hand and squeeze it. He kissed her cheek and nodded confidently. 'Of course, love. You know Huw! If he fell in the midden he'd come up with a bunch of violets! Don't worry. He'll be home before you know it. And probably a lot wiser for the experience, mark my words.'

Nan gave a shaky smile and went on her way. Davy sighed heavily and sat down in his armchair by the fire and stared into the flames. He hoped he was right but he had terrible feeling that there was a long haul in front of them and that there would be a lot of horrors to face on the way.

When Nan arrived at Pool Road, Mama took the bread from her with her usual fervent thanks and pressed her to sit down and have the ritual cup of tea. Dada made sympathetic noises through his whiskers. He was aware that Huw was only the first of his grandsons to go and suddenly he felt very old and confused. He muttered to himself in Welsh and when Mama asked him if he wanted a cup of tea he frowned and shook his head, his blue eyes looking quite fierce. Mama frowned back and then, in a rare soft moment, leaned down and patted his hand, gnarled with rheumatism, as it lay on his knee. He looked up at her with a pathetic air and then down at his hand wonderingly. She turned and reaching for the kettle, singing above the fire, she poured boiling water into the teapot and sat down opposite Nan, pouring tea for herself and the younger woman.

'Nell has gone down town for a few things,' she sipped the hot tea, her blue-veined old hands wrapped around the cup. 'The others are working till dinner-time. Nell fetched a bit of shin beef from Maurice Powell's yesterday so I have made a pot of stew for us today. Pity our Davy did not come down with you. You could have stayed for to have some. There will be plenty to go round.'

Nan smiled. 'You still want to feed us all, Mama,' she said. 'But no, thanks all the same. I'll get back shortly now. We're only having a few sausages for dinner, but Edward will be in at half-past twelve. He'll be in a hurry, I daresay. I think he's taking Ruth to watch the football. Town playing Caersws, I think he said.'

'Nell and Elwyn are talking of going to see Meg and Reini tomorrow in this car that Elwyn has bought. He wanted us to go with them, but indeed I do think it would be a bit too much for us. And then it does get pretty cold these nights, and that would be a bit too much for this boy here,' looking over her shoulder at Dada, who pricked up his ears.

'What would be a bit too much for me?' he asked, indignantly.

'To go to Meg's in that old car of Elwyn's. It would surely get cold by the time we would set off back. That wouldn't do your rheumatics any good, boy.'

'I want to go!' Dada said, petulantly. 'I will wrap up warm. I would only be sitting in this car. Then I will sit by the fire at the Walkmill. What harm? Yes, I do want to go. Tell Elwyn we will come with them.' He bent a fierce look on Mama who shrugged and raised her eyebrows at Nan. 'He is still ready for any mischief.' She sighed and shook her head.

'I don't think it would do either of you any harm. Be a bit of a break,' urged Nan, 'Only put warm things on, isn't it? Meg would love to see you, I know. Well,' she rose from her chair. 'I must be getting back and get the spuds on. Think on and go you for that little trip out. Do you the world of good. A bit of something different.'

And so it was that on Sunday, after Elwyn and Nell had been to Church and they had all had dinner, Dada and Mama were dressed in warm clothes, they were tucked into the back seat of Elwyn's second-hand Morris, with a blanket over their knees and off they went, Dada's old eyes sparkling under his wiry, white brows and Mama looking a little apprehensive by his side. Nell sat proudly beside Elwyn, and Rhiannon and Gareth stood on the doorstep, waving them off. The morning mist that had drifted up from the river had cleared and the September sun had struggled through, although it was cold and a few ragged clouds sailed above the surrounding hills. The leaves were beginning to change colour, especially those of the wild cherries in the woods beyond Abermule, which had turned to crimson. Here and there the chestnuts were golden, and bore the spiky green casings which held the rich brown nuts. The beech trees had not yet lost their green to the golden brown which would come in October but there seemed to be a waiting hush in the countryside, which heralded the dying of the year. The hillsides were rich with the bronze of the bracken and the leaves had begun to thin out on the hedges. As Elwyn drove slowly and steadily along, Dada was gazing eagerly at the countryside around and even Mama had relaxed and was obviously enjoying herself. They had been unable to go to Manafon for some years now, since Dada's old pony Mog had died and Dada had become too infirm to drive the trap anyway. The only other member of the family to have acquired a car was Reini, Meg's husband, and his son Heinrich known in the family as Henry, was learning to drive it.

They were all enjoying the journey, especially the old ones, to whom it was a great adventure. Dada had perked up no end and even Mama was almost sorry when they eventually drove slowly through Manafon and the drive was almost over. But they all looked forward eagerly to seeing Meg, everyone's favourite, and Reini and Henry, now regarded as an integral part of the Rees family. The car turned into the lane leading up to the Walkmill and Elwyn changed gears to begin the stiff climb through the high hedges and the tall trees beyond them, already scattering a carpet of fallen leaves on the rough surface of the lane. At last they reached the top and their first sight of the Walkmill, standing whitewashed and trim in the misty September sun. An old collie ran out to meet the car, barking furiously and followed by another, younger dog. The front door opened and there was Meg, a smile of welcome on her face, the old scar from the fire at the Gwalia Mill so familiar to the family that they no longer noticed it, but saw only the sweet smile and the contentment in her blue eyes. Her thick fair hair was streaked with grey now and the once-trim waist-line was a little thicker, but she was still their much-loved Meggie.

She was expecting Nell and Elwyn, but she exclaimed in delighted surprise at the sight of Mama and Dada, beaming at her from the back seat. She came forward to help and they were extricated from the car with some difficulty and helped into the house that had once been Mama's home amid much exclamations of welcome and warm counselling to 'take their time' and 'mind the step!' Eventually they were installed in wooden armchairs near the fire which blazed merrily in the hearth, and Mama looked round, relieved to see that nothing had altered and everything looked cherished and well cared-for. The flames were reflected in the shining dark oak of the dresser, in the china displayed there and in the brass handles on the drawers and whilst the blue jugs still stood on the window sills, instead of gillyflowers they held branches of Autumn leaves and scarlet hips and haws. Mama gave a sigh of contentment and watched Meg excitedly bustling around to give them a cup of tea in their hand, helped by Nell, whilst Elwyn let himself out of the back door saying he would go and find Reini and Henry. Meg called out to him that they were on the top field, trying to get the last of the hay in before the weather broke. 'I know they shouldn't be working on a Sunday,' she said, as she poured out strong cups of tea, 'but we can't afford to lose any hay. Its too dear to buy in for the animals and you never know what sort of a winter we will get.'

When Mama and Dada had their cups in their hands and were sipping gratefully, she and Nell took their seats at the table, and they all settled down for a cosy chat. When Meg asked what sort of a run they had had, Mama answered with a wry smile. 'Well, this car does not have to stop at the Beehive for a drink before it can go any farther, like Mog used to, and somebody else I could name.'

Dada ducked his head to hide a sly smile. 'Well, now. That was a good pint of ale they kept at that old Beehive, too. And Mog did stop there always. Would not go past, no matter what. I did only have a drink to pass the time while Mog did drink his bucket of water. It did help him to climb this old lane yonder.'

Mama sniffed, 'I did always wonder how Mog did know that there was water for him at the Beehive in the first place. Funny thing, too. That old Bold that you did have before Mog did know about that water as well. Indeed, a very funny thing that.'

Dada shook his head and adopted an innocent air. 'Well now, there is no knowing the ways of animals. Mebbe they can smell out the water when they pass, like. Who knows?'

'Funny how they can smell out that water and not any other on the way here. I think that ale does surely smell a lot stronger than the water.' Mama sipped her tea and shrugged.

Nell and Meg looked at each other and laughed. Meg said, 'Never mind, Dada. Reini has got some good ale in the cellar. You shall have some later on.' Dada brightened and Mama clicked her tongue and looked up at the ceiling.

'We have had enough trouble getting his legs into that car as it is. If he has got ale in him we will be in worse trouble.'

'No, no, Mama,' soothed Meg, smiling. 'Just a drop to cheer him up, isn't it?' Dada nodded his enthusiastic agreement and drew more tea through his whiskers. 'Aye, aye. I will not drink enough to go down into my legs, woman dear. Just a drop to wet my whistle. Nothing like a drop of ale to lay the dust from the road, I do find.'

Nell drained her cup and set it down in the saucer. 'Anyway, how are you all? There's a terrible thing this old war. At least Reini and Henry won't have to go will they?'

She plucked at the tablecloth and her face took on a worried expression. 'No, they won't have to go to the war. But Reini is worried he may be interned. Because he is a German, see.'

Nell frowned. 'What do you mean, interned?'

'Well, he says that they could take him away from us and lock him up somewhere while the war's on. Because he's a German and we're at war with Germany.'

'Sort of put him in prison, d'you mean?' Nell was horrified. 'Why on earth would they do that? What harm would he do here on the farm, even if he is a German? Good Lord, he's been here ever since the last war and done nobody any harm. A good man like that, surely they wouldn't do anything that daft?'

Meg sighed. 'I don't know. I just know he's worrying about something. He told me about this internment thing when I asked him what was wrong. He said we'd better be prepared, in case. Henry won't have to go to the war because of the farm, and so Reini is getting him ready quietly in case he has to take over. Oh, Nell, I don't know what I'll do if they take him away from me. We've never been parted since we married, and I never thought we would be. I suppose Henry and me will manage, we'll have to. It's just that I can't bear to be parted from Reini.' Her eyes brimmed with tears and she dabbed at them with the corner of her apron, while Nell looked across at the old couple by the fire anxiously. However, Dada was dozing off in the heat of the fire, his teacup balanced precariously on his lap, while Mama sipped the last dregs from her cup, oblivious of the low voices of her daughters at the table.

She rose and rescued Dada's cup and saucer. 'More tea?' she asked Mama, brightly, but her mother shook her head. 'I will wait now for my tea proper, ' she said. 'It is nice and warm here. I could nearly doze off myself, indeed.'

'Well, there is nothing to stop you,' laughed Meg. 'Have forty winks while I take Nell for a look around.'

'Yes, go you two,' Mama replied, contentedly. 'I will be all right resting here, and that one,' nodding at Dada,' that one will snooze for a bit now. You would need a wheelbarrow to take him for a look round the farm, anyway.' She chuckled and nodded at them as they gathered up the cups and saucers and carried them out to the back kitchen to be washed up. When this was done the two women let themselves out of the back door and strolled arm in arm across the yard, scattering the big brown hens, who squawked indignantly before resuming their scratching in the dirt.

They peeped into the barn, but at the moment it housed only a large old Fordson tractor and a few hens pecking among the straw. 'No horses now?' asked Nell. Meg shook her head. 'It's sad, really, isn't it? Reini would like to have kept the two big plough horses on and carried on using them, but Henry has more modern ideas and persuaded him to buy that old tractor. Right enough it does the job quicker but oh, I was so sad to see the lovely old horses go to be sold. That's an ugly old thing, isn't it?'

Nell shrugged, 'You must go with the times, I suppose. Henry has taken to the farming well, they tell me.'

She nodded. 'Oh, he loves it. He is a born farmer. It is just as well. There is a lot to do. Reini has bought in quite a bit more land. We have sheep on the hill yonder and the milking cows in the next field. Then there are the store cattle on the bottom meadow and we have four fields for crops. Anyway, come and see the pigs. I love pigs.' She drew Nell round the corner of the barn and over to the pigsties, where they leaned their arms on the top of the wall and gazed down at four large white pigs snuffling in the trough in the one sty and in the other a massive sow with nine piglets lying against her vast side. She looked up at them with small, suspicious eyes and gave a warning grunt.

Nell felt a cold nose against the back of her calf and jumped, startled, but it was only a black and white sheep-dog. It flopped down on its belly when Nell turned and wagging its tail, grinned ingratiatingly up at her. 'Hello, boy,' she said, bending to stroke its head, causing it to roll over and present a muddy underside to her. 'That boy is a girl,' laughed Meg. 'That's Floss, Henry's dog. Very good with sheep. Henry has trained her well. He is good with the dogs. There are four of them. Floss's grandmother, Fly. She's too old to work much now, but she is at Henry's heels all day long. Then Floss's mother, Judy, and lastly the old collie you saw out the front, Ben, who is Floss's Dad and has always been Reini's dog. Good dogs are worth their weight in gold with sheep. Let's go down to the stream. Its lovely there now the leaves are changing colour. There's a lot of blackberries down there, too. I have picked a fair few pounds already. Made jam with some and tarts. There's a basketful in the house you can take home with you to make tarts with and I will give you a couple of pots of jam.'

They made their way through a small wicket gate and descended a steep, rough path, bordered with beech trees, their leaves turning a rich golden brown. Birds rose from the blackthorn bushes as they disturbed them and the willow trees along the banks of the stream drooped yellowing leaves down to the surface of the water. Brambles covered the slope and a lot of the berries still clung to the thorny branches, although the leaves were turning into crimson around them. Nell plucked a large and juicy berry and popped it into her mouth, savouring the sweetness of the purple juice. They came upon a crab apple tree, covered with small rosy apples. 'I must pick some of these this coming week,' said Meg, 'Make some crab apple jelly. I don't look forward to it. Its a messy old business, but the men both love the jelly, which turns out nice and pink. What with the fruit all coming at the same time, there is so much to do at this time of year, with jams and chutneys. I feel like a squirrel sometimes,' she laughed. 'Getting ready for the winter.'

They stood for a while watching the stream as it flowed between the lush vegetation of its banks then they turned and climbed back up the path and through the wicket gate.

'You seem to have really taken to this life, our Meg,' said Nell.

'Oh, yes. It is a hard old life sometimes, but I would take to any life as long as it is with Reini. There are times when it is not easy and it is really not the life Reini was used to. He was a scientist, you know, but he was looking into the growing of grains and so on, so of course he knew about farming and I believe his people had a big farm in Bavaria, so he wasn't ignorant about it. He does work very hard and Henry, as well. Especially in the springtime when we are lambing. Then we must all get up before the light and sometimes it is very cold, especially when there is snow on the ground. Reini does try to lamb in the barn as far as he can, but they must still go up on the hill at night in case some old awkward ewe is dropping her lamb early or they have missed the signs. Then there are still all the other jobs, the feeding and the milking and the pigs. The pigs will farrow at an awkward time or the cows will calf in the middle of everything. No, it is not an easy life but I love it and Reini is a good, kind man. But what about you, our Nell? Are you contented now you're home again?'

Nell shrugged, 'Oh contented enough. Glad to be back home again. Canada was all very well, and like you I am contented enough as long as I am with Elwyn. He is a good man, as well. We have been lucky in our men, haven't we?' She smiled at Meg, who nodded in agreement, then she went on, 'I did think to buy Mrs Moses Owen's shop and start my own millinery business, like I had in Canada. But it didn't turn out that way. First of all, Mama and Dada really need somebody there all the time. Mama cannot do what she used to, though you have to let her think she does. There is a lot to do with the two old ones, as well as my own lot. Nan is very good, she still does the baking for us and the heavy washing. That is a big help, indeed. And Mattie does all our sewing for us, another good girl, she is. Indeed, we have all been lucky in our partners, apart from Davy's first and I suppose Llew's first wasn't much cop, although she had two grand kids in Owen and Esther.'

'Well, they were Reeses, weren't they?' put in Meg, laughing.

Indeed,' smiled Nell. 'Anyway, it wasn't all down to looking after them all at once that I gave up the idea of the hat shop. It struck me that there was really no longer much call for the sort of hats I'd been trained to make. Remember them? Great big things with ruching and tucking, flowers and feathers and yards of ribbon. Nowadays the hats are mostly felt, and cheeky little shapes, at that. Maybe a feather but not much else in trimming. I saw a girl the other day. She had long dark hair, falling in waves and curls, and perched on the top was a little red pillbox with two bobbles hanging from the crown on strings. Lord, but it looked cute. I'd like to have seen old Madame Beynon's face if she'd have been alive to see it!'

Both women were giggling when they heard the sound of men's voices nearby and turned to see Reini, Henry and Elwyn coming towards them, deep in conversation. They stopped speaking when they saw the women and Reini hurried forward with outstretched hand. 'Nell, it is very good to see you.' Henry, christened Heinrich but only called that by his father, also stepped forward, a tall, fair young man, with his father's steady grey eyes and his mother's thick fair hair. He smiled with great sweetness at Nell and as she took his hand she notices his knuckles were bruised and the skin broken and when she looked up into his face, he was sporting a fine black eye. He had obviously been in a fight, she thought and felt some surprise as he did not seem to be the fighting sort. However she made no remark and Meg spoke then, telling Reini with some eagerness that Mama and Dada had come, too.

Reini smiled warmly at her, 'So Elwyn tells me. That is good. We will go in to see them. I have heard all the news from the family of

Newtown. This is a terrible business, this war, Nell. I suppose your Gareth will have to go to fight. And Davy's Huw has gone already. The man Hitler is a madman, and has to be stopped of course. It is easy for me to say that and very selfish, for my Heinrich will not have to go, I think.' He put his arm round Henry's broad shoulders and then drew Meg into the circle of his other arm. 'We will keep the home fires burning, hein, and provide you all with food. If they will leave me alone to stay.' Meg's face clouded and Henry's eyes were bleak, but he rallied them. 'Come, let us go into the house and see Mama and Dada. It will soon be time for the meal, anyway. We are getting hungry, eh, Heinrich?'

The three linked together made their way to the house and when they went through into the kitchen Mama and Dada woke with a start, although Mama assured them that she had not been asleep, just resting her eyes for a moment. Reini went forward to shake her hand and then Dada's, followed by Henry, who kissed his grandmother and shook hands with Dada.

'Diawl, there is a big fellow you have got now,' said Dada and looking up at him, studied the ripened black eye for a moment. 'What did the other fellow look like?' He chuckled hoarsely and Henry flushed and looked across at his mother. Meg turned away and Nell, sensing something sensitive, joined her, murmuring, 'Shall we start getting the tea on, then? We shall have to start back before dark, anyway.' Meg nodded and they went through into the back kitchen, where they piled china onto a big tray, and bustled back and fore with plates of sweet pink boiled ham, jars of pickles and chutney, plates piled with thickly buttered fresh home-made bread, a dish of floury scones with a pot of raspberry jam, and last, but not least, a fine big fruit cake. Reini helped Mama across to her seat at the table then fetched in a small table which he set beside Dada's chair. He brought Dada a plate of the ham, which he had cut up into small pieces, and Dada settled back with a fork in one hand and a folded a piece of bread in the other and forked ham into his mouth with great enjoyment. After he had demolished his plate of ham he was handed a cup of tea, which he drew thirstily through his whiskers. After that he managed a scone and a piece of cake, followed by a further cup of tea. Replete he lay back in his chair and overcome with a full stomach and the warmth of the fire, found himself slipping into one of his easy dozes again. His last thought was of Henry and his black eye. 'He didn't look like a fighting man,' thought Dada, drowsily.

Eventually the time came for them to get Mama and Dada into their layers of clothes and Reini and Elwyn helped them out to the car. Meg carried out a large tin full of blackberries and a square basket containing two blackberry pies, two packs of farm butter and a round yellow cheese. Henry followed with a small grain sack filled with potatoes, carrots and three swedes. These were all stored in the boot and with Meg, Reini and Henry standing at the top of the lane smiling and waving, the little Morris bumped down the lane.

As soon as they were out on the open road again Nell turned to Elwyn and lowering her voice, asked 'Come on. Tell them. What was wrong with Henry? Why had he been fighting? He's not that sort of lad.'

Elwyn stared out at the unfolding road and shook his head doubtfully. 'Trouble there, I'm afraid. Not from Henry, mind. It seems he's been courting a girl from a neighbouring farm. She's got two brothers. One of them's been called up. Seems the powers that be reckon only the one is needed to run the farm. The family's pretty sore about it. Seeing as Henry won't have to go they're jealous, I suppose. Anyway they've started calling him a dirty Hun and a Jerry and the other night they egged some village boys on to set on him and thrash him.'

Nell drew her breath in with horror. 'Oh Lord, poor Henry. He went to school with the village boys, too. There was never any trouble before. Nemma God, he was born in Manafon! What are they thinking of?'

'That's it,' grunted Elwyn. 'They're not thinking. Government propaganda stirs up anti-German feelings and the likes of Henry suffer. It's pretty nasty. What's more, the girl's father has forbidden her to see Henry. I think they're meeting in secret, but that's dangerous. He'll likely get a worse pasting if they're found out. Too bad. He's a nice lad, too.'

'Oh, deary me. What a worry for Meg and Reini. And they're already worrying about something called internment. Means men might come and take Reini away and lock him up while the war is on. Meg'll be in a state if they do that.'

Elwyn nodded slowly. 'I'm afraid everybody will suffer in some way through this war. It will be long and hard on us all, I'm thinking. We've all got troubles to face.'

Nell sighed and as if to accompany her there was a soft snore and a bubbling breath from the muffled figures on the back seat as they drove into Newtown as darkness fell.

6

Christmas and Pianos

Christmas that year was subdued. The only joy was the sight of Huw in his Air Force uniform, home on a forty-eight hour leave for Christmas Day and Boxing Day. The sight of him looking so dashing and handsome, with his blue forage cap perched on his dark curls and his eyes sparkling with the old mischief caused a painful clutch at Nan's heart, but she kept up a smiling face and enfolded him in the warmth of home.

However, Huw missed his brother. He hadn't realised how much old Ned had been part of the home scene but Edward was now in the Royal Engineers and somewhere in France with the British Expeditionary Force. Nan had had a card from him just saying that he was all right at the end of November and on Christmas Eve there had been a Christmas card addressed to them all. Huw wondered what had made Ned choose the R.E.'s. Gareth and Jim had both chosen the Royal Welsh Fusiliers and had been mobilised in Newtown before being transferred to Wrexham. From that time onwards Newtown became a garrison town.

The family all gathered at Pool Road for Christmas tea: Llew and Mattie, Davy, Nan and Huw, Owen and a very pregnant Lena, and Esther and Martin with their three. Esther was also pregnant again and soon retired to a corner of the old sofa with Lena to compare notes while Rhiannon watched them with a bored curl of the lip. Nell and Nan laid the table and carried in the food, a large cake which Nan had made and warm mince pies which Nell had baked on Christmas Eve and warmed through in the oven. Plates were brought in with slices or ham and tongue on them, to be eaten with various pickles and freshly baked bread, generously spread with farm butter from the Walkmill.

Llew looked at the laden table and gave a rueful shake of the head.

'Make the most of all this, you lot. They tell me rationing's on the way. We'll be limited to a bit of this and a bit of that. We'll be lucky having Meggie on the farm. She'll be able to help out a bit with butter and cheese and maybe the odd bit of home-cured bacon and so on when they kill a pig. That'll be more than most poor devils will get, I'm thinking.'

Mama was sitting in her chair opposite Dada. They both had a plate on their lap and were savouring small bits of bread and meat, and both nodding with satisfaction at the sight of their family seated round the board enjoying the good food. Suddenly Dada stopped his chewing and struggled to say something. He was frowning anxiously and fixed Llew with a stern eye.

'What is it, Dada,' asked Llew. 'Do you want something?'

Dada nodded and wiped his whiskers with the back of his hand. 'The boys,' he managed to get out at last. 'Where are the young ones? Why are they not here? Nobody tells me anything. They should come to see for me and Mama.'

They all looked at each other and Huw rose from the table and went over to his grandfather. 'I'm here, Dada,' he said, softly. 'I have come to see for you,' and he squatted down beside the old man's chair grinning up at him.

Dada nodded and sat back against his cushions again, 'Oh, aye. Huw. Good boy, good boy.' He peered a little closer at Huw and the wiry eyebrows went up. 'What for are you dressed like that, boy?'

Huw was silent for a moment then he shrugged, 'I am in the Air Force now, Dada. Flying in aeroplanes.'

Dada looked horrified. 'I do not hold with it. The good Lord would have given us wings, did he want us to fly. No, I don't hold with it.' He subsided, muttering into his whiskers and gazed into the fire with a bewildered air.

'Do you take that plate off his knee, good boy, before it does land on the floor.' Mama's voice was uncertain and lacked her usual sharpness. Truth to tell they were both failing and the family round the table shook their heads and looked at each other sadly. They tried to keep as much from them as possible regarding the war and were grateful that they did not seem to take in the seriousness of it.

Owen took a piece of bread and folded it over. Half of it disappeared in one bite and his voice was muffled as he turned to Llew and asked, 'D'you feel guilty, Dad? You know, not going to the war this time.' His eyes twinkled knowingly as he swallowed the other half of the bread.

Llew snorted, 'You know better than to ask me that, boy. I did my stint in the last one. I swore I'd never go and fight another war for them and I haven't changed my mind.'

Owen nodded, 'I shan't have to go, being a teacher. I'm glad. I think I'm a pacifist. Mind if somebody attacked Wales, maybe I'd fight back. Defend my own, isn't it?'

Davy grinned at him. 'Maybe you could join this new lot. What do they call them? L.D.V.?'

'What does that stand for?' asked Owen, suspiciously.

'Local Defence Volunteers, I think. There's a few drilling already. Bring your own broom handles.'

Huw burst out laughing, spraying crumbs and making Nan shake her head and tut-tutted smilingly. 'Bring your own broom handles!' he echoed. 'What good would they be against machine guns, or whatever it is that Jerry is using.'

'Oh, they've been promised guns eventually. Though half of them wouldn't know what to do with 'em. Good God, can you picture some local characters running amok with guns? They'd soon clear the streets of Newtown, let alone frighten the Jerries to death!' Davy chuckled at the thought.

'I might join something like that,' replied Owen, thoughtfully. 'That would be defending my own, wouldn't it?'

'Oh dear,' Nan sighed. 'Surely it's not going to last all that long, is it? I thought the French had got the Maginot Line and nothing could get past that?'

'Aye, and Jerry's got the Siegfrid line,' grunted Llew. 'I'm sorry to say, I think it's going to be a long haul.'

Esther and Lena had been listening from their seats on the sofa, balancing their plates on their laps. Lena stared at Owen, her dark eyes big with worry. 'This L.D.V. thing isn't dangerous, is it, Owen?'

'Of course not, love,' he responded, heartily. 'Ah, Jerry's not going to get this far! Why would he want to take Newtown, anyway?' He chuckled. 'It's not got much strategic value, now, has it?'

'I don't know what strategic value means,' Lena retorted. 'Do you have to join this thing?'

'No, of course I don't. But it might be a good idea. Save me being handed the white feather.' He gave a short laugh. They all knew how often that had happened to Davy in the last war by idiotic women who had no idea of the heart condition which had kept him at home.

Huw shook his head in despair. 'God, it all sounds so dull. Being in the RAF is so exciting. I had hoped to be a pilot, but it would have taken too long to have trained. Anyway, being a rear gunner is pretty vital. Gives me a real go at Jerry. There's something about being up in the clouds that beats anything. I think I may stay in the Air Force after the war's over. It's the life for me!'

Davy felt Nan shudder next to him and his own breath caught in his throat. 'You always were up in the clouds, lad,' he said, striving for lightness, but his eyes were bleak and he reached for Nan's hand and squeezed it.

Esther gazed across at her husband as he sat quietly between Mary and Alun and cut up their meat for them, encouraging them to eat up their bread. The baby, Johnny, was upstairs on Nell's bed, worn out by the excitements of the day, the wonder of the Christmas tree and the bewilderment at the presents and particularly the wrappings. He was charmed with the coloured paper and when held up to inspect the tree, had to be restrained from pushing a shiny gold globe into his mouth under the impression that it was some exotic fruit.

'Shall you be joining this L.D.V., Martin?' she asked him, trying to keep the concern out of her voice. She had felt so lucky that he wasn't going off to the war, but surely if they were going to give guns to the men left behind, they must expect the Germans to get through into Wales? Suddenly the war loomed too near for comfort.

Martin looked across at her and smiled lovingly. 'I don't think so, dear. I'll have too much to do now they've taken Edward from me. I thought I might have been able to make a case for him to stay but they obviously didn't think my office merited two lawyers, and the fact that he hadn't yet taken his finals was against him. We're pretty busy actually and I've only got Miss Morris and she's slowing down a bit now. I don't know how old she is. One daren't ask and there's nothing in the records.

I suppose when my Dad took her on he wouldn't have asked her age. It wasn't done then.' He grinned. 'Anyway, I doubt if I'd be much use with a gun. Better I get on with what I'm doing and make money to keep my ever-increasing family!'

Esther stifled a relieved sigh. 'Couldn't you get a young girl for Miss Morris to train up to help?'

Martin shook his head. 'Easier said than done. I've heard they're going to build a munitions factory here which will mean higher wages than I can afford to pay a girl, so they'll all flock there when it comes, no doubt.'

The soft voice of Mattie broke in then, 'Maybe I could get a job at these munitions when they come. It would be better to be doing something all day than to be sitting at home worrying about our Jim.'

Llew looked at her in surprise, 'You go to work in a factory? You wouldn't like it. Besides, you've got enough to do looking after me!' He laughed. 'Anyway, we're not short of money, are we?'

'No, no. I'm not saying that, Llew. But it would be nice to be able to put a bit away, so as to set Jim up a bit when he comes home.' Her eyes were wistful.

'Ah well. We'll see. The factory hasn't come yet. Anyway, I'm hoping that after the war the people will have the sense to oust the Tories and put in a Labour government. Then maybe there will be some good jobs going, even here.'

'Come on, Llew,' grinned Davy. 'It's Christmas. No politics at Christmas, is it.'

Rhiannon had been watching Huw and thinking how much more attractive he looked in his uniform. She still dreamed of Edward and was thankful that he hadn't married Ruth before he went. She was still determined to get him somehow, but in the meantime Huw looked dashing. 'There's a good picture at the Regent next week. D'you fancy coming?' she asked him.

Huw looked at the pretty face and was relieved to find himself unmoved. 'Won't be here, Rhiannon. Only got today and tomorrow and then back to base early the next morning.' Seeing her face fall, he couldn't resist adding, 'Wouldn't be right for me to take you, anyway. Got a girl of my own now, back at the base.'

His mother looked at him with interest. 'One of many, I suppose?'

'Not this time, Mam,' He shook his head and grinned. 'This time it's the real thing. Lovely girl, works in the NAAFI, called Roma. Next time I get a leave I'd like to bring her to meet you, if she can come. I've met her folks, she lives not far from the base, and they're really nice people.'

'Well, well,' Davy's eyes widened. 'It's happened at last. I believe he's really serious!'

'Sure am, as the Yanks say,' Huw nodded.

There was a babble of teasing and Dada stirred and came awake. 'Eh, eh.? What has happened? What are you saying? Where is Mama?'

'I am here, boy. What is with you. They are saying Huw has a girl.'

He pushed himself up a little straighter and looked around him. 'Where is this girl of Huw's? I don't see her. Bring her to me. I want to see her. Edward brought his girl to see me. Nice girl. Duw, I have forgotten her name. A nice girl. Where is Edward, did you say?'

'Edward has gone to the war,' replied Mama, sighing. 'Gone to fight the Germans again. Llew went to fight the Germans a while ago, and now they are giving trouble again, seems like. Some old bad one called Hitler.'

Dada frowned and searched his memory. 'Wasn't he something to do with Sam Smout?' he asked, looking confused.

Davy stifled his laughter. 'No, no, Dada. Its just that he was a housepainter, like Sam Smout.'

'I did think Sam Smout wouldn't be causing trouble like that. Quiet man, is Sam Smout.'

'Why are you talking about Sam Smout?' asked Mama, herself puzzled now. 'He hasn't gone to the war, has he? Too old surely. Maybe he had a son that went?'

Davy turned to the others and threw up his hands. They were all trying to control their giggles and he shushed them. It hurt him to see the old people failing and yet it was hard sometimes not to laugh at some of the things they came out with in the innocence of their confusion. He looked round at his family and felt how good it was to see them gathered together there with their families and how sad that the three young men were missing from the gathering. He looked across at Huw and his heart constricted. Huw was so devil-may-care, would he be all right? Many of the battles in this war were going to be fought in the air. The boys in the planes would be so vulnerable.

Suddenly he turned and put his arm round Nan and hugged her. She looked up at him and smiled and knew what he was thinking.

A row of men sat like crows along the Bridge Wall on a Tuesday at the end of January. They were watching some fifty or so soldiers marching in ragged fashion down Kerry Road, a red-faced and exasperated sergeant yelling at them to 'Keep in step, you lot!' The men on the wall watched dispassionately as the soldiers shuffled past and turned in the direction of New Road.

'Hm,' grunted Gwilym the Sticks. 'Why should England tremble!'

'Nemmind England. God help Wales if them are the best they can send!' snorted Bill Owen Neaudd.

'Well, fair play,' put in a thin dark man, judiciously. ''They'm only just been called up. Give 'em time, boys. Dessay they'll shape up soon enough when they got to.'

'Ah,' another nodded. 'It wunna make a lot of difference the way they march when they'm stuck in the trenches. We dinna 'ave much shape when we went to the last lot.'

'I wonder will there be much trench warfare this time?' Bill Owen put in.

'They do say this lot'll be mostly fought in the air. Dropping bombs an' suchlike. Wunna want the Poor Bloody Infantry this time.'

' Dunna talk so daft, mun!' Gwilym the Sticks was scornful. 'They canna fight a war proper without the infantry. They'll always need the footsloggers to do the dirty work, I hear they'm havin' a fair tough time in France. Up to their necks in snow and that Maginot line fell apart first whack.'

'Poor sods,' said the dark man. 'It'll be trenches there, all right. God, I can still feel what it was like the last time, stuck in them trenches. Rats fightin' you for your bit of hard-tack. And the lice!' He shuddered at the memory. 'I think the lice was worst of all. Sometimes it was nearly a relief when the order come to go over the top. You'd forget what was bitin' you then when you was dodgin' Jerry's shells.' He looked down at his stiff leg, sticking out in front of him, the result of a shattered kneecap which still gave him pain on damp days. 'I dunno what it was all about then. Didn't seem no sense to that war. I suppose the Generals enjoyed theirselves. We poor devils didn't. I never give much for that King and Country bull. Maybe this time there's a bit more reason for it. That oul' Hitler 'as to be stopped, I suppose. But I'm glad I wunna 'ave to go. I 'ad enough.'

'Dunna thee want to be an 'ero, then?' asked Owen Neaudd, grinning.

'I was an 'ero last time, mun, an' it didn't do me a bit of good. Only buggered me leg up!' The dark man gave a bitter laugh.

'Well,' put in a small, wizened man on the edge of the group, 'I dunna think war was ever any good to the poor fools what had to fight 'em. The only lot to do any good out of the wars is them as make the guns and the mortars and so on. They make plenty and they anna got to go and fight. Tinna fair, is it?' he asked, pathetically.

The others shook their heads solemnly and watched the last of the militiamen march off up New Road.

'It's Tuesday,' pointed out Gwilym the Sticks, as though just discovering the fact. 'Open all day! I'm goin' for a pint. You comin?' He turned to Owen Neaudd.

'If thee't payin'. I got no money.'

Gwilym grunted. 'I'll buy thee one. Only one, mind. Allus the same. You anna got any money.'

'Well,' Owen Neaudd pointed out, 'The dole dunna go very far. The kids is gettin' big and they eat a lot. Maybe there'll be jobs when this factory comes down Pool Road. Maybe I'll get a job there.'

'Then I'll 'ave a long wait to get a pint back off thee, for they anna started to build it yet. Might look for a job there meself. Make a better living than selling sticks, surely.'

'Oh, I dunno,' chimed in the dark man, 'Owl Charlie Carter dinna do too bad out of it, I'm told. They say as he had a tidy bit put by when he went.'

'Lot of good that would do 'im. You canna take it with you; though I dessay Charlie would 'ave a good try. Somebody told me he'd 'ad an 'ole drilled in the top of 'is wooden leg an' 'e kep' the money in there!'

Gwilym raised his eyebrows questioningly. 'Would he be wearing his wooden leg when got to heaven?' he asked, seriously.

'Sure to,' said Owen Neaudd, with a solemn face. 'Be awkward trying to play an 'arp, 'oppin' around on one leg.'

'That's it! That's enough daft talk.' Gwilym jumped down from the wall and dusted the seat of his trousers with a brisk hand. 'Come on if thee's want that pint, Neaudd. We'll go across to the Queen's Head. They keep a tidy pint there. Any of the rest of you comin'?' There was a murmur of assent and they all slid down from the wall and made their way over the road to the Queen's Head.

When they entered the dim interior it was to be met with a thick atmosphere of tobacco smoke from the various pipes and cigarettes and a smell of beer, together with the stale smell of suits and coats brought out only on Market Day, as the farmers, having left their wives in the Market Hall disposing of the last of their wares, or taking advantage of the chance to go round the shops, had escaped to spend a little of their takings from the Smithfield. Some were sustaining themselves with thick wads of bread and cheese with home-made pickles on the side, the only fare obtainable. Others leaned elbows on the bar and bemoaned the poor price of fat lambs or the store cattle they had sold that morning, as farmers have done since markets were invented. Here and there the lilt of Welsh could be heard from those who hailed from the more remote hill farms. One round-faced man with rosy cheeks was swaying in his corner seat and softly singing a hymn in Welsh. A farmer seated nearby finished the last of his pint and joined in. Without looking at each other they harmonised together and were joined by two others, providing further harmony. No-one took any notice of them and they took no notice of each other except when the round-faced man embarked on another hymn and they waited to lend their voices softly to his.

Gwilym the Sticks and his companions pressed up to the bar and ordered their pints and halves, according to the state of their finances. There was much scratching about in trousers pockets to find the requisite amount, made up mostly of pennies and half-pennies. There was very little money about in Newtown since the depression which had begun in the late twenties. Jobs were scarce and the dole was meagre. However, with the young men going to the war, there would be openings for the older men, relics of the last conflict, and with the anticipated coming of the new factory, hopes were high among men and women that at last they would be needed again.

Gwilym took his first pull at his pint of bitter and exhaled with satisfaction. He knew he was going to be in for a tongue-lashing when he got home and his wife smelled the ale on him, but that was nothing new. He drank very little but his wife was strict Calvinist and that little was too much for her. However Gwilym took it all in his stride and never answered her back. Each day he handed over to her the small amount he made by selling his bags of logs and morning sticks, always keeping back enough for a pint for himself and one for some other poor soul like Owen Neaudd who had no money. This way he felt he was fulfilling his Christian duty, although he never told his wife of this. He looked around now and his eyes fell on the men in the corner, softly singing their hymns. His face softened. That's what he called churchgoing. Nice hymns and doing your friends a favour when you could. He was brought up a Baptist, but he only went when the Anniversary was on. His wife kept on reminding him that he was on the downward slope to hell, but he was totally unable to reconcile the idea of a loving Saviour with the 'black chapel' image of a God with a flaming sword of retribution, thundering curses at him because he enjoyed a pint of beer occasionally. Maybe his missus was on the right road to heaven, but it seemed to Gwilym that it wouldn't be a heaven that suited him. If his wife was anything to go by it would be scrubbed clean and very cold, a bare place with not much love around. Gwilym liked to imagine his own heaven, with lots of colour and music, warmth and love, with St Peter at the door, welcoming him in and saying, 'Come on in Gwilym. You've not been such a bad sort. You always bought a pint for them what needed it and gave free wood to some of the old folks who couldn't afford coal.' Then Gwilym would look round for his wife, to make sure she hadn't heard what St Peter had said. He sighed when he thought they might end up in the same heaven. He was hoping for some peace when his time came to go there.

The small wizened man who had come in with Gwilym and company and whose name was Eddie Bowen leaned his shoulder against the bar and stared at his boots, worse for wear and tied up with string. His glass of mild ale sat untouched on the bar as he brooded. Gwilym's eye fell on him and he raised enquiring eyebrows.

'What's with thee, Eddie? Thee hasn't touched thee ale!'

The small man looked up at Gwilym and his eyes were bleak and beaten. He heaved a deep sigh and shook his head. 'It's this Transitional. It's near killed my missus.'

The group looked puzzled and Gwilym regarded him with a frown. 'How d'you mean, Eddie. You on the Transitional?'

Eddie nodded. 'Aye. When I was laid off from the Kymric six weeks ago I couldn't go on the dole straight away. You has to go on the Transitional for a few weeks, first, an' they send a chap round to your house to see if you've got anythin' you can sell before they start to give you dole. Well, of course, we anna got much, but we 'ad the piano.' He paused and shook his head sadly. 'Its our Frank, see. He's musical.' He looked round them with a diffident air of pride. 'He allus was. Well the missus was determined to get 'im a piano, by hook and by crook. And her got one, too. Saved a bob here and a tanner there an' bought one for two pounds from Gladys Oliver, who'd got a near new one. Well, her was playing in that dance band so I s'pose her had to have somethin' decent. Anyway we was payin' Ernie Oliver sixpence a week to teach our Frank and Ernie said he was a natural. Lord, he was comin' on well. Then this chap came. Well we dinna 'ave nuthin' else, only the piano. He told us we'd 'ave to sell that before we could 'ave any dole. What could we do? Elwyn Breeze bought it off us for his little gel to learn on. Only give us thirty bob for it, too. It's 'it my missus somethin' awful. Her's gone all quiet, won't talk about it. Cries on the quiet, too. It took 'er two years to save them tanners an' bobs to buy it. Our Frank tells her not to take on. He'll get another some day. But the life's gone out of 'er. Oh, 'er was that proud of getting our Frank the piano!' He sniffed and dragged his frayed cuff across his nose, then to hide the tears in his eyes he buried his face in his glass.

The group were silent, taking this in. They all knew what poverty was but this story of the end of a dream touched them all. Gwilym patted Eddie on the back awkwardly, but could find no words of comfort for him. They all sipped morosely at their drinks and the small choir in the corner softly sang 'Bread of Heaven', most of those around them humming a background harmony.

Owen Neaudd broke the silence, clearing his throat. 'Any of you lot goin' to join this Fred Carno's Army they're settin' up?'

'The broomstick army, you mean,' replied Gwilym, scornfully. 'Let's see if they get 'em some guns and a uniform, first. I inna goin' to march around Newtown with a broomstick over me shoulder for nobody. Anyway, do you see the need for it? Who's goin' to attack Newtown? What for? It wouldn't do 'em much good, would it?'

'Oh, I dunno,' mused Owen Neaudd. 'Maybe when this munitions factory comes 'ere they might think to attack that.'

'I thought that was all very hush-hush?' put in the thin dark man.

'Huh!' Gwilym snorted. 'Hush-hush in Newtown? They know 'ow many times thee's blown thee nose afore breakfast in this town, mun. And they bury thee afore thee't dead. Oh, tell us somethin'. Is it true that oul' Councillor Giles is dead?'

'Well, they'm buryin' 'im on suspicion, anyway. Funeral's on Thursday.' Owen Neaudd supplied the information.

'Well,' said Gwilym, shaking his head. 'One thing I will say, Council meetings won't be the same now without him. He was a funny oul' stick, but 'e talked a lot of sense at times and shook some o' them other fools up anyway. An' they need it.'

'Ah,' said Neaudd. 'They'm a dozy lot. Well, I dunno about the rest of you buggers, but I'm goin' 'ome. The oul' 'ooman'll murder me if 'er thinks I'm spendin' money that should be comin' to 'er.' He drained his pint pot and looked round for Eddie Bowen. The little man had crept into the corner to join the hymn singers and was giving a lachrymose rendering of 'Abide with Me', tears softly coursing down his thin cheeks.

Gwilym pointed him out . 'Look at that. On half a pint of mild. Oh well, poor devil. Not much comfort at home, I dessay. I'm sorry for Mrs Bowen. Tidy 'ooman, too. An' their Frank. Oh well, summat'll come for them, no doubt. We'm all goin' to be rich. There's a war on.'

With that they all drifted out, leaving little Eddie Bowen to his hymns and tears and the company of the choir.

7

Small Boats and Bombshells

The end of May in that year of 1940 brought news of the retreat of the British forces to Dunkirk, where they were hemmed in by the Germans. Gathered on the beach there they were bombarded by shell fire and strafed by German planes. The only way out was by sea and a flotilla of boats of all descriptions was organised to bring the beleaguered troops off the beach. Edward was among those waiting there, tired after a three day march with practically no sleep and little food. He felt he was in a horrific nightmare, following on a winter bogged down in snow and surrounded by confusion. He had become resigned to the fact that he was unlikely to come out of this lot alive, but was almost too exhausted to care. When his platoon commander asked for a volunteer to swim out to a waiting steamer to take the rope line out and secure it so that those who were unable to swim could use the line to get to the boat, he was the first to step forward. He could swim, yes, learnt up Severn Green, but whether he was a strong enough swimmer to get to the boat was another thing. However, anything was better than standing there waiting to be mown down and he took the rope end, took off his boots, handed his rifle to the man nearest him and plunged into the waves.

He struck out towards the boat, which seemed a very long way off, and soon found that swimming in the gently flowing Severn in his bathing trunks was a far cry from struggling through the sea with wet khaki weighing him down. Luckily the sea was fairly calm and not too cold and he battled on. Soon the struggle was adding to his exhaustion and his arms and legs began to ache and the dragging rope was becoming a burden. His heart was pounding under his ribs and he began to swallow water as the weariness caused his head to dip under the waves. Suddenly he knew he could go no further and with a despairing cry he turned over onto his back and began to lose consciousness. He had been unaware of how close he had come to the steamer but felt arms reach down to heave him aboard, and he was soon laid down on the deck while the rope was untied from round his wrist and made fast to a bollard on the deck.

He came to to find someone helping him to his feet and guiding his stumbling footsteps towards the funnel. There he was put to sit, with his back to the funnel and with a prayer of thankfulness he relaxed against the warm metal and promptly fell asleep. The next thing he knew he was feasting his eyes on the white cliffs of Dover and although it was not Wales, at that moment it was the most wonderful sight in the world.

Meanwhile, at Plasgwyn Nan and Davy were out of their minds with worry. They had heard nothing from Edward for some weeks, the last thing had been a letter from somewhere in France which told them very little but enclosed a snapshot of Edward, looking incredibly young, standing between two older soldiers who flanked him protectively, as he stood, looking slightly bewildered, in an over-long army greatcoat, his hands plunged into his pockets for warmth, his forage cap over one ear and his boots sunk into about a foot of snow. Nan's heart ached when she studied it and thought of what her boy was going through. She grew to depend on Davy for comfort and his arm around her shoulders as they listened to the wireless avidly. Little was given away, however, for security reasons, presumably, and it was not until the second of June that they received a brief note, 'Back in Britain. Coming home. With you twelve o'clock Saturday. Edward.' Nan and Davy clung to each other, their cheeks wet with tears of relief and as soon as they had recovered they hurried down to Pool Road to tell everyone there. The talking and relieved laughter left Dada totally bewildered but eventually it got through to him that Edward was all right and was coming home on Saturday and he was too overcome at the news to get any words out and the little tear that ran down his old cheek went unremarked. Rhiannon sat on the old sofa and said nothing but hugged the news to her. She would be there to meet his train, no-one would stop her. Never mind that Ruth would be there, she supposed. She just had to see him and then she would plan what to do about getting him. She ignored the excited chatter around her and fell to her fantasies in which Edward took her into his arms and told her that it was she that he really loved. This ended with a lingering kiss and the image of Ruth walking away defeated. She smiled to herself. It had to happen. She would make it happen!

Nell was asking Davy whether they had heard anything from Huw lately. Davy grinned. 'We've had a letter rhapsodising over his plane and over his girl, and sometimes it's not clear which one he's talking about. But he seems in good spirits. Same old Huw. It'd be nice if he could get leave while Edward is home, but he hasn't mentioned anything. In fact he hints, without saying much, that things are hotting up as far as bombing raids are concerned.' He looked across at Nan and sighed. He knew that relief at Edward's safe return still left the worry over Huw. 'What about Gareth? Still in Northern Ireland?'

'Yes.' Nell nodded. ''Though what on earth they're doing there, I don't know. Elwyn says something about 'covering their backs' but I don't understand. I'm just glad that he sounds fairly safe for the moment. Mattie's Jim is there too. They seem to be in the same barracks in Londonderry. That's nice for them, isn't it. I hope they stay there. They say the people are very nice to them. They'll be coming home with Irish wives, I shouldn't be surprised.' she added with a twinkle.

'Who's got Irish wives?' asked Mama, frowning.

'Nobody yet, Mama,' chuckled Nell. 'I was just saying, Gareth and Jim might fall for Irish girls if they stay over in Ireland much longer.'

Mama sniffed. 'Welsh girls is good enough for anybody, I should think. Better than marrying wild Irish.'

'Mama! All the Irish are not wild! Anyway, I hear that the militiamen are moving up to Wrexham shortly and then over to join Mattie's lads in Ireland and that an Irish regiment are coming here. So maybe the Newtown girls will marry Irishmen .'

'And why not,' put in Davy, with a smile. 'All Celts together, isn't it.' But Mama only shook her head in disapproval. 'I don't hold with it,' she said, stubbornly.

And so it came about that the same train which brought Edward home from Dunkirk also brought the first contingent of the Royal

Inniskillin Fusiliers to Newtown. When the train steamed into the station, the Rees family, consisting of Davy and Nan, Owen and Lena and Ruth, with Rhiannon standing a little apart, stepped forward eagerly, but had to search for Edward among a bewildering crowd of strange soldiers, speaking with a strange accent.

'Irish.' remarked Davy, and on that Edward broke through the crowd and hurried towards them, hugging first his mother, then his father and looking eagerly towards Ruth, who came forward shyly for his kiss. Owen wrung his hand and Lena squeezed his arm and reached up to kiss his cheek. Rhiannon hung back for a moment, feasting her eyes on him but when he turned to her and hesitatingly held out his hand, she stepped forward boldly and stretched up to kiss him on the mouth. He drew back with a small frown and hastily turned to his mother.

'Good to be home, Mam,' he said, grinning down at her. 'Hope you've got the kettle on. I haven't had a decent cup of tea since I left!'

'Come you, boy,' Nan answered, her eyes shining with unshed tears of joy and the group gathered round him as he caught and held Ruth's hand and tucked her arm through his.

Rhiannon bit her lip and remained standing there for a moment after they had all moved off towards the bridge. One of the Irish soldiers who had watched the scene with interest, kept his eyes on Rhiannon's face and thought she was the most beautiful girl he had ever seen. He hadn't missed Edward's quick withdrawal when she tried to kiss him nor the expression of revulsion on his face and it occurred to him that the man must be blind or daft to turn away from a girl like that. The chap had obviously preferred the other girl, who wasn't a patch on this one for looks. He picked up his kitbag and hefted it onto his shoulder moving off after his mates in the direction of the bridge. He found himself walking alongside Rhiannon and couldn't resist giving her an appreciative grin. Her chin was high again and she stared at him assessingly.

'Hello,' he said, tentatively. 'You live in this place?'

'At the moment, worse luck.' she replied and tossed her dark curls back over her shoulder. She peeped up at him from under her lashes and took in a square face, the most compelling feature of which were a pair of brilliant blue eyes with curling dark lashes. His mouth was generous, with a full lower lip and his black hair sprang in curls from under his forage cap.

He looked puzzled. 'You sound American?'

'Canadian,' she corrected. 'My parents are Welsh, that's how I'm over here. But I shan't be staying. Once the war is over I'll be off.'

'Where?' he asked.

'Don't know yet. I'll see what turns up.'

'You should try Ireland,' he grinned. 'God's own country.'

She shrugged and tried to hurry on, but his long strides kept up with her. 'Any chance I could see you some evening?' he ventured.

'You're a fast worker!' She raised her eyebrows. 'Anyway, my cousin just got back from Dunkirk. I don't know how long he'll be on leave , but I expect I'll be busy in the evenings while he's here.'

He looked at her quizzically. 'Looked to me like he was likely to be pretty busy himself.'

She coloured up and her eyes flashed temper. 'That's all you know. Leave me alone!'

He put up a hand in surrender and fought with a grin, but before he could reply there was a barked order from the Sergeant of the platoon as he attempted to bring order to his troops on the other platform.

'And you, Kerrigan!' rang out the Irish voice. 'When you can tear yourself away from the local talent, perhaps you'll fall in with the rest.'

'Yes, Sarge. Coming, Sarge.' Sean Kerrigan saluted Rhiannon. 'See you around.' he said softly and ran after the squad, to take his place as they formed fours to march out of the station. As they disappeared through the door he looked back at Rhiannon and winked and then he was gone out of sight.

She couldn't resist smiling to herself, ruefully, at the bare-faced cheek of him, but she had to admit that she could understand what they meant when they talked of the Irish charm. He had certainly kissed the Blarney stone, as they say. Then through the station railings she could see the Rees's moving triumphantly along, with Edward in their midst and her mouth tightened as she saw that Edward still had Ruth's arm through his possessively. She felt the hot tears sting her eyes, but she dashed them away impatiently. She wouldn't give up. She'd think of something.

After a celebration tea at Plas Gwyn, for which Nan had outdone herself, they all went down to Pool Road where Edward had a warm welcome home from Nell and Elwyn. When he went over to kiss Mama, the tears ran down the old, wrinkled cheeks and she put up a trembling hand to touch his face. He touched the tears with his finger and shook his head.

'Now, come on, Mama. What are these for? I'm back safe and sound, isn't it?'

Mama was ashamed of her weakness. She had never been one to cry, but lately the tears came too easily, She resented the fact that she couldn't work like she used to, and it upset her to see Dada confused and bewildered and constantly asking where the boys all were. She looked across at him now as he stared around him from under the bristling eyebrows, frowning and shaking his head in confusion.

Edward then stepped across to speak to Dada and gently took the gnarled old hand in his. 'Well, I'm back, Dada,' he said, softly.

The old man looked up at him. 'Is that old war over now, then?'

'No. no, Dada,' Edward smiled. 'Wish it was. No, I am back from France. Had to swim for it, too!' he laughed.

'Swim for it?' The old man frowned. 'Didn't they have boats to cross the sea, then?'

Edward chuckled. 'Oh there were plenty of boats. We had to swim from the beach to get on to them, is all.'

Dada shook his head, unable to comprehend, but then the dim blue eyes lit up and he bestowed a sweet smile on Edward. 'I am right glad to see you boy. But where are the other boys? They don't come to see for me?'

'Never you mind, Dada. They'll all be home before long, coming to see for you. Just now Jerry's got the upper hand, but never fear, we'll have him beat in the end.'

'Who is this Jerry, then? I thought as you were fighting against that Hitler. That housepainter, wasn't it?'

'Aye, aye, Dada. He won't be painting many houses after we've finished with him.'

The old man nodded and heaved a deep sigh. 'I do hope you will not take too long about it. I would like to be here when all the boys come back home. I am old,' he said with an air of pathos, 'And I can't wait very long.'

Edward patted his shoulder. He felt sad as he regarded the feeble old figure in the armchair, with the rheumatic-twisted limbs, the faded blue eyes and the once wiry white hair now lying in lank wisps on his collar. Mama too, was failing now he could see more clearly, and the indomitable old lady had only a sharp tongue left to show the strong will. 'Oh you'll still be here when we all come marching home, Dada, never fear. We'll have a high old time then, you'll see.'

Dada nodded and smiled vaguely at him. 'A high old time,' he echoed. 'Aye, aye boy. A high old time.' and he sank wearily back against the cushions.

'You will have a cup of tea in your hands?' queried Mama, looking round.

'Oh, of course,' Nell got up and moved the kettle over the fire. 'I am forgetting. Mama will scold,' she smiled at the old woman in the chair who nodded back. Nan rose also and went to fetch the cups and saucers. Elwyn and Owen, who were sitting at the table began to talk about the Local Defence Volunteers.

Much to Rhiannon's chagrin Edward and Ruth made their excuses and left to go and visit Ruth's parents at The Bryn. The rest sipped their tea and talked among themselves. Suddenly the wailing sound of the warning air-raid siren filled the air with its ululating message and everyone looked up, startled.

'Had we better go down in the cellar?' Nell asked urgently, looking round for Elwyn.

'We'd never get Dada down there.' Elwyn shook his head.

'I'm not going down no cellar,' protested Dada, struggling upright. 'Why for would I go down the cellar?'

'The aeroplanes, Dada!' Nell explained, breathlessly. 'The German aeroplanes are coming!'

'Well, they can't see me in my house!' Dada said, irritated.

On that there came the heavy drone above them and they all looked fearfully at the ceiling, rooted to the spot. They held their breath and waited as the threatening sound of the German bombers sent shivers through them. At last the sound receded into the distance and after a while the all-clear siren went. They all breathed a sigh of relief.

'How do you know they were Germans?' asked Rhiannon, adopting a scornful air.

'Because the siren tells us,' her father answered her, shortly. 'That's what it's for.'

'I don't see what they want to come and bomb Newtown for, there's nothing here.' Rhiannon shrugged.

On that there was a sound like a distant thud and the ground shook a little under them. 'My God,' breathed Owen. 'That was a bomb!'

'Some way off.' Davy said. 'They've gone now. I daresay they're coming back from a raid on Liverpool or one of the cities in the Midlands. Maybe they're unloading their bombs in case they run into ack-ack flack.' using the new wartime slang picked up from Huw's stories of 'sorties' and 'bombers' moons' etc. 'That's my guess, anyway.'

'Was that thunder?' asked Mama, confused.

They looked at each other. ' I daresay, Mama,' Nell soothed. She looked towards Dada but he had fallen asleep and was snoring gently.

Rhiannon went to the front door and opened it in order to see what was going on. She stood for a few moments silhouetted in the doorway with the light from the kitchen shining behind her. Suddenly a voice in the darkening street bellowed out, 'Put that light out!' and she hastily withdrew, muttering under her breath.

Nan turned to Davy. 'Time we were going, boy. It's getting late. Thanks for the tea, Nell. You'll be all right now, won't you? There won't be anything else tonight, I shouldn't think.'

'I hope not,' Nell answered, fervently. 'We can't take these two to the cellar.' she added, dropping her voice and nodding her head towards the two old people in their chairs.

Suddenly Lena let out a cry and clutched her swollen stomach. Owen stared at her and then put his arm round her. 'Are you all right, love?' he asked anxiously.

She let out a long breath. 'I think you'd better get me home, now,' she answered, a little shakily. 'I think its the baby!'

'Can you walk home?' asked Owen in a panic.

'Of course I can, silly.' she smiled at him. 'Come on. Goodnight everybody. Maybe I'll soon have some news for you.'

'I'd better come with you,' offered Nan. 'Make sure things are OK. You go on home, Davy love. Don't worry if I stay the night with Lena.' There was a general murmuring of concern, then Lena left, supported by Owen's strong arm, with Nan following them. Davy made for home shortly afterwards.

As he walked up Stone Street in the encroaching dark, he remembered his own feelings when Nan had been having her babies. He recalled the awful feeling of panic and helplessness, the fear of losing her, she who had become the very mainspring of his existence. It brought back to him the tragic night when his first wife had died in childbirth, died carrying a child that wasn't his. But that was behind him now and all he felt was the residue of pity for the wild and ill-fated Elinor. He moved his shoulders as though to shake off the thoughts and said a polite goodnight to a figure looming out of the dark. There were no street lights now and one had to have one's own radar in order to negotiate the dark pavements. He recognised the answering voice as that of Jack Richards, the Milk, and called to him by name.

'That Davy Rees?' asked Jack.

'Aye, it is. Jerry been having fun with his bombs, Jack.'

'Seemingly,' Jack answered, laconically. 'Didn't hear yet where it dropped, but not on the town anyway, dunna think. Probably killed a cow somewhere, like as not.'

'Poor old cow!' Davy grinned in the dark. 'Goodnight, Jack.' 'G'night.' Jack the Milk answered and his footsteps died away down the street.

Later it turned out that Jack the Milk guessed right. The bomb dropped in a field in the Mochdre district and left a large crater and a very dead cow!

Davy was finishing his breakfast when Nan walked in and sank into a chair at the table, opposite him. She looked tired but satisfied.

'A little girl,' she said, with a contented sigh, as Davy poured her a cup of tea. 'Lovely, too. Spittin' image of Owen. Lena was fine. 'Course Sister Lloyd-Jones come quite quick and as soon as she took charge everything went well. Oh, she's a marvellous nurse. I know they always used to swear by Nurse Latham in the old days, but nobody could have been better than Sister Lloyd-Jones. Owen is like a dog with two tails. They are going to call her Kathleen, I think. A bit of Irish that, yes?'

'I'll take you home again, Kathleen.' sang Davy. 'Aye, its a bit of Irish all right. Nice, though. I thought Owen would have wanted a Welsh name, all the same.'

' Her second name's to be Welsh.' nodded Nan, sipping her hot tea gratefully. 'Eluned. Kathleen Eluned Rees. Goes right nice together, I think.'

'Oh, well. The main thing is that mother and baby are all right. Anyway, what do you want to eat. There's some porridge left, plenty in fact. I made extra for Edward, but he's not surfaced yet. I didn't call him. I'll bet he's very tired. Hasn't had much sleep lately, seems like. Best to let him lie till he wakes of his own accord.'

Nan yawned and nodded. 'Yes, leave him. I know how he feels,' she smiled ruefully. 'I'll have a bit of that porridge and maybe a bit of toast after. Delivering babies is hungry work!'

'You ought to have a bit of a lie down, yourself,' Davy said, anxiously, as he stirred the porridge on the hob and ladled a generous helping into a bowl.

'Oh, I'll be all right,' Nan covered another yawn with her hand and tackled her porridge. 'I must set the bread to go and then it will be time to start the dinner. We'll not get to church this morning, but we could go this evening. I feel I must go and give thanks for Edward getting home safely. God help the poor boys left on that old beach. I wonder how many of them got away alive?'

'Oh, I think quite a lot got away onto various ships. They seem to think so in the Daily Despatch, anyway. A good few poor devils got killed, though. Edward was lucky. Good job he could swim!'

Nan shuddered. 'Oh dear, and that old water would be icy cold, too. Still, he seems to be all right, except real tired, doesn't he?'

'Well,' Davy answered, pouring himself another cup of tea. 'He'll soon get over that. We must see that he gets a good rest on leave, anyway. I daresay he'll want to be with Ruth as much as he can. He's only got fourteen days and he doesn't know where he'll be sent after he goes back. There's a lot going on in North Africa at the moment. Still, it's not for us to speculate.'

Nan sighed and shook her head. 'There's Huw to worry about too. It frightens me to think of him up in those old planes, even though he loves it. I couldn't help thinking Lena was lucky that the baby was a girl. Any more wars, at least she won't have to go. God doesn't make it very easy for mothers, does He?' she smiled ruefully.

'Nor for fathers,' replied Davy quietly.

The following week passed all too quickly for Edward. He tried to give as much time to his parents as he could, helping Davy in the garden, and running errands for Nan. He spent an hour here and there with the old ones at 46 Pool Road, who once again took him for granted, not understanding that he would be going away again soon. He tried, as far as possible to avoid Rhiannon, with whom he felt very uncomfortable, but she never left him if she was in when he called and the intensity of her gaze made him very hot under the collar. Most time, however, he spent with Ruth, either up at the Bryn farmhouse, where her parents made him very welcome, or he brought her down to Plasgwyn. She and Nan got on very well together and Nan looked forward to the time when Edward could get married and she could have her as a daughter-in-law.

In fact, she felt that Ruth could very well become the daughter she'd never had, and all she wanted was the war to be over so that her boys came back and they would all settle down in peace again.

Saturday evening came round, bringing the usual dance in the Church House. These 'Shilling Hops' were very popular, especially since the soldiers were stationed here, providing plenty of partners for the local girls, now that the Newtown boys were almost all away at the war. The girls were particularly keen to see what the Irish boys were like and there was a good attendance this Saturday when Edward and Ruth turned up along with the young people of the town. Ruth was looking very pretty in a red dress, which set off her dark curls and sparkling dark eyes.

She held proudly to Edward's arm, clutching the rough khaki of his sleeve possessively. Under the bright lights a crowd of soldiers and girls in bright dresses were circling around in a slow fox-trot, played with plenty of tenor saxophones and a clarinet, under the leadership of Richie Richards, a tiny figure, well under four feet tall, with a fine head on a crippled body, but who used his baton with confidence. The locals were well used to Richie, and seemed not to notice his hunched back and his lack of inches, but the newcomers stared at him in amazement. However, the band was very good and they soon became used to the tiny figure in his immaculate evening dress. The slow fox-trot ended as Edward and Ruth entered the hall and as Richie turned to bow to the dancers. Ruth heard a soldier close by turn to his mate and say 'I didn't think that little band leader was real. I thought he was a clockwork figure!' Ruth was very indignant. Everyone in town liked Richie, and she felt like telling the man off, but at that moment Richie turned and announced The Hokey-Kokey and Edward and Ruth found their hands grasped and they were drawn into the nearest circle. As the lively music started they flung their arms out with the others while all chanting, 'You put your left arm out, your left arm in, your left arm out and you shake it all about!'

Breathless and laughing they went through all the actions, flouncing into the middle until they reached the end and were released by the others. Edward put his arm round Ruth and looked down at her lovingly. She returned his look and she rested her head against his shoulder briefly. When she looked up she was conscious of a pair of dark eyes fixed on her from across the room. She recoiled a little as she recognised the burning intensity of Rhiannon's gaze and the naked venom in it. She was well aware that Rhiannon wanted Edward for herself but it had not occurred to her that this would generate such a hatred of her, Ruth, and she shivered a little. Edward looked down at her. 'Not cold, are you, love?' She shook her head and as Richie announced a waltz, Edward drew her into his arms and they danced dreamily to the strains of the wailing saxophones.

Meanwhile, Rhiannon was surrounded by khaki-clad Irishmen, foremost of whom was Sean Kerrigan. Eventually he drew her away from the rest and they slipped into the waltz, his arm encircling her slender waist, while she looked up at him provocatively. It was in her nature to flirt and he found her enchanting. He had forgotten how she had revealed her attraction to Edward when he had first seen her on the railway station, and he set out to charm her in the inimitable Irish way.

After two more dances Richie announced a 'Ladies Excuse Me'. Before Edward and Ruth could get up from where they were sitting, Rhiannon had brushed off Sean's arm, which was possessively round her waist and had darted across the floor, fetching up in front of Edward, and ignoring Ruth, pulled Edward up from his chair. 'Dance with me, Edward!' she demanded. 'It's a 'Ladies Excuse me'. You have to dance with me if I ask you.' She tugged him onto the floor and Edward looked back imploringly at Ruth, but there was nothing she could do to save him! Reluctantly he put his arm round Rhiannon's waist and guided her onto the floor.

'Don't look so miserable!' she taunted, whilst he held himself rigidly and gazed over her shoulder. 'Why not let yourself go and enjoy it? Quite a few fellows would like to be in your place, you know. Oh, Edward,' she attempted to press herself closer to him, 'You know I'm in love with you. Why don't you like me? I'm pretty, aren't I?'

'Look, Rhiannon,' Edward muttered, uncomfortably. 'I'd like you a lot better if you'd leave me alone. As you say, there are plenty of fellows who would be only too glad to have you. I've got Ruth and she's the only one for me. We shall be married as soon as the war is over. If you keep on like this you'll only make me dislike you.' He looked around and trying for a lighter note, laughed and said, 'There's a chap over there who can't take his eyes off you. Handsome chap too. An Irishman, I expect. He obviously fancies you. He'd be a lot better bet than me. After all, I'm taken.'

She sighed and pouted. 'But its you that I want, Edward.' Before she could say any more the music stopped and Edward, relieved, withdrew from her and courteously led her over to where Sean stood. He nodded to Sean and with a small mock bow to Rhiannon, hurried back across the room to where Ruth sat waiting.

'Whew!' he muttered, wiping his forehead with his handkerchief, ' That girl is the limit. She's spoiled rotten. Auntie Nell and Uncle Elwyn should have taken her in hand long ago. Anyway, let's forget her, eh? Come on, it's the Lambeth Walk. Doing that's fun,' and he took her hand and drew her onto the floor, where they were soon marching along to the music and forgetting Rhiannon.

Soon it was time for the Last Waltz, the couples drifting around together under lowered lights, the saxophones and clarinets sounding plaintive and the vocalist, a local lad with a soft tenor voice, voicing the question: 'Who's taking you home tonight?' A question echoed in whispers into the ears of many a girl there in the Church House. Then it was time for coats to be fetched and girls who had whispered 'Yes' to the question found themselves claimed by their swains and guided down the steps and into the darkness of a town with no street lighting.

Edward gave his arm to Ruth after first taking advantage of the darkness to kiss her thoroughly. The night was warm and balmy and they strolled through the town on their way to the Bryn Road, couples giggling as they bumped into each other in the blackout on a night without a moon. They paused at the gate leading into the farmyard, whispered all the things which lovers have whispered through the ages, held each other and kissed passionately and after a quick arrangement to see each other the next day they parted, Edward cautiously feeling his way back to the road in the total darkness and then hurrying through the town and up Kerry Road, the road familiar even in the darkness. He passed the dark, looming bulk of Pryce Jones's on the right and as he stepped onto the pavement outside Merton Terrace, a row of four Edwardian dwellings, he smelled the heady scent of a rosemary bush in Mrs Meredith's garden, the perfume of which filled the summer darkness. He sniffed appreciatively and strode on with confidence, knowing even in that darkness the feel of familiar ground beneath his feet.

He reached the door leading into the yard at the side of Plasgwyn and was about to lift the latch quietly when a shape detached itself from the shadows. He turned sharply as a voice whispered, 'Edward!' Edward recoiled. 'Rhiannon! What on earth are you doing here?' he hissed. 'Waiting for you,' came the unwelcome reply. A questing hand reached for him in the darkness, as he asked harshly, 'What do you want from me?'

'Don't be like that,' Rhiannon murmured. 'I want you to please take me home.'

'For God's sake, girl,' Edward ground out furiously. 'Where have you been till this time of night? The dance finished over an hour ago. Your Mam will be worried.'

'I know,' came the reply. 'That's why I want you to take me home. If I tell her I've been with you she won't give me a hard time.'

'Look here! You're not going to use me like that!' exploded Edward. 'I'm going in now. You must make your own way home and take the consequences!' and he moved once again to lift the latch. Rhiannon's arm shot out of the darkness and grabbed his sleeve. 'Edward, please! I'll have a terrible row if I go home alone now. I've been with Sean Kerrigan, the Irish lad and Mam'll do her nut!'

'Then why didn't this Sean Kerrigan see you safely home?' he asked, impatiently.

'Oh come on, please Edward. You're wasting time and its just getting later and I'm in for a most terrible row if you don't see me home.' and she began to sob hysterically.

Edward hesitated and then gave in. 'Oh, come on then,' he said, grabbing her arm. 'Just this once. But don't you ever let me in for anything like this again. If Ruth got to hear about me taking you home, she may not understand.'

'Thanks, Edward,' Rhiannon whispered in a small voice and slipping her arm through his, allowed herself to be hustled unceremoniously along the dark street on the way to No.46 Pool Road. As they reached the house and Rhiannon was about to mount the step she suddenly turned and pressing herself against Edward, reached up and kissed him passionately on the mouth. Before he could extricate himself from the embrace the door opened suddenly and Nell was standing there with an astonished look on her face and the light from the room shining out from behind her, revealing what looked like a very warm 'goodnight'.

'Edward!' Nell's voice was shocked. ' What on earth are you thinking of? And you supposed to be engaged to Ruth! For shame!' She reached out and pulled Rhiannon roughly into the house. Rhiannon just managed to call out 'Goodnight, Edward, darling, thank you for a lovely time!' when the door was shut decisively on a stunned and stuttering Edward. He stood on the pavement staring at the door, paralysed with disbelief. My God, that girl had really dropped him in it. Suppose Ruth got to hear about it? He shuddered at the thought. And how could he explain to Auntie Nell without giving Rhiannon away. She deserved it, but he knew he couldn't do it. 'Dammo!' he shouted aloud, sounding in that moment like Dada in a rage, then turned on his heel and strode away in the darkness, cursing Rhiannon under his breath and bumping into an unlit lamppost, and ending up in a worse temper and with an egg-like bump on his forehead for his pains.

8

Broomsticks and Nemesis

It was the following Monday evening and Llew and Owen were making
their way to the Armoury in Severn Place. As they turned the corner
from Broad Street they met a trickle of other heroes on their way to join
the L.D.V. - Local Defence Volunteers. Llew recognised Gwilym the
Sticks and lengthened his stride to catch him up, Owen following suit.

'Aye-up, Gwilym,' Llew was grinning. 'Now I know we'll win this
old war. Good God, and Owen Neaudd as well! Hitler anna got a chance,
mun.'

'Well, the old war is draggin' on a bit,' answered Gwilym. 'I thought
it was time I give an 'and. I dunna think the lot that are runnin' it 'ave got
much idea. It'll take somebody who was in the last lot to sort 'em out a
bit. Thee wast in the last lot. What dust 'ee think?'

'The same as thee,' replied Llew nodding. 'If they'll let us at the
Jerries we'll soon sort 'em out. What d'you say, Neaudd?'

'Well,' Owen Neaudd blinked solemnly. 'We canna do any worst
than them buggers at the top now. We 'ad to fetch the poor devils back
from Dunkirk in boats, and they'm talking about that as though it were a
victory. Ah, but,' he continued, doubtfully, 'We canna do much with
broomsticks, mun. They'll 'ave to give us guns to do any good.'

'Oh, we'll get guns bye'n bye, dessay,' opined Gwilym the Sticks.
'There'll be some from the country, you know, farmers and the like, as'll
have their own guns. They canna leave the rest of us with broomsticks.
I'm lookin' forward to 'avin' me own gun, too. There's one or two sods
I'd like to shoot in Newtown,' he added, darkly.

'Now, now, Gwilym,' warned Llew, stifling a grin as he glanced
sideways and caught the merriment in Owen's eyes. 'If the big men hear

thee talk like that they'll never give thee a gun.'

Gwilym grunted. 'If they dunna give me a gun I shanna play. Then there'll be one less to look out for 'em when the Jerries reach Newtown!'

'Dust'ee really think Jerry'll get as far as Newtown?' asked Owen Neaudd with raised eyebrows. 'I canna see it, somehow. 'Less they come up the Severn in a gunboat.' He chuckled. 'We should 'ave to call in Dick the Boats to repel 'em!'

Laughing heartily at the picture this conjured up they all trooped into the Drill Hall. There some forty-odd men stood self-consciously round the hall, men of various ages and sizes, about half-a-dozen country types smugly carrying shotguns over their shoulders and looking ready for action. The rest, mostly weaponless, stared resentfully at these superior beings and those one or two who had brought broomsticks tried to pretend they didn't belong to them. At the far end of the hall three men stood looking doubtfully at the volunteers, obviously trying to picture them as a fighting force and failing! Two of the men were locals, in civvies, Eddie Probert, who kept a small cafe in Town and who had at one time been a Sergeant-major in the Territorials, and Jack the Fish, whose name indicated his trade, who also had done time in the 'Terriers'. The third man was in khaki with a couple of pips on his shoulder and an air of authority. It was the latter who eventually started the proceedings.

'Right, men,' he began, drawing himself up and trying to put confidence into his voice. 'If you'll just form lines up here in front of me, I'll try to give you some idea of what we hope to do.'

The would-be fighting men shuffled forward, those with the broomsticks abandoning them against the wall hurriedly, and after much confusion, which did nothing to increase the officer's confidence, they managed to form into lines with a dozen men in each. When the command 'At ease!' rang out, those who had fought in the last war took up the position automatically, and the others copied them as quickly as they could. When the shuffling finished the uniformed man began to address them, flanked by Eddie Probert and Jack the Fish, attempting to look knowledgeable and superior.

' Well, men,' the officer began, tentatively. 'As you probably know, the object of this exercise is to form a fighting force of local men to guard local towns, villages and installations, so that the regular fighting forces can be released to engage the enemy elsewhere.' The men all looked up at him with varying degrees of eagerness and nodded to show that they were with him so far. He went on to tell them how this was going to be achieved, through meeting to drill under a proper instructor, and how their local knowledge would be invaluable. They looked pleased at this and drew themselves up a little straighter. He then introduced them to Captain Probert and Sergeant Price, both of whom had trained with the Territorial Amy and will be in charge, with help from time to time from a non-commissioned officer from regular army units stationed locally, wherever possible. He told them that at the moment it would be a Sergeant from the Royal Inniskillin Fusiliers who would be helping out with the training. They would be meeting twice a week for the moment and he hoped that the uniforms and rifles and possibly other weapons (which caused an excited stir in the ranks!) would be available fairly soon. This caused a sigh of relief to those with and without broomsticks. 'However,' he went on, 'will you please bring along broomsticks or pick-axe handles in the meantime, so that we can simulate weapons so as to get on with the training. Understood?'

The fighting men nodded and shuffled again, looking at each other as though to say 'Is that it?' Then the officer began again. 'Before I dismiss you, you will be required to attend for training here in this Drill Hall on Thursday evening this week and on Mondays and Thursdays each week thereafter. Understood?' he barked. 'Right, then. Dismiss!'

The ranks broke raggedly, those with guns marching away with them over their shoulders, those with broomsticks surreptitiously collecting them and carrying them away as inconspicuously as possible. The rest, aware that they too would be carrying these undignified weapons next time forbore to tease them as they might have done otherwise. As they all scattered and made their way up Severn Place and into Broad Street, Llew and Owen found themselves once again walking beside Gwilym the Sticks and Owen Neaudd. 'Well, what d'you think, Gwilym?' asked Llew. 'Ready to defend Newtown with your last drop o' blood, are you?'

Gwilym made a rude noise through his pursed lips. 'They inna gettin' my blood if I can 'elp it. But dessay I'll 'ave a go. Hope they'm not too long gettin' the guns though. We canna do much 'arm to Jerry without 'em.'

'Thee cust 'it 'em over the 'ead with thee broomstick, mun,' chortled Owen Neaudd. 'See they wunna be expectin' that and thee'll take 'em by surprise. A few of us settin' about 'em with broomsticks could do a fair bit of damage, thees know.'

'Oh, Ah? An' what'll they be doin' in the meantime? Layin' down their arms an' lettin' us whack em to death? I should cocoa!'

'Oh well, lets 'ope they come up with the guns pretty soon then, whilst Jerry's still trying to find 'is way down over the Anchor,' replied Owen Neaudd, philosophically. 'You comin' in the Black Boy for an 'arf, Gwilym?'

'On a Monday? Don't be daft, Neaudd. Where'd I get the price of an 'arf on a Monday,' Gwilym replied, shaking his head.

'Come on, I'll stand thee an 'arf and thee can pay me back when thee't flush.'

'Flush?' Gwilym gave a hollow laugh. 'When shall I ever be flush? Flushed down the drain, mebbe.'

'All right, lads,' laughed Llew, 'I'll buy you all a quick half. Coming, Owen, lad?'

'Wouldn't miss it for the world,' grinned Owen. 'Can't stay long though. Left Lena at Pool Road with the little 'un. Last I saw of them Mama was having a lend of Kathleen Eluned on her lap. They'll be all woman talk. Won't miss me for another ten minutes. I thought we'd be there longer than this, anyway.'

They drifted into the Black Boy and Llew ordered four halves of mild, all he could afford himself on a Monday night. He and Mattie were working hard and trying to save up to buy the little cottage they lived in, thinking they would have some security for their old age. Mattie was a very careful housekeeper and made quite a bit with her sewing. The landlord in the Black Boy was glad to see them. Monday was a quiet night these days with so little money about. Maybe if this factory came off down the Pool Road there'd be a bit more about. It'd take a war to bring money into this town, he thought, bitterly.

'Where 'ave you lot been tonight then, lads?' he asked, as he pulled the four glasses of beer and put them one after another onto the counter.

'We bin joining the army, mun,' replied Gwilym the Sticks, sinking half his beer in one desperate swallow. 'Ooh, that was good, I was ready for that. Ah, you can all rest easy in thee beds from now on. We'll be takin' care of Jerry if he dares to come this way. Dessay they'm got their spies. They'll know that we lot 'ave joined up so they wunna try it on 'ere. Mark my words.' He returned to his beer with little sips to make it last.

'Good God,' the landlord's eyebrows rose to his hairline. 'Have we got to rely on you lot to protect us? God help us, is all I can say! We may as well surrender quick and get it over with.'

'Now then!' Gwilym replied, wounded. ' Thee's may be glad of us yet. We shall have guns shortly, the man said.'

'Lord! that's worse still!' the landlord replied. 'It dunna bear thinking of, you lot running round loose with guns. Nobody'll be safe!'

'Dunna fret,' put in Owen Neaudd. 'We'm a fine body of men. A fighting force. The man said so.'

The banter went on until the half-pints were finished. Llew and Owen parted outside in Broad Street, Llew setting off over the Long Bridge for home, while Owen walked with Owen Neaudd as far as the turning for Ladywell, when Neaudd bade him goodnight and Owen made for Pool Road. When he arrived and let himself in the lamp was lit. Dada was nodding off in his chair, and Mama half-dozing with baby Kathleen on her lap, fast asleep, the little round head with its cap of dark hair peeping out of the old woollen shawl, which had held many of the Rees's babies over the years. Lena and Nell were sitting at the table, their arms folded and heads together, talking quietly. They looked up almost guiltily when Owen came in.

'Right then, you two. Who's getting their character pulled to pieces, now?' He asked, and winked at Elwyn, who had looked up from the newspaper he was perusing and nodded at Owen.

'Cup of tea, Owen?' asked Nell, all innocence, while Lena lifted a flushed face and grinned at him.

'Aye, may as well,' Owen replied, pulling a chair up to the table and sitting down, while Nell bustled off to wet a fresh pot of tea from the kettle already singing on the hob. Owen leaned over and ruffled Lena's hair. 'All right love? Has Kathleen Eluned been good?'

' Like an angel,' replied Lena. 'Just slept on Mama's lap all night.'

'Well, I guess that old lap has got a bit of magic on it after all these years of nursing babies.' Owen smiled. 'I was one of those babies, so I ought to know. I'll just have this cup of tea and then we must go and get that infant into her bed.'

'Who is that there now?' came Dada's querulous old voice from the fireside. 'I cannot see so well now. Is that you, Llew?'

'No, Dada. Its me, Owen. How you feeling tonight, anyway?'

'I am all right except for me rheumatics. I cannot move much. This old age is not a good thing at all.' Dada shook his head sadly and looked across at Mama in the opposite chair. 'Even your Mama is feeling it these days. She cannot do what she used to. It is as well our Nell is here to look after us. Plenty for her to do indeed there is. I hope it is not too much.' He looked across at Nell with an air of pathos.

'I dessay I shall manage,' put in Nell with a smile.

Owen drained his teacup and turned to Lena. 'Well, girl, its time we were getting that small one back home and into her cot.' He rose and went over to gently lift the sleeping infant out of Mama's arms. Mama started and in the confusion tightened her grip on the baby. Owen grinned. 'It's all right, Mama. I am just taking her home to bed now.' Mama loosened her hold on Kathleen and nodded, sitting up a little and sighing. 'She has slept like a little angel here on my lap,' she said with an air of satisfaction.

'I just hope she keeps that up all night,' Owen answered, ruefully, drawing the shawl more closely round the baby, who whimpered a little in her sleep. 'Right now, Lena. Goodnight all. Thank you for us.' Lena murmured goodnight and followed him through the door. As they made their way along Pool Road towards Woolpack Row where they rented the little cottage in which Lena's mother had lived, Owen looked down at Lena and with a grin said, 'Well, let's be having it. What was all the gossip about? You and Nell had your heads together there. I'll bet somebody's reputation was getting a going over.'

'I don't know what you're on about.' Lena's tone was defensive.

'Aw, come on. What was it all about? Something pretty serious by the guilty looks on your faces. You may as well tell me.'

'Well, if you must know. It seems that Edward is two-timing Ruth. Guess who with?'

'Look,' Owen stopped in mid-stride. 'I don't believe that. Not Edward. He thinks the world of Ruth. They're engaged to be married, for God's sake.' He started walking again with quick, irritable strides and Lena trotted indignantly beside him. 'Well, wait till you here who the other girl is. Would you believe.. Rhiannon?'

'Oh, well, now I know its rubbish!' Owen retorted. 'Rhiannon! Edward can't abide Rhiannon. You know that.'

'Well, I wouldn't have believed it if it hadn't been for Nell telling it. It seems Rhiannon was very late coming from the dance in the Church House on Saturday night and Nell was waiting up for her. She heard somebody on the doorstep and opened the door to give Rhiannon and whoever was with her a piece of her mind, and lo and behold there were Rhiannon and Edward in each other's arms. You have to believe Nell, surely. She wouldn't make that up. She's very vexed about it. She likes Ruth and she knows that Nan and Davey'll be in a right state about it.'

'I should think they would,' Owen grunted, as he turned into the alleyway that led down to the cottages, watching his step carefully in the dark, while Lena clung onto his sleeve. 'Anyway, there's something fishy about this, mark my words, love. I don't trust that Rhiannon a bit. She made a set for poor old Edward from the start and he didn't want her. Couldn't stand her, in fact. I just don't believe it of Edward. He's always been a jannock bloke. Steady as a rock.'

'Well, you've got to admit Rhiannon's very pretty.' Lena said, doubtfully, as they reached their door and she pulled the key out of her pocket and let them in, switching on the electric light, which Owen had had installed recently. She took the baby out of Owen's arms and hushed her when she whimpered. 'There, there, my little love. Let Mammy change you and then you shall have a nice warm bottle. Reach me a clean nappy off the pulley, Owen love.'

As they settled the baby and then got ready for bed themselves, Owen was very quiet. He felt there may be trouble brewing in the family and knew that Nan and Davy had enough worries at the moment, what with not knowing where Edward would be going when his leave was up at the end of the week and hearing daily of the losses the Air Force were reporting, even as they claimed their high quota of enemy planes shot down.

Owen would have been even more worried had he known that Rhiannon planned to tell Ruth about Saturday night, at least her own version. With this in mind, and telling herself that all was fair in love and war, she set off down in her dinner hour on the off-chance of seeing Ruth about. As luck, or mischance, would have it she bumped into her coming out of the Market Hall into Market Street, laden down with shopping.

'Hello, Ruth. My, you're carrying a load.'

Ruth gave Rhiannon a smile and a nod. 'Hello, Rhiannon. How are you?' She made as if to edge round the other girl, feeling her usual distrust of her but trying to remain pleasant, since they would soon be related.

'Where's Edward, then? Why isn't he around to help you. Oh, perhaps he's told you about Saturday night! Oh, dear, maybe I wasn't supposed to mention that.' She hurriedly put her hand over her mouth. 'You never know with fellas, do you?' she added with a little laugh.

Ruth stared at her. 'Told me what?' she asked, frowning. 'About Saturday night? What about Saturday night? We were together Saturday night. You saw us, at the Church House. You saw us there, didn't you?'

'Oh, yes. I saw you at the dance. I don't suppose he told you about after the dance, did he?'

'He took me home after the dance,' Ruth said, frowning. 'I don't know what you mean.'

'It was after that. Oh, these men, they're too bad, aren't they. I feel awful about it all, but then its not my fault, is it? He was waiting to see me home, after he'd taken you home. I thought perhaps you'd had a quarrel. Well, I wasn't to know, was I? Did you quarrel? Or maybe he'd just been waiting his chance with me? He was all over me. My mother caught us on the doorstep.'

Ruth flushed and then the colour drained from her face. 'I don't believe you!' she said hoarsely. 'He wouldn't. We're engaged.'

Rhiannon shrugged. 'He wasn't acting much like an engaged man, I must say. You don't believe me, do you? All right, ask my mother.

She'll tell you. She wasn't very pleased. I was really late and she was waiting up for me. Look, Ruth, its no good blaming me, if that's what you're doing. I should think you'd be better off without him if he doesn't care enough to be true to you. After all, there's plenty more fish in the sea. Irish fish, too!' She giggled. 'Get yourself an Irishman, why don't you. There's some lovely blokes among them.'

Ruth turned away as though in a daze and made her way slowly along Market Street. Rhiannon watched her go, a triumphant smirk on her face. So far, so good. That'll put a spoke in her wheel, she thought. Ruth wouldn't be the sort to put up with two-timing, she was sure. What a bit of luck that Mam had seen Edward on the doorstep with her, Rhiannon. It probably looked as though he was embracing her, not the other way round. Mam couldn't deny it if she was asked. She made her jaunty way home, satisfied with the results of her conniving. She'd probably have to give Edward a while to get over Ruth, but she'd get him in the end. She'd be so sympathetic and loving. Oh, how loving. She had a qualm of conscience for a split second, but quickly shrugged it off. You had to fight for what you wanted in this world. And she wanted Edward.

Edward was due to go to tea at the Bryn that afternoon and he set off at three o'clock on his bicycle. He had only three more full days at home before he went back on Friday. Where they'd be sent next was anyone's guess, although a strong rumour was going the rounds of his Company that it might be North Africa. If that was so it could be a long wait before he got home again. Sometimes he wished they hadn't been so cautious and had just gone ahead and got married. But then again, what if he didn't get back? Oh, hell, he thought. Why did his generation have to get stuck with a war? Europe was only just getting over the previous one. As he pedalled hard up the Bryn Road he tried to put all such thoughts away from him. In a moment he would see Ruth and he hoped to persuade her to spend even more time with him for the next three days. God alone knew when they'd see each other again. He felt very tender towards her. He couldn't wait for this cursed war to be over and they could marry and settle down.

He reached the gate of the farm, half expecting Ruth to be waiting there for him. However it was Ruth's father who came out of the farm house and down the path to the gate. He carried in his hand a small dark blue velvet-covered box, but Edward's eyes were on his face which was grim and frowning.

'Hello, Mr Jones.' he called, trying to sound cheerful, but wondering at the forbidding expression on the other man's face.

Ruth's father came up to the gate but did not open it to let Edward through. Instead he stood on the other side and faced the young man with a steely look. 'You are not welcome here any longer, Edward Rees. It's sorry I am that you have turned out to be a bit of a rotter. We were pleased for Ruth at first. Thought you were a steady chap. But since her trip to town today and meeting with your cousin, Rhiannon, she has been breaking her heart. She doesn't want to see you again, and to be honest I can't blame her, for she's a good girl and doesn't deserve to be treated as you've treated her.'

Edward stared speechlessly at the older man. He shook his head and tried to gather his wits together. His body was rigid with shock and the blood had drained from his face. 'I-I don't understand!' he stammered, but a glimmer of what must have happened began to penetrate.

'I think you understand right enough,' Mr Jones said, grimly. 'Your cousin was only too pleased to inform Ruth that you had gone straight to her on Saturday night after you left Ruth, and her mother found you kissing and cuddling on the doorstep. According to Ruth that Rhiannon has been after you ever since she came. Well she's got you now, seemingly, and welcome to you. I daresay my girl will get over you in time, but you've hurt her bad and I can't forgive you for that. Here, take this.' He handed the blue velvet box over the gate to Edward. 'It's the ring. She'll have no use for it now. Asked me to give it to you.'

Edward drew himself up and put the little box into his pocket. He faced the older man squarely, pale but with his head high. 'I could explain this,' he said in a tight voice, 'But then, you wouldn't believe me,' he added, bitterly. 'I never thought Ruth would have condemned me without giving me a hearing, but it seems her love for me didn't include trust. You may tell her that I love her and her alone, and always have and always will. If she can't believe that, then there's nothing more to be said.' He turned and began to walk away, pushing his bicycle over the rough ground of the lane and the other man stared curiously after him, watching the rigid back and the proud tilt of the head. He took off his cap and scratched his head, frowning. Dammit, he didn't look guilty, either. Had Ruth got it all wrong? Or had that Rhiannon been telling a pack of lies? But no, she'd said that her mother had caught them on the doorstep, so that could have been checked. She wouldn't have dared lie about that. He shrugged and made his way back to the house. He didn't know what to make of it. He sighed. Suppose it'll sort itself out, he thought.

Meanwhile, Edward continued unseeingly down the Bryn Road towards the town. There was a dark anger within him, something unusual for Edward, and with it was mixed a bitter hurt. To think that Ruth would believe what Rhiannon said, whatever it was, without giving him a chance to tell her whether it was true or not. The colour mounted his face. That was the trouble, there was that little grain of truth in Rhiannon's version, whatever it might be, which made it difficult to deny outright. His thoughts were a confused mixture of pain and a bitter anger against Rhiannon. If she thought that he would now turn to her she'd soon find out her mistake.

He trudged on with a heavy heart, pain like a lump in his chest. He hadn't the heart to mount his bike but pushed it through the dead leaves at the side of the road. He thought savagely that he was glad he was going away on Friday. Wherever he was sent no doubt he wouldn't have time to think much. But before he went he would tackle that Rhiannon, if it was the last thing he did. This was the second time she had tried to come between Ruth and him. It looked like she'd succeeded this time, but he'd have his say before he left Newtown.

When he finally reached Plasgwyn he pushed open the gate into the yard and, moving like a zombie, put his bicycle in the shed and let himself into the house. He made straight for the stairs and mounted them to his bedroom. Nan and Davy, who were in the kitchen, looked at each other in surprise. They hadn't expected him home so soon, knowing that he had gone up to Ruth's house and that he was staying for tea. She raised her eyebrows at Davy but he shrugged and shook his head.

'Funny,' Nan said. 'He's back early. Something's wrong, sure to. Did I ought to go up to him.'

'No,' Davy answered. 'He's a grown man, now, not your little boy.

Leave him be, love. He'll tell us if he wants us to know .'

'I suppose so,' Nan answered doubtfully.

Edward flung himself down on his bed, his right arm covering his eyes. He felt the tears well up and did nothing to check them. The deep hurt at what he saw as Ruth's betrayal filled his mouth with gall. How could she have believed Rhiannon, of all people. Why didn't she give him a chance to tell her the truth? Surely a love like theirs would include trust, he thought bitterly. As for that Rhiannon. Anger surged through him and he sat up and swung his legs over the edge of the bed. He would go now, down to Pool Road, and confront her while the anger was white hot in him. He knew his own nature too well and thus knew that in time he would calm down. But he wanted to wound her as she had wounded him. He crossed to the wash-stand and poured cold water into the basin and splashed his face with it. Then he towelled his cheeks fiercely and with the front of his hair still wet, flung out of the room and down the stairs. His mother was in the hall and he brushed past her, his face pale and tight with fury. Nan stepped back, one hand to her mouth and the other reaching out to touch his sleeve. 'Edward! What's wrong boy? Where are you going?'

'Pool Road!' He flung the words back at her and went out, banging the door behind him.

Nan hurried back into the kitchen. 'Oh Davy, I've never seen our Edward look like that before. He's in the most terrible temper. He says he's going to Pool Road? Whatever for? Something's happened!'

Davy got up and put his arms round her and stroked her hair. 'There, there, love. You know our Edward. He's never in a temper for long. Pretty placid lad.'

'I know,' replied Nan, frowning. ' That's the trouble. I never saw him look like that before. What d'you think he's gone to Pool Road for?'

'I don't know,' Davy said grimly, releasing her,' But I'm willing to bet that Rhiannon figures in it somewhere. She's been up to some mischief, mark my words. She tried before to come between him and Ruth. If she's tried to do it again, especially now when he's got to go away again on Friday, God knows where, well, she'll get the length of my tongue as well as Edward's, Nell or no Nell.' He patted Nan's shoulder. 'Come on now, girl. It'll sort itself out, no doubt. We shall find out, soon enough.'

Edward reached No.46, his anger still at boiling point and pushed his way in, banging the front door shut behind him. As he strode into the kitchen, Mama and Dada looked up from their seats by the fire and smiled when they saw who it was. Nell was beginning to lay the tea-table and stopped, startled at the sight of Edward's face. Elwyn and Rhiannon were still at work, which Edward had forgotten.

'Rhiannon not here?' he asked harshly. 'I want to see her. I have something to say to that girl, and you may as well all hear.' His hands balled into fists and his shoulders were rigid.

Nell stared at him. 'Sit down, boy,' she said, frowning. 'Whatever is the matter with you?' She pulled out a chair and sat at the table opposite where he had slumped down, his fingers tapping tensely on the tablecloth. 'What has Rhiannon done now to upset you? I take it it is Rhiannon?'

'Oh yes, its Rhiannon alright. She's only told a lot of lies about me to Ruth and now our engagement is off. That's all!' He gave a bitter little laugh.

'What lies?' asked Nell, regarding him steadily. 'D'you mean about you bringing Rhiannon home and kissing her on the doorstep? Don't forget that I saw you, Edward. Yes, I was surprised, knowing you were engaged to Ruth. Shocked, really. I suppose you didn't want Ruth to know, but I suppose Rhiannon has told her. I think that was pretty rotten of Rhiannon, but it wasn't fair on Ruth what you were doing. It wasn't like you to do such a thing either. But, there, the temptation of the moment, I dessay.'

'But you don't understand!' Edward protested. 'It was all Rhiannon's doing. She was waiting for me outside Plasgwyn when I got home from sending Ruth to her door that night. She said she was afraid to come home because you would be in a temper with her for being so late and begged me to see her to Pool Road. I couldn't do anything else, could I. And then,' he flushed, suddenly embarrassed, 'When you opened the door she flung her arms round my neck and kissed me. She did it purposely. But how do I explain that to Ruth? Especially as she won't even talk to me. Just sent her Dad out to give me the ring back.' He fished in his pocket and brought out the blue velvet box. He opened it and gazed down sadly at the little diamond ring inside. 'Its only a small diamond, I know,' he said, almost apologetically, 'but Ruth was quite satisfied and I promised that when I came back from the war I should be able to afford something better. And of course a wedding ring. But now,' he shrugged and his eyes were bleak, 'Now that's all over. But Ruth should have asked me if it was true and given me a chance to tell her. She should have.' He shook his head and stared at his fingers, plucking the table cloth.

'What is with that boy?' came a querulous voice from the direction of Dada's chair and then Mama chimed in. 'What does the boy want? Is there trouble at Plasgwyn? Nell, you are too fond of keeping things from us. We are not dead and gone yet you know. What is going on? What does the boy say?'

Nell gave an exasperated sigh. ' Nothing is wrong, Mama,' she answered, raising her voice. 'No trouble at Plasgwyn. Edward has just come to say goodbye to Rhiannon before he goes back to the Army.' She turned back to Edward with a wry smile. 'I daresay that is no lie! Well, I am sorry that Rhiannon has caused this for you. She deserves all you will no doubt say to her. But I am sure that Ruth will believe you if you explain it all to her. Do you go up to the Bryn and park yourself on the doorstep until she will come out to you. You mustn't give up like this.' Nell sighed wearily. 'I don't know what is with that girl. I don't understand her. Nobody does. She will try to get her own way, no matter who suffers.'

Edward shook his head. 'No,' he said, grimly. 'It's up to Ruth now. If she's going to take someone else's word and not give me a chance to give my version, then she doesn't trust me, does she, and that says something about her love for me.' He was sitting and brooding on this when the door opened and first Rhiannon came in, followed by her father. She stopped in the kitchen doorway when she saw Edward sitting at the table and the colour fled from her face. Without a word she turned and made as though to go to the staircase that led from the kitchen. Her mother's voice halted her.

'Just a minute, Rhiannon. Come back here. Edward has something to say to you.' Elwyn looked questioningly at Nell, but she jerked her head in the direction of the back-kitchen and after a curious look at

Edward, he followed her out of the room. Rhiannon stood in silence for a moment then decided to brazen it out.

'I suppose this is all about me telling Ruth about Saturday night? Well, she was quick enough to believe me, which shows she doesn't think as much of you as you like to think.' As he made no answer she was emboldened to go on. 'Well, it's true, isn't it? If she was that keen on you she'd listen to you, not to me. Have you thought that perhaps she was using this as an excuse to finish it? I suppose she has finished it? I can see she has. Well, you know, there's plenty more fish in the sea. And there's one here who'd be only to glad to take her place.' She gave a strained laugh and then came to sit down opposite him. 'I mean it, Edward,' she went on seriously. 'I've been in love with you ever since we came to this God-forsaken country and its the only reason I've stayed. Oh, I've had plenty of chances with other fellows, including your brother Huw, as you know. But it was you I wanted and I've waited my chance. Oh, Edward, you know how I feel about you,' and she reached out her hand as though to touch his.

Edward had been listening to her in mounting disgust and he drew his hand away as though it was burned. He stood up and stared down at her, then he bent his face towards her and spoke very slowly. 'I hate you, Rhiannon. Get that through into your thick skull. I hate you. Nothing will ever change that now. If I never see you again it will be too soon. Just keep out of my way, and thank your lucky stars that I'm not a violent man. I'm going back to the Army on Friday, so just try to keep out of my sight until I've gone. Because of you, I'm not sure I want to come back.' he ended, bitterly. He swung round and made for the door, banging it after him.

Rhiannon sat white-faced and still. Her mouth felt dry and the cold anger in his voice seemed to echo in her ears. She realised this was the end. She'd really done it this time. She got up slowly and made her way up the stairs to her room, where she closed the door and flung herself face-down on her bed and wept gut-wrenching tears.

When Nell and Elwyn returned to the room they looked round then at each other.

'What was all that about?' Elwyn asked.

'It's a long story,' Nell said, shaking her head.

9

Evacuees and Bricks

Nan and Davy stood on the Station platform, waving as the train steamed out. As it vanished round the corner Nan blew her nose and wiped her eyes with her handkerchief. Davy put his arm round her shoulders and gently urged her towards the exit. They descended the station steps in silence. Out on the pavement Nan stopped and looked up at Davy miserably. 'If only he wasn't going away so miserable,' she said, sniffing and blowing again. 'If only he'd made it up with Ruth, it wouldn't have been so bad.'

'I know,' Davy muttered. 'But they were both too stiff-necked to make the first move. They both felt betrayed, I suppose. That damned Rhiannon. I could screw her neck. Edward wasn't going to be thrilled to bits going back anyway, I know, but it wouldn't have been so bad if all had been well with Ruth.' He slipped his arm under her elbow. 'Come on, love, let's get home and make a cup of tea. Daresay things will sort themselves out. Nothing we can do about it, anyway.'

'Well, I'm going to see what I can do about it, anyway,' Nan said resolutely. 'I'll take a walk up to the Bryn one of these afternoons. Mebbe get Nell to go with me. We'll make sure that Ruth gets the true story, anyway. It'll be up to her then, won't it? At least we'll have done all we can.'

As they walked down Station Road they met Dick Pugh going to his allotment up Brimmon Lane. He had the next one to Dada's, which Davy and Owen kept going between them. As an excuse to catch his breath, which was laboured after coming up the incline, Dick stopped and addressed them. 'Another oul' bomb dropped las' night, then.'

Davy nodded. 'Aye, Dick. Did you hear where it landed?'

'Llanmerewig, I did hear.' Dick coughed. 'Another cow gone, seems. Funny oul' war. They canna win it jus' by killin' cows, surely? Is that what we'm doin' as well? Killin' their cows? Dunna make sense to me. Poor oul' cows. They inna to blame for that Hitler, is they?'

'Well no, Dick.' Davy grinned and watched Dick climb laboriously up the Brimmon Lane and then stop and, turning, remark over his shoulder. 'Aye indeed. A funny oul' war, in't it. No shape, somehow.'

When they reached home Davy put the kettle on and when it boiled, wet the tea, while Nan fetched out the cups and saucers, sugar and milk. While she did so she reviewed the last two or three days and her heart ached for Edward. The fact that Ruth had chosen to believe Rhiannon without giving him a chance to explain had hurt him very badly. He was not her Edward at all, very withdrawn. It was almost as if he was glad when the day of his return to the army had come. He still did not know where he was due to go, but felt it would be North Africa. Nan sipped her tea and wondered what was in store for her sons.

After dinner Nan took up two loaves from the morning's baking and putting them in her basket, covered them with a clean white napkin, left Davy with his Daily Despatch and set out for Pool Road. When she let herself in she heard voices and found Meggie and Henry sitting at the table drinking tea. It was plain that Meggie was very upset and the lad looked angry. She handed the basket over to Nell, who was hovering over Mama and Dada, watching that they didn't spill their tea and encouraging them to eat some thin bread and butter which was placed on stools near them.

'Sit you down, Nan.' Nell said, nodding to her and Meg looked up and gave her a watery smile.

Nan sat down opposite Meg and Nell passed her a cup of tea. 'What's wrong?' she asked apprehensively. 'What's the matter?'

Meg's eyes filled with tears again, but it was Henry who spoke. 'They came yesterday and took my Dad away,' he said tersely. 'He's to be interned for the duration of the war. Because he's German. My Dad!' he added bitterly, 'Who's never hurt a soul! But he's an alien now. Argh!' He banged his fist on the table. 'It makes me sick!'

Dada spoke from his chair. 'Who is thumping? What is going on? Why is nobody telling your Mama and me what is going on? I myself will start thumping in a minute!'

Nell turned to him. 'Hush, Dada. It is Henry, he is upset. They took Reini away today to be interned'

Dada struggled to sit up in his chair, his face working, his eyes wild, while Mama went pale and whispered, 'Oh, my God.'

'You people are wicked!' Dada managed to get out, his voice a croak. 'You have never told us that Reini is dead. When did he die? Why were we not told? You are always keeping things from us!'

'Reini dead?' cried Mama. 'Oh my God. Meggie!'

'No, no!' shouted Nell, distracted. 'No! Reini isn't dead. He's been interned.'

Dada looked from one to the other, bewildered. 'But I did think interred did mean buried! If he is not dead they cannot bury him! I don't understand.' he added, pathetically, while Mama searched each face, frowning and shaking her head

'Not interred, Dada,' broke in Henry hysterically, 'Interned! That means that they have taken him away and will keep him locked up until the war is over. Because he is a German.'

Dada sank back against his cushions again. 'I do not understand,' he repeated, sadly. 'I know he is a German, but he is a good man. He has been good to our Meg. I would tell anybody that.'

Mama nodded in agreement. 'Meg,' she called querulously. 'What does Meg say?'

Meg dried her eyes and went over to Mama. 'Its all right, Mama. Reini will be back soon. He will be quite safe. Henry will run the farm while he is away. And I can help. We'll keep going all right until Reini comes back. Don't you fret.' She turned to Dada. 'Reini will be fine, Dada. He will be safe now until the end of the war. We will miss him, of course, but then there's a lot of women missing their men nowadays, and at least mine is not fighting. And then they will not take Henry, because he will have to run the farm, so I am better off than most.' She smiled bravely, then kissed Dada on the forehead and squeezed Mama's hand. She returned to her chair and reached out to touch Nan's hand. 'Your Edward went back today, so Nell tells me,' she said, with her head on one side and her eyes sympathetic. 'You will be missing him now, and Huw. Oh, dear. when will this horrible war be over? Making a mess

127

of everybody's lives. I could strangle that old Hitler.'

'We all could,' soothed Nell. Let's all have another cup of tea. Come you, Nan. Drink up. You will be feeling low, seeing Edward off. He doesn't know where he is going, I suppose?'

'No,' replied Nan, stirring sugar into her fresh cup. 'But that's not the worst of it. He's been so upset over this business with Ruth. If only they'd made it up before he went. I think he would have had more heart to go. Mind, his heart isn't in the soldiering, anyway.' She sighed and sipped the scalding tea as if she found solace in it.

After a while Meg and Henry announced that they would have to go to be back in time for milking and to get the hens in. Nell and Nan saw them to the door and watched as they climbed into their old car. They waved as the car rumbled off down Pool Road, then Nan went back in to say cheerio to Mama and Dada who still looked a little shaken, and set off back to get tea for Davy, while Nell sighed and began preparing the evening meal for when Elwyn and Rhiannon came home.

Next morning Nan and Davy had some news that cheered them up. There was a letter from Huw to tell them that he was coming home on the following Tuesday and bringing his girl, Roma, with him. There followed a flurry of activity as Nan rushed around putting hot water bottles into beds to air them, cleaning an already spotless house, and planning all the baking she would do on Sunday, to be ready.

'Thought Sunday was a day of rest,' teased Davy. 'I can see little rest for us Sunday or Monday, come to that.'

'There's a lot to do,' protested Nan defensively, and Davy let her get on with it, feeling, rightly, that all the activity would help her to come to terms with worry over Edward, and fussing over Huw and Roma would fill a gap in her life.

When Tuesday came round Nan was in a state of high excitement, as they went up to the station to meet the twelve o'clock train. When it drew up with a belch of steam, she and Davy scanned the doors until they saw Huw step out and turn to give a hand to a pretty girl, with hair the colour of ripe corn and a comely figure. The first thing Davy thought was how like Nan when she was young, the same straightforward grey eyes, broad cheekbones and fresh complexion. Huw led her forward proudly and when Nan enfolded her in her arms she gave a smile of great sweetness.

'Well, Mam, don't I get a hug and a kiss then?' laughed Huw and Nan drew him to her and after she had kissed him, she whispered in his ear, 'She's lovely!'

'I know!' he whispered back, then turned to give his father a hug, while whispering in his ear 'Looks like Mam, doesn't she?' When Davy grinned and nodded, he went on, 'That's why I picked her!'

Roma proved to be a most pleasant guest, fitting in perfectly at Plasgwyn, pleased with all that was done for her and obviously head over heels in love with Huw, who, in his turn, was overjoyed to see how much his parents liked Roma. They confided in Nan and Davy that they were engaged. Roma showing her modest ring proudly, but were both agreed they should wait until the war ended before they got married. 'It'll not be long now,' Huw told them buoyantly. 'I think we've got 'em in the air now. We'll soon finish 'em off. Then we'll be coming home to settle down in Newtown, won't we love. Roma's persuaded me not to stay in the Air Force and, well, she's the boss now!'

'D'you think you'll be happy to settle in this little town?' Nan asked, smiling at Roma, who answered,' Yes, I like the look of it, but I'll be happy anywhere that Huw wants to settle.' and she turned such a look of love on Huw that Nan's heart was quite satisfied.

Huw took Roma up to Bay House to meet Esther and her family. Esther had her hands full with Mary, Alun and little Johnny, who was now toddling around, into everything. Added to that she had taken in two evacuees from Liverpool, a brother and sister, the boy ten years old and the girl eight. At first they had been very difficult, bewildered and lost, the little girl crying for her Mammy and the boy bottling up his misery in silence and a refusal to cooperate. But gradually Esther had broken down their reserves, giving them the same love that she gave to her own three, so that in time they became adjusted to their new life. From time to time they needed reassurance that they would be going back home to their Mammy and Daddy when the war ended and it helped that their mother kept in regular touch with letters and little gifts to show that they were not forgotten. At least there was plenty of room at Bay House and although Esther was kept very busy, she was ably helped by Edie Davies, who extended her hours and took a lot of the burden of the housework off Esther's shoulders. Martin played his part too, being father to the two little strangers, Teddy and Gwenny. Truth to tell, He and Esther were as much in love as ever and he was enjoying his role of paterfamilias to his children, which he regarded as an extension of his devotion to his beloved. It was indeed, a boisterous and happy household and Esther, whose love of children had begun with Edward, was totally fulfilled with the children round her skirts.

Roma was charmed with Esther and with Johnny, who took to her immediately and demanded to climb up onto her knee. Esther was horrified to see his sticky little hands grasping at Roma's pale blue blouse, but Roma only laughed and hugged the plump little body to her. Huw looked on fondly. He knew she was the right one for him and thought how good it would be when they could finally get married and Roma could have a baby of her own to bounce on her knee. Huw and Roma were invited to stay for tea and they were there when the four children came bursting in from school. They crowded into the living room and then stopped, abashed, in the doorway at the sight of cousin Huw in his Air Force uniform, and a strange girl with him. Esther drew them forward, introduced them to Roma, and watched, smiling, as the boys, Alun and Teddy, approached Huw, tentatively at first, and as they got bolder, plied him with questions about his aeroplanes and how many German planes had he shot down. He answered them good-humouredly and he and Roma were kept busy with the children, while Esther and Edie went into the kitchen to make the tea. After a while Martin arrived from the office and they all sat down to a good high tea, Huw and Roma eventually leaving as it came time for the children to be put to bed, a task shared by Esther and Martin and actually enjoyed by the children, as Martin read stories to the boys and Esther did the same for the girls.

As they walked back through the town Huw found Roma very quiet. 'What's up, love?' he asked, tenderly. She shook her head and he stopped and tipped her chin up with his finger. There was moisture in her eyes and he frowned and put his arm round her. 'Come on!' he said softly. 'Tell Huw! What is it?'

'I wish we could get married so that we could start a family like your cousin's.'

Huw shook his head. 'Look, love, we've been though all this. You know there's nothing I'd like better than for us to be married, but its too risky just now.' He walked on, his face shadowed with a dark emotion which he was at pains to hide from her as best he could. Only he knew the uncertainty of his war. He never spoke of the nights when the glib words 'some of our aircraft are missing' meant that two or three of his comrades never returned from their mission. None of them knew when it was going to be their turn, and the tightening of the stomach when the command to 'scramble' came was now part of life. There was no time to brood on it when you snatched what sleep you could and kept up the febrile banter with your pals, although they knew only too well what you were feeling. How could he marry Roma, when he didn't know how many days or nights he'd got left. And yet, he told himself, it couldn't go on for ever and some of the boys would come back safely to civvy life.

He forced a grin and took Roma's hand. 'Trying to seduce me, are you? Better be careful. You may not have to try too hard.'

Roma gave a watery smile. 'Sorry, Huw. Sometimes I get impatient for this war to be over so that we can settle down. It was just seeing Esther with all those lovely children, and a loving husband, made me envious.'

'You'll get a loving husband one of these days, sweetheart, and as many little dabs as you like. We're all impatient for the end of this old war. We must just keep going and keep believing. OK? Now come on. We've only got a couple more days left and we're due to go to Owen and Lena's tomorrow night for a meal and I must have another session with Mama and Dada at Pool Road tomorrow morning. It's hard to see them like they are. I'd love you to have known them in the old days. They were great.'

'You are so lucky to have such a big family, Huw. They're lovely people, too. I'm looking forward to coming to live among them.' Huw hugged her to him and they made their way more happily to Plasgwyn.

Huw and Roma were kept busy for the rest of the leave, having a meal with Owen and Lena in Woolpack Row, where another baby helped to fuel Roma's envy, and visiting Llew and Mattie, where they had news of Jim, still in Londonderry in Northern Ireland. Nell's Gareth was there also and both he and Jim had had seven-day leaves recently, which had pleased their respective parents. They were still to have a trip to

Manafon on Sunday in Elwyn's car, but before that Huw wanted to take Roma to the dance in the Church House on Saturday night, in order to show her off to the locals.

When Saturday night came round Roma put on a pretty mauve dress and tucked a pink flower in her thick tawny hair. With little silver sandals on her feet she looked a picture and Huw was immensely proud as he walked along New Road with her hand tucked into the crook of his elbow and her loving face turned up to his. He squeezed her arm as they began to mount the steps into the hall and she whispered, 'Will I pass?' Inside, Richie Richards' band was just tuning up and the three and a half foot figure of Richie was turned to face the dancers as he scanned the room. Huw waved to him and led Roma across the room to the stage to meet him. He had not warned Roma about Richie's lack of inches and she had to fight hard to prevent herself staring at him. He was dressed in a perfect little evening suit, and his handsome head with its wavy dark hair, so at odds with the deformed body, inclined regally towards her. 'How do, Huw boy,' he said in his rather harsh voice. 'Who's this then?'

'This is Roma,' Huw answered, grinning up at Richie. 'And you can keep your beady eyes off her, 'cos we're engaged.'

'Ho! That's how it is, is it? Well, look out, I may try to cut you out anyway. I'll start by dedicating the first number to you. What shall it be?' He looked down at her thoughtfully. 'I know, what about 'Jealousy? D'you tango?' She nodded and moved into Huw's arms. They led off as the band struck up the haunting strains and Richie leered over his shoulder at her. As they executed the steps with a flourish Huw caught sight of Rhiannon watching them from the sidelines. He had heard what she had done to Edward and Ruth and his face darkened. Her keen eyes noted his expression and with a toss of her dark curls she turned to Sean Kerrigan, who was never far away from her, waiting hopefully, and catching his hand, drew him into the dance. She engineered their steps to bring them closer to Hugh and Roma and when they drew alongside she called out 'Hello Huw! Nice to see you!'

Huw shot her a steely look. 'Sorry I can't say the same,' he gritted between his teeth, while Roma looked up at him in astonishment. When the tango finished and they made for a couple of empty chairs, she asked 'Who was that? You were very rude to her, Huw.' she added reproachfully.

Huw grimaced. 'That was my fair cousin, Rhiannon, the one who came between brother Ned and his girl, Ruth and ruined things for them. If we hadn't been in a public place I'd have been a lot ruder. And to think I fancied her once!' he snorted.

Roma gazed across to where Rhiannon was standing, hanging possessively onto Sean's arm, while he looked down at her with a besotted smile. 'She's very pretty,' Roma said. 'She looks as if she's keen on that soldier now, anyway.'

'Poor devil. Little does he know what he's taking on if he messes with her. I'd as soon go out with a tarantula! Anyway, she's probably chatting him up for our benefit. I believe Edward let her know what he really thought of her before he went off leave, so she's showing us she doesn't care, I expect. Oh, forget about her. Come on, the bands playing a St Bernard's waltz. I like that. Gives me a chance to twirl you about.' He grinned at her wickedly and they returned to the floor, Huw calling out greetings to friends from time to time, mostly girls, since his contemporaries were nearly all in the forces. Huw had always been popular and many an envious eye was cast on Roma since Huw looked very attractive in his R.A.F uniform, with his black curls and merry dark eyes. In between dances he led her round the room to meet his friends and Rhiannon's eyes followed them, her expression bleak. Sean noticed this and said 'Isn't that your cousin? Brother to Edward that you used to be in love with?'

Rhiannon tossed her curls and laughed. 'Goodness, that was a long time ago! I've grown up since then. It was only a girlish crush.'

'So maybe there's a chance for me?' Sean queried, smiling down at her. 'You know I'm in love with you, don't you. Have been since the first time I saw you on the station. But you had no eyes for me then,' he added, ruefully

She looked up at him, the blue Irish eyes serious now and a dark curl flopping over his forehead. She took in the broad shoulders in the khaki uniform, the trim waist and the long legs, and then her gaze returned to his mouth, with the full lower lip and the little quirk to the upper lip.

She knew a lot of the girls in Newtown would have given anything for a chance with him and suddenly she felt a frisson of excitement run through her body. He was very attractive and was obviously serious about her. 'Perhaps you should try again,' she said softly.

His eyes were intent on the beautiful face turned up to him. 'If I thought you really meant that, Rhiannon, I'd be thrilled to bits. But I don't just want you flirting with me. I'm serious about you and I don't want to be messed around. You're very lovely and I daresay a lot of blokes are after you. If I take a chance, how do I know I won't get hurt?'

Rhiannon pouted. 'You never will know if you don't take a chance, will you?'

'Let's go outside and walk for a while,' Sean urged. 'We can't talk in here, and I need to know if you're serious. I warn you, I'm not the sort you can play around with.'

Rhiannon looked up at him and had the feeling that she had met her match. She nodded. He was very masterful and she found she liked it. They left the dance hall hand in hand. Huw saw them go and felt relieved. He could never forgive her for what she had done to poor old Ned, who'd had to go back to the army miserable, so his mother had told him, and that had upset his mother too. It was to be hoped this Irishman could handle her. They were supposed to be pretty hot-tempered, the Irish. Huw grinned. Good luck to him.

The rest of the evening passed pleasantly and Huw and Roma danced the last waltz, 'Who's Taking You Home Tonight', dreamily in each other's arms, then with a roll of drums and the lights going up, they sighed and made their way out into the night.

The next day, Huw and Roma set off for Pool Road. The weather was close and humid and people were making their way towards the fields for their usual Sunday walks, dressed in their thin summer clothes, children gambolling beside the more languid grown-ups who were feeling the heat. One or two families stopped to greet Huw, who was always a favourite locally, and to be introduced to Roma, and they were a little later than expected arriving at No.46, where Elwyn was waiting to take them to Manafon.

Nell waved them off from the doorstep. She had hoped to go herself, for she was worried about her sister, Meg, knowing that she would be feeling bereft without her Reini. But she couldn't leave Mama and Dada, and Rhiannon who planned to meet Sean Kerrigan, had refused to stay in with them. So the little party set off without her, driving fairly steadily down Pool Road, with the odd bang from the exhaust which made Huw and Roma jump but which was ignored by Elwyn who was used to the vagaries of his old car.

Heat hung like a miasma over the water meadows that flanked the river Severn and cattle huddled under the shade of the trees, lowing from time to time, or lying down quietly chewing the cud. Up along the hillsides the air was still and silent, with few birds hovering there, most preferring to shelter in the leafy trees below.

'Wouldn't be surprised if we had a storm,' remarked Elwyn as he drove fairly sedately along the dusty road. They met one or two cars and a few walkers who hugged the side of the road and turned hot faces towards them as they drove past.

'If a storm is coming I hope it holds off until we come back,' Huw answered, squeezing Roma's hand as they sat close together in the back. Elwyn only grunted in reply and Huw turned to watch Roma's face as she gazed out at the countryside, bathed in the hot summer sun and yet still lush due to the heavy rain during the previous month. When they finally rolled into the village of Manafon, Roma gave a murmur of pleasure as she took in the lovely old church with its lych gate and the Beehive Inn opposite, the black and white cottages to the right of the church and the background of rolling farm land which acted as a backdrop to the scene. Soon they were entering the leafy shade of the steep lane that led up to the Walkmill and the welcome coolness beneath the arching branches that met overhead. Waiting for them outside the long, low whitewashed farmhouse was Meg, with Henry standing beside her, his hand protectively on her shoulder.

'Oh, it is good to see you!' Meg cried. 'Come in, come in! It is cooler inside. There's hot it is, isn't it?' She put her arm through Roma's and drew her into the house and down the cool, stone-floored passage to the kitchen. She had let the fire in the range go out after cooking the Sunday dinner and planned to put a kettle to boil on the little primus stove in the back-kitchen to make them all a cup of tea.

'Will you take a cup of tea in your hand?' she asked, looking from one to the other. 'They do say as it cools you down better than a cold drink, but I have squeezed some lemons and made a jug of lemonade if you'd rather have that? It'll be nice and cold. Its been sitting on the cold slab in the dairy all morning. The man at the shop did say that these would be the last lemons we should see for a bit.' She sighed. 'This old war! Anyway, which would you like, dear?' She smiled at Roma, who found that when she gave that sweet smile one failed to notice the livid scar running down her cheek, the result of being caught in the fire at the Gwalia Mill a long time ago.

'I'd like some lemonade, please,' said Roma, smiling back at Meg, and Huw joined in, 'Me, too!'

'I'd still like a cup of tea, Meg, if its no bother?' said Elwyn, his head on one side, apologetically.

'No bother, Elwyn love,' Meg answered. 'Henry, good boy, fetch in the lemonade from the dairy and a couple of glasses. Maybe you'll have a glass yourself, too. I'll make some tea for Elwyn and me.' and she bustled off into the kitchen while Henry disappeared in quest of the lemonade.

'What a lovely room!' exclaimed Roma, her glance taking in the gleaming blue and white willow-pattern china on the polished Welsh dresser with its brass handles on the drawers shining as a shaft of sunlight caught them. On the window sills at each end of the long room sat the blue jugs that had stood there in Auntie Martha's day, and were even now filled with the velvety gilly-flowers which Martha had loved so much, the perfume of them filling the room. There were one or two rag rugs, their bright colours contrasting with the cool slate slabs of the kitchen floor and the big deal table stood in the centre of the room, its top scrubbed until it was almost white. In the middle of the table, on a round crocheted mat in cream-coloured fine wool, sat an earthenware bowl filled with nasturtiums, their gold and orange and burgundy making a splash of glorious colour as the sun poured onto them through the south window.

Meg came back with a tray bearing a brown tea-pot, a glass sugar bowl and a matching glass cream jug filled with creamy milk, closely followed by Henry carrying a large brown earthenware jug, drops of cold moisture beading the outside. Meg fetched cups and saucers from the dresser and Henry brought glasses from the cupboard and soon they were all sipping their drinks and nibbling Meg's home-made shortbread, a plateful of which she had produced from another cupboard and placed before them at the table.

'I love this room,' Roma told Meg, at the same time savouring her cool tangy drink.

Meg looked around at all the familiar things which had been there in Auntie Martha's days and in Granny Evans's before that, and nodded in agreement. 'Indeed I'm fond of it myself,' she smiled. 'Homely, isn't it? I always loved it, even when I was little and came here to visit Granny and Auntie Martha and her sons.' She sighed at the painful memories.

'Are they all dead now?' ventured Roma, her grey eyes fixed on Meg's face.

'Aye, all dead now. The farm came to me and Reini - well its a long story but it was through Mama that it came to us. Reini worked here for Luke, Auntie Martha's son, when he - Reini - was a prisoner.' She smiled lovingly at her son. 'Henry was born here and he farms it for us now, while Reini is away.'

'Have you heard from Reini since he went?' asked Elwyn, putting down his cup and reaching for another shortbread.

'Oh, yes. He is in a camp in Cheshire. They are allowed to write home. The letters are censored but that doesn't matter to us. There's not much in Reini's letters or mine that they have to black out!' She laughed but her eyes were moist with unshed tears.

Elwyn turned to Henry. 'Managing all right, are you?' he asked and Henry nodded. 'Between Mam and me we aren't doing too badly. We're kept on the go morning till night, of course, and we miss Dad, but we'll keep it all going till he comes back. Hope that won't be too long. But, yes, we're managing.' and his chin went up in a proud lift as he turned and grinned at his mother. Then he turned to Huw and Roma. 'If you've finished your drinks would you like to come and have a look round the farm?' They rose eagerly and then went out after him. Elwyn stayed behind to talk to Meg, whose eyes had followed the tall figure of her son with pride.

'He is a good boy,' she said, softly. 'He works very hard and never grumbles. Its not easy to get help now, and what we'll do when it comes to the shearing and dipping I don't know. A lot of the farmers round here have stopped helping us. The Francis's, Henry's girl's family, have a lot of influence round here and they've persuaded the other farmers not to offer help. Well, we managed while Reini was still here. Henry is a big strong boy, but there are busy times when it really needs two men.' She sighed and stared out of the window. 'Reini is a good man, Elwyn. He has helped other farmers round here in the past. Why should they turn against him because of this old war? He's still the same man that helped them with their shearing and in the harvest. The Francis's are being very nasty to Henry. Why?' She turned an agonised face to Elwyn. 'Henry was born in Manafon. He's a local boy. But Henry and Olwen, his girl, have to meet in secret, like as though its shameful! Poor Olwen. Her brothers watch her like hawks and threaten Henry with all sorts if he doesn't keep away from her. And, oh dear, they really do love each other. I feel so sorry for them. It'll come to a head one of these days and somebody will get hurt.' She wiped a tear from her eye with the edge of her apron and gave a shaky laugh. 'Dammo! as Dada would say. You didn't come here to listen to my tale of woe. Have another cup of tea to keep you going till I get the proper tea later. How are all at Pool Road, anyway? I hope Mama and Dada are not too much for Nell?'

'No, no. She manages. Nan is very good. She does a lot of the washing and bakes our bread every day. Poor Nan. She worries about her boys. Huw goes back tomorrow and nobody knows when Edward will get home. It turns out his mob has gone out to North Africa, just as he thought, and to add to that worry was the break-up of his engagement to Ruth. Caused, I'm ashamed to say, by Rhiannon.' He shook his head grimly.

'What happened, anyway?' asked Meg, frowning. 'I never heard the full story of that. Will they get together again?'

Elwyn shrugged. 'They're both too proud to climb down, I think,' and he proceeded to tell Meg all the details he knew of the story, while she tutted and shook her head in sympathy. 'And what about your Gareth? Is he all right? In Ireland, isn't he?'

'Aye, so far, anyway. What they're doing there I don't know, but I'm glad they're there, anyway. It means that Nell doesn't have that worry.' Elwyn made a face. 'Rhiannon is enough of a handful, believe you me. I think very often I could shake her, but I'm afraid if I started I wouldn't know when to stop!' He gave a short laugh and shook his head.

Suddenly Meg frowned and went to the window. My word, it is getting dark. I think we are in for a storm. Oh! here comes the rain.' As large drops pattered against the window pane. 'Those youngsters had better run for it!' she added and then squealed as a loud peal of thunder shook the house, accompanied by a flash of lightning. The back door flew open and Roma tumbled in, laughing, followed by Henry and Huw, wiping the rain off their faces with the palms of their hands.

'There now, you are wet!' exclaimed Meg. 'I'll get you a towel to dry yourselves,' and she hurried into the kitchen, to return with a snowy white towel which they passed among themselves.

Another loud clap of thunder rattled overhead and Meg, who had never liked storms, winced and clapped her hands over her ears. Roma put her arm round Meg's shoulders and led her to the old rocking chair. Just as she settled her down there was a crash from the window that looked over the yard and the sound of breaking glass as the panes of the window smashed inwards, letting in the torrential rain. Meg screamed and struggled out of the chair, while Henry ran to the window and was in time to see two figures fleeing across the farmyard. He flung out of the house and gave chase, Huw following. Elwyn approached the window and stooping down picked up a half-brick which lay on the floor among the shards of glass. With a grim face he lifted it and showed it to Meg and Roma, who looked on, horrified.

'The Francis's...' whispered Meg. 'It must be. Oh, I wish Henry and Huw hadn't gone after them. They'll get hurt, sure to!'

On that the back door opened and the boys came back, dripping wet and furiously angry. 'Too late,' panted Henry. 'But it was the Francis's all right. We can report it to the police, but it'd do no good. They'll deny it. Why can't they leave us alone?' he shouted, bitterly. What have we ever done to them? People have gone mad in this old war. Anyway, we'll have to get this window boarded up. There's some old pieces of plywood in the barn. Will you give us a hand Huw, till I nail some over the window or we shall be flooded in here.' Both young men hurried out again, while Meg stood staring at the window, her hand over her mouth.

'Where is your broom, so I can get this broken glass up?' asked Elwyn. 'And a mop or something.'

Meg straightened. 'Oh dearie me, what am I thinking of. I'm not usually so helpless! I'll get a broom and pan. Then we'll mop the wet up.' She quickly left the room, followed by Roma, calling out 'I'll help you, Auntie Meg!'

The boys returned carrying pieces of plywood and Henry brought in his father's tool-box. They soon had the wood nailed up and Meg and Roma cleared up the broken glass and mopped up the puddles on the floor. By the time they had finished the storm had passed and the sun was out. Meg set about getting the tea with Roma helping her, and although pale, Meg was more composed when they all sat down at the table. Elwyn was concerned, but Henry assured him that he could handle the Francis's and although Elwyn wasn't entirely happy, there was nothing much he could do about it and he said no more for fear of making Meg more anxious.

Despite all that had happened, they made a good tea, with succulent boiled ham and sweet tomatoes, plenty of fresh bread and farm butter, Meg's home-baked scones, a raspberry tart with thick cream and finally a cake rich with fruit and cherries.

Elwyn sat back replete, patting his stomach and sighing pleasurably. Then he became serious. 'You must report this to the police, Henry,' he urged. 'Unless they're stopped you don't know what they'll do next. If you need me to give any evidence I'll come right away.'

'Yes, all right, Elwyn. I guess I'd better do that. I'll have to come into town in a day or two to fetch some glass to mend the window, so I'll call and tell you what the police say.'

'Don't forget,' chimed in Huw. 'I'm going back tomorrow, but Dad or Llew or Owen would all be glad to come if you need them, and Elwyn has seen what happened and can back you up.'

'We'll be all right,' Henry said, squaring his shoulders. 'I'll look after Mam. I don't think old man Francis knew anything about this. Words are his style, not this sort of thing. He'll likely put a stop to their capers if the police call and accuse those idiot sons of his. Don't worry about us. We'll cope.'

Meg nodded. 'Henry'll sort it out. Just so long as Reini doesn't get to know about it. I wouldn't want him to worry about us. We're doing very well, really,' and she gave a tremulous smile.

Eventually it was time for the visitors to go. Roma and Meg hugged each other. Meg really liked Huw's girl and felt she would be good for him. Henry and Meg stood at the top of the lane to wave them off, Henry's arm round his mother's shoulders as his tall frame towered above hers. It was a reassuring sight and Elwyn felt better as he drove through the cooling evening, the countryside looking fresher after the storm, the birds singing their evening chorus and the cattle peacefully cropping the grass in the translucent light of the water meadows.

10

Enemies and Bedsheets

It was Monday, and Huw and Roma had departed by the two-fifteen train, leaving Nan and Davy missing their company once again. They decided to walk down to Pool Road. Nan had a large loaf of bread for the family there, anyway. When they settled down round the table with the inevitable cups of tea, it was to talk about Huw and Roma, and all agreed that Roma was a lovely girl and would be good for Huw. 'Calm him down a bit,' said Davy, grinning. 'Nothing wrong with Huw when he stops to think, but he's inclined to go off at half-cock, as you know. Not like Edward, who thinks everything through carefully before he does anything.'

'Well, we're not all alike,' offered Elwyn. 'Huw is a good lad at heart. I thought him much quietened down this leave.'

'Aye, that's true,' Davy agreed. 'Maybe that's to do with Roma. But there again, what he's going through would make him grow up pretty quick, I should think.' Davy saw Nan's eyes widen and recollected himself. 'Mark my words, he'll have tales to tell when this is all over, and if I know Huw they'll be pretty tall tales, too.'

On that the front door opened and Owen entered, ushering Lena before him with Kathleen Eluned in her arms. Owen was dressed in khaki uniform, a rifle on a sling over his shoulder and a forage cap at a rakish angle on his dark curls.

'Aye up!' exclaimed Davy. 'Why should Wales tremble? Haven't seen you in uniform before. Very fetching. When did you get issued with this lot? Oh, we'll be safe in our beds now, girls,' and he grinned at the women who were casting admiring glances at the dashing figure which Owen cut.

'All right, you lot,' Owen grinned back. 'We got this lot last Thursday evening. This'll be the first parade in uniform and with guns instead of broom handles, thank God. I felt a right Charlie walking down to the drill hall with a broomstick over my shoulder. I was right fed up with meeting kids from our school and having them shout after me, 'The end of your broom's fell off, sir.' I did forget my dignity once or twice and swung my broomstick at them, but they were always too fast for me, little blighters.'

'Well, I think you look very handsome and a real soldier,' Nell said, soothingly. 'You mind, Lena. All the girls'll be after him.'

'Nah,' Owen shook his head. 'Not with all these Irishmen spreading their blarney around. Us local blokes don't stand a chance. Anyway, I've got to go or I'll be late. Little Eddie Probert is a right little Buonaparte. Talk about discipline! Don't know what he was in the last lot, but I should think a Brigadier at the least. I'll call back for you here then, shall I Lena, love?

'Yes, if Nell doesn't mind me stopping for a bit. I don't fancy sitting down in Woolpack Row all night on my own with Kathleen. I get morbid.'

'You know you're welcome, Lena.' Nell assured her and poured her a cup of tea while Owen hurried out and Lena went round the table to offer the baby to Mama, who reached out for her eagerly, smoothing back the shawl from the little face and cooing to her in a language as old as time. Lena passed Dada on her way to her place at the table and he beckoned to her with a gnarled finger. As she bent down to him she could see the worried frown on his face and he whispered to her, 'Who was that soldier who was here just now? Nobody does tell me anything. I think he had a gun. What was he doing in my house?' He grew agitated and grasped her arm.

'Oh, twt, Dada, that was only Owen,' Lena told him, patting his hand reassuringly.

'Owen? Our Owen?' Dada lifted a puzzled face to hers and shook his head. 'Duw, why haven't I been told. I didn't know as Owen had gone to this old war. I thought he was a teacher. Who is to teach the children, then?'

'No, no, Dada,' Lena stifled a fit of giggles. 'Owen is in the Home

143

Guard. They are not real soldiers, well, what I mean is that they won't have to go away. They will stay here in Newtown to look after us in case the Germans come.'

Dada's eyes widened in horror. 'Are them Germans coming here, then?' he asked hoarsely.

Lena saw Nell roll her eyes and hastened to comfort Dada. 'No, of course not, Dada. They'll never get here. They haven't even managed to get to England yet, let alone all the way to Wales. If they tried to land in England all the soldiers and sailors and airmen would jump on them. No, I think our Owen and his mates are just dressing up to try and be big.' She nodded to him and grinned and went to sink thankfully into her chair at the table and drained half her cup of tea at one swallow, pulling a wry face at Nan. Dada muttered for a while, but soon sank into one of his little dozes.

Meanwhile Owen had met Llew and his mates, Gwilym the Sticks and Owen Neaudd at the end of Severn Place and they all made their way to the drill hall. It was a blustery evening, a strong westerly breeze blowing up the valley, as though yesterday's storm had upset the spell of good weather. However there was no sign of rain and Gwilym the Sticks remarked that it was a pity to be going indoors. It was a nice night for a stroll up Severn Green, said he.

'What you on about, Gwilym.' Owen Neuadd stared at him. 'We'm goin' to 'ave a go with our guns, all dressed up like real soldiers. That's better'n a stroll up Severn Green, mun. Thee cust do that any time.'

Gwilym sighed. 'I dunna think I was ever cut out to be a soldier, somehow. 'Ow'm I goin' to get the 'ang of this gun. To tell you the truth, it frightens me to death. I'm afraid I shall shoot somebody I know.'

'There's no ammo in the guns yet, Gwilym lad,' Llew reassured him. 'You can't shoot anybody without ammo. Bullets, you know. We shall be issued with them tonight. You'll soon learn to be careful. That's what these drills are all about. Teaching us to use the guns properly.'

'S'alright for thee,' grumbled Gwilym. 'Thee wast in the last lot. Thee knows what thee's doin'.'

'Well, I had to learn first, same as you, mun,' said Llew. 'Anyway, here we are. Get inside, you old fool. You'll soon enough pick it up.'

Soon the men were immersed in the mysteries of loading with

real ammo, those who had been through the last war lending a hand to those who had never handled a gun before. They were initiated into sloping arms with a proper gun instead of a broomstick and various other activities designed to make soldiers of them. Although from time to time Eddie Probert shook his head in mock despair and bellowed at them 'You 'orrible lot!' in true Sergeant-Major style, they all appeared to enjoy the action and felt like real soldiers.

They were all standing easy while Captain Probert told them that they would all be going out to the shooting range at Mochdre next Monday night, after some more drilling and training on Thursday, when the door to the hall burst open and Sergeant Edwards from the Police Station next door stumbled in.

'Cap'n Probert, Cap'n Probert,' he shouted hoarsely. ' We've just had a phone call from somebody in Cambrian Gardens. A Parachutist has landed on the Rackfield!'

Eddie Probert looked stunned. 'A parachutist!' he repeated, dazedly. 'On the Rackfield? I never heard any aircraft? Good God!' He looked round, then suddenly sprang into action. 'Attention!' he bellowed. 'To the right! At the double! To the Rackfield!'

The men wheeled round and began running through the door, Probert at their head. Down Severn Place they poured, faces grim and set. This was war! It had caught up with them. Eddie Probert led them behind the Elephant and Castle and along the bank of the river, below the Tannery. Eventually they reached the Ha'penny Bridge and streamed across this. By now a small crowd had spotted them and sensing something was up, followed after the thundering boots as they crossed the bridge. Past the disused waterwheel of the old mill which sat on the bank of the river on the right of the bridge they ran on until they were in Cambrian Gardens and in sight of the Rackfield, which at one time had belonged to the Mill, and on which the woollens had been hung on racks to dry, hence the name. The gate to the Rackfield was open and Eddie Probert, their dauntless Captain halted them when they were all through and motioned them to silence.

There in the middle of the field they saw a large white shape, and as they crept nearer, holding their breath, with eyes popping out of their heads, they saw movement under the material, as of someone thrashing about, trying to get out. 'Right, men!' Eddie Probert said, his voice cracking with tension.

'Form a ring around it. Weapons at the ready. I'm going to try to peel back the parachute. Now you cover me,' he pointed to Llew, 'The bugger's under there and he's alive. You can see him move. Anybody know any German?'

They all shook their heads, but Llew remembered a jumbled phrase which sounded like 'Henda Hock' which he reckoned meant 'Hands up!'

'Right then,' croaked the Captain. 'When I give the signal you all shout 'Henda Hock!' as fierce as you can, and keep those guns trained on the soddin' Jerry.'

Breathlessly they took up their positions and Eddie Probert braced himself and bent down to begin lifting up the edge of the parachute. Everybody's eyes were fixed on the writhing form underneath. Eddie Probert gave the signal and there was a mighty shout 'Henda Hock! Henda Hock!' On that a crumpled form emerged from the parachute on its hands and knees and blinked wildly round at the ring of soldiers with their guns trained on him. He gave a terrified cry and tried to crawl back under the material, but Eddie Probert was too quick for him and hauled him out by the collar. There was a groan from the assembled army.

'What the hell! Its Jack Evans!'

A sweating and bewildered and somewhat drunk and incapable Jack Evans, current owner of the Rackfield, his hair standing on end and his eyes wild, struggled in Captain Probert's grasp. 'Lemme go! Wot you tryin' to do to me? 'Ave you all gone mad? I'shnt it enough that this oul' sheet blowed on top of me from shomewhere! I 'an't done nothin'. I'll 'ave you in court for falsh arresht, Probert.' He twisted out of Eddie Probert's grip, his indignation lending him strength. He pushed his sleeves up and took a fighting stance more or less in front of the Captain. 'Come on then, you devil! One to one, man to man.' He staggered round the embarrassed Probert, his fist raised ready to land a punch if he could decide which Probert to hit, when they were all startled by a loud scream and a fat woman in a white pinafore lumbered towards them.

'What you doin' with my sheet?' she screeched. 'What you think you're playing at? Haven't you got anything better to do, grown men!

Look at the state of my sheet.' She bent down and gathered up a large white sheet, now dirtied and bearing grass stains. 'Look at it! Its one of my best pair! Real linen! You'll pay for this, Eddie Probert, and you Jack Evans.'

'Your sheet, ish it?' cried Jack Evans, indignantly. 'You want to watch what you're doin' with your oul' sheets. If it hadn't been for your bloomin' sheet I wouldn't 'ave been frightened half to death. First it landed right on top of me and then these idiots was coverin' me with their guns when I crawled out at last. 'Nuff to give a man an 'eart attack, it wash! What you doin' throwin' your oul' sheets about?'

'I wasn' throwin' my sheets about. An' they're not oul' sheets, I'd 'ave you know, Jack Evans! Best linen is what I 'ave on my beds. This must 'ave blown off the line. An' now look at it! I'll 'ave to wash it all over again.' She gathered her sheet to her substantial bosom and marched off towards the gate, muttering about Jack Evans's origins and questioning the sanity of daft clots pretending to be soldiers. As she passed through the enraptured little crowd at the gate she wondered aloud about louts with nothing better to do than play games with her sheet.

Captain Eddie Probert cleared his throat and with a barked command, called his troops to order. As they shuffled into line he had time to think up a face-saving speech. 'Well, lads, it seems we've been victims of a mistake. But it's not been wasted. We've shown the people of the town how quickly we can respond to an emergency. Well done, chaps. Attention! To the left - quick march!' The gallant band swung out through the gate, ignoring the hysterical laughter and catcalls of the onlookers and, albeit with red faces, they held their chins up, and marched back to the Drill Hall, where they collapsed into helpless laughter and hilarious remarks, and Eddie Probert joined them.

Owen was still laughing to himself when he bounded up the steps of No.46 Pool Road. Nell, Lena and Elwyn looked up in surprise when they saw him. 'You're early!' Lena grinned at him with raised eyebrows.

'Didn't bother going for a pint after the session,' Owen answered, smothering a laugh. 'Don't think we could have stood the barrackin' we'd have got in the pub tonight. So we all crawled home, hanging our heads in shame!'

Lena frowned. 'What are you talking about, boy? What have you idiots done now?'

'Not so much of the idiots, girl,' Owen frowned in mock ferocity. 'Brave fighting men, us, and we proved it tonight.' He collapsed into hysterical laughter, while his listeners looked at each other, mystified. At last Lena gave his arm sharp pinch, at which he stopped laughing, rubbed his arm and said 'Ow!' reproachfully.

'Tell, then,' Lena said, threateningly.

'All right, all right! No need to pinch. It was like this, you see. It all began when a parachutist landed on the Rackfield.'

There were squeals from the women and 'Good God!' from Elwyn and Owen hastened to say 'But it wasn't really a parachutist, you see. It was Jack Evans under Mrs Moses Owen's sheet!' He started to laugh again, but they all looked at him blankly. 'Jack Evans under Mrs Moses Owen's sheet?' Nell repeated slowly and incredulously. 'What in God's name was Jack Evans doing under Mrs Moses Owen's sheet. Don't tell me Mrs Moses Owen was under the sheet with him?' Nell's eyes were wide with horror. 'On the Rackfield? In broad daylight!'

Owen shook his head but he was choking too much to reply. Mama had looked up from nursing Kathleen Eluned and she watched Owen anxiously. 'What is wrong with that boy? Will somebody see to him. He is having a fit!

This made Owen choke even more and Lena thumped him on the back, making him shout. This woke Dada from his little doze and his eyes fixed on Owen from whom great whoops were issuing forth. Dada started forward in his chair. 'There is that soldier with the gun again! What is he doing in my house. Throw him out, Elwyn,' and he wagged an accusing finger at the bent figure of Owen. At last the latter sobered up and wiping his eyes, turned to Dada and showed his face. 'It's me, Owen, Dada! Don't you know me?'

'I told you, Dada,' said Lena. 'Its only Owen. He's not a real soldier. Remember I told you about the Home Guards?'

'Oh, aye,' Dada said doubtfully. 'They are going to stop the Germans from coming to Newtown. And our Owen is one of them, is he?'

At last Owen recovered his breath and related to them all that had happened during the evening. They all had a good laugh, but as Lena said, at least it showed how quick they could be at getting after a Jerry if he did land, and with that comforting thought Owen took Lena and Kathleen Eluned home to Woolpack Row.

Two days later Henry called. He was in town to fetch the glass to mend the window. He looked a little happier when he sat down at the table, after greeting Mama and Dada. Only Nell was there at eleven o' clock in the morning and as he accepted her offer of dinner, she went off into the kitchen to peel a few more potatoes and chop up two more large carrots. Home made faggots were cooking in the oven and the savoury smell of them was making Henry's mouth water. Nell made him a cup of tea and gave him a piece of her currant loaf to tide him over until dinner time. Then she sat down opposite him.

'How are things at the Walkmill now, then?' she asked, anxiously. 'Elwyn told us all about the bother on Sunday night. Did you go to the police about it?'

'Yes, I did and I'm glad I did, now. I didn't want to bother, I didn't think it would do any good, but it did!' Henry grinned at her and took a sip of his hot tea. 'I met with Olwen last night down by the stream.' He made a face, but went on, 'We have to be careful. Her old man still doesn't like her going out with me and gives her a rough time if he catches us. Anyway, we did meet for a while last night and she told me what had happened when the police went to Francis's farm, Brynteg. When they asked for the two boys, Bernie and Ivor, the old man wanted to know what it was all about, of course. When he found out he went roaring after them, gave them both a good hiding - he's a big strong chap - and told them never to go near our place again. 'Our quarrel is with the German and his whelp,' he said. 'There is a woman at the Walkmill and there's no need to frighten her.' So I don't think we shall see them round our way again. The police asked me if I wanted to press charges, but I told them, not this time. But something else good came of it. It got around the local farms what the Francis blokes had done and two farmers, Lewis, Cae Glas and Jones, Brynsiriol, came to see me. They were pretty sheepish, but after havering about a bit they said they'd come to offer help when I'm ready to get the harvest in. I thanked them and told them I'd be glad of their help. They told me a lot of people were sorry to hear of our trouble and they didn't hold with what the Francis's had done. They even went so far as to say that Dad had been a good neighbour to them in the past. So things are looking up and I'm glad of it for Mam's sake. She was very upset on Sunday, and the Lord knows she's got enough to put up with just now. She misses Dad badly. It relieved her mind that some of the neighbours are coming round, anyway. I just wish I could court Olwen openly, but that will come, maybe. We were all right until this old war started.' He sighed and drank his tea gratefully.

Nell had been making sympathetic noises as he talked and she was relieved to hear that things were better with them, for she was very worried about her sister, living among such hostile neighbours. She poured Henry another cup of tea and excused herself while she went to check on the dinner.

Henry chatted with Mama and Dada, who were at their brightest in the morning, giving them news of the farm and painting a bright picture of how well they were managing. The old people had now understood and accepted that Reini was in the internment camp, and as long as he was safe and Meg was all right, they were satisfied.

Later, after Henry had enjoyed dinner with them all and set off back home, Nan came down bringing the day's bread with her. Esther also turned up with her three children and the two evacuees in tow.

When do they go back to school?' asked Nell.

'September the Third,' Esther replied.

'You'll be glad to see them go, I should think,' Nell said, smiling.

'Oh, I don't know,' Esther shrugged. 'They're not a lot of trouble. The weather's been pretty good so we're out a lot of the time. I take them up the Bryn Bank or fishing in the Ffrydd brook. They don't catch anything, but they're content to paddle up and down and build dams and so on. We take picnics and I think I enjoy it as much as they do!'

'Well, you always did want a lot of children and now you've got them.' Nell ushered the four bigger ones out to play and Esther released Johnny from his pushchair, He immediately made for Dada's chair and lifted up his arms for Dada to take him up.

'Somebody lift this boy onto my knee,' ordered Dada, pleased, and Nan went over to him and put the little boy onto his knee. He promptly snuggled down against Dada's chest and the old man wrapped his rheumaticky arms round him and kissed the top of his downy head.

Johnny snuggled closer and while the three women round the table talked, Dada and the little boy slipped into a doze. Mama sat quietly gazing into the fire, but unnoticed by the others her hand went to her flat old chest from time to time and she frowned and winced. After a while Nell got up to make them all a cup of tea and as she drew the kettle off the hob and on to the trivet over the fire, she glanced at Mama and asked 'You'll have a cup of tea, Mama, yes?'

Mama raised a pale face and nodded. 'Can you get me a bit of bicarb in a drop of milk first, Nell?' she asked and Nell looked at her anxiously. 'You got a bit of wind, Mama? The faggots a bit rich for you, I expect,' she said. She went out to the kitchen and came back stirring the bicarb in a drop of milk. Mama pulled a face as she drank it and Nell laughed. 'You shall have a nice cup of tea to wash it down now,' she said and spooned tea into the old brown pot before pouring boiling water in. After pouring out four cups of tea she carried one over to Mama. The old woman's hands shook a little when she took it from Nell, however she sipped the tea and seemed to draw strength from it, for she smiled up at Nell who was reassured and joined Nan and Esther at the table.

Esther was talking about Ruth. 'I met her in town on Tuesday and she was walking around with one of the Irish soldiers.'

'What!' Nan cried. 'And I was going to take a walk up to the Bryn this evening, to try and put Edward's side of the story and persuade her to write to Edward. 'Well! Would you believe it It didn't take her long to forget him, did it? She must be fickle. Maybe Rhiannon did Edward a good turn!'

Nell shook her head. 'I still feel bad about what Rhiannon did, but I did think at the time that Ruth should have waited to hear what Edward had to say. She was pretty quick to chuck him up, wasn't she?'

'Poor Edward!' Esther said. 'He thought such a lot of Ruth. He'd not bothered much about girls before that, had he?'

'Edward's pride will keep him going,' said Nan, 'But its been a blow to him. He's already gone out to North Africa. I had a field card from him. He didn't say where they were, of course, but he let a couple of hints drop that Davy recognised.'

'Yes, and I've heard the RWF's are moving from Ireland shortly, too,' said Nell. 'It's a pity. I thought that Gareth and Jim would be pretty

151

safe there. I wonder where they'll be sent next? Oh, I hate this old war!'

'Well, we're luckier than some,' Esther pointed out. 'The poor folks in London are having a bad time, sleeping in shelters or down the underground. At least we can sleep in our beds.'

On that there was a crash of breaking china and they turned, startled to see Mama's cup in shards on the floor and the old woman lying back in her chair, her face pallid and beads of sweat on her forehead. She was clutching her chest and her eyes were stricken.

'Mama!' cried Nell and flew across to her mother. 'What is it? D'you feel bad?'

Mama struggled for breath but was unable to answer. 'Quick, Esther, run for Dr. Shearer,' Nell urged and Esther was bounding through the door before she'd finished speaking. Nell stroked Mama's hair and Nan chafed her wrinkled hands, but the old woman's eyes closed and her breathing became very laboured. Nell looked across at Dada but was thankful to see that he and little Johnny were fast asleep.

When Dr Shearer came hurrying through the door fifteen minutes later the three women presented a tableau, with the two younger women on each side of the old one's chair as though frozen. Esther had not come back with the doctor but had run to Woolpack Row for Owen and once he was alerted she had rushed up Kerry Road to fetch Davy.

Meanwhile Dr Shearer, after a swift glance at Dada in passing, bent over the old woman and took her wrist in his fingers. After a moment he let her hand drop to her lap and lifted an eyelid. He sighed and straightened up. 'I'm afraid she's gone,' he said slowly. 'Heart, without a doubt.'

The door opened and Owen came rushing in. He halted when he saw the doctor, who turned and nodded to him. 'Your grandmother?' he asked.

'Its Mama!' Owen said, shaking his head, and then, recollecting himself, he stammered 'Y-yes. She's my grandmother. Is she ...?' he couldn't bring himself to say the word.

'I'm afraid so, son,' the old doctor said, softly.

The door opened again and Davy hurried in, white faced and breathless. 'What's wrong with Mama? Esther said -' his voice trailed off as he saw the doctor and his eyes questioned him.

Nan went to him and squeezed his arm. 'Oh, Davy, love. She's gone, I'm afraid.'

Davy shook his head in denial. 'Not Mama!' he cried hoarsely. He went up to his mother's chair and touched her hand. 'Mama! It's Davy.'

The doctor caught his arm and turned him round. 'Come now, lad. There's things to do. Now, can you and this young man carry your mother upstairs and lay her on her bed? Then I'll give her a proper examination so that I can write the certificate. Can you do that?'

Davy and Owen looked at each other and then nodded. They gently lifted the thin frame that was all that was left of their Mama and bore her carefully up the stairs. They were surprised to find how little she weighed. They laid her gently on her bed and Owen pulled the eiderdown up over her as though to keep her warm. He stared down at the woman who had been his 'Mama' since he was a small boy and his mother had died giving birth to Esther. He remembered no other mother and a sob escaped him and tears rolled down his cheeks. Davy put an arm round his shoulders and drew him close, feeling his own throat tighten as he looked down at his mother, that pillar of strength for the whole family. Suddenly the thought of Dada was like a clamp round his heart. What would happen to the old man? She had been his strength and his rock all through their life together. She had chivvied him and scolded him but they had understood each other and were quietly devoted. Whatever would Dada do now?

Two weeks later Dada joined Mama, lost and bewildered without her and though the family grieved for him too, they knew that his place was at her side and he could only be happy reunited with his Susan.

PART TWO

1

Nuptials and Toasts

The war rolled on and the winter of 1941 approached. In June the Germans had broken their non-aggression pact with Stalin and had invaded Russia. Llew, who had long wondered what the heck Stalin was doing signing a pact with the arch-fascist-enemy was relieved, especially now that the Germans were having to fight on two fronts and he could tell his detractors that it had been a clever tactical ploy by the USSR, and that now they were on our side we'd have the beating of Hitler and his lot. However it seemed that the Nazi's massive war machine hardly halted despite the Allies' efforts.

On the whole, morale in Britain remained high. People put up with the minor irritants of food rationing and the recently introduced clothes rationing. Martin, who had to keep up appearances, quietly complained that if he'd been able to replace his old raincoat it would have taken sixteen coupons, seven for a new pair of boots and two for a pair of gloves which was all he ended up buying, as he'd ruined his old ones changing a tyre after getting a puncture on a cold muddy visit to one of his farmer clients up near Kerry.

A boost to the morale was the wireless, where the most popular light programme was Tommy Handley's ITMA, much enjoyed by Edie, the Phillips's help, who never tired of parrotting its famous catchphrases: 'Can I Do You Now, Sir?' made immortal by 'Mrs Mopp' and 'I Don't Mind If I Do!' from the tipsy 'Colonel Chinstrap', until the whole Phillips family wished that ITMA would come up with some new ones, sooner rather than later.

Vera Lynn, the 'Forces Sweetheart', caught the sentiment of the people and had everybody singing along in pubs and social gatherings to 'We'll

Meet Again', which also found a poignant echo in the hearts of lonely and longing loved ones.

The Rees's kept going, although with the death of both Mama and Dada something of the heart had gone out of the family. Those of them who visited No.46 were continually conscious of something missing and eyes went to the two chairs by the fire which no-one really felt like occupying. Offered them by Nell they sat uncomfortably, as though they were taking a liberty, and preferred to sit at the table, which had been their more natural habitat.

On a cold and dreary day in November, Nan sat with Nell over a cup of tea and Nell confided that she had decided to go out and get a job. 'It's no good me thinking I can start up making hats again. Women don't want my kind of hats any longer. Goodness knows, a lot of them are just wearing headscarves. That looks sloppy in my opinion, but there you are, I suppose you can't expect people to keep up standards in wartime.' She sighed and poured herself another cup. 'I hear they'll be opening that factory on Pool Road soon, making munitions of some sort. I might try to get in there. Elwyn's not keen on me going out to work, but being here all day on my own since Mama and Dada went, I'm getting morbid. I brood on what might happen to Gareth. Well, you know only too well what it's like. You've got two to worry over.'

Nan nodded. 'I know what you mean. If Davy wasn't retired and home all day I should go spare. I think sometimes he worries that he's not doing anything to help the war effort, but he can't go in the Home Guard like Llew and Owen because of his heart. He thought he might apply to be one of these A.R.P. wardens, but then his eyesight's not that good and he'd break his neck in the dark, I'm sure.' She smiled and shook her head. 'I keep telling him that we've sent two of our boys to the war. That should be enough, surely.'

'Aye, of course it is,' Nell agreed. 'There's plenty that have used their influence to keep their boys out of it. Let them go first before we sacrifice all the men we've got in the family. I was talking to Llew's Mattie the other day and she says she's going to apply for a job at this factory. It was her gave me the idea. Elwyn and Rhiannon will have to do more jobs around the house if I do go out to work. Elwyn'll shape up when he gets used to the idea, I know. As for Rhiannon, it's time she did a bit about the place. She's been mooning around ever since that Irishman, Sean Kerrigan, went. Seems to have really fallen for him.'

'It didn't take her long to get over Edward.' Nan said, smiling ruefully.

'No,' Nan shook her head. 'And after all the mischief she made between him and Ruth. Oh well, there's no accounting for Rhiannon. But from what I've gathered this Sean Kerrigan is a pretty tough proposition. She doesn't get all her own way with him, seemingly. Maybe she's met her match. I don't know what to think about him. Seems a steady sort of a lad and he's certainly good-looking. He could charm the birds off the trees with that Irish brogue. But you know he's a Roman Catholic.'

'Do you mind about that?' asked Nan, raising her eyebrows.

'I don't know,' Nell responded, doubtfully. 'The Rees's have always been strong C.of E. I asked Elwyn what he thought and he told me not to jump my fences before I got to them!' She laughed. 'Anyway, he said that in the event that they did marry and Rhiannon turned Catholic, the discipline in that Church might be good for her.'

'Well, there is that,' Nan chuckled. 'Myself I wouldn't care what religion my lads married into as long as they're good women. So long as they don't go in for anything weird, that is. Not that there's anything very weird round here. The religions are all pretty tidy. And we're all hoping to go to the same place, after all.'

'That's true,' Nell agreed with a smile. 'Anyway, we'll have to wait and see what happens with Rhiannon and her Sean. I'd have liked her to find a tidy local lad, but I expect there'll be a few will marry the Irish. Rhiannon is going up to Bangor on Sunday. A load of local girls who were going out with the Irish till they were moved to North Wales have hired a small bus to go up and see them and Rhiannon has joined up with them. She hasn't had time to tell this Sean that she's coming. I hope she doesn't find that he's got another girl when she gets there! But it would serve her right if she had the tables turned on her for a change!'

'You are cruel, Nell!' Nan laughed. 'Poor Rhiannon. I'm sure she'll settle down eventually. She's so pretty that she's had things her own way up to now. Maybe this Irishman will tame her. To tell the truth it's Edward that worries me. It looks like Ruth is going seriously with her Irishman, too. I expect she'll be going on the bus to Bangor, as well. We send letters to Edward through the BFPO, but we never mention Ruth, and of course we only get these old field cards in reply. At least they tell us Edward is all right up to now. We hear from Huw regularly but there's no chance of leave just now.'

Nell shook her head. 'Field cards are all we're getting from Gareth, too, but that's better than nothing. Mattie's getting them from Jim as well, so our boys are safe so far, thank God. Now then, another cup for you?'

'No thanks, Nell. I seem to do nothing but drink tea all day and Davy's just as bad. A couple of old tea-chops we are, I tell him. By the way, have you had that Bob the Barn round at night? He's been made the ARP Warden for Kerry Road, Pool Road and New Road, and it hasn't half gone to his silly oul' head. He's a devil! If he finds a crack or a little hole in the black-out he pounds on the door and roars and curses. I'm sure they're not allowed to curse people, are they?'

'I'd like to see him try to curse me!' said Nell, indignantly. 'I should be down to the offices to complain sharpish if he tried it. Honestly, some of these little officials forget themselves when they're made up and given a bit of a uniform and a title. Who the devil does Bob the Barn think he is?'

'God knows.' Nan shrugged.

'Anyway, to change the subject, what do you think of this new lot of troops that have come here now? The Royal Artillery. I wonder will the local girls fall for them like they did with the Irish?'

'Oh, I daresay,' Nell grinned. 'Its the uniform, you see. Makes all the difference. I've heard of one or two married women in the town who've seem to have conveniently forgotten their married vows, too.' She pulled a face. 'Its rotten when you think of their men off at the war, fighting, too. I doubt that there'll be a few marriages break up after this old war is over.'

Nan nodded sadly. 'It's a shame, isn't it. But there, this whole war is a crying shame. Why can't men live in peace with each other? I'm sure if they left it to us women there wouldn't be any wars.'

'I wouldn't be too sure of that,' Nell chuckled. 'Ever heard two women quarrelling? They can be pretty vicious too! Oh, I must tell you, give you a laugh. Rhiannon came into the back kitchen the other day and asked to borrow the gravy browning. I looked at her like a fool. I mean, it wasn't dinner time and anyway she never makes gravy. D'you know what she wanted it for? She couldn't get any more silk stockings and she won't wear lisle ones, so it seems what they do now is colour their legs with gravy browning and pencil a line up the back to look like a seam! Did you ever hear anything like it?'

'Ugh!' Nan pulled a face. 'That means they'll be going through this winter with bare legs, really. They'll catch their deaths!'

'Pride will pinch! I told Rhiannon that I'm not nursing her if she gets pneumonia! She wants to buy a new winter coat, but she's used up most of her clothing coupons already, that's why she couldn't get any stockings. She'll be sweet-talking me soon to try and get some of mine, you watch. Well, she's not getting mine. Her Dad'll probably give her some of his. She could always wind him round her little finger, for all he grumbles about her.'

'Oh well,' Nell rose from her chair, 'I'd better think about getting their tea ready. They'll be in soon.'

It was a dark and dismal Sunday morning when Rhiannon climbed onto the small bus which was to take eighteen Newtown girls up to Bangor. They started at nine o'clock and they settled down for the journey. Rhiannon was sitting next to a girl called Betty Williams, a plump fair-haired girl who had been going out with an Irish soldier ever since he had landed in Newtown. They were more or less engaged and were hoping to be married before Christmas, since no one knew how long the Inniskillin Fusiliers would remain in Wales. It looked like there would be a number of marriages before they left for their next destination.

Rhiannon listened to the other girl with half her attention. She was absorbed in thoughts of Sean Kerrigan. She felt he was serious and would like to marry her, but being Rhiannon she wanted to know more about him and his prospects before committing herself. She was aware that he excited her, even more than Edward had done, and she was also aware of a sternness in him and the knowledge that she wouldn't always get her own way with him. Yet he moved her more than any other fellow ever had and when she was with him she had no doubts at all. However, when she said goodbye to him a few weeks ago she had refused to give him any commitment and although he had promised to be true to her, she didn't know what she would find when she got to Bangor. What if he had found another girl? She couldn't think of that without a cold clutch at her heart. Well, she supposed that meant she was in love with him. And if he asked her to marry him, what would she say. Maybe she should put him off until after the war. But she couldn't bear to do that. She had the feeling that no matter how much he cared for her, she couldn't play fast and loose with him. She pictured him in her mind, tall and broad-shouldered, with those intense blue eyes fringed with curling black lashes, that beautiful mouth and the dark curls which fell over his forehead. She closed her eyes for a moment while the girl next to her prattled on. When she opened them again they were passing through the mountains of Snowdonia, but they were shrouded in mist and a thin drizzle was falling. The time seemed long and Rhiannon couldn't wait to get to Bangor.

At last their journey ended and they stopped in a car park at the top of the town. They all got out and Betty Williams and Rhiannon began walking along the main street. There were a number of Irish soldiers strolling about and the two girls scanned them in the hope of seeing the ones they were looking for. It was fifteen minutes later when Betty gave a squeal and left Rhiannon's side to charge across the road shouting 'Jimmy! Jimmy! I'm here!' A stocky young man turned an astonished face which soon split into a delighted grin. Rhiannon was left standing on the pavement staring round her. After a moment she carried on walking down the street. She spotted a Catholic church and soldiers still coming out of it so she stopped nearby and watched. She could hardly believe it when she saw Sean lighting a cigarette while chatting to another man. Her heart turned over. He looked so handsome. She edged a little nearer and suddenly he looked up and stared at her as though he was seeing an apparition. She smiled at him and nodded and slowly he moved towards her, hardly able to believe his eyes.

'I don't believe this,' he said, his brogue thick on his tongue. 'Rhiannon. Is it really you?' He shook his head in wonder. 'Do you know I was thinking about you in church when I should have been praying, and yet here you are, an answer to all my prayers.' He took her in his arms, deaf to the small, good-humoured cheers from the group of men by the church gate, and kissed her thoroughly. 'You are real,' he

162

said breathlessly when he let her go. I feel like pinching myself in case its all a dream. But if it is, I don't want to waken.'

Rhiannon laughed shakily. 'Yes, I am real. I came up on a bus with a lot of girls who have come to see their fellows.'

Sean grinned. 'Well I hope they find their fellows behaving themselves. And what have you come to find?' She shrugged with a flirtatious smile. 'For me it's a mystery tour. Are you the official guide?' He laughed and drew her hand through his arm and guided her back up the street. 'Come, I'm sure you could do with a cup of tea and something to eat. There's a great little cafe just up the street from here where they do a grand Welsh Rarebit. I usually call in there after Mass. The girls behind the counter tease me because I'm always on my own. Well, now they'll see why. Oh, Rhiannon!' He stopped and drew her round to face him. 'We need to talk, wee girl. I want to pin you down.' He then went silent for a moment as they walked on.

'Here we are, lets get a cuppa and something to eat and talk in comfort somewhere warm.'

They entered the steamy interior of the small cafe and they were immediately the focus of all eyes. There were wolf-whistles from the other soldiers sitting at the tables, and envious stares from the girls behind the counter. It was obvious that more than one of them would have liked to change places with Rhiannon. Suddenly she felt very proud of Sean and thrilled that he had taken his commitment seriously and at once she was aware that she was eager to hear what he had to say to her.

They settled at a table for two in the corner and Sean removed his cap and tucked it under the epaulette on his shoulder. He ordered two teas and two Welsh Rarebits from the waitress and then reached over to take Rhiannon's hand. He gazed at her in silence for a moment taking in every feature of her lovely face, now flushed with excitement. Then, very seriously, he asked.

'Does this visit today mean what I think it means? What I want it to mean?'

'What do you want it to mean? Isn't it enough that I've taken the trouble to come all this way to see you?' Rhiannon's smile was provocative.

Sean shook his head reproachfully. 'You know I want to marry you. I haven't asked you outright before because there are some things we have to get straight. You have to know what this involves, what my prospects are, in other words.' He smiled, but his eyes were serious. 'You may not be aware of it over here but to be a Catholic in Northern Ireland is to be a second-class citizen. We are only allowed the humblest of jobs, unless you want to be a priest or a teacher. Well, obviously I'm not cut out for a priest, and I don't want to teach. However, I'm lucky because my father has his own business in Derry - or Londonderry as you know it over here. He has a furniture business and I shall have a place in that when the war ends. So I'm secure in that way. The next thing is my faith. I wouldn't pressure you to become a Catholic if we married, but of course it would please me more than anything if you did, not least because any children we have will have to be Catholic. Then again, we would have to be married in a Catholic church, mainly because we would not be married in the eyes of the Church otherwise, but also because my brother, Seamus, is studying at Maynooth to become a priest, and it may go against him if I was to marry outside the church. They are very strict at Maynooth. So you see, my love, these are the things I want you to know before you give me an answer. It's only fair. It's asking a lot of you, I know, and you may think I'm doing the dictating, but I pray you won't see it like that. It's just that my faith is not negotiable, not even for you, the love of my life. I hope you'll understand. If you want to lay down any ground rules yourself, then feel free. I'm here to listen.' He gazed at her with so much love in his eyes that her heart turned over. Maybe you want time to think about it all and about what you are taking on. Perhaps talk to your folks about it? But I hope you won't take too long about it because things are very uncertain now, and I don't know how long we'll be in Wales, or where we'll be sent next and I'd like to marry you before that and make sure of you!'

Rhiannon was silent, thinking of all he'd said. He was asking a lot too. She'd have to marry in his church, probably convert to his religion, bring his children up as catholics and live over in Ireland. If any other man had dictated to her like this she would have given him his marching orders. Yet she felt sure that if this was the price she had to pay to have Sean Kerrigan she believed she would pay it. She realised with surprise that she had barely taken in the fact that he had a secure future in the family business, which she presumed would be his some day. It sounded as though they would be comfortably off.

He had been watching her closely and he reached for her hand again. 'Well, my love, how does it sound to you? On the romantic side, I promise to love and cherish you all my life.' He grinned. 'Does that help?' She smiled quizzically. 'In other words,' he continued buoyed up by her smile, 'Do you love me enough to take me on, Rhiannon?' He turned her hand over and planted a kiss on the palm. Every nerve in her body responded, and she wondered and yet knew what was happening to her.

'I say yes,' she whispered. 'Yes, yes.'

'Oh my God! Let's get out of here! I have to hold you! I have to kiss you! Do you realise we've just got engaged?' He gave a mighty whoop which brought all eyes round to them. 'Congratulate me!' he called out. 'She's said 'yes!' and he grasped her round the waist and waltzed her towards the door, while she laughed breathlessly. They left the cheering behind them as they went out and he led her towards a small park and there under the dank and dripping trees he held her and kissed her and they were lost to the world.

For the rest of the day they roamed around Bangor in a daze, until it was time for her to go to the bus. As the bus moved off she waved through the window to him as he stood there looking bereft. When he was out of sight she lay back against her seat and hoped Betty Williams wouldn't talk too much as she wanted to think and ponder the future. However Betty was quite silent, with a small, satisfied smile on her face, planning her own wedding and her own future.

Nell and Elwyn received the news of the engagement without surprise, but with mixed feelings. They felt relieved that Rhiannon was serious about someone at last but they listened with awe to all the conditions which she had accepted. This Sean must be quite a man! No doubt they would come to terms with the change of religion eventually. They had seen enough of the Catholic church in Canada to know something of its strict rules, and Nell was coming round to Elwyn's way of thinking, that it would do no harm to Rhiannon to have a bit of discipline. The fellow seemed to be very strong-minded, which was no bad thing where Rhiannon was concerned. When they heard that Sean was to come to

Newtown on leave in a fortnight, they issued an invitation for him to stay at No.46 so that they could get to know him better. Although Nell was sad that her daughter would be going to live in Ireland, she realised that Rhiannon would never have stayed in Newtown, anyway, and on top of that they were pleased that the young man had a good job to go back to after the war in his family business

And so Sean Kerrigan came to No.46 and charmed his way into the hearts of all the Rees family. The marriage was talked over and plans laid for it to take place at the end of December. They fixed a date provisionally and Sean and Rhiannon travelled on the train to Welshpool to see the Catholic Priest there, Father Adolph Evans, who covered the Newtown parish as well as Welshpool. Despite his unfortunate Christian name they found him a kind and helpful man and arrangements were made for the wedding to take place in the little church of Saint Frances of Rome which was really a private chapel belonging to the Briscoe family of Newtown Hall, but which was open to all Catholics of Newtown on a Sunday and on Holy days. Sean went back to Bangor to arrange a couple of days leave for that time and to write to his parents in the hope that they could get over for the wedding, although he wasn't hopeful that they would be able to do so. Not only was travel restricted in wartime, but they had the business to run. However he had told them before about Rhiannon and how he was determined to marry her and they were willing to trust his judgement, providing there would be guarantees regarding his religion. He was happy to tell them that Rhiannon was prepared to adopt his faith and they wrote giving the couple their blessing, and also sent a letter to Nell and Elwyn telling them that they were pleased to welcome Rhiannon into the family. Sean had another brother besides Seamus called Francis, who was training to be a teacher, and two sisters Eileen and Bernadette, one who worked as a clerk in the family store and the other who was a bookkeeper in the city. The Rees's thought they sounded like a lovely family and Sean planned to take Rhiannon over to see them if he could get a fourteen day leave in the New Year.

So all was preparation at No.46. There would be no bridal gown and all the trappings, but they would beg, borrow or steal enough coupons to get Rhiannon a smart suit to get married in, while the rest of the family relied on their best clothes. Nell began to plan the wedding cake. 'I read a good tip in the paper the other day. How to make imitation almond paste. You use Soya flour and icing sugar, and flavour it with almond essence. You have to have a couple of eggs to bind it, but I can get eggs from Meg and she's also promised to give me some dried fruit, which she had from the village shop.'

'I'll ask Mr Swain our grocer if I can have some dried fruit, too. We can do without a Christmas cake this year,' Nan said, sighing. 'Huw says he can't see any sign of leave for a while, so it'll only be me and Davy. I just don't feel like making a fuss over Christmas this year. I'll just get presents for the small ones of the family, Esther's lot and her little evacuees, poor little things, and Lena's Kathleen.'

'I don't know why you say 'poor little things' about Esther's evacuees. She spoils them more than she does her own. Well, she acts as though they were her own. I don't know what she'll do when they have to go back home. Surely break her heart, you'll see.'

'Well, you know what Esther's like with kids. I remember how she doted over Edward when she wasn't a lot older than him herself. Then she couldn't wait to have babies of her own. Its a good thing Martin is able to afford a big family and has got the patience for it. Because I doubt very much whether Esther's finished yet!' Nan chuckled. 'She thinks we're a poor lot with our two apiece!'

'Well,' said Nell, 'Two's enough for me, especially when one of them is Rhiannon!'

'Oh well, you may not have her much longer if they're going to live in Ireland after the war. What does she think of that?'

Nell shrugged. 'Its a city she's going to. Londonderry, or Derry as she's told me to call it. She says the people there don't call it Londonderry. Only the English do. Anyway, at the moment it seems that she'd go to Timbuktu if Sean was going there. Can't believe it, can you? She's really fallen hard for him and he certainly seems to have got the upper hand, which is no bad thing when you're dealing with Rhiannon.'

'Well. anyway, I'm glad she seems to have found her Mr Right and I hope she'll be very happy. She'd never have been happy with Edward. Even if he'd have agreed to have her, which is unlikely, he'd have been far too soft with her. I think he was too soft with Ruth, he should have made her listen to him. But there, it was not to be and perhaps it's all for the best if she can forget him so soon.'

'Maybe he's got over her by now, anyway. Out in North Africa I daresay he's got other things to think about.'

They went on to talk about plans for the wedding and how to gather together enough food for the reception. All the family had offered to chip in and they decided that a buffet would be the easiest. The men would provide the beer and a couple of bottles of sherry and that was all that could be expected in wartime.

'It will cheer us all up,' Nan said, smiling. 'A bit of excitement to take our minds off our worries.' She bit her lip. 'I worry most about Huw, you know. Every time I hear them say on the wireless 'One of our aircraft are missing', I wonder if it's Huw's.'

'Oh, you mustn't worry so much,' Nell patted Nan's shoulder. 'Your Huw has surely got a charmed life. You've heard from him lately, haven't you?'

'Oh yes. I had a letter the day before yesterday. And I had a letter from Roma today. She seems such a nice girl and thinks the world of Huw, by her letters. It'll be nice when this old war is over and they settle down in Newtown. She can be the daughter I never had.'

Nell nodded. 'It'll be lovely for you and for Davy. Is he all right? He seems pretty quiet these days.'

'Yes, he's all right, I think. But he follows the war more closely than I do, which means that he worries a lot about the boys, though he doesn't let on. He tries to cheer me up. Well,' she rose from her chair and reached for her coat. 'I must go back to him.' She turned back when she reached the door. 'He's a good man, Nell. I don't know what I'd do without him.'

The weeks went by quickly, filled with the wedding preparations. At last the great day arrived and although it was very cold, at least it was dry. Sean had arrived on the six-thirty train the night before and had quickly joined in the task of preparing the food and generally making himself useful. Under his firm guidance Rhiannon worked hard and Nell and Elwyn looked at each other from time to time and grinned. On the wedding morning, Elwyn's car was pressed into service and after taking Sean and Owen down to the little church, where Owen was to be best man, he came back and ferried Nell and Lena with little Kathleen, coming back eventually for the bride, who looked very lovely in a pale mauve suit and a pretty tip-tilted felt hat in the same colour. Her bridesmaids were to be Esther's Mary and little Gwennie who were brought to the church by Martin in his car, this time without a puncture, along with the three other children. Llew and Mattie made their own way to the little Church as did Nan and Davy and they all settled themselves in the unfamiliar pews with some trepidation. However Father Evans came over to shake hands with them all and to welcome them with a kindly smile and briefly explained the service, which in the event did not seem so strange after all.

Rhiannon looked radiant and Sean was very handsome in his walking-out uniform. Nan whispered to Nell, 'Aren't they a handsome couple!' and Nell nodded, too choked with pride and emotion to answer. When the priest said, 'You may kiss the bride now!' with a benevolent smile, there was such love behind that kiss, on both sides, that the family were moved and all the unpleasantness with the old Rhiannon was forgotten. The couple knelt for Father Evans's blessing and Rhiannon became Mrs. Kerrigan.

There was no time for a honeymoon as such since Sean had to go back up to Bangor the following day, but he had booked a room at the Elephant and Castle for the night and in the meantime the wedding party returned to No.46 where the buffet wedding breakfast awaited them. Meg and Henry had arrived by then, having had to see to the animals before coming, so that all the Rees's were present with the exception of the young men away at the war.

Nell looked around the gathering. There were her brothers, Davy and Llew, her sister Meg, there were Owen and Esther, Nan and Mattie, and the young ones. Of her generation only Reini was missing and she felt sorry for Meg without her partner. She slipped her arm through Elwyn's as she stood beside him, and thought with affection of the whole family and how close to each other they were. 'I wish Mama and Dada had still been with us,' she whispered to Elwyn. 'How they would have loved today, to see us all together and to see Rhiannon settled.'

Elwyn smiled down at her lovingly and squeezed her hand. 'We're really not all together yet, though, are we?' He said, ruefully. 'Not until

Reini and the boys all come home. It would have been difficult for Mama and Dada to have understood that. They'd have wanted to know where the boys were. Never mind, we'll have a great get-together when they all come marching home.'

Nell offered up a silent prayer that all the boys would return safely and for a moment yearned after her Gareth. If only this old war would end so that they could get on with their lives without the old worry nagging at them all the time. On that, the bridal pair came up, hand in hand and obviously consumed with their own happiness. 'Sean wants to make a speech!' Rhiannon said, laughing.

'Go ahead, Sean lad,' Elwyn said, grinning. 'Wait till I get a bit of hush.' He banged his fist on the table and everybody stopped talking and looked expectantly towards Rhiannon and Sean, where they stood hand in hand at the head of the big table, around which they had all sat over the years. 'Let's have hush for Sean, my new son!' said Elwyn and stepped back, leaving the limelight to the big Irishman.

'I'm not going to say 'Ladies and Gentlemen' although that's what you are. But you're my new family and I would like you to think of me now as part of that family. I fell in love with Rhiannon the very first time I saw her,' he looked down at a blushing Rhiannon and smiled lovingly. 'I didn't think I had a chance then, but I kept on trying and I think she's given in now because I've worn her down. I'll do my best to make her happy, I can promise you, and my family in Ireland have asked me to tell you that they will welcome her warmly when I'm able to take her over to meet them. In fact I know they will make her as welcome as you have all made me. Finally, I just want to ask Nell and Elwyn if I can start calling them Mam and Dad?'

There was an enthusiastic cheer as Nell and Elwyn smiled and nodded and Owen, as Best Man proposed a toast to the happy pair and glasses were filled to the brim.

Suddenly there was a small, indignant voice from among the crowd. 'What about us? Can we have some toast as well?' and Mary pushed forward, together with Alun and Teddy and Gwennie bringing up the rear, struggling with the effort of carrying a solid Johnny in her arms. 'And my cousin Kathleen will want some as well!' she announced imperiously, pointing at Kathleen Eluned, perched up in Lena's arms and looking round in wonder.

Amidst the laughter Nell hastened to fetch the lemonade and to fill six glasses which were presented to the children. 'There! Now you can make your own toasts!' she told them, as round-eyed they sipped their drinks. Johnny was most puzzled. He'd never been given lemonade when he'd asked for toast before, but he stored it in his memory to try out at breakfast the next day.

2

Telegrams and Tears

At the end of March 1942 the RAF started a campaign of saturation bombing of industrial targets in Germany. One Sunday night, the Krupps works at Essen was pounded by massive 4000-pound bombs carried by the new four-engined bombers, escorted by Spitfires. For the crews, these were days and nights rolling into a blur of nightime raids. They would return, if lucky, in the early hours and snatch a little sleep. Then they'd have de- briefings of the night's work followed by briefings for the next night's sortie which would mean facing enemy fighters from as early as the Luftwaffe's forward base at Le Havre, and then ever more intense ack-ack as they approached their targets. They released their bombs into a pyrotechnic chaos, and then had to endure the painfully long and risk-heavy flight back to base. As the number of sorties increased, so did the casualty rate.

Some days after that fateful Essen raid, the much-dreaded telegram boy knocked at the door of Plas Gwyn and brought Nan and Davy the news, from which they never really recovered.

Huw was dead. Bright, cheeky, loveable Huw. Huw who had always wanted to fly, had loved flying and had died flying.

When Nell entered through the back door later that day, having learned the news from a shattered Esther who had been there at the time, it was to find Davy sitting alone in his chair in the kitchen, staring in front of him, his eyes dry and expressionless and his body slumped in the chair. Nell knelt beside him and put her arms round him. He looked at her with a lost air, then held onto her arms and put his head down on her shoulder. The tears poured down her cheeks and dropped onto his greying hair. Suddenly he whispered, 'Nell?' and lifted his face.

172

At once the tears came, gleaming on the grey stubble on his cheeks, and Nell thought fleetingly how old he looked, he who had been her baby brother. His mouth worked and he tried to say 'Huw is...' but he couldn't bring himself to say the word. He began to shake and Nell tightened her hold on him. 'Hush now, good boy,' she said, 'Hush now.' But he shook his head. 'I can't believe that Huw... I can't believe it. My Huw. My son. And oh, poor Nan. I have to be strong for Nan, Nell, and I'm afraid. I don't know whether I can comfort her, when I can't comfort myself.' His eyes were full of pain as he gazed at her helplessly, then dropped his head into his hands.

'You will comfort each other,' Nell said, reaching up to touch his hand and draw it against her wet cheek. 'Where is Nan?'

'She is in her bed, God help her!' Davy replied. 'Doctor Shearer came and gave her a sedative and she went to sleep. Oh, Nell, what am I going to do?' A deep groan escaped him and they both turned towards the door to the passage, where the groan had been echoed, and where Nan stood, swaying, her face white beneath the blotches left by her tears. Nell rose to her feet and stepped away and Nan crossed to Davy, her arms out. 'Nan!' he cried and went to meet her, drawing her into his arms, while she reached out and touched his wet cheeks. Nell watched for a moment then nodded and went to fill the kettle to make tea, the balm for all crises.

That night they came, the Rees's, in twos and threes, finding no words for their grief, but a comfort to Nan and Davy by their presence. They could not believe that never again would they see Huw, who had charmed them, annoyed them, made them laugh and rollicked through their lives over all his years. Their hearts were sore, but they clung together and helped each other through the days that followed. This was something they were glad Mama and Dada didn't live to see.

Life went on and the summer passed. Nan and Davy had had a letter from Roma, bewildered and grief-stricken, and Nan had written back to tell her that she would always be welcome at Plasgwyn, whenever she would have a chance to come over. They also had an official letter from Huw's squadron, confirming his death and offering condolences. That letter went unanswered.

The German war-machine just seemed to roll on, and their bombers started targeting towns such as York, Bath and Exeter, as well as their usual cities like Liverpool which was the target that usually brought their frightening drone over Newtown with some regularity. But their resources were becoming stretched because of the push they were trying to make on the Russian front. And the British people were beginning to feel more hopeful since the Americans had come into the war following the Japanese bombing of Pearl Harbour. Most of the first American soldiers were initially stationed in Northern Ireland, much to the bewilderment and suspicion of the people there. However, not everyone was thrilled to see them. The phrase was coined regarding the 'Yanks' - 'They're over-paid, over-sexed and over here!' This was mainly the attitude of the British soldiers who couldn't compete, for they weren't paid as much, they hadn't the same glamour, their uniforms were a joke compared to the Americans and they hadn't the same chocolate ration! So naturally the girls liked the new exotic species and there would be many a 'G.I.Bride' going to America after the war.

As the days began to shorten again and August was almost past, people were beginning to tire of the war and even Churchill had to face a censure motion in the Commons over his direction of it. However he survived the motion with a large majority and remained in charge.

In Newtown the people were also tiring of the war. They followed it in the daily papers but it all seemed remote. Those who had husbands, sons or lovers away fighting saw the war only in terms of where they were and what might be happening to them. The Home Guard still met regularly and drilled under the command of Captain Eddie Probert. They marched out to the shooting range and perfected their skills in that direction but Hitler seemed uninterested in Newtown, and even the teasing they had endured following the Rackfield parachutist had died down. A few more bombs dropped in the vicinity, making holes in the good Welsh earth, but not even a cow was killed. Life descended into routine.

Owen was on his way to the Drill Hall one Monday night, meeting up with Llew in front of the cinema. When they arrived in the hall it was to find Gwilym the Sticks there among the other heroes, as usual, but a sadly battered Gwilym, with two black eyes, a swollen lip and a more than usually bulbous nose.

'Aye up, Gwilym,' Llew said, staring at him. 'What you been up to? The missus caught up with you at last, has she?'

'Thee's look as though thee's gone ten rounds with Joe Louis!' Owen Neuadd put in. 'What shape is the other chap in?'

But Gwilym refused to be drawn and the evening went forward with the usual drill. After they had packed up, Llew and Owen, together with Gwilym and Neuadd went across to the Black Boy for the one pint they indulged in on these nights. They carried their drinks across to the table in the corner and after they had settled and tested the quality of the beer, Llew tackled Gwilym again. 'Come clean now, Gwilym, lad. Who have you had a dust-up with? Somebody didn't like you, that's a fact.'

Gwilym took a long and healing draught from his pint pot and wiped his mouth with the back of his hand, wincing as he touched his sore lip. He sighed and settled back in his chair, looking round at his friends lugubriously.

'It was las' night,' he began. 'Me and the missus was sitting listening to the ten o'clock news when there was all this shoutin' an' bad language outside. Well, you know what my missus is like about bad language. Her goes spare if her hears as much as a damn or a blast, and there was a lot worse than that goin' on outside. Anyway, her was makin' such a fuss that I 'ad to get up an' go an' see what was up. Her followed me to the door, o' course, ready to 'ave a go at whoever was cursin'. Who should it be but Bob the Barn, goin' on somethin' awful at the old lady next door 'cos she'd been showin' a bit of light through her curtains. Well, they'm pretty tattered anyway. They was some oul' sheets died black, I think. Well, the oul' biddy was shoutin' back at 'im, givin' 'im 'is family history, which made 'im madder and 'is language was gettin' wuss and wuss. I can stick a bit of cursin', can do a bit meself when needs be, but what he was shoutin' was beyond, specially with women-folk about. Anyway, I told 'im to shut up and get off home, which was a mistake.' Gwilym looked sadly at his pint and took another swallow, before resuming his story. 'The bugger swung round at me an' smashed me full in the face with some stick he was carryin'. Well, that got me dander up good an' proper and I landed 'im with a tidy left hook to the chin which floored 'im. My missus an' 'er next door was 'anging on to each other by now and squawkin' like a couple of oul' hens. Bob the Barn got up an' looked round sort of dazed for a bit, then it come to 'im that it was me as 'ad floored 'im. He come up right close to me an' shook 'is fist in me face, spittin' tacks at the same time. 'Right you, Gwilym Evans,' he said in an 'orrible voice. 'I'll 'ave you up for this, I will. Assault and Battery. I'll see you in court for this.'

'You can try it,' says I. 'But I got two witnesses 'as can say you 'it me first, an' with a weapon. An' you was swearin' at a woman. Just because they give you some sort of a uniform, they dunna pay you to go round shoutin' an' swearin' at people, 'specially women. So mebbe I'll see you in court first!'

'Well, he went off after that, did'n he, still cussin' under 'is breath an' threatenin' me with 'orrible things. An' would you believe it? When me an' the missus went back in, I got a tongue-lashin' from 'er! 'You should'n 'ave knocked 'im down,' says she. 'You'll get us into trouble for that!' I ask you! You canna win, can you. Not with wimmin, anyway.'

As Gwilym supped the last of his ale, Llew winked at Owen, who had been listening with an appreciative grin on his face. 'You should report him, Gwilym,' Llew urged. 'Then perhaps he'll get the sack. That'd be a tidy job for you. Only have to go round after dark, and you get a free uniform and a bit of extra money.'

Gwilym put his head on one side and considered the suggestion. 'Right enough it would get me out of the house an' the missus couldn't grumble at me for gettin' in late, could she?' Then he shook his head sadly. 'Oh, I dunno. What can you do with the silly oolerts round 'ere. 'Alf of them anna got tidy blackouts, an' you won't believe this, but the oul' 'ooman next door goes out into the yard when 'er hears a German plane go over at night, an' shines a torch up into the sky to try an' see which way it is goin'!'

They were still laughing over this when they left the pub and Owen bade Llew goodnight and walked along as far as the entrance to Ladywell.

'Dust 'ee think Gwilym the Sticks is right in the 'ead?' asked Owen Neuadd, stopping before turning into his street. He looked up at Owen, his face solemn, and shook his head. 'Knockin' an Air Raid warden down is no way to go on. Thee cust get into bad trouble for that, I should think.' But Owen shook his head. 'Bob the Barn needs taking down a peg or two. I'd like to have been there to see him get his come-uppance. Goodnight now!'

It was on the following Saturday, Davy and Nan were eating their dinner when they heard a knock at the front door. Davy looked at Nan and raised his eyebrows in query. None of the family came to the front door, simply walking in through the back door, which was never locked. 'Wonder who that can be?' Nan said, and got up to go and answer the door. When she opened it she was shocked to see Roma standing on the step, a pale and exhausted Roma, who looked to Nan as though she were about to faint any minute. Nan drew her inside. 'Oh child, come in, come in. Why didn't you let us know you were coming? Davy would have met your train. You've carried that big old bag from the station and you look ready to drop.' Nan looked closer at her after she had lifted Roma's bag in and shut the door. 'Are you all right, girl?'

Roma steadied herself against the hall table and looked pleadingly at Nan. 'Do you think I could lie down for a little while? I feel a bit faint.'

'Of course, my dear,' replied Nan, concerned. 'Leave your bag here and we'll bring it up later. I take it you've come to stay for a few days,' she said, smiling. 'You can have Huw's room, it seems right you should, somehow. Come along.' and Nan led the way up the stairs and into a large, light room at the front of the house. 'This was Huw's room,' she said, looking round sadly. 'Edward always said Huw had the best room in the house, but it used always to be untidy. I keep the bed aired. We were always hoping you would come to see us! Take your coat off, dear, and I'll bring you up a cup of tea. You shall lie down a bit before you have something to eat.'

Roma hesitated and then turned away and took her coat off. Then she turned back towards Nan and faced her, her hands raised supplicatingly, her eyes desperately pleading.

Nan gasped as the realisation struck her. 'You're pregnant,' she whispered and put her hands to her cheeks. Roma nodded and her head drooped forward hopelessly.

'Huw's baby?' The colour had fled from Nan's face and she sat down suddenly on the side of the bed.

Roma's head went up and she stared challengingly at Nan for a moment. 'Of course,' she said. 'Its Huw's baby. That's why I've come. My mother turned me out when she knew. I had nowhere else to go. I thought that as it was Huw's baby you wouldn't turn me away? But if you want me to go, then I must find somewhere else. Just let me rest for a while and try to think. Its been so hard to think since Huw died and then I knew I was pregnant.' Her voice trailed away and she sat down wearily beside Nan, the tears running down her cheeks as she stared hopelessly in front of her.

Nan gave a sob and turning to Roma, put her arms round her and held her close. 'You poor little girl,' she murmured. 'How you've suffered. Don't worry any more. We'll take care of you. After all,' she gave a watery smile, 'You're carrying our grandchild. Huw's baby. The child has a right to a home with us.' She kissed Roma tenderly on the cheek and the girl clung to her like someone drowning. 'Come now, Take off your jumper and skirt and slip into bed. I'll go and make a cup of tea and fill a hot water bottle. You need rest more than food at the moment, I think.' She rose from the bed, patted Roma's shoulder and looked down at her compassionately. 'How far gone are you,' she asked, shyly. 'Seven months,' the girl replied. 'I only knew for sure on the day before I heard that Huw ...' Her voice choked, and it was with an effort that she went on.' I was planning to tell him the following weekend, and I hoped that we could get married quietly as soon as he could get a licence. But he never knew.' The tears came again and Nan bent and kissed the wet cheek. 'There now, get into bed. Have a rest. We can talk about it all later. I won't be long with a cup of tea and a hot bottle.'

Roma lay down as she was and drew the counterpane over her. She looked up at Nan with brimming eyes. 'You're very kind,' she said, brokenly. 'But what about Mr Rees? What will he say?'

'He'll be all right,' Nan soothed. 'You leave Davy to me. He's a good, kind man. You've nothing to fear from him.'

The girl sighed and closed her eyes wearily. Nan left the room and paused on the landing. It was all too much to take in. What that poor girl must have gone through. And her mother turning her out. Nan thought she could never have done that to a daughter if she'd had one. But the one thing that stood out in her mind was the fact of Huw's baby. A part of Huw had come home after all. She pressed hands to hot cheeks and tried to think, but she felt she couldn't take it all in. She started slowly down the stairs, only to find Davy waiting at the bottom, frowning and looking anxious.

'Who was that?' he asked. 'Whose bag is in the hall?'

Nan went to him and put her arms round him, but he put her away and stared at her. 'Nan, what is it? You've been crying too. What's going on?'

'Oh Davy, its Roma. Roma's come to stay with us for a while!'

'Roma?' Davy's eyebrows went up. 'Oh well, it'll be nice to see her. Daresay it's been hard for her to lose Huw, too. I keep forgetting about Roma. Fetch her down for some dinner. There's enough there. And you haven't finished yours yet. I put it in the oven to keep warm.'

'It's all right. I couldn't eat any more. I just want to make Roma a cup of tea and fill a hot water bottle for her. The poor girl is exhausted. She needs a rest before food.'

'Well,' said Davy, shaking his head. 'If that's all she wants just now, the kettle is boiling. I was just about to make myself a cup. There's enough in that old kettle for tea and a bottle. I'll just wet the tea in the pot and then you can have the rest of the water for her bottle. Poor girl!'

Nan said no more, but carried a cup of tea up the stairs in one hand and a hot water bottle in the other. Roma was still lying there, staring up at the ceiling, but already she seemed to Nan to have a little more colour in her face.

'Here, sit up, love, and drink this. I'll just slip this hot water bottle to your feet and that will warm you up. What a time of it you must have had, you poor thing. Never mind, we'll soon have you right again, ready for your baby. And poor Huw never knew?'

Roma sipped the hot tea and shook her head. 'As I said, I'd meant to tell him the weekend he died. He was going to meet me for a couple of hours. I'd sent a message to the base to tell him I wanted to see him on the Sunday night, but he never came. I never saw him again. I didn't know what to do. I kept it all from my mum. I knew she'd never understand. She's very strong in her church.' She dropped her voice to a whisper. 'We only slept together twice. It was my fault, I sort of made him. I wanted him to marry me, but he said we had to wait till the war was over. He said it was too risky, every time you went up you never knew whether you'd be among the ones that came back. I've felt since, that he somehow knew.' She gave a dry sob, then buried her nose in her cup. 'It was all my fault, Mrs Rees. I don't want you to put any blame on Huw. You don't have to take me in if you don't want to, but I came because I had the feeling that Huw would have wanted me to come to you.'

Nan sat on the edge of the bed and stroked Roma's hair away from her face. 'Of course Huw would have wanted you to come to us. Where else would you go? Anyway, snuggle down now and get some sleep, and when you're ready come down and I'll make you something to eat.' Nan pulled the counterpane up round Roma's shoulders and took the cup and saucer downstairs.

When she got to the kitchen she put the crockery in the sink and went to sit down in a chair opposite Davy. He looked at her with raised eyebrows. 'What about her dinner?' he asked. 'She'll be hungry, won't she?'

Nan shook her head. 'She's going to have a little sleep. I'll make her something when she wakes up. Look. Davy. There's something I have to tell you.'

'Come on then, spit it out,girl.'

'Roma is carrying Huw's baby!'

Davy stared at her for a moment then took a deep breath. 'Huw's baby? But, but how can that be? They weren't married. I mean, he didn't want to get married until after the war. He told me so. Oh, he was going to marry Roma, that's for sure, but he said they were going to wait. Oh, well, I see. They didn't wait, obviously. I mean .. Oh I don't know what I mean.' Davy shook his head as though to clear it. 'Has she come here to stay? You know, to have the baby here?'

'Would you mind very much?' asked Nan, her eyes appealing. It was quite evident to Davy that Nan had set her mind on it and he reached forward and took both her hands in his. 'Not if that's what you want, love. It seems fitting, somehow. What about her own mother? What does she think about it, I wonder? Don't tell me she's turned the poor girl out?'

'It seems so,' said Nell, shaking her head. 'Can you believe that her own mother would be so hard? I couldn't do that. No matter how disappointed I was.'

'Yes, I guess they only jumped the gun a bit,' Davy said with a rueful grin. 'And how can you blame them, God help them. That boy was dicing with death every day. I suppose they saw each other as some sort of security in a shifting and frightening world. We must do the best we can for the poor girl, Nan. And for Huw's baby when it comes. Somehow I feel we'll have a little bit of Huw to keep on loving.'

'Oh Davy!' Nan said, going over and putting her arms round him. 'I'm that glad you feel like that about it. It's the way I feel, too. We'll manage.'

'But what's she going to live on in the meantime,' Davy asked. 'She can't go out to work. Daresay we could afford to feed her and perhaps clothe her, but she'll want some money of her own, I shouldn't wonder.'

'Oh well, we'll talk about that with her later on. In the meantime we'll just make her welcome and look after her. Oh!..' she put her hand over her mouth. 'What are the rest of the family going to say. What will Nell and Elwyn think?'

'Does it matter, love?' Davy patted her shoulder and smiled. 'Its our business. Our grandchild. Anyway, you know the Rees's. They'll adapt to anything within reason. And they liked Roma when they met her. They're not stiff-necked, you know. You wait, Nell will start making baby clothes and Esther will be full of it and her and Lena will be rooting among the things their kids have grown out of. They'll have a whale of a time, you'll see!'

And of course he was right. When they got over the initial shock they took Roma to their collective bosom. Nell got out her knitting needles to make matinee coats and booties, and hunted through her remnant bag for lengths of flannelette for nighties and barras. Kathleen Eluned was out of nappies by now and Lena brought a pile of snowy nappies round, together with lots of other first size things. She offered to lend Roma her pram, 'I won't give it to you,' she explained, ' 'Cos I hope to have a boy next! I shan't stop at one!'

Esther came with armfuls of baby clothes and a Moses basket, which again she said she would lend to Roma but might want returned later when another baby came along. She also offered a cot on the same terms.

'Just think,' she said, her eyes shining. 'A little Huw for us to love.'

'Hang on a minute!' protested Nan, laughing, 'It might turn out to be a little Roma!'

'We'll love it just as much!' said Esther stoutly.

Roma was reduced to tears by all the kindness and quite overwhelmed. She looked much better since she was rested and well-fed and fussed over by Nan. Each day that went by saw an improvement in her. She often smiled now and was much more relaxed. She began to look forward to the coming of her baby, happy that its place in the lives and affections of the Rees family was secure. As the days passed the very raw grief that had weighed her down began to ease a little, enfolded as she was in the affection and genuine care of Huw's family. At times, when her relief and gratitude overwhelmed her, she thought she heard him whisper, 'I told you so!' and then she hugged his memory to her, and strained towards the day when she would hold his child in her arms.

Her dream came true on a crisp December morning, as she lay in Huw's bed, in Huw's room and felt closer to him than she had since the day he had left her. Her pains had begun in the night but she held the knowledge to her, only calling out for Nan when she heard her getting up at half-past seven. Nan came hurrying in, and after exclamations of concern, went off to get Davy up and sent him for Sister Lloyd-Jones, the midwife, who had been booked. By twelve o'clock Roma was sitting up, a little tired, but flushed with joy, gazing down at a miniature Huw in her arms. No-one could have doubted who the little one's father was and tears of happiness ran down Nan's face as she watched the tiny replica of her lost son. He weighed seven pounds and was perfect. Nan looked so wistful that Roma held out the baby to her and Nan took him in her arms and held his tiny soft face against her wet cheek. He stirred and pursed his lips and looked so like Huw that Nan gave a shaky laugh.

Davy came in with two cups of tea, which he put down on the bedside table. Nan held out the baby to him with a tremulous smile and he took it gently into his arms and gazed down at this little Huw. He cleared his throat. 'What are you going to call him? Not Huw?' he ventured.

'No,' Roma smiled and shook her head. 'Not Huw. There was only one Huw. I was going to ask you if you'd mind me calling him David? We could keep it as David, and not shorten it.'

'Fine by me!' Davy grinned. 'I'd be flattered. Little David he shall be.'

Nan nodded agreement and took the baby back. 'Drink your tea now, love,' she told Roma. 'I'll lay this little one down in his cot and then I'll go and make you something to eat. What do you fancy?'

'Oo! I could eat a boiled egg with toasted fingers,' Roma said, eagerly.

'Right you,' smiled Nan. 'That's what you shall have. Mind, you deserve a full chicken dinner for producing this little angel for us. Our little David.'

'I'll settle for the boiled egg, please.' Roma laughed then became serious. 'You have all been so kind to me. I nearly didn't come, I was so afraid. But now you've all made me so welcome. I do really feel that Huw wanted me to come here. Thank you for me and for David.'

3

Absent Friends and Orphans

Once again the Rees family spent a quiet Christmas. Fighting was intense in North Africa and those within the family who had boys in the RWF who were fighting there, were in a constant state of worry. Edward too, was known to be somewhere in that vicinity. By now it was thought that he would have received the letter telling him of Huw's death, a letter very hard to write and news that would have been easier to break face to face. They pinned their hopes on 1943 and their longing that this would at last bring an end to this war.

Whilst they all ate dinner in their own homes, this year they were all invited to Bay House for tea with Esther and Martin. All had contributed something from their rations towards the spread. Small packets of fruit for the cake; Lena had gleaned some icing sugar from her grocer, Mr Swain, taken instead of ordinary sugar, which wasn't a very great sacrifice as Owen didn't take sugar. Nan brought bread and a tin of the inevitable Spam, and Meg and Henry brought butter, eggs and a cooked chicken. Nell had made a sponge with eggs she had from Meg and filled with her own raspberry jam. Mattie brought scones and another tin of Spam, and when eventually they all sat down around the big dining table in Bay House, with the big middle leaf extending the table to its utmost, they all agreed it was a feast indeed.

The talk ranged from the present state of the war and the Government's handling of it, about which Llew had quite a lot to say, to local gossip and news from the boys. Mattie had heard nothing from Jim for a while and she and Llew were more than usually worried about him. Field cards had been received from Gareth and Edward, which told them very little but at least they knew they were alive at the time they

184

were sent which was a relief.

While Llew and Martin at one end of the table discussed the war and the fact that it looked as though Germany was losing on its Eastern front, and Meg and Henry gave the family the latest news they had had from Reini, the other women gossiped about the latest wedding in the Catholic church, details of which were furnished by Rhiannon, who was attending the church for Mass on Sundays and instructions in the Faith on Saturday nights, after Father Evans had heard confessions. She told them that Ruth had married an Irish soldier, one Jimmy Quinn, in a very quiet wedding, and that rumour had it that her family, strict Presbyterians, had refused to go to the wedding because it was held in the Catholic church and that Ruth herself had refused to change her religion. Rhiannon seemed to think that this boded no good for the marriage if Jimmy was going to the Catholic church and Ruth to the Presbyterian. Sean, who was stationed in the South of England and had been back to Newtown recently on a weekend leave, had told Rhiannon that if Jimmy took Ruth back to Northern Ireland with him, their life would be near impossible, since the bitterness between the Catholics and the Presbyterians, in particular, there was so rife. 'I think they'll probably settle in Newtown.' said Rhiannon, whom Ruth appeared to have forgiven for her loss of Edward, and talked to her freely when they met. 'I think Ruth would be made miserable going to live among Catholics. I shall be all right,' she added, smugly. 'By the time we go to live in Derry, I shall have been received into the Catholic Church.'

'Are you happy about that?' asked Nan, with curiosity.

'Oh yes, very happy,' returned Rhiannon, tossing her dark curls and looking around challengingly.

On that there was a small cry from the Moses basket in the corner and Roma excused herself and went over to pick up a scarlet-faced little David. 'I think he wants his feed,' she said, apologetically. 'Could I use your bedroom or somewhere, Esther?'

'Oh don't get up,' she urged as Esther rose with a fond smile.

'Well,' said Esther, sinking back onto her chair again. 'It's the door facing you at the top of the first flight of stairs, Roma.'

After the girl had gone upstairs, Esther turned to Nell. 'She's really nice, isn't she, Nell? I'm glad she screwed up her courage to come to

Newtown to have the baby. It is Huw's baby, after all, and it's what he would have wished.'

'Oh, its Huw's baby all right,' laughed Nell. 'There's no mistaking that! You've been very good to her, Nan.'

'She's easy to be good to,' Nan said, smiling. 'And we love having our grandson. Whether we'll have any more I don't know,' she went on with a sigh. 'That depends on Edward. He still doesn't know about Ruth. He's never mentioned her from that day to this, so we can only hope he's got over her and that it won't put him off women. He thought such a lot of her, you see.'

'So you haven't told him about Ruth?' asked Nell, while Rhiannon played with the edge of the tablecloth, wishing they wouldn't talk about the love affair that she had been instrumental in breaking up.

'No. Well, as I say, he never mentioned her and so we didn't. We must just hope he's forgotten her when he comes back.'

To change the subject Rhiannon asked Nell in a whisper,' What is Roma going to do? I mean, for money. Will she go out to work later on? There's the baby, isn't there?'

Nan shrugged. 'We haven't talked about it much. I've told her that I'd look after the baby if she wanted to go out to work, but she doesn't seem to want to leave him. And I can't say I blame her.' Nan added, with a smile.

'Yes, but how's she going to keep herself?' Rhiannon said.

'Well now, that's not a problem at the moment. She told us when she came that she had some money in the bank. She'd saved up nearly a hundred pounds before she ever met Huw, out of her own earnings, and she was putting so much a week away for the wedding. On top of that her Dad left her two hundred pounds. He had a little grocery business it seems and it was sold after he died. She had two hundred and her brother had two hundred, and her mother had the business, which she still runs. So she's got enough to keep her for a while. We don't take anything from her for her keep, although she offered it. She's a big help to me in the house and I don't grudge her her food. She's a grand little worker and a very sensible girl with her money, so we go along very nicely just now.'

They were interrupted by a loud laugh from Martin at the top of the table. Llew was chuckling too, along with Owen and Davy. 'Tell us what the joke is,' said Esther with a grin.

'Oh, nothing much,' said Llew, his shoulders still shaking with mirth.

'Oh come on, Llew,' said Mattie. 'Tell us.'

'Well,' began Llew, 'It was little Alfie Williams, who works in the pattern office at Pryce Jones's. He came in yesterday morning with a real shiner of a black eye. Now Alfie is a very quiet little man, a bachelor, about fifty, I should say. Never bothered with women, frightened to death of them seemingly. He lives in that row of houses in Park Street next to the Plymouth Brethren Chapel. It seems that Lily Golightly lives next door to him. Lily has been no better than she should be, but now she's getting a bit long in the tooth, Lily's looking for a steady man to provide for her in her old age, and it seems Alfie measures up. Well, she's not had much luck with him up to now. In fact, he's run a mile every time he sees her. Until last night. He was coming from a meeting at the Baptists and the night was as black as the hobs of hell and no lights about, of course, and didn't Alfie mistake the house. Walked into Lily Golightly's by mistake! Before he could turn round and run she had him in an arm lock. 'I knew you fancied me,' she squealed, covering his face with kisses. 'Geroff, woman!' yells Alfie. struggling with her. When he gets free he says 'Fancy you! Fancy you! If you were the last 'ooman on this earth I would'n fancy you!' Before he could get to the door she landed him one and gave him a black eye, poor little devil!'

'Llew! How do you know all this?' asked Mattie, giggling.

'Had it straight from the horse's mouth,' Llew said, with a grin. 'And a pretty frightened little horse it was, too.'

Nell shook her head. 'Poor little man. Lily Golightly is enough to frighten anybody. Is that her real name?

'No,' replied Llew. 'I think she's one of the Jones the Muck-Sweepers. They call her Golightly 'cos she wears a long old coat, and when she takes her soldiers for a walk down Pool Road, they say the bottom of her coat sweeps the pavements, so the council men don't have to sweep them. So they say!'

The children were sitting up at the table, Kathleen Eluned with the help of a cushion which she was in danger of slipping off. They were interspersed with the grown-ups, so that the latter could keep them in order. Now Mary piped up, demanding a piece of the Christmas cake. 'I want the piece with the reindeer on,' she told her mother.

'No Christmas cake until you've finished what's on your plate, Mary.' Esther's voice was firm, 'Look at all the stuff left on your plate. Bread and butter, Spam, a pickled onion. You must finish that up before you get to the cake.'

Hot tears welled up into Mary's eyes and she gazed at her mother with a tragic air. 'I'm nearly full now and I just know that if I eat all the stuff on my plate I'll never have room for my cake! And then I can't have the reindeer off the top!'

'I want cake as well,' Alun chimed in. 'And I want the snowman off the top. And I don't want any of those silver balls on my piece. You can break your teeth on them!' he added, anxiously.

Gwennie and Teddy also looked anxious, but they said nothing, waiting to see the outcome of Mary's demands. Kathleen repeated 'Cake,' proudly, but Johnny had other ideas. 'Me no want cake. Me want pickly oonion,' and he displayed his teeth as though to show his readiness.

There was general laughter. 'Oh, give them cake,' said Martin, grinning. 'It is Christmas, after all.' 'Yes, yes. Cake, cake!' they all clamoured. 'And us as well,' whispered Gwennie, and Teddy nodded silently.

As Esther was cutting the cake and distributing pieces to the children, Roma returned with David, replete on her arm, fast asleep, with a trickle of his mother's milk on the corner of his rosebud mouth. Roma laid him down in the Moses basket and took her place at the table next to Nan. They smiled at each other affectionately.

Martin rose from the table and returned in a few moments with a bottle of port. 'Get some glasses, love,' he said to Esther. 'We must have a toast to absent friends.' When their glasses were filled and raised to 'Absent friends' Nan reached for Roma's hand and they both thought about Huw, who would forever be absent now.

After Christmas the New Year brought news of the German surrender in Stalingrad in January, but it seemed that the Germans were now concentrating their resources once again on their Western front. In February, thirty-eight schoolgirls and six teachers were killed in a direct hit on a school in Catford. It was thought that as this was a daytime attack, the Germans were testing the British defences. Certainly they stepped up their attacks on London and the South of England and it was in April that Esther received a letter from a Mrs Johnson, written on cheap, lined paper.

'*Dear Mrs Phillips*, (she had written)

I am sorry to ave to tell you that my sister, Mrs Smith, and Mr Smith, who was the mother and father of Gwennie and Teddy, what are staying with you in Wales, has both been killed in an air raid. Their house is gone too. It was a direct hit. I dont know what is to happen to those two poor children. I would take them but I cant because I have five of my own and only two bedrooms and my Bert isnt erning very much anyway and its ard making ends meet as it is with our five. It looks like they will have to go in a home because theres nobody else to have them as our Mum and Dad are dead and our brother died in the war and Mr Smith hasnt got nobody. You can write to me at the address I have give you and tell me what you think. Must I look for a home for them or will you look. I am sorry to have to tell you this bad news and for you to have to break it to those two poor children.

Yrs truly,

Mrs Melia Johnson'

Esther was at the breakfast table when the letter arrived and she read it in stricken silence. 'Anything wrong, love?' Martin asked, his eyes on her shocked face. She shook her head and looked back at him beseechingly. Then she pulled herself together and attended to the children's breakfast, hurrying them along, but treating Gwennie and Teddy with special gentleness. When they were all bundled into their school clothes and each given a small packet to eat at playtime, she settled Johnny down on the floor with his toys and went to sit close to Martin, who was having his last cup of tea before leaving for the office. His eyes fixed on her face, he said, 'Come on, love, what was that letter all about? Bad news of some sort by the look on your face.'

Esther took the letter out of her apron pocket and after smoothing it out she gave it to Martin, while her hands plucked at the hem of her apron and her eyes were filled with tears.

Martin finished reading the letter and laid it down by his plate. 'Oh, my God! What are we going to do now. Poor kids! How are we going to break it to them? And what's going to happen to them? Doesn't sound as if there's anybody at the other end who's going to help out. Or even take any responsibility for them! What on earth happens in a case like this?'

Esther shook her head. 'I don't know,' she whispered in a choked voice. 'Poor little ones. Mam and Dad and home all gone! How are we to tell them? I don't know how to do it.'

Martin got up and put his arm round her shoulders. He dropped a kiss on her hair and held her tightly against him. 'Look, sweetheart, I must go, but I think we must wait until tonight and talk about it some more. Don't say anything until then. And don't go worrying, you hear. We'll work something out. We'll tell them together when we know what's going to happen. Say nothing until then.' She lifted up her face for his kiss and he ran a finger through the tears on her cheek. 'And no more of these!' he whispered.

Shortly after he left Edie Davies arrived. Esther followed her into the kitchen and once again pulled the letter from her apron pocket and handed it silently to Edie. Esther had come to rely on Edie, who although a bit of a gossip was nevertheless full of sound common sense, old-fashioned remedies and shrewd old sayings. Edie read the letter through slowly, then handed it back to Esther, her lips pursed in a soundless whistle. 'Oh, dearie me! Poor little dabs. Orfins. Have you told them yet?'

'No!' said Esther with a shudder. 'And I don't know how I'm going to, Edie. What a job I've been landed with! They're going to be in a terrible taking.'

Edie looked thoughtful. 'I wonder will they? I've been thinking lately how well they fit in here. Get on with your kids like anything, they do. Looks to me like they're beginning to look on you and Mr Martin like you're their Mam and Dad. Like this is their home, too.'

Esther stared round-eyed at Edie, then reached blindly for a chair and sat down by the kitchen table. 'But - but what you're saying is that they should stay with us? That we should take them over? For good?' Her voice faded into a whisper.

'Well, what you goin' to do with them then? Send them to that Dr Banana's? There's no place for orfins round here, is there? There used to be the workhouse, but them has gone now. And sounds like them folks up in London aren't goin' to do much for the poor little blighters. Still, p'raps they'll put 'em in Dr Banana's for you. Its sure to be nearer London than here.' Edie watched her mistress's face, knowing full well that the soft hearted Esther could never bear to send Gwennie and Teddy out into the unknown.

Esther bit her lips and bllinked back tears. 'Oh no! Poor little things,' she whispered. 'Whatever would become of them? But could I really keep them? What would Martin say about it? They're nice little children, no doubt. Not much trouble and ours do seem to get on with them. But I don't know. Its a big step, isn't it? I'd have to see what Martin says, discuss it with him. But yes, I wouldn't mind.' She lifted her face and smiled at Edie through her tears and the older woman thought to herself that if she looked up at her Martin like that he'd surely melt. Anyway, he was so daft about her, thought Edie, that she could wind him round her little finger, though, fair play, she didn't try it on purposely.

'Oh well,' said Edie, briskly, running hot water into the washing-up bowl and starting on the breakfast dishes, 'Talking won't get the work done. You'll have to see what your Martin says tonight. Best to know what you're goin' to do with them before you break it to them about their Mam and Dad. At least if they're going to be able to live with you, that'll be some comfort to them, won't it, poor little dabs'.

Esther went slowly up the stairs leaving Johnny to play in the kitchen under Edie's eagle eye. Her first task was to make the beds, but she was moved to go into Gwennie and Teddy's room first. She sat on Gwennie's little single bed, ignoring the rumpled bedclothes and stared thoughtfully into space. She'd had the two little evacuees for well over two years now and had grown very fond of them. They were quiet children and she'd rarely had to scold them. After the initial bewilderment when they first came, they had settled very quickly and now rarely asked about their mother, and never mentioned their father. Her own children had accepted them, understanding that they had come here to escape the bombs. Gwennie accepted Mary's slight bossiness and they had become great friends, whilst Alun had taken Teddy under his wing, stuck up for him at school and generally enjoyed his role as 'big brother'. As for Johnny, they were welcome to his world, he was such a placid child.

All this passed through Esther's mind as she stared across at the other rumpled little bed. It all made sense, she told herself. She'd always wanted a big family, so what did another two matter? She'd enough love for all of them. It would make it easier to tell them about their parents and their home if she could offer them a home at Bay House. She felt that they were really happy here and there was plenty of room for them and a good big garden for them to play in and plenty of outbuildings for wet days.

All that remained was to persuade Martin. Surely he wouldn't insist that they go? Not her lovely, kind Martin. No, she was sure he would let her keep them. Especially as the alternative was Dr Barnado's or somewhere like it. Good places, no doubt, but not a real home. She'd talk to Martin tonight. Show him how easily she could manage. Hadn't she had them for all this time and managed perfectly well. He'd say yes, she felt sure.

Her spirits raised she set about making all the beds, going from room to room, exulting in the blessing of all these children round her, and giving thanks for her beloved Martin who made it possible, bringing her to her beloved Bay House, which always seemed to open its arms to all who needed its shelter. Martin would surely let her gather these two poor children in, to give them a home and plenty of love. She began to sing softly to herself and Edie, listening downstairs as she took the Ewbank cleaner across the carpet in the dining room, grinned and knew that the seed that she had planted had borne fruit.

When all the children had been put to bed that evening and Esther and Martin were settled in front of the fire, Martin still catching up with the news in the Daily Express, Esther fidgeted and mentally reviewed the best way of broaching her plan. Martin hid a smile behind his newspaper as he guessed what was coming. He knew his Esther and it had come to him during the day that it looked as though they were going to increase their family by two, permanently. He couldn't see Esther turning the two poor little orphans out, to go into a home. So he waited, pretending to be absorbed in his newspaper and at last Esther took a deep breath and, all diplomacy fled, burst out, 'Can we keep Gwennie and Teddy, Martin? Please say yes! I'm quite willing to take them on. We can't just send them off to a home. I feel as thought they're mine, anyway. I've had them so long. And they're company for our children and they all get on well together. And we could adopt them properly. I'm sure those people in London wouldn't object. We've got plenty of room and we can afford two extra. What do you think, Martin?'

'Martin, are you listening to me? I said, what do you think?'

Martin laid his paper down on his knee and stared into the fire, appearing to think hard. Then he raised his head and looked at her solemnly. 'Do you know what I think? I think we should keep those two kids and adopt them. That's what I think.' He picked up his paper again and pretended to read it.

Esther stared at him for a moment then she flew across to him and hugged him tightly round the neck. 'Oh, thank you Martin, love! I knew you'd see it my way!'

'Esther!' he croaked. 'Don't strangle me, or I'll not be able to go to work to earn enough for all these children you're saddling me with! And anyway, I'm not just seeing it your way. I knew straight off that this would be what you'd want to do and I've come to terms with it during the day. That is, if you're sure you'll be able to cope with five kids?' The paper abandoned, he pulled her down onto his lap and kissed her. When she emerged breathless she cupped his face with her hands and gazed into his eyes. 'You are the best husband in the world,' she whispered. 'I love you.' 'I know,' he said, smiling, and kissed her again.

When the next evening they called the two little evacuees in from play and shut out their own children, they broke the news as gently and tactfully as they could, Martin hugging Teddy, who was seated on his knees and Esther cuddling Gwennie. Both children were quiet. They eventually asked where they were to go if they had no home, but asked no questions about their parents. 'Where would you like to go?' asked Martin, gently. Gwennie hung her head and whispered, 'Can't we stay here with you? Can't this be our home and you be our Mam and Dad?' Little Teddy looked up hopefully at Martin, tears gathering in the corners of his eyes.

'Would you like that?' Esther queried, softly. Would you like to be our little boy and girl?'

Gwennie peered up from under a curtain of hair. "For ever?' she asked, her voice trembling. 'For ever and ever?' Esther nodded. 'For ever. Yes'

'For ever and ever, amen!' Teddy echoed, knuckling the tears from his eyes. 'You'll really be my Daddy then, won't you?' and he wound his thin arms round Martin's neck.

'Steady on!' said Martin, grinning. 'Why is everybody trying to strangle me today?'

'And you'll be my Mam, won't you,' Gwennie said, gazing in wonder at Esther. 'My real Mam. You wouldn't ever send me away, would you, not like our other Mam. She sent us away.'

Esther hugged her tightly and kissed her cheek. 'No, I'll never send you away, my love. Never.'

Meanwhile, on the last Sunday in May, Nell and Elwyn set off in Elwyn's car to go to Manafon. Nell wanted to see Meg and as it was a lovely May day she announced at breakfast that they should make the trip today. Rhiannon didn't want to go, she was bent on writing a long letter to Sean, who was still stationed in the South of England. The trees and hedges were dressed in their new and tender green foliage and the summer flowers appeared in the hedgerows. The bright purple of the foxgloves contrasted with the fresh white cloud of the lady's lace and here and there a few bluebells still nodded in the soft breeze. The blossoms from the fruit trees were lying in pools round their bases and the dog roses had unfurled in the hedges, together with the pink and cream honeysuckle. Nell felt that maybe May was the loveliest month of the year, still spring, but with the promise of the lushness of summer. She crooned to herself the words of the song 'One morning in May' and Elwyn glanced affectionately at her and smiled. 'You sound happy enough, love,' he murmured and Nell stopped singing to consider her words.

'I don't know,' she said slowly. 'I can never be really happy until I know that Gareth is safely home with us. That's always in my mind. But on a day like this I can believe that it will happen. I don't know how to say it, I'm not much with words, but today seems like a promise that it will be all right some day. Do you see what I mean?'

'Yes, I see what you mean, love. And I think you've got a very good way with words!'

'Oh, not really,' Nell's tone was rueful. 'You know me, I'm a blunt old thing.'

'You used to be when I first knew you,' conceded Elwyn. 'But you've mellowed over the years, don't you think? You're getting to be a real old softy!'

Nell smiled to herself and said nothing for the moment. Then she reached out and touched his hand on the steering wheel briefly. 'I'm still soft about you, anyway,' she murmured, then put her hand back on her lap.

Elwyn grinned. 'Likewise,' he said as they turned into the village of Manafon, sleepy in its Sabbath calm. The little car chugged up the steep lane until eventually the welcoming sight of the Walkmill came into view at the top.

One of Henry's sheepdogs rushed out of the gate barking madly, which was a signal for the front door to open and Meg to appear, beaming a welcome. They climbed out, the dog backing away as Meg scolded him, and they were drawn into the cool old passage and down into the farmhouse kitchen, which looked the same as it always had, except for the quiet figure of a girl sitting at the table with her chin in her hands. 'This is Olwen, Henry's young lady,' Meg told them, her eyes warm with affection as they rested on the girl. Nell took in a round face with russet cheeks, large brown eyes and a cap of soft dark hair, caught back with a large tortoise shell slide, as the girl rose and with a shy smile advanced to shake hands. Nell noticed that she had a trim figure and was of medium height and took a liking to her straight away. They exchanged greetings and Olwen offered to make a cup of tea for them to have in their hand and trotted off into the kitchen. When she was gone Meg whispered, 'She's staying with us just now. I'll tell you about it later. Poor girl. But Henry and me will look after her.'

Nell raised her eyebrows but no more was said, as Olwen came back into the room bearing a tray with an old brown teapot and the glass cream-jug and sugar basin which was so familiar to visitors to the Walkmill. Olwen seemed at ease there and fetched cups and saucers and spoons and poured out tea for them. A plateful of chocolate digestive biscuits was brought to the table and they all settled down with their refreshments.

Olwen listened quietly while Meg plied Nell and Elwyn with questions regarding Gareth and the other boys who were away at the war.

'It must be awful for you wondering about Gareth and worrying all the time. I miss Reini, but at least I know he's safe in Cheshire. And of course I'm lucky to have Henry here with me. He's a good boy and he runs the farm well. I help him all I can, but now that the other farmers are willing to come and help at busy times like dipping and shearing, we're managing pretty well. And Olwen does a lot outside, as well as helping me in the house, don't you, love?' Meg smiled at Olwen and the smile was returned with a shy nod of the head. Nell was dying to ask how long the girl was going to be there and what the story was, but she contained her curiosity until she could have the chance of talking to her sister alone.

On that Henry came in, walking in his stocking feet, having taken his dirty boots off in the back kitchen. He grinned all round and greeted Nell and Elwyn. 'I heard old Fly bark, so I guessed you'd arrived,' he said, but his eyes soon slid round to Olwen and they exchanged loving looks and smiles. She poured him a cup of tea which he drank thirstily and afterwards also asked for news of the other boys in the family. They sat talking for a while and then Henry asked them would they like to come and have a look at a couple of Hereford cows which he had bought recently, and Elwyn rose to follow him. Nell said she'd stay and have a chat with Meg and come out later, but Olwen rose and left with Henry and Elwyn.

'Now then,' Nell leaned forward eagerly, as Meg poured them another cup of tea each. 'Tell me what's going on. That Olwen seems a nice girl, but how come she's living here?'

'Well,' said Meg. 'Its like this. Henry and Olwen were courting in the woods between our place and the Francis's. And of course didn't old Francis come along and catch them. Well, he dragged Olwen off home by the scruff of the neck and Henry couldn't do anything to stop him or he would have made things worse. As soon as he got her home seemingly he really lost his wool and gave her a terrible hiding. That night she ran away when it was dark and came to us, crying to be taken in. I didn't know what to do for the best, but she was in such a state, with bruises on her arm and marks of the stick on her back and Henry was firm that she was to stay. Next day when the family found she was missing they came straight here, at least old man Francis did. Well, he shouted and stamped and carried on and I tried to calm him down. When he got a bit quieter he asked Olwen was she coming home with him. She looked across at Henry and he shook his head. 'I'm not willing for Olwen to go back with you and got knocked about again,' says he. 'We love each other and we're going to get married. We're both of age and there's nothing to stop us.' Well, the old chap went a funny colour and I thought he'd have a stroke, but he just gave Olwen a nasty look and said she needn't think she was coming home if she changed her mind. He marched off then and although Olwen was a bit quiet for a while after that, she's settled down now and the upshot is that they're going to be married. The banns are being read on Sunday week and they'll be married the first Saturday in July. I'm right pleased for Henry. He didn't like sneaking around to meet her. Henry's always liked everything up front. She'll be a big help to me too. Being a farmer's daughter she knows all about churning and seeing to the butter and she's a right good little cook and not afraid to have a go at the outside jobs. I think she'll make a good wife to Henry, and they think the world of each other.'

'Do you think you'll have any more trouble with old Francis himself?' Nell asked.

'I don't think so,' Meg said, finishing the last dregs of tea in her cup. 'I think part of the trouble was that she was the only woman in the house. Did I tell you her mother died? So either one or both of the sons will have to get themselves a wife each, or they'll have to hire a housekeeper. They've got plenty of money, it's a very good farm, so they can afford to get a woman. We've had no more trouble with the two sons since the police warned them off and now that the other neighbours have come round and are friendly with us again, the Francis's are on their own and I think they're afraid to start anything.'

'I hope so,' said Nell. 'Anyway, shall we go out and have a look round I hear Henry is making a very good job of the farm. He's a good boy.'

'Yes he is. I'm very lucky, really. But I do miss Reini very much. He's a good man and when I think of how it all worked out, with Mama giving us the farm so we could get married, I thank God for all my blessings. I just pray that Reini will be alright and back home with me soon. He writes me such loving letters,' she added, fondly. 'He doesn't seem to care about the censor. Well, why should he? We're married, aren't we? Sometimes, being German, he says things in a funny way. I think that's what happens when I see words crossed out. I wish this old war would end,' she sighed and rose from her chair. 'Come on, before I get maudling. We'll find the others and have a look round before I get the tea. Its lovely to see you, Nell love!' She hugged Nell's arm for a moment and Nell patted her hand and drew her out through the door.

They found Olwen and the two men leaning over the half-door of one of the barns, inspecting a cow and her new brown and white calf. The cow watched them suspiciously and nudged her calf, which then began to suckle eagerly. 'A heifer?' asked Elwyn and Henry nodded. 'Nice looking little article,' Elwyn said, approvingly and Henry smiled and put his arm round Olwen's waist, while she lifted her face with an answering smile.

'Well,' said Nell, when she and Meg joined them. 'Congratulations! I hear you're getting married, you two. I hope we'll be invited to the wedding!'

'Of course, Auntie Nell!' Henry laughed. 'All the Rees's will be invited and I hope they'll all come.'

'What about the Jones's?' teased Elwyn. 'Don't forget that I belong to the big tribe of Jones's and so does your Auntie Nell now.

'Well, of course. You know what I mean,' answered Henry with a grin. 'All part of the family. The banns are being called in Manafon Church next Sunday week and for the two Sundays after and then we'll be married on the first Saturday in July. The sooner the better, isn't it, love?' he added, looking down into Olwen's upturned face. She nodded and Henry went on, 'Then she'll belong to me and there'll be no more old nonsense from her family. I just wish Dad could have been here to be with us that day, but we've written to tell him all about it and anyway he knows Olwen and always said he liked her. It'll be great when he does come home. It must be awful to be locked up when you've done nothing to deserve it!' Henry's tone was indignant but then he glanced at his mother's face and he went on, more briskly,' Come on, let's see the rest of this great estate of ours! I'm beginning to feel hungry and it'll soon be time for tea, eh Mam?'

They completed the tour of the animals and Henry pointed out various innovations he'd made, then they repaired to the house, where Meg set about making the tea, Olwen bustling about helping her. Nell could see that the girl was going to fit in very nicely and she was glad for Meg's sake. It would give her a bit of company while Henry was about the farm all day, she mused. And certainly the two young people seemed to be very much in love.

Soon there was a substantial meal of home grown produce: cured ham, thinly sliced with parsley sauce, cheese from the dairy, new potatoes with chopped spring onions and melted farm butter, and an egg, radish and lettuce salad, on the table and they all sat down and enjoyed it, forgetting for once the privations of rationing, and washing it down with many cups of tea. Meg asked after Rhiannon and Sean, and Nell was able to tell her that Rhiannon really seemed to have settled down to wait for Sean and that they would be going to live in Ireland when the war was over. 'Won't you miss her?' asked Meg, to whom the thought of parting with a child made her shiver. 'Well, it's like this. I think this Sean is good for Rhiannon. She's never been an easy girl to deal with, has she?' she appealed to Elwyn, who shook his head. 'It's good to know there's someone who'll stand no nonsense from her and will look after her.'

They went on to discuss the news of Esther and the new additions to her family. As Meg remarked, Esther would manage if it was anything to do with children.

Soon it was time for Nell and Elwyn to leave and as they set off down the lane, they looked back to see the reassuring sight of Henry standing there with an arm round each of his women, and somehow that, coupled with the sense of the constancy, give or take the the odd natural rebellion, of the land that had given them such a simple but fine, fresh meal in such hard times, planted in them the seeds of an optimism that after this horrible old war came to its conclusion, and gains and losses were calculated and borne, life would go on, even though it would never again be quite as before.

4

More Telelgrams and Secrets

Nineteen-forty-four saw the final turning point in the war. Britain became an armed camp as troops were gradually gathered in the South in preparation for the invasion. Nan and Davy lay in bed at night and heard the convoys of trucks roll down Kerry Road in the darkness. Minor roads were used to move these convoys at night, all to prevent the Germans from finding out what was going on. Troops were being moved from garrisons all over the UK and all leave was cancelled during May as the preparations built up for the great day. Letters from Sean Kerrigan already in the South of England gave no hint of what was going on, but most of the troops gathering along the coast were no doubt aware of what was coming, but not when.

Before this, however, the Rees family suffered another blow. Mattie and Llew received a telegram to say that Jim had been posted missing. No further information was given and the family were stricken. Llew tried to keep Mattie's hopes up: 'It doesn't say he was killed,' he argued, holding her close and stroking her hair, but she clung to him, totally devastated. 'It doesn't even say 'Missing presumed killed!' he went on. 'Mattie, love, maybe he's been taken prisoner.' She looked up at him for a moment with a wild hope in her eyes. 'Do you really think he could be alive, then, Llew?'

Llew was torn between raising her hopes, perhaps falsely, and giving her comfort at the moment. She saw the conflict in his face and she drooped in his arms. Jim, or 'Little Jim' as he had been known in the family until he grew to five foot nine, was the only child by her first husband, who had been Llew's friend and whom he had seen drowned in an icy river, whilst fleeing from the Germans in the First World War.

His body was never recovered and Mattie was left a widow with a small boy until Llew asked her to marry him. They suited well. She supported him loyally in everything, even his politics, which she did not entirely understand. But if Llew believed in a newly emergent socialism, then that was all right by Mattie. In return Llew was devoted to her and adopted Jim as his son. Although Llew had the two children, Owen and Esther, by his first wife, he made no difference between them and Jim, which was made easier, anyway, by the fact that Mama had insisted that the two children she had taken in and brought up after their mother died, Esther as a new-born baby, should remain at 46 Pool Road, and Llew hadn't the heart to take them off her.

And so this news felt to Llew like the loss of his own child and he devoted the days that followed to comforting Mattie and trying to bolster her courage. The rest of the Rees family rallied round and Mattie was rarely left alone to brood. Nan was particularly sympathetic because of her own loss and sometimes their tears mingled as they held each other and gave way to their grief.

On the sixth of June came the news of the invasion. Rhiannon was certain that Sean was among those who went over that morning and landed on the beaches of France. She had no thoughts for anyone but Sean and hung over the old wireless at No.46, eagerly awaiting whatever news came through. Then, during the battle for Cambes Wood, Sean stopped a sniper's bullet in his arm and was brought back to Britain to be hospitalised. He landed up in a hospital in Scotland, and although it was good to know he was in this country and that his wound was not too serious, it was too far for Rhiannon to travel to see him. However, his letters were frequent and he assured her that he would get leave before he had to go back out again.

'It's just not fair,' she cried, indignantly. 'He shouldn't have to go back out there again after being wounded. I can't believe they are going to send him back to the front again!'

'You'd better believe it,' her father told her, shaking his head. 'It's probably the last push of the war and they need every body they can get. People with worse wounds than Sean will have to go back, I daresay.'

Rhiannon had to content herself with writing long letters to Sean, while her parents marvelled at the change in her which the young man had wrought. 'She doesn't seem like the same girl, does she?' Nell said, wonderingly. 'She used to seem so spoilt and selfish. And look what she did to poor Edward!'

Elwyn shrugged. ' Maybe she did Edward a good turn after all. If Ruth could forget about him this quickly, she couldn't have thought much of him.'

'Yes, but perhaps Edward still loves her, Elwyn. We don't know, do we?'

'Still carrying a torch, as they say in the movies?' Elwyn shook his head. 'Edward was always a bit stiff-necked and proud. He'll have got over it by now, I bet you.'

'I hope so,' said Nell, thoughtfully.

The only thing that had lightened the run-up to the invasion had been the wedding of Henry and Olwen. All the Rees family had gone down to Manafon for this and the ceremony had been held in the charming old church in the centre of the village. The couple made their vows, Henry in his best suit and Olwen in a cream dress which Mattie had made for her and a little pink hat which sat on the side of her thick dark hair. She was not beautiful like Rhiannon, but looked sweet, rosy and wholesome, and as they gazed lovingly at each other, the hearts of the onlookers were touched. There were many who turned out from the village, partly in curiosity as to whether the Francis family would come to make trouble, but there was no sign of them at the church, although the rumour went round that old Francis had disowned her.

Such a rumour had reached Olwen and was a cloud hovering over her joy. He was her father, after all. On Meg's advice she had sent an invitation to her father and her two brothers, but there had been no reply and although Olwen shrugged it off, Meg knew that she was hurt and wished she could comfort her.

After the marriage ceremony was completed and the register signed, the family all packed into the cars available and made their way to the Walkmill. One or two neighbouring families, who had helped Meg and Henry whilst Reini was away, had been invited and these were waiting in the house, some of the women bustling around, laying out the wedding breakfast until the table groaned with good things. As the family came in there was a silence at first, and every eye turned, not to the wedding party, but to three chairs in isolation in the corner of the kitchen. Meg's eyes followed that direction and her face flushed and a smile broke over it. She turned to Olwen and putting her arms round the girl's waist, drew her gently over to the occupants of those chairs.

Olwen stopped in front of the three men sitting sheepishly in the corner, stiff in their best clothes, the colour high in their cheeks. 'Dad?' she whispered, uncertainly. His voice was gruff as he looked under his eyebrows at her and said. 'Olwen.' then glanced at Meg.

'You're welcome, Mr Francis,' Meg said quietly and turned to the two younger men. 'You too. You're welcome to your sister's wedding.'

They nodded, embarrassed, and muttered their thanks in gruff voices. A concerted sigh of relief went through the room as Henry came forward to shake hands with his new brothers-in-law and his father-in-law. Then he put his arm round Olwen's waist and looked down to see the complete happiness in her eyes and was glad.

Meg was kept busy attending to the wants of her guests. The food was plentiful, considering it was wartime, but Meg was a good cook and had been saving various rations for this day. Nell had made the wedding cake, complete with her imitation marzipan, which everyone said they couldn't tell from the real thing! Owen stood as best man, in the absence of any of the younger men of the family and made a speech, warmly welcoming Olwen to the family. When he had finished he looked round for Mr Francis and nodded to him. 'Would the father of the bride like to say a few words?'

Olwen's father hesitated, looking across at his sons as they stood stuffing themselves with cake. The young men stood still, frozen, their cheeks bulging, as they stared back at their father. Then Mr Francis coughed. 'Aye,' he said, his voice rough. 'I reckon it's time to say sorry to Meg Bauer for a start and I hope as how she'll accept it. And I say sorry on behalf of my sons, the daft oolerts, for the bother they caused her. I say to my daughter, Olwen, shall us let bygones be bygones, my girl? And lastly, I hope as Henry here will let bygones be bygones as well. I think as he is a tidy boy whatever his origins, and he is welcome to my girl. There!'

He blew a relieved breath and sat down. Everyone clapped and

Henry went over and once again shook hands with Francis and his two sons, old Francis by now, grinning from ear to ear.

Although Olwen had winced at the mention of Henry's 'origins' she had no desire to make an issue of it. She knew how much it had cost her father to make that speech and she guessed that Henry knew too. She was happy now with a husband she loved very much and her father's approval at last.

Meanwhile the British and American invasion army made progress in France and during July they drove the Germans from Normandy. However the people of London were suffering the daily terror of 'buzz bombs' and many children who had gone back to their homes in the south of England had now to be evacuated over again. Esther was glad that Gwennie and Teddy were settling well and tried to give them extra love and care to help them get over the first trauma of losing their home and their parents. She had to be careful, in case her own children became jealous, but her three were safe in their parents' love and showed no sign of this happening. At this time she also found that she was again pregnant, which would make six children, but far from being dismayed by this, she rejoiced in her large and expanding family. Martin would have been a little anxious, but he knew full well that this had always been Esther's ambition and as his practice was doing well he could afford to feed the extra mouths and as long as Esther was happy, Martin was happy.

It was a sunny August morning and Mary was sitting on the steps of Bay House. She was looking forward to her eleventh birthday and to sitting the scholarship to go to the County School. She was bright and hoped next year to pass the exam. She would have liked to have gone this coming September, but because her birthday fell at the end of August she had not been able to sit the scholarship last May. It was early and a heat haze hung over the tops of the hills, promising a hot day to come. Mary's blonde hair hung to her shoulders, a shining corn-colour like her mother's and her brilliant blue eyes scanned the street, quiet with a summer sleepiness. She watched Harry Bennett leave his house opposite, carrying a flask of tea, on his way to open his corner shop at nine o'clock. The shop stood between Bryn Street and the side street known as Union Street, because it connected Bryn Street and Crescent Street. It was a small, old-fashioned shop but it did a good trade and was a centre for gossip and news-gathering. Mary felt in the pocket of her cotton dress and found a penny nestling in the corner. It was, as she knew full well, much too early to start eating sweets, but she thought she could get an apple for a penny, so she tightened the straps on her strong brown sandals and trotted up the street to Harry Bennett's shop.

'Hello, Mr Bennett,' she said brightly, tapping her penny on the counter.

Harry looked at her benevolently over the top of his steel-rimmed glasses. 'Hello Mary. What can I do for you today?'

'I've got a penny,' explained Mary. 'Is it enough to buy an apple?'

Harry drew in his breath judiciously and regarded her with his head on one side. 'Ooh, I should think so, miss. Being as it's you. Have a look at them apples over there and see which one you like the best. Good apples, them. Worcesters.'

Mary trotted over and picked out the largest and rosiest she could find, then went back and gave Harry Bennett the penny. He thanked her solemnly and put the coin in the till. She polished the apple against her stomach, then took a large crisp bite out of it. She chewed meditatively for a moment, searching for a topic of grown-up conversation. She swallowed and leaned against the counter with a negligent air. 'How do you think the war is going, Mr Bennett?' she asked.

Harry began to tidy a shelf behind the counter: 'Well, now. I think as we're winning at last, Mary. This invasion seems to be doing the trick. We shall win, right enough, and the sooner the better, I say.'

Mary nodded and took another bite of her apple. ' Our evacuees are going to live with us for ever, Mr Bennett,' she offered, when she'd chewed and swallowed the apple in her mouth. 'Their Mam and Dad have been killed by a bomb and their house is all gone, as well. So Mam is keeping them and they're going to be my sister and brother now.'

Harry Bennett nodded. 'So I hear. Very good of your Mam to keep them. Well, they'll have a good home with you. Now there'll be five of you, won't there?'

'Six,' Mary said.

'No no. Five, isn't it. You three and the two little Londoners.'

Mary chuckled. 'You don't know the secret yet, do you, Mr Bennett. You see, Mam's ordered another baby for us. She'll have it sometime in the New Year. I heard her tell my Dad.'

Harry Bennett, an old bachelor, looked round swiftly, then shook his head at Mary. 'I don't think you ought to be talking about this to people yet, my girl.' Then, curiosity overcame him and he leaned a little nearer. 'And what did your Dad say?' he asked.

'I didn't hear him say anything for a long time,' Mary mused. 'Then he sort of choked and said 'Six!' in a loud voice and my Mam shushed him. I didn't hear any more.' Of course the news wasn't long spreading out from the little shop but Esther was bewildered to know how people had come by it so soon.

It was on September the third, the fifth anniversary of the start of the war, that Mattie and Llew had the news that Jim was a prisoner of war and a day or two afterwards they had a letter from him, with much crossing out by the censor, but telling them that he was all right and giving them an address through the Red Cross where they could write to him. There were tears from Mattie, but this time tears of joy. Jim was alive! A prisoner, but alive. They could send him parcels from time to time, they were told, so they bought him cigarettes, warm gloves and socks and a bag of treacle dabs, which he was fond of. These were quickly packed up and sent to the address they were given, and there was much rejoicing in the Rees family. It transpired that he had been taken prisoner at Tobruk, but communications at that time were so confused that it was some time before the Red Cross traced him.

That week Llew went to Home Guard with a lighter heart and Owen slapped him on the back when they met. 'Great news!' he said. 'At least old Jim's alive and out of the war. We can write to him now, can't we?'

Llew grinned and nodded. 'Yes we can write to him and send him parcels through the Red Cross, it seems. It's good news, right enough. I hope he'll be all right,' he said, sobering. 'Actually, I don't know how the Jerries treat their prisoners. I don't say anything to Mattie. She's so relieved, I'm not going to worry her. Oh, I daresay he'll be fine. The Red Cross are supposed to keep an eye on things. The Geneva Agreement and all that.'

Before Owen could reply they were hailed by Gwilym the Sticks and Owen Neaudd who caught them up in Severn Place. 'Thee't lookin' right pleased with thyself,' said Gwilym, eyeing Llew, who then told him his good news. 'Well, surry, that is good news,' said Owen Neuadd. 'Right you, come on. Lets go an' practice killin' Germans in case we're needed. We anna seen much action up till now, 'ave we?'

'Oh, I dunno,' put in Gwilym. 'We know 'ow to capture a Jerry parachutist, dunna we? We'm ready if another one comes floatin' down on the Rackfield!'

His companions made as if to set on him, but he ducked inside the Drill Hall, laughing and there they were all called to order by Eddie Probert.

After the session was over they made their way over to the Black Boy. The nights were already beginning to draw in a little and the town was blacking out. 'Be right nice when the lights go up again,' Llew said, as they walked across Broad Street in the dark.

Owen Neuadd shook his head. 'I dunno about that. This black-out covers a multitude of sins.'

Gwilym stopped and peered at him through the darkness. 'What sins hast thee got, Neuadd?' he asked, his voice rising. 'Come on, let us know!'

'No fear,' chuckled Neuadd. 'Me sins are me own. Tell 'em to you? I should cocoa!'

'Come on, mun. Gis' a laugh,' Gwilym urged. 'I could do with a few sins meself. Fat chance. My old ooman is gettin' worse. To 'ear 'er you'd think the way I go on was the cause of the war! Sins! She's never done tellin' me about mine. Well, I tell 'er, what 'opes 'ave I got of a few sins?' He gave a deep sigh and Llew clapped him on the shoulder. 'Cheer up, Gwilym. You're about to commit one now. I'm going to buy you a pint and you're going to drink it. Your missus'd say we were both sinners. Dyed in the wool, mun.' 'Ah,' answered Gwilym, cheering up, 'And damn thirsty sinners, too.'

They carried their pints over to their favourite corner and settled down. After taking a long pull at his ale, Gwilym wiped his mouth with the back of his hand and said, 'I see they've liberated Paris. What does that mean, Llew?'

' Well, Jerry took Paris early on in the war. Now the Allies, that's the British and the Yanks have driven them out. Old General De Gaulle was one of the first in. Well, that was fitting, I suppose,' added Llew.

'Is he the bloke with the big nose?' asked Gwilym.

'Aye, that's him.'

'D'you know, I've always thought I'd like to go to Paris.' Gwilym mused, wistfully.

His friends turned and regarded him with surprise. 'Oy, oy!' Llew said, with raised eyebrows. 'What you fancy about Paris, then, Gwilym boy?

'I dunno, really. I think its them French gels going Ooh la la. I dunno what it means but it sounds hellish good, mun. I canna see my old 'ooman saying Ooh la la. Not even when we was first courtin'. Not that we did much courtin', really. Seems like 'er 'ad me picked out an' I never 'ad a chance.' Gwilym shook his head sadly. 'That's somethin' I never did understand, you know. If 'er wanted me an' went all out to 'ave me, why did 'er go off me from the day we were married? I never done nothin' to 'er! But 'er seemed bent on making me life a misery!'

However, the other three had heard it all before, so Owen changed the subject. 'I wonder how much longer they'll keep the Home Guard going? I mean there's not much chance of Jerry coming over here now, is there? It looks like they're on the run, surrendering all over the place. Its mostly the buzz bombs that are the danger now, and that's only in the South of England. Nasty things, right enough. Killed a lot of people.'

'Is it right they dunna need aeroplanes to drop 'em from?' asked Owen Neuadd.

'That's right,' said Owen. 'They target the things on London and when you hear the engine in them cut out, then look out, the bombs drop straight down.'

Neuadd shuddered. 'They wunna target 'em on Newtown, sure not?'

'No, no,' Owen reassured him. 'I don't think the things would travel that far, but in any case,' he grinned, 'They wouldn't waste them on Newtown. Its not important enough.'

'Well, it's important to me!' said Neuadd, indignantly. 'An' London inna. I've never bin there an' I dunna want to go. D'you know,' he added, shaking his head in disgust, 'Them Londoners walk around in suits all covered with pearl buttons! D'you ever hear the like? Pearl buttons sewed all over their clothes. How d'you like to go to work covered in pearl buttons?' He gave a loud guffaw at the thought.

Llew grinned. 'I think they only put them on on special occasions. They dress up as Pearly Kings and Pearly Queens. But they don't wear those things all the time.'

Neuadd grunted. 'Sounds daft to me, anyway. No I dunna fancy London. I'd as lief go to Aber, any day. I do love oul' Aber. You get the best fish an' chips there I've ever tasted. They used to do nice trips up to Aber on a Sunday night before the war. You could go up on the train about four o'clock an' stroll along the prom all evening. There'd be fairy lights along the front and a band playing hymns in the bandstand. It was lovely, mun. Bit of community singing as well. All for one an' ninepence, if I remember right. Oul' war put an end to all that.'

'Never mind, Neuadd,' Llew said. 'It'll soon be all over and Aber'll still be there, and your band and your hymns and your fish and chips. And the castle'll still be there, even though Oliver Cromwell knocked it about a bit.'

'Was that Oliver Cromwell?' asked Neuadd, indignantly. 'Lord, that fellow got about, didn't 'e! Did more 'arm than our council!'

Llew laughed. 'I don't know was it Oliver Cromwell or some English King, but they made a good job of it anyway. But I agree, it was nice sitting up there on a Sunday evening, listening to the sound of the waves and smelling the sea air. Our Davy's lad, Edward, was at Aber Coll, and we used to go up to see him in the summer. A lovely old college that. Was meant to be a posh hotel, but the owner run out of money. Then the miners of South Wales bought it with their pennies, so the story goes, so that their bright boys needn't go down the mines. Well, whatever the truth of the matter, it's turned out some good scholars. The Welsh were always a brainy lot. Poets and politicians.'

'Aye, well,' Gwilym said, with a sigh. 'We'd better be gettin' home or we shall be dead poets and politicians.'

They drained their pint pots and shuffled out into the gathering dark.

Gwilym looked up at the dark shape of the hills that loomed protectively over the little town. 'Damn me, but I dunna think I'd change this for Paris, even if the gels dunna say Ooh la la.'

At the end of September, Sean came on leave, his wound almost healed. He was thinner, but his blue eyes were as bright as ever and his lips as ready to break into his heart-wrenching smile. He arrived on a Saturday afternoon and Nell laid on a good tea for him, with ham and eggs courtesy of the Walkmill, followed by a sponge as light as air, thanks to the eggs from the same source. There would be no more fruit cakes until Christmas, for Nell had started saving the fruit for the Christmas cake.

It was a long journey down from Scotland and Sean dozed on the old horsehair sofa after eating enough for two. Rhiannon sat on the chair opposite and gazed at him as he slept. She almost grudged him this time out from what was to be a long weekend leave, and yet it was good to see him there, his face open like a boy's while he slept, a black curl falling over his forehead and a hand under his cheek. She wondered if he would wake if she stole a kiss, but decided it would be a shame to rouse him, he had obviously been tired. Besides, she was hoping to drag him off to the dance in the Church House, to show him off, and above all to feel his arms round her as they danced. She was amazed herself at how deeply she had fallen for this man. The thought of Edward meant nothing to her now, and yet there had been a time when she would have done anything to make Edward love her. She felt no real guilt about having caused the break between Edward and Ruth, especially as Ruth found someone else very quickly. As for Edward, surely he had forgotten and forgiven by now? Well, maybe by the time Edward got back from the war, she and Sean would have left for their life in Ireland, and she strained to that day, to a life with Sean always at her side. She continued to gaze at him and he stirred in his sleep, as though he felt her thoughts concentrated on him. However, he didn't wake, and she sighed and she settled down to wait, as her mother came in from the back-kitchen, where she had been washing up the tea dishes.

'Now you let that poor boy sleep,' Nell ordered. 'He must be fair worn out, coming all the way down from Scotland.' She kept her voice low as she added, 'Its a long old journey and him with a wounded arm.'

'I know, Mam,' whispered Rhiannon. 'I'm just glad he's here. But he'll have to go back out to France or wherever they've reached by then. It doesn't seem fair. Oh, if only this war would end quickly. I can't wait to get settled in Ireland!'

Nell pulled a face. 'Can't wait to leave us, is it?'

'Oh no, you know its not like that,' Rhiannon protested. 'But you know I've never settled in Newtown. I was always going to leave sometime. And we'll be coming back and fore to see you from time to time.'

'I know, love,' Nell sighed. 'So long as you're happy, isn't it. That was a nice letter you had from Sean's mother last week. They sound very nice people and I like your Sean. I'm sure he'll look after you.' She smiled down on the sleeping man, seeing the lines of strong character in his face and knowing that just such a man was needed to curb her wayward daughter.

Elwyn came in from chopping sticks in the yard and Rhiannon put a finger to her lips and pointed to the sofa. Elwyn smiled and nodded, whispering, 'He could do with that, poor lad.' and took up the daily paper and sat quietly at the table. It was almost an hour later before Sean stirred and opened his eyes. He looked around him confused for a moment, then sat up and ran his fingers through his hair. 'Good Lord, how long have I been out for the count?' he asked, smiling at Rhiannon to pull on her heartstrings. 'I'm sorry. That was bad manners.' He blinked and swallowed a yawn. 'But gosh, I was pretty shattered. Och, but I'm ashamed of myself. I'd better get a wash, I think. See if that'll wake me up. Lead me to a cold tap, acushla, and I'll be a new man, you'll see.'

He did indeed look like a new man when he emerged from the back kitchen a quarter of an hour later, his curls still damp and his face flushed from the towelling. Rhiannon had been up to her room to change in the meantime and came down again looking quite beautiful in a white dress with a broad scarlet belt fastened round her neat waist. Her hair was a dark cloud of curls round her pale oval face and Sean caught his breath when he saw her. She had a white flower tucked into her hair and bright red sandals on her feet. When she saw the expression on his face she blushed with pleasure.

Sean whistled his appreciation. 'Whew! You're a wee smasher!' he said, grinning. 'And where are we bound for tonight, wee girl? Are we going to dance the night away?'

She laughed. 'Well, until eleven o'clock, anyway. Richie Richards only plays till eleven o'clock.'

'Right, then,' Sean said, briskly. 'It's now seven o'clock. We've got four hours. I think that'll probably be enough. I've got civvy shoes on and I haven't had a chance to break them in yet. My feet are killing me!'

'That's a good start!' Rhiannon said, indignantly.

'Whisht, now, Mrs Kerrigan, dear,' said Sean, in his best blarney. 'Whenever I get you in my arms, sure I'll be dancing on air, anyway. Come, Cinderella, your coach awaits! Well, Shanks's pony, at least.'

They went out of the door, laughing, and Nell looked after them with a fond smile. She didn't think she would have to worry about Rhiannon in future, provided of course that Sean came safely back from the war. She said a little prayer and crossed her fingers for good measure.

Sean and Rhiannon climbed the steps to the Church House and could hear the band tuning up in the hall. They left their coats in the cloakroom and went in arm-in-arm. The hall seemed to be full of soldiers, with here and there a civilian man standing out in a suit or a sports coat and flannels. For the most part the girls tended to ignore the civilians, except where there was an understanding. The small figure of Richie could be seen in front of the band on the stage, but most of the newcomers had got used to the sight of the tiny conductor by now. He raised his baton and the band began to play a quickstep. Sean took Rhiannon into his arms and they moved expertly around the dance floor, many an envious eye of both sexes following them. This was followed by a waltz. 'Nice and smoochy!' whispered Sean as his arms tightened round her and they danced cheek to cheek to the languorous strains. She was careful not to press on his upper arm where the wound was healing, but apart from that she gave herself up to the closeness of his hard body against hers. Oh, how she loved him, and she knew that her love was returned. He lifted his head and looked down at her, his blue eyes filled with that love, unable to resist a swift kiss planted on the soft pink lips so tantalisingly close to his. Those same lips brushed his ear as she whispered: 'Behave yourself, Sean Kerrigan!'

'I'm impatient!' he whispered back, then laid his cheek against hers again. She closed her eyes and drifted with the music and his nearness, while Richie's soloist sang :

'He holds her in his arms, would you, would you?

'He tells her of her charms, would you, would you?'

'I would, would you?' sang Sean in his rich baritone, drawing smiles from the couples nearest them.

The mood changed as Richie announced the Lambeth Walk and they all marched around, punctuated by cries of 'Hoy!'. This was followed by the dreamy 'Mexicali Rose' and as they danced Sean sang:

'Kiss me once again, and hold me,

'Mexicali Rose, Good bye!'

Rhiannon felt her throat close for a moment as she thought of Sean saying goodbye on Tuesday, to go back to the war. She blinked back the tears and smiled up at him, but he had guessed what was going through her mind and his arm tightened around her. 'Hey!' he murmured. 'It won't be for long this time. It's nearly all over, and then I'll be marching back to claim you and take you across the sea to Ireland.'

'I can't wait!' she breathed and squeezed his hand.

The evening drifted on, waltzes and fox-trots interspersed with the 'Hokey-Cokey' and 'Underneath the Spreading Chestnut Tree,' with its accompanying actions. They quickstepped round the room to the jerky rhythm of 'Oh, Johnny, oh Johnny', followed by the measured and graceful steps of the 'St Bernard's Waltz'. At last the band was playing a dreamy 'Goodnight Sweetheart' and the evening was over.

Sean and Rhiannon collected their coats and made their way down the steps and out into a slightly frosty night. The sky was bright with stars and Sean pointed out a crescent moon shining with a cold, clear light. He hummed the last tune the band had played and with his arm round her waist, they walked along New Road. They passed the old Church School at the bottom of Kerry Road, its pale stone looming behind the big oak tree which stood in the playground. On the other side of Kerry Road, on the corner, the Queen's Head was closed and shuttered, although lights showed in the bar where the landlord cleared up after the Saturday night rush. Sean drew her across Pool Road to look over the Bridge Wall to the dark waters flowing beneath. He turned her towards him and his arms went round her urgently and his mouth came down on hers in a lingering kiss.

'I'm coming back, acushla,' he whispered. 'Don't forget that. I'm coming back. And that's a promise. I must come back. We've got a whole lifetime to share yet.'

5

More Reunions and Reminiscences

Nell was getting ready to go to work at the Accles and Pollock factory on the Pool Road. She had been there for almost a year now and although she didn't like it very much, the extra money was useful. Elwyn's wage from Pryce Jones's just about kept them but didn't allow for any extras. Rhiannon paid for her keep, of course, but running the car ate into their capital. She thought she would stay at home when the war ended and Gareth came back. She sighed for that day and longed to see her son again. She was tying a cloth turban-wise around her head to protect it from the oil in the section where she worked when Elwyn said; 'Oh, no! Dear God!' from the depths of his newspaper. 'Listen to this! The Russians have found Nazi death camps in Poland. They reckon one and a half million dead in one camp alone! They've found gas chambers where they killed the poor souls and a crematorium where they burned the thousands of corpses.' He lifted a shocked face and stared at Nell over the paper. 'What sort of human beings would be capable of that?'

Nell shuddered. 'I don't think they can be human beings. They must be monsters. Oh dear, I wish you hadn't told me about that. I shall be thinking of it all day.'

'Well,' Elwyn said, sternly. 'So we should be thinking of it. I hope the top brass are thinking of it, as well. To make sure it's never allowed to happen again.'

'The Germans must be a terrible bloodthirsty people!' said Nell, shaking her head. 'And yet they can't all be bad. Look at Reini. As nice and gentle a man as you could wish to meet.'

Elwyn nodded. 'Ah, no. They're not all bad, of course not. It's just the Nazis, those that followed Hitler. I daresay a lot of the German people had to do what they were told or be shot. Did the ordinary people not know what was going on in these camps, do you think? Seems funny to me. But then, if it was happening in Britain, maybe we wouldn't know about it. I daresay we don't know the half of what our lot get up to!' he added, darkly.

'Oh, be quiet, Elwyn,' Nell scolded. 'You're beginning to talk like our Llew! Anyway I must get to work. Where's that Rhiannon? Time you and her were out of this house as well.'

'Oh, she's had a letter from Sean this morning. I expect she's mooning over that. They weren't long in sending him back out, were they? Oh, well, I don't think it'll be long now till it's all over. They're talking about lifting the black-out for this coming winter.'

'Well, that'll be something,' said Nell, with a sigh. 'We've had enough of walking about like moles, some nights you can't see a hand in front of you. There's been more broken limbs and bumped heads. Yes, it'll be good to see street lights again. When are they going to do that then?'

'I don't know. This month, I think. The same time as the clocks go back.'

Rhiannon came down the stairs, her coat on, ready for work. She looked dreamy, clutching Sean's letter in her hand. To their enquiries as to how he was she replied, airily, that he sounded all right, then she smiled, kissed the letter and stuffed it in her pocket before waving goodbye as she went out of the door. Nell raised her eyebrows at Elwyn and shrugged, before following her out. Elwyn folded his paper, drank the last remnants of his tea and left for work himself. The house was now silent, except for the ghosts of Mama and Dada, and what would they make of an empty house? Mama must have shaken her head and wondered what the world was coming to!

An even more significant letter had arrived for Meg in Manafon. She was alone when she read it and she had to sink onto a chair by the table and read it over again, her hand clutched to her heart.

'My dear one,

I think that I will be home with you before long, now. It would seem that preparations are being made to release us. The news is that Germans are surrendering in Italy and other places and therefore I am no longer a threat.' The next phrase was violently blacked out, but Meg was used to this and read on as Reini told her how he was looking forward to seeing her and Henry again, that he was well and had great plans for the future. It was a brief letter, but Meg had read all she wanted to know, and hugged the letter to her with tears in her eyes. Those tears fell for all the long years apart, for the fact that Reini had missed his son's wedding and for the loneliness she had endured. She thought back to the early days when they had first met and how she had thought that he was staring at her scar when he didn't seem to be able to take his eyes off her. She shook her head and smiled ruefully to herself. Her Reini would never have been so cruel. She soon found out how gentle and caring he was, and yet so proud that it hurt that he did not provide the farm for them himself. However, that fence was mended when at last the money came through from Bavaria from the sale of the family farm when there was no-one else but him to inherit it, since his older brother had been killed in the first World War. That money had paid for more land and improvements to the house and farm, and at last Reini was happy that he was providing for his family himself.

She sat staring into space, tears still hovering on her eyelashes, until Olwen came into the room, carrying a can of milk and a bowl of big brown eggs. She put these down on the table, then looked more closely at her mother-in-law.

'What's wrong, Mam?' she asked, anxiously. 'Not bad news, is it?' nodding towards the letter in Meg's hand.

Meg shook her head and gave a soft laugh. 'No, no. Not at all. Good news, in fact. Reini says he should be back home soon. I suppose I'm crying for joy. Can you understand that? Daft aren't I?'

'Oh, that's wonderful!' cried Olwen. ' I must run and tell Henry! Oh, sorry, you probably want to tell him yourself.' She looked embarrassed.

Meg smiled at her. 'Not at all, love. You go and tell him. Maybe he can spare a few minutes to come in and have a cup of tea. To celebrate, isn't it!' She rose and went into the back kitchen to put the kettle on and make a fresh pot of tea. It wasn't many minutes before Henry came bursting in, followed by Olwen. 'Mam!' he cried excitedly, 'Is it right? Will Dad be home soon?'

'Read the letter, Henry, love. I think I've got it right.' Meg poured boiling water onto the tea and carried the pot into the kitchen, placing it on the old tea-pot stand painted with pansies, that had been Granny Evans's. Using her best china defiantly she poured out three cups and sat down, watching Henry's face, with a smug smile.

'Sounds right enough, Mam.' Henry perused the letter once again. 'Lord, I can hardly believe it, after all this time. Oh, it'll be good to see Dad again. I wonder will he think I've made a good job of the farm?' he added, anxiously.

Meg patted his hand. 'You've made a wonderful job of it, love,' she said. 'He couldn't have done better himself. I've been telling him so in all my letters. And I've told him all about you, dear,' she said, turning to Olwen. 'I've told him what a big help you are and how fond I am of you.'

Olwen blushed. 'D'you know, I can hardly remember what Henry's Dad looked like. I didn't see much of him before I started going out with Henry. I just remember he was tall and had a kind face.'

Henry laughed. 'He's no oil painting, but just the same he's pretty special. And yes, he's kind. The kindest man I know,' he added, proudly.

Meg's eyes had misted over again and she took a handkerchief out of her apron pocket and blew her nose. 'Oh, yes,' she murmured. 'He is very kind. We used to laugh together when we were first married, trying to understand what we were both saying. I thought he said such funny things in his German way, and he thought what I said was funny. But he was always kind. He never cared about my scar, you know, and after a bit he made me so that I never cared about it either.' She put her hand up to her face to cover the livid scar reminiscing, and Henry reached out and took the hand down again, giving it a gentle tap. 'That's what Dad would have done if he'd seen you trying to cover that up again,' he chided her, and she nodded and laughed self-consciously.

'Its funny,' said Olwen, 'But I never notice that now. I don't think I ever did take much notice of it. I thought you were lovely,' she added, shyly, 'And I envied Henry having a mother like you.'

'Well, there now,' Meg said, ' You'll turn my head. And I am your Mam as well, now, Olwen love. And wait till Reini comes home. He'll love you as much as I do, I know.'

So it was that on a dark and dreary November day, Henry took the car to Welshpool station and waited for the twelve o'clock train from Crewe to draw in. As the carriage doors opened and the porter shouted 'Welshpool!' Henry stared anxiously at the people descending onto the platform. At last, with a gasp of joy, he saw the tall rangy figure of his father step down, hefting an old kitbag, which he lowered to the ground when he saw Henry coming towards him. He looked even thinner than Henry remembered, paler and tired-looking, but his face lit up and his arms went out to embrace his son, with a long and heartfelt sigh. He put the young man from him eventually and held him at arms length, feasting his eyes on him. 'Heinrich!' he said softly. 'My son!'

'Dad!' said Henry, suddenly shy. 'How are you, Dad? Good to see you!'

'And it is so very good to see you, my son,' Reini answered, warmly. 'And your mother, how is your mother?'

'She's fine, Dad, fine. She stayed behind to cook a grand dinner for you.' Henry picked up the kitbag and heaved it onto his shoulder. 'Come on, she'll be waiting. Dying to see you.'

'Dying to see me?' repeated Reini, smiling. 'And I have been living just to see her. But forgive me, I have not asked after your wife. I find it hard to think that my son now has a wife! She is Olwen, yes? I look forward to meet your Olwen.'

'I think you'll like her, Dad,' Henry said, confidently as they reached the car and he opened the back door and slung the kitbag in. Then he went round to the passenger side and opened the door for his father. Reini grinned. 'This is, how do you say, the VIP treatment, yes? It is good. I feel important!'

Henry climbed into the driver's seat and started the engine. 'You are important, Dad. Very important. I guess I'll let Mam tell you just how important,' he added, laughing.

The journey from Welshpool to Manafon was only a few miles, but to Reini it was interminable. He strained towards the moment when he would hold Meg in his arms again and hoped that he would be man enough to keep back the tears. They had been long years in the internment camp, boring and mindless. There were few books and although they took exercise, it was not enough to tire him so that he could sleep at night. The guards had not been rough, simply uncaring and as bored as the inmates. Only the thought of what awaited him after his incarceration was over kept him sane. It had been worse in some ways than when he had been a prisoner-of-war in the last conflict, for then he had not cared how long he remained locked up. He had lost everything and everyone that he cared about and he was numb, he felt nothing. This time, having been wrenched away from everything that he held dear, his Meggie, his Heinrich and his precious home, the impatience to get back made each day an agony of waiting. But now it was over, soon now he would see his Meggie and hold her. He felt a lump in his throat and turned to look out of the side window, so that Henry couldn't see his face.

At last the car coughed and grumbled its way up the steep lane, and there at the top stood Meg, her face wreathed in smiles, her arms already open to receive him.

Henry stopped the car at the top of the lane and Reini clambered out. He walked towards Meg, holding out his arms, and as they folded round her he bent his head and buried his nose in her hair, still golden with streaks of silver. Then he tipped her face up and gazed down for a moment into the blue eyes that blazed with love for him, before lowering his lips to hers in a long and sweet kiss. 'Oh my Meggie,' he whispered. 'At last!'

Henry slipped the car into gear and drove round to the yard at the back, leaving them to their private homecoming. He felt choked up himself, and entered the house, calling for Olwen. She came out of the kitchen to meet him. 'He's come then?' she said, smiling. Henry nodded and drew her into his arms. 'Give us a kiss,' he said, smiling. 'They'll be busy for a bit, I'm thinking!' She drew away after kissing him thoroughly. 'I hope they won't be too long. Dinner's ready. It'll go cold.' 'Daresay they won't notice,' he grinned, 'but I'll go and call them. I'm starving myself, and I should think Dad is.'

On that Meg and Reini came in, arms entwined and broad smiles on their faces. Henry drew Olwen forward. 'Dad, this is Olwen, my wife. Olwen, my Dad. The best in the world!'

Reini folded Olwen's little hand in his big ones. 'Olwen. Now that I am your other father, is it that I can kiss you?'

Olwen nodded, shyly and lifted her face for him to gently kiss her cheek. 'Right then,' said Meg, smiling round her little family. 'Olwen has laid the table, so take your places and we can eat. Everything is from the farm, chicken, vegetables, potatoes and for afters, apple Charlotte and custard. What about that then? War or no war we are eating well!'

'You sit down by Dad, Mam,' said Henry. ' Me and Olwen will serve you This is your day, yours and Dad's, and you both deserve it.' So Henry and Olwen bustled out and in a few moments came back with plates full of succulent chicken and bowls of chopped carrots, yellow buttery swede and roasted parsnips. Another larger bowl contained a mound of floury potatoes, and they placed a jug of rich-looking gravy in the middle of the table.

Reini looked at the good things on the table and then at the smiling faces round the table and for a moment was silent. Then he said, quietly, 'This is indeed a moment for us to thank God for all our blessings. We have much that is good to eat, we are all together again, and we are all safe. Many have not these good things. Many are not safe. Let us bow our heads and say 'thank you' to the Lord.'

Meg smiled tremulously at Reini and nodded. They all bowed their heads for they were truly grateful that they were all together at last and they knew quite well that not all families were so fortunate.

Henry demanded that his father come out and inspect the farm after dinner. Reini was reluctant to move from Meg's side, and Olwen saw this. 'Go you with them, Mam,' she whispered. 'I'll wash up. I can see Dad doesn't want to let you out of his sight!' she added with a light laugh.

Meg flushed. 'Well, it has been a long time. Thank you, love. I do want to be with him. We'll get used to each other after a bit, I expect. I'm getting to be an old woman, but today I feel like a young bride!' And, indeed, with her cheeks flushed and her blue eyes sparkling, she looked like a young newly-wed, too. So she joined Reini and Henry outside and walked around in the circle of Reini's arm, returning his loving looks from time to time, while in between he praised Henry for his husbandry of the land and the animals and even the November day failed to damp their spirits.

News of Reini's return was greeted with relief and great pleasure by the family in Newtown. Many were the messages that were sent to Manafon to welcome him home. It was taken as further proof that the war was entering its final stage, and everyone strained towards the day when it would finally end and the boys would come back home again.

In the meantime, news reached the Home Guard in Newtown that they were to be stood down. It was greeted with mixed feelings among the troops. Llew met Gwilym the Sticks on a Saturday morning in town, coming out of Griffiths and Griffiths, carrying his paper.

'Aye, aye, Llew,' Gwilym greeted him. 'How's it going, boy? Have you heard as we're goin' to be stood down? Us Home Guards, I mean. Seems they dunna want us any more.'

'Aye, I heard it on the wireless, Gwilym,' said Llew. 'They think there's no chance of the Germans invading us now. They're pretty well finished, they do reckon. There's still the Japs, of course, but I daresay the Yanks'll see them off. Anyway, they're not likely to invade us. So, it looks as though we're not wanted any longer.'

'Looks like it,' said Gwilym, sadly. 'Pity. I did like bein' a soldier. Not a shot fired in anger, mind you. But it did give me a good excuse to get out nights. Between that an' the black-out bein' lifted, life wunna be worth livin'.' He sniffled, drew a large red and white spotted handkerchief out of his pocket and blew his nose loudly.

'Aren't you glad for the war to be over, Gwilym?' asked Llew, shocked.

'Oh, aye, dunna get me wrong. I'm glad for them as is really fighting. Glad for their families as well. Its just that it was a bit of excitement. I anna 'ad much excitement in my life. An' it was good, walkin' around like Lord Muck in me uniform and a gun over me shoulder. I really felt like I was somebody. You know, mun.'

Llew laughed, wryly. 'Tell you something, Gwilym, lad. There'll be a few that'll have to come back down to earth after this lot's over. I don't mean blokes like you, Gwil bach, but them that have been given a bit of power, you know, these desk-soldiers. They've had the chance to throw their weight about these last few years and they haven't half used it! All these little Caesars, like them in the fuel office, and you've only got to think of Bob the Barn, with his tin hat, going around putting the fear of God into folks. I mean, who'd have taken any flaming notice of Bob the Barn before he got made an A.R.P. warden? I ask you! And there are Bob the Barns all over the country, mun. And worse. Oh, there'll be a reckoning after this is over , mark my words'

'Ah, I dessay,' said Gwilym, shaking his head. 'Anyway, I'm going to miss the oul' Home Guard. Oul' Eddie Probert wasn't a bad oul' stick, was 'e? 'E taught us a fair bit, only we never 'ad a chance to use any of it. I wouldn't 'ave minded 'avin' a bit of a go at a Jerry. The nearest we come was when one landed on the Rackfield. God, that was excitin' if you like!' Gwilym's eyes lit up at the memory.

'Ah, but that wasn't a Jerry. That was Jack Evans under Mrs Moses Owen's sheet and another three sheets to the wind!' Llew laughed.

'Ah, I know that, mun. But we did'n know when we went into action, did we. We thought it was the genuine article. God, my knees was knockin', I can tell you. But we went in, lad, an' it would 'ave been all the same if it 'ad been a Jerry. See what I mean?'

'Aye, I see what you mean, Gwil.' Llew smiled rather sadly. He knew just what Gwilym meant. Men like Gwilym the Sticks who led such colourless lives, had at last had some excitement, felt themselves valued and of some importance. They would sink back into oblivion when the war ended, as it looked like doing soon. Llew himself would be glad. He still felt uncomfortable wearing army uniform after he had sworn 'never again'. Almost as though he had betrayed his own principles. He shrugged and chided himself for being foolish. He would certainly never have gone in the army proper again. He would have gone to prison first, but he had been too old, anyway, and was glad of it. Playing soldiers in the Home Guard and helping to train the others didn't count.

'Never mind, Gwil. When they stand us down we'll have a pint to celebrate,' he said.

Gwilym sighed. 'We 'ave a pint anyway. So what'll be different?'

'Well, then,' grinned Llew. 'We'll go mad an' have two pints! I'll treat you!'

Christmas 1944 was a more cheerful time for the Rees family, gathered round the festive board at Bay House, the biggest house in the family, which was needed for all of them to get together. They gave Reini a great welcome when he and Meg, with Henry and Olwen, arrived, laden with goods from the farm; fresh butter, vegetables, ham and bacon, home-made sausages and black pudding from a recently killed pig, together with a piece of fresh pork for Boxing Day for Esther's family.

For that day they had a large goose, bought in the Market Hall and they were reminded of the time Dada had bought a live goose from the same source, thinking to save money. He had rued the day, having had a terrible time bringing the thing home, and Owen told how he had come home for his dinner to find Dada chasing that recalcitrant bird round the yard at No 46 and how he, Owen was almost too weak with laughter to help capture the creature. Dada had taken great satisfaction in carving the thing up on Christmas Day.

They reminisced about Christmases past, when Mama and Dada were alive and fell to looking forward to next Christmas, when they hoped the boys would be back to join them round the Christmas table. There was a sadness in the eyes of Davy and Nan, and Roma too, as they thought that Huw would never sit with them again, and yet their thoughts turned to young David, now sitting up in his pram in the corner, chewing valiantly on a turkey bone with his two teeth and looking so like a miniature Huw that it was almost comical.

Rhiannon sat next to her mother, looking very pretty and smiling to herself. She had had a letter from Sean yesterday and it was cheerful and full of anticipation. She felt sure that next Christmas she would be over in Ireland with her new family and above all, her beloved Sean. She was going to be received into the Catholic Church in February, sponsored by a nice lady, a member of the small parish in Newtown, and already felt at home in her new Church, which seemed to suit the romantic in her soul. She wished Sean could have been there for the ceremony, but Nell and Elwyn said they would come, and Esther also volunteered to go along to support her.

Martin sat at the head of the table and carved the goose. There was a little grey in the fair hair at his temples, but his kindly grey eyes shone behind the gold-rimmed glasses, especially when they rested on Esther. He had loved her since he was a small boy and that love had not diminished over the years, but was stronger then ever. She sat at the other end of the table, the bloom of pregnancy already on her. She was one of those women who enjoyed pregnancy and were at their best when expecting a baby. She was beaming round the table now, Johnny sitting next to her on top of a large encyclopaedia which was on the seat of his chair. Mary sat between him and Alun, wearing her new Christmas dress of red velvet with a little white lace collar and cuffs of the same lace. Her blonde hair was brushed until it shone and was tied up with a red ribbon to match her dress. She felt her consequence and sat up very straight, minding her manners and helping Johnny to cut up his dinner, with her mother's approving eyes on her. As for Alun, he was most interested in the food. He seemed to be always hungry, although his father said he must have hollow legs, for he remained thin and wiry. He was a little bit worried about the hollow legs, and from time to time tapped them with his finger nails, but they didn't sound hollow to him and certainly they didn't look any different from the legs of other boys, as far as he could see. He shrugged and waited for his plate of goose to be handed to him.

On the other side of Esther sat Gwennie and Teddy. They had settled down very well, adjusting to the fact that this was now their home. They met with nothing but kindness and affection from their new Mam and Dad and casual acceptance from Mary and Alun. In their turn, Gwennie adored Mary, copied her in everything and would willingly have been her slave, whereas Teddy hero-worshipped Alun, which was pleasant for Alun after the bossiness of Mary. As for Johnny, he loved everyone and simply went his own way

Llew and Mattie were a little quiet. Mattie had been upset when the papers were full of the horrors of the concentration camps that had been uncovered during the Russian advance, so afraid that the prisoner of war camps would be like that, but Llew had reassured her that they would be different, that the Red Cross and the Geneva Convention would prevent anything like that happening to the prisoners of war. Still she worried about Jim, only consoling herself that he was alive, for she had had a card from him, and also that at least he was out of the fighting. But she knew he would hate being locked up. 'If only this hateful war was over,' was her litany these days, and she was glad that she was going out to work at the Pool Road factory, which helped to take her mind off things, and also gave her the company of Nell, who was always kind to her.

Owen and Lena sat on each side of Martin, and Kathleen Eluned was also propped up on the second volume of the encyclopaedia beside her mother. She was a dark, solemn child, with her mother's straight dark hair like a raven's wing and the Rees's large brown eyes. Her smile was wide and sweet and showed tiny, pearl-like teeth. She particularly adored her father and loved to travel on his shoulders, grabbing handfuls of his thick dark curls to steady herself. Lena was secure in Owen's love now, and could barely remember the days when Owen loved Mary Ann and she, Lena, thought she would never have a chance. Then poor, frail Mary Ann had died and eventually Owen had turned to her and their love had strengthened through the years. Occasionally over the years she had wondered whether Owen had ever thought of the lovely, fair Mary Ann, who had been his first love, but if he had, he never mentioned it, and although Lena had a quick temper, probably born of a certain insecurity, Owen was phlegmatic and patient with her and their rows were rarely serious. Now she hugged to herself the thought that she may be pregnant again, and hoped that if she was, she would have a little boy who looked like Owen. She smiled to herself now and Owen, watching her, raised his eyebrows. She grinned and tapped her nose at him and Kathleen Eluned smiled to keep them company.

This then was the Rees family at Christmas 1944, with hopes that the war would end soon, with Reini restored to them and Meg full of happy smiles.

With two young girls joining them, Roma and Olwen, with a new generation of children round the table and all waiting now for the end that would bring the boys marching home.

1945 came in and the news continued to favour the Allies. In February came the shocking news of the controversial bombing of Dresden. Most people in Britain were uncomfortable about this event, since it transpired that the City, ancient and very beautiful, was full of thousands of refugees. It was the result of 'Bomber' Harris's strategy of blanket bombing of German cities, which he claimed, by terrorising the German people, would shorten the war. However, people put this behind them and by March the Allies, led by General Montgomery, were closing in on Berlin. It certainly looked very much as if Germany was in its death throes.

At the standing-down ceremony of the Home Guard they were told that they were to keep their uniforms and their rifles, which was a consolation to those like Gwilym the sticks and Owen Neuadd, who had enjoyed their spell as soldiers while still in the safety of civvy street. After the ceremony was over and they were marched through the town to show off for the last time, rifles over their shoulders and moving in step, looking disciplined, they said their goodbyes to the Drill Hall where they had trained over the last few years and wandered out on to Broad Street, feeling somehow part of an anti-climax. Llew and Owen, with their pals Gwilym the Sticks and Owen Neuadd made their way over to the Black Boy, as usual, and settled in their usual corner, carrying their usual pints with them.

Owen Neuadd took a deep draught of his ale and wiped his mouth, sighing with satisfaction. 'We wunna 'ave an excuse to do this from now on, lads. Well, here's to peacetime when it comes, but there's a lot to be said for wartime, too.' He gave a wicked grin and looked challengingly all round.

Llew shook his head. 'You can keep war, for me. I see nothing good in it, Neuadd. I haven't forgotten the last lot. That was enough for me. We didn't even know what we were fighting for! God, what a mess it was. I suppose this lot had some sort of reason to it, Hitler had to be stopped, but I can't help thinking there should have been some way of stopping it in the beginning. And stopping that idiot Mussolini. I mean, he started his career trying to pinch Abyssinia. Somebody should have stopped him then.'

Owen nodded in agreement. 'Aye, and Hitler got his practice helping Franco in the Spanish Civil War. Surely somebody at the top could have seen what was coming and clamped down on those two with sanctions or something, before it came to a war that has killed millions.'

Neuadd was silent for a while, then he stared coolly at Owen and asked, 'D'you ever feel sort of funny that you never went to fight? A young fellow like you. Us here was too old to go, but you wasn't'

Owen stared back. 'No, Neuadd, I never did,' he answered, deliberately. 'I never would have, even if I hadn't been in a reserved occupation. I suppose I would have had to declare myself a conshie and been a stretcher bearer or something, or even go to clink. But I wouldn't have fought. Don't get me wrong. I'd fight if Wales was threatened, because Wales is my country, but I don't reckon to fight for somebody else's country, see?'

'You one of them Welsh Nationalists then?' asked Neuadd, round eyed.

Owen laughed. 'I 'spect I must be.' he agreed. 'Anyway, that's how I've always felt. I'd have followed Glyndwr if I'd have been alive back then.'

'Ah, but Owain Glyndwr is dead, mun,' said Neuadd, doubtfully.

'Aye, an' I see in today's paper as Lloyd George is dead, as well!' Gwilym put in. 'What did you think of 'im?'

'Not a lot.' Owen dismissed Lloyd George with a wave of his hand. 'He didn't do much for his own country, and he split up Ireland, which I reckon is a recipe for trouble.'

Neuadd, feeling the discussion was getting to deep for him, began to sing:

> 'Lloyd George knew my father,
> Father knew Lloyd George.'

'Huh!' interrupted Gwilym. 'Lloyd George was more likely to know thy mother, from all accounts. Bit of a devil for the women, I did hear.'

'Good Liberal, though,' Neuadd defended the statesman. 'My oul' 'ooman is a big Liberal. Photo of Clement Davies in the house. I dunna bother to vote, me. They dunna seem to do anythin' for me, so why should I trouble meself to go to the pollin' station for them?' He sniffed. 'Politics is a mug's game unless you're gettin' summat out of it. There's them as does, but I inna one of them.'

Llew tutted and shook his head. 'And people have fought and died for universal suffrage!'

'What's that when it's at home?' asked Neuadd, suspiciously.

'Well, your right to a vote,' explained Llew. 'You know, democracy.'

Neuadd sniffed. 'Big words. Politics is all about big words. Blokes trying to blind us with science. They'm clever at big words, but its all about jam tomorrow. I could do with a bit of jam today, me.'

Llew laughed. 'You're a cynic, Neuadd!'

'Ah, I'm sure to be,' he agreed, draining his pint. 'I dunno what it means, but you an' Owen here are scholars, so you'm sure to be right. If I'm one of them, then I want to know whether we'm going to have that second pint you was talkin' about. Talkin' politics is thirsty work, thees know!'

'My treat,' said Llew, grinning. 'And worth it to hear you lot on politics!'

6

Ends and Beginnings

It was the end of April 1945 and virtually the end of the war. News came through first of the death of Mussolini, who had been shot by his own people and strung up by his heels, together with his mistress, Clara Petacci, from the facade of a petrol station in Milan. Two days later, on the 30th of April, Hitler killed himself in his bunker and his wife Eva Braun took poison. This was the end of a twin regime which had terrorised Europe and caused a war in which at least fifty-five million died.

A sigh of relief was breathed right across Europe, and that included the Rees family in Newtown. They now waited for their menfolk to return: Edward and Gareth, who had fought their way up through Italy to link up with the Allies who had over-run Germany; Jim from the prison camp and Sean from Monty's H.Q. in Northern Germany. The Armistice had not yet been signed, but it was only a matter of time now and then the long six years of war would finally be over. Nan and Davy had had a letter from Edward to say he was well and looking forward to demob and home. Nell and Elwyn had had the same from Gareth, who couldn't wait to get back and resume his work with Norman Oliver. Rhiannon had had a long and loving letter from her Sean who never tired of writing about the life they were going to have together in Ireland, and Rhiannon never tired of hearing about it. She had been quietly received into the Catholic Church back in February during a Sunday morning Mass, with Nell and Elwyn sitting behind her, along with Esther, who had also brought Mary. They were made welcome by Father Evans and although the service seemed strange to them, they were very impressed with it, and even more so with Rhiannon's confidence as she made the responses and seemed quite at home and comfortable with her new faith. Now she felt she was ready to meet her new family and strained towards the day when Sean would come home.

Llew and Mattie had not heard from Jim for a few weeks. Llew tried to tell Mattie that things would be difficult for a while as the war wound down, but he felt anxious himself although he put a good face on it for Mattie's sake. She had been a good wife to him over the years and he had never regretted marrying her, although it was second marriage for both of them and built on mutual respect and a quiet affection, which had grown over the years. He had never had children by Mattie, but had shared in the bringing up of Jim and was as fond of the boy as though he was his. Mattie was always a quiet woman, but now she was quieter than ever and Llew knew that she was worried about Jim. When they went to All Saints on Sunday evenings it was to pray fervently that he was safe and not suffering too much.

The Allies were finding more concentration camps as they pressed more deeply into Germany, and what they found was so horrendous as to be barely credible. Mountains of emaciated bodies were piled up on the ashes of those which had been burned. The gas chambers through which had passed millions of Jews, men, women and little children, still stood, a terrible memorial to man's inhumanity to man. The soldiers who had liberated Belsen had wept at the sight of the walking skeletons, rooting among the rubbish dumps, looking for food. But mostly the inmates were too weak to rise and helping them was an almost impossible task, for thousands were too far gone to respond. Those who were strong enough to talk of their ordeal told of an unbelievable savagery, starvation, humiliation and of being treated as non-people. Millions had been processed through the gas-chambers and then shovelled into mass graves or burned in the huge incinerators built for the purpose. This must surely have been the most terrible genocide in history.

To the people of Newtown this was a remote happening. They tutted over it as they read their daily papers and shook their heads at the horror of it, but they could not really imagine it, and it had to be pushed to the back of their minds so that they could concentrate on the coming end to the war and the thought of the boys marching home. Many of the boys, like Huw, would never come home again, and the end of the war meant less to their families, nursing a heartache which would stay with them for the rest of their lives. On Kerry Road alone, three only sons failed to return to their parents: Kenneth Gwalchmai, Derek Pugh and Harry Bithell, leaving those parents with an empty future. The list of names on the war memorial lengthened sadly.

When eventually the news came through that the armistice had been signed in May the town went mad. Those troops which were still garrisoned there took to the streets, mingling with the townspeople, the foundry hooter went and the church bells began to ring. The schools declared a half-holiday and the children streamed out, chattering excitedly. Owen hurried home to Lena and they put Kathleen Eluned into her pushchair and hurried over to No 46. Davy and Nan, with Roma carrying little David, had got there before them and Nell had come home from the factory and Elwyn and Rhiannon from Pryce Jones's. Soon Llew and Mattie came, followed by Esther and her brood and Martin, who had given himself the day off and closed the office. They all had cups of tea and then decided to go down into the town to see what was happening.

There was a carnival atmosphere in the town, the pubs were all open and people were standing around on street corners, talking eagerly and yet not quite realising what it all meant. There was almost an air of bewilderment about. There was, as yet, no tangible evidence that the war had ended, everything looked the same, and gradually it was borne upon the people that until the men came home again, their relief was almost premature.

'I guess we'd all feel differently if we lived in London or round the south coast of England where they've really suffered,' said Martin. 'We haven't known very much about it here, have we? Apart from a few bombs in the countryside and a couple of cows killed.' he grinned. 'No, we've been pretty fortunate. And thanks to Meg and Henry we haven't starved.' They were standing with their backs to the Bridge Wall, and Llew, who was next to Martin, nodded agreement.

'I'm sorry for Nan and Davy, though,' he said. 'Losing Huw. When all the others come marching home, they're going to feel it. I wonder what Edward will think, with Huw gone and Roma here with Huw's child. It'll be a funny sort of homecoming for the lad, won't it?'

'Oh well, I think Edward will cope. He's a pretty steady lad. When he gets back he'll have to study to get his final qualifications, which he shouldn't have any trouble with. He'd worked hard up till he went away, and as long as the war hasn't taken anything away from him, he should do well. He's got the makings of a good lawyer, you know, the right sort of brain.' Martin said.

'Hope he's not still hankering after that Ruth,' Llew said. 'He was pretty struck with her. I wonder if Davy's told him she's married? I know they've been careful what they told him while he was away. It's been enough for him to handle Huw's death, I should think.'

'It'll be good to see them all come back, anyway,' Martin said. 'Have you had news of Jim yet?'

Llew shook his head, a worried look on his face. 'Not yet. I suppose there's bound to be a lot of mess and confusion while these mopping up operations are going on, as they call them.' He glanced across to where Mattie and Nell were in close conversation, and lowered his voice.' I don't say anything to Mattie. She's worried enough as it is, but when I see the pictures in the papers of the things that have happened in the concentration camps, I go cold all over. I think that the same savages as did that could have been handling our prisoners, and I have nightmares thinking what they might have been suffering.'

'Oh, Lord,' said Martin, shaking his head, 'I'm sure you needn't worry on that score. They'd never dare to do those things to the proper prisoners of war. After all they're supposed to allow Red Cross access to the camps. Then there's the Geneva Agreement that controls how prisoners of war are treated.'

'Huh!' Llew gave a derisory laugh. 'I'm afraid I've not got much faith in those Nazi hell-hounds abiding by any agreement.' He sighed. 'I daresay I'm making a mountain out of a molehill. But I can't help worrying. Both my own kids, Esther and Owen are safe. I just hope to God, Jim is. Mattie'll do her nut if anything happens to him.'

'Well, what are we doing standing here,' Martin said, looking round at them all. ' Let's move up town and see what's going on. They won't have got anything organised yet, don't suppose. Probably have a big day later. Anyway, lets go and mingle.'

And mingle they did, chatting to friends who lined Broad Street, waiting for something to happen. After a while, all eyes turned to Wesley Street, from where the sound of drums came and then the Newtown

Silver Band hove into view, marching importantly with Nattie Corfield at their head, blowing away at their instruments as they played 'Blaze Away' with verve enough to make everybody's pulses race. It wasn't the complete band, but as many as could be contacted and pressed into service at short notice, and they gave of their red-faced best. They got a rousing cheer as they passed down Broad Street and wended their way up High Street, to end up on the Cunnings, the ground where the sports were held. There they formed a circle and played a selection of stirring marches, whilst the townspeople, who had followed after them, gathered round. After a while they changed to Welsh hymn tunes, and the spectators joined in singing 'Bread of Heaven', 'Ar Hyd y Nos' and 'Calon Lan', finally ending up with the Welsh National Anthem, loud enough to shake the leaves from the trees, before they reluctantly scattered, the men and some of the younger women, to gather in the pubs later on.

Esther and Martin invited the family to Bay House, so they all made their way back up Broad Street and over the Iron Bridge. They called greetings to Martin Harris as he stood in the doorway of his shop with a broad smile on his face. Already the Grapes Hotel had opened its doors and there was singing going on there. Esther told them all to go on into the house, then gathered the children together and ushered them into Clayton's shop to buy sweets. They were all looking bewildered and Mary's lower lip was jutting out dangerously.

'What's going on, Mam?' she asked, frowning. 'What's all the fuss about?'

Mrs Clayton leaned over the counter, her cheeks as pink as her freshly ironed overall. She smiled at Mary. 'The old war is over, dear. That's what the fuss is about!'

Mary looked up at her mother. 'Is the war over now, Mam? Did we win?' she added, anxiously.

'Of course we did, silly,' said Alun, scornfully, proud that he knew more than his bossy sister. 'That old Hitler is dead. We beat him!'

Mary decided to ignore him. 'I'd like those chocolate buttons with hundreds and thousands on them. Please. What do you want, Gwennie?'

'I want the same as you,' Gwennie said, shyly.

'Say please, then, 'scolded Mary and turned to Kathleen Eluned, holding onto Esther's hand. 'What would you like, Kathleen?' but

Kathleen shook her head, overwhelmed. 'Best get her the same as me and Gwennie,' said Mary, sagely. 'She's only little. She doesn't know what she wants.'

Mrs Clayton looked at Esther and laughed. 'Well, nobody can say that about you dear, can they, ' she said to Mary. You know just what you want and I've got the feeling you always will. Just like your Mam!'

Esther laughed and turned to the three boys. 'What are you having then?'

'Bullseyes!' they chorused and waited, hopping up and down, while Mrs Clayton weighed out all the choices and handed the separate bags to the children.

'Nice that the old war is over, dear, isn't it?' she said to Esther. 'At least your man didn't have to go, did he?'

'No, he didn't,' Esther replied, taking out her purse to pay for the sweets. 'But I had nephews and cousins that did. And one, our Huw, that won't come back.'

'Ah, that was sad,' Mrs Clayton shook her head. 'Your Uncle Davy's lad, wasn't it? In the Air Force. Awful risky, the Air Force, I always thought.'

Esther shepherded the children across Commercial Street and into Bryn Street, where they all climbed the steps into Bay House. Esther was now seven months pregnant and moving more slowly now, but she was looking well and straining towards July when the baby would be born. Lena's baby was due in August so they were able to compare notes. Lena wanted a boy, but Esther didn't care what hers was, she was broody, as Martin said, and just wanted a baby.

At last the day in July came, but it was a Sunday, with all the children at home. They were sent out to play in the big garden at the back of Bay House and told that if they were good children they would have a new brother or sister later in the day. The two girls, Mary and Gwennie, sat on the lawn, while the boys climbed the old apple tree, made easy by the gnarled bark of the trunk, and from time to time picked the small hard fruits and threw them at the girls sitting talking below.

'Stop that!' shouted Mary, rubbing an ear which had received a painful direct hit. 'I'll tell on you, our Alun. Dad said if you pick those little baby apples, there'll be none when apple time comes and then you'll get no apple pies, so there!'

'Tell-tale-tit!' chanted Alun, but the thought of being deprived of apple pie put a stop to the game and the girls were left in peace to talk about the fascinating subject of the new baby.

'Is it going to be a girl or a boy?' asked Gwennie, round-eyed.

Mary shrugged. 'Dunno. I asked Mam, but she said we'd have to wait and see. I don't see why you can't order what you want. It'd be a lot easier. You'd know what colour to knit things in then, wouldn't you. Mam has been knitting everything in white wool. I thought they'd be nicer in pink, but she said p'raps it would be a boy and you couldn't put pink things on a boy.'

'I wonder what would happen if you did?' Gwennie speculated, biting a thumb nail. 'Would it be something bad? Would they get sick, or something?'

'I don't think so,' Mary answered, shaking her head. 'I think it's just that nobody'd know it was a boy. They'd 'spect it to grow up into a girl, wouldn't they? They'd call it a girl's name and put a frock on it.' She giggled at the thought. 'No, they got to dress it in blue so's they know its a boy. And girls is in pink always. So they don't dress them in trousers.'

Gwennie contemplated this for a while but it was above her head. She returned to the age-old question instead. 'Where does your Mam get her babies from?'

'I think she orders them from Sister Lloyd Jones. I 'member her coming when we had Johnny, and now she's come again today, so it must be her that brings them. Dunno where she gets them from.'

Mary looked very doubtful. 'But I saw her come in before your Dad shooed us out and she only had a very little bag with her. It didn't look big enough to put a baby in.'

'Babies is very small, anyway,' pointed out Mary, sagely. 'An' they don't have any clothes on. You've got to have the clothes ready to put on them.'

'Don't they cry when they're put in the bag an' its zipped up?' Gwennie asked, horror-stricken. 'I'd bawl like mad if somebody tried to put me in a bag an' zip it up!'

'I s'pose they're too little to know where they are. An' they surely put holes in the bag for them to breathe. You know, like you have to when you put caterpillars in a matchbox.' Mary pursed her lips and looked knowledgeable.

Gwennie accepted this, as she accepted most things that Mary told her. 'What d'you hope it is?' she asked.

'Oh, a girl,' said Mary, firmly. 'We've already got three boys, and they're a right nuisance.' She peered up the tree with a severe air and received a raspberry from Alun in reply. 'Well, I hope it's a boy,' he said and Teddy nodded agreement. 'Girls are bossy. They're no good. They can't climb nor do nothin' but talk.'

Johnny said nothing. He was too busy clinging to his perch on the lowest cleft of the tree, where Alun and Teddy had dragged him up to and left him. He was a bit frightened, but he didn't want to admit it even to himself. He looked up through the branches apprehensively to where Alun and Teddy were perched precariously. He wished he could get down and sit with the girls, but Alun would accuse him of being babyish if he asked to get down, and that was out of the question. He gazed imploringly down on Mary's golden head, willing her to look up and take pity on him. As though she felt his gaze she looked up and fixed him with an assessing stare. 'Our Dad's going to be right mad at you, Johnny, if you fall and break your neck. He'll kill you. You'd better come down right now.'

'I can't,' Johnny replied, sniffing. ' I don't want Dad to kill me. Can you get me down, Mary?'

With some difficulty Mary and Gwennie reached up and began to ease Johnny from his perch. He slid a little way but gravity was too strong for him and he landed in a heap on top of poor Gwennie, knocking the breath out of her. He himself was unhurt and he rolled off Gwennie and sat up.

Mary bent over Gwennie. 'Are you all right, Gwennie?' she asked, anxiously.

Gwennie looked a little pale, but she drew a deep breath and found it didn't hurt very much so she too sat up, albeit a little dazed. The two boys at the top of the tree had been unsure as to whether to laugh or not, but now that it looked as though no-one was badly hurt, they gave a derisive chuckle, begun by Alun and copied by Teddy.

'You two shut up!' hissed Mary, furiously. 'Gwennie could have been killed with our Johnny dropping on her. I shall tell our Dad on you two.' She gave an exasperated sigh. How much longer were they going to have to stay out here?

'Why's it taking so long for Sister Lloyd-Jones to hand over the baby?' asked Gwennie, echoing her thoughts. 'I mean, she's only got to give it over to Mam, hasn't she?'

'I don't know, do I?' replied Mary, irritably. Then, as a sudden thought struck her, 'Suppose they've brought the wrong baby and had to take it back?'

'Why would it be the wrong baby?' said Gwennie, shaking her head. 'You know Mam said she didn't care whether it was a boy or a girl. There's not any other kind!'

'P'raps they've brought a black one!' said Alun, eagerly. 'Hey, that would be good, wouldn't it? I hope they wouldn't send a black one back. I'd like that. I don't think Mam would send a black one back, anyway. She likes any kind of babies, I 'spect.'

'I don't think they send black ones to white people,' said Mary doubtfully. 'I wish they did. I've seen little black babies on the pictures and they're heckish cute. I think I'll go and tap on the back door and ask if it's a black baby. I'll come back and tell you.'

Alun and Teddy came slithering down the apple tree, leaves in their hair and scrapes on the toes of their boots. They sat down beside Johnny and Gwennie to wait in eager anticipation for news, almost convincing themselves that it might be a black baby.

Meanwhile, Mary tapped sharply on the back door. She had been told not to come in until they were called, but she wouldn't be going in, would she? After a long interval the door was opened a crack and the flushed face of Edie Davies peered out. 'What you want, Mary?' she asked, hoarsely. 'You've been told not to come in till you're called, haven't you?'

'I'm not in,' pointed out Mary, with justification. 'We just want to know what colour is the baby?'

Edie Davies opened the door a little wider and stared at Mary, frowning. 'What d'you mean, what colour is it?' she asked suspiciously.

'Is it a black one, Edie?' Mary whispered, eagerly.

Edie's expression was horrified. 'A black one!' she shouted, then covered her mouth with her hand. 'You wicked girl. What d'you mean by a black one? I'll tell your father on you, coming here saying nasty things like that. Clear off, now and leave us in peace. A black one, indeed,' she muttered, glaring at Mary. 'The very idea!' and closed the door on a bewildered and disappointed Mary.

She returned to the group at the foot of the apple tree who waited for tidings with bated breath. 'Well?' said Alun. 'Was it a black one? Don't tell me it was an' they've gone and sent it back?'

Mary shook her head. 'Nah, it's not a black one. Edie came to the door and she was real cross when I asked her if it was black. I dunno why. 'Less they asked for a black one an' they couldn't have one cos they're white. Though I don't see why not. Anyway, we still don't know why they're taking so long about it. I did'n have time to ask Edie 'cos she shut the door in my face. Oh, well, never mind. There's a ball in the shed. Go and get it Alun, and we can have a game of catch. They surely can't be very long now.'

And it wasn't much longer before Esther was delivered of a baby girl, seven pounds, two ounces, plump and compact, and very soon washed and tucked into a nappy much too bulky for her tiny legs and a flannelette night-gown with bluebirds embroidered on the bodice. Then she was put into Esther's eager arms and Martin was called up to the bedroom to view the latest addition to his family. He took her gingerly into his arms and touched his lips to the downy cheek. 'She's a peach!' he pronounced 'A real angel!'

'There now,' Esther smiled up at him. 'There's her name for you! Angela!'

'Angela!' he repeated. 'Yes, I like it. What about Angela Susan, after your Mama. She was a great lady, wasn't she?'

'Angela Susan! Lovely. There now,' said Esther. 'Go and fetch the children, Martin'. So Martin put Angela Susan back in Esther's arms and went out into the garden to find the children. When he found them he called out, 'Come and meet the new baby. She's called Angela Susan!'

Alun and Teddy groaned their disappointment. 'Oh heck, another girl. And we were hoping it would be a black boy!' said Alun, pulling a face.

Martin regarded his son with a puzzled smile, but decided it was a joke.

It was on the Saturday afternoon a week later that Mattie was making pastry in her little kitchen. Llew had called at Bay House to view the new arrival, but Mattie had voted to stay at home. To tell the truth she had not been feeling much like socialising these last few weeks, although she had gone up to Esther's to the the baby last Monday evening and had felt her anxiety melt away for a while as she held the sweet-smelling little bundle and kissed the downy head. How could you feel miserable with a tiny new baby to hold? But now her heart was heavy as she rolled the pastry and filled two enamel plates with it. She had sliced up a few apples from the store which Meg had given her. They were last Autumn's apples and a little wrinkled, but they smelled nice and the insides were good. She was just shaking sugar over them when the latch on the outside door rattled.

'Just a minute', she called, remembering that Llew had snicked the Yale latch down before he went out. This would be Llew coming back early. Why hadn't he got his key with him. 'Coming!' she called again, and wiped her floury hands on a damp cloth. She bustled through the front kitchen and unlocked the door. 'Where's your key...' she began, then stopped and gave a gasp. Her hand flew to her heart and she stared speechless as her eyes took in the sight of Jim standing there, a tentative smile on a pale, tired face.

'Hello, Mam,' he said. 'You look as if you've seen a ghost. Yes, it's really me.' He gave a short laugh. 'At least, I think so.'

As he bent to kiss her she put up her hands to cup his face and after he straightened up she still clung to his arms, as though to reassure herself that he was real. She hadn't uttered a word, but two big tears rolled down her cheeks and she shook her head slowly from side to side unbelievingly.

'Jim!' she faltered. 'Jim! Oh Jim!'

He gave a weary smile and his kit-bag slid down onto the step. He leaned against the door-post. 'Aren't you going to ask me in then?' he teased, trying for lightness.

Leaving the kit-bag on the step, Mattie ushered him in and put him to sit in the armchair by the fire. He reached out a thin hand to the flames and she realised he was shivering. Her heart was so filled with joy and thankfulness at the sight of him sitting there that it was a while before she could tear her gaze away.

'Oh Jim!' she said, breathlessly. 'I can't believe it! You're really home! We hadn't heard anything. We didn't expect you!'

'No,' he said quietly. 'We only docked yesterday. I just got on a train. I fell asleep on Crewe platform. Tired, you see. So tired.' He stopped and gazed into the fire. 'So tired.' he repeated, and shivered again.

'Oh, my love, and here I am like somebody daft, when you could do with a hot cup of tea to warm you right now. Stay you there and rest yourself . I'll make you a cup this minute. Then while you drink it I'll cook you something to eat.'

He shook his head. 'Just a cup of tea for now, Mam. I'm not hungry yet. I'll have something later when you and Dad eat. Where is Dad?' he asked, as though it were an effort for him to talk.

Mattie regarded him anxiously. 'Dad's gone up to Esther's. She's just had another baby, a little girl. He'll be back soon. Oh, he won't believe it! We've been so worried.'

He nodded and laid his head against the back of the chair. 'Good to be home,' he murmured and suddenly there were tears in his eyes and he turned his head away.

'I'll go and get you that tea,' Mattie muttered and hurried into the back-kitchen, ignoring her abandoned pastry and spooning tea into the pot, while the kettle began to sing on the small, newly acquired gas stove. While she waited for it to boil she hugged her joy to herself. Her boy was home! He was very thin and very tired, but she'd soon feed him up and he should have all the rest he wanted. He'd soon be their own, cheerful Jim again, she told herself. She wet the tea and poured it out into one of her best cups. She put a couple of ginger biscuits onto the saucer. He'd always liked dunking ginger biscuits in his tea . Then later she'd make them all a good meal. Oh she wished Llew would hurry up home so she could share her joy with him. She carried the cup into the front kitchen. 'There now, drink this. It'll warm you up!' but Jim was already fast asleep, the lines of his face showing his exhaustion. She sighed and put the cup down on the table. She stood gazing at him, drinking in the fact that her son was home, safe and sound. He should sleep, God bless him. That's what he needed most just now.

She suddenly remembered the kit-bag abandoned on the step and went out to get it. As she looked up the street she spotted Llew just turning the corner from Chapel Street into Frankwell, and forgetting she was a middle-aged woman, ran up the street to meet him. He stopped, surprised to see her sprinting towards him and when she reached him he held her shoulders, staring at her with a frown. 'Whatever is it, Mattie? What's wrong? What's happened?'

Breathlessly she clung to him. 'It's Jim! It's Jim! He's home! He's here!'

He continued to stare at her incredulously, but she nodded, laughing. 'Yes, he's really here! He's come home!'

A broad grin spread over Llew's face. 'By God. Is he really home? Come on, girl. Why are we standing here?' and he set off down the street at a run, pulling Mattie by the hand after him. When they reached the door and he saw the kitbag lying on the step he gave a half laugh, half sob and would have burst into the house, but Mattie held him back, with a finger to her lips.

'Sshh!' she warned. 'I left him asleep. He was so tired, poor lad. I made him a cup of tea, but he fell asleep before he could drink it. We mustn't waken him . He just looks worn out.'

Llew nodded and picking up the kitbag carried it into the house, walking with soft and careful steps to where Jim lay sleeping. He stood and gazed down at him, taking in the pale, exhausted face and the thin hands lying on his knees, twitching from time to time. An occasional frown passed over the high, pallid forehead and he muttered restlessly in his sleep. Llew lightly touched Jim's cheek and it was still very cold, despite the warmth of the fire.

Llew put the kit-bag safely in a corner and drew up a chair to the table, where he could watch the boy he had thought of as a son. He could feel a cold anger gathering in him as he contemplated what had turned a strong, healthy young man into an emaciated shadow of himself. Mattie crept into the room and placed a steaming cup of tea in front of Llew. Llew picked the cup up and sipped from it, welcoming the scald of the hot tea in his mouth, and not taking his eyes off the sleeping young man.

Mattie sat down at the table, too, and feasted her eyes on her son. 'He's very thin, isn't he?' she said. 'But I'll soon build him up again. Good grub will make a difference in no time. And he'll be better when he's rested. Oh, dear, he was staggering tired when he got here, love him. I think we'd better leave him sleep as long as he wants to and then he may be ready to eat. He must be hungry. He said he was travelling all day yesterday, after he got off the boat, and then fell asleep on Crewe station! Fancy that!'

Llew nodded and took another gulp of the hot tea. Mattie was reluctant to tear herself away from contemplating her son, but remembered the apple tarts almost ready for the oven and crept out to finish them and put them to bake. She would make some custard later and that would tempt Jim. He'd always loved apple tart and custard.

Llew continued to sip his tea and gaze at Jim as he slept an uneasy sleep. He wondered what the boy had been through to leave him as exhausted as this. What had he suffered over the last two years. Certainly he would have hated being shut up. Eventually, he thought, they would have the whole story from him, but in the meantime, as Mattie said, plenty of rest and good food were the order of the day. But there was something about the lad that worried Llew. He could understand him being tired; wherever he'd come from, it had been a long journey. But this seemed more than tiredness. Once again Jim stirred and muttered in his sleep. He seemed agitated about something. Llew sighed and shook his head, and wondered about the future.

7

Barbed Wire Blues and Birds

Jim's unexpected return home brought joy to the family, but it was tinged with concern when Llew told them that the boy had retired to his room and rarely left it. Mattie had to take most of his meals up to him. He ate some of the food, but the plates which he left outside his bedroom door were rarely cleared, and although the weather was good, he adamantly refused to go outside, except for visits to the 'ty bach' in the yard. Although he didn't lock his door there was that in his attitude which discouraged Llew and Mattie from going in, and he refused point blank to discuss the prison camp. Various members of the family called to see him, but Mattie had to tell them apologetically that he wasn't well enough to have visitors yet. Mattie remained calm and patient with him, so glad to have him back safely that she was willing to put up with his strangeness, feeling that he would come round in time if she kept on taking him nourishing food and letting him rest. But as the weeks went by and there was no improvement, Llew became very worried, and talked of calling in the doctor. However, this upset Mattie.

'You think he's gone mad, don't you?' she hissed angrily at Llew. 'You've just got to give the poor boy time. He'll come round, you'll see. There's no need for the old doctor to come and bother him. He needs time to get used to everything again. He's reading books up there, so he's not daft. Owen sends him books and he seems to be glad of them.'

Llew sighed and shrugged, still convinced that the doctor could help, but unwilling to push the matter for fear of upsetting Mattie. But then he read an article in the Daily Herald, headed 'Barbed Wire Blues'. It was written by a psychiatrist and he described the very symptoms displayed by Jim. He wrote that these were common among returning prisoners of war and were the result of an inability to come to terms with what had been a longed-for freedom. In other words they simply could not handle the freedom to come and go as they liked after years of being locked up. The outside world, even that peopled by loved ones, frightened them. The only cure was time and patience and loving care until eventually they were willing to talk about their experiences and gradually come to terms with the demands of everyday life.

Llew breathed a sigh of relief at the thought that this was a recognised state of mind and that Jim was not alone. He looked up over his paper and grinned at Mattie. 'Good old Doctor Mattie,' he said. 'You were right all along. I should have known you would be!'

Mattie poured herself a second cup of tea to wash down her breakfast toast, and frowned across at Llew. 'What you talking about?' she asked, suspiciously.

'That you were right about Jim! He's got something they're calling 'Barbed Wire Blues'. Returned prisoners of war get it. Its on account of them being locked up. Here, you can read about it in the paper It tells you all about it, and the only cure for it is just what you're doing. Good old Matt!' He handed over the paper to her and took another piece of toast.

Mattie read the article slowly, nodding from time to time. 'Yes,' she said thoughtfully. 'Sounds just like our Jim, doesn't it? So we just got to be patient and be kind to him and not ask him a lot of old questions. I always said he'd come round in his own good time, and this man seems to think they do. I mean the poor boys that have this 'Barbed Wire Blues'.' She shuddered, and handed back the paper to Llew. 'Sounds horrible, doesn't it. These poor fellows. What they must have gone through!' She got up and began to clear away the breakfast things. 'Never mind, is it? He's come home to us now. We'll soon put him right. I told you he didn't need no old doctor.' She went off into the back-kitchen, humming a little air, and Llew thought, not for the first time, of the calming influence of Mattie's common-sense, down-to-earth attitude which seemed to put all problems into perspective.

When he got to work it was to hear another piece of good news. Elwyn met him with the tidings that they had had a letter from Gareth that morning, telling them that he would be home on the 20th, which was tomorrow. 'Nell's beside herself,' he chuckled. 'Running around like a chicken with its head off. Ah, well, you can't blame her. I feel a bit like that myself. It'll be good to see the lad again. Anyway, you know what its like with your Jim. How is he, by the way? Any better?' He looked with concern at Llew.'

'Not yet,' replied Llew. 'But I think he's going to be all right,' and he told Elwyn about the article in the paper.

Elwyn nodded, slowly. 'Well, that seems to make sense. 'Barbed Wire Blues' eh? I suppose its going to take him a bit to get used to freedom, and even to civvy life. A couple of years in a prison camp is bound to have an effect on the poor chaps. At least our Gareth won't have that problem.'

'No,' Llew said. 'I daresay he'll just be glad to get home and get back to his carpentering. He really took to it, didn't he? Old Norman was telling me the other day how much he's looking forward to Gareth coming back. He's had a boy to help him, but not a patch on Gareth, he reckons. Well, I'm glad to hear your news. He's a nice lad, is Gareth. It'll be good to see him back.'

'Well, this is just the demob leave, he's got to go up to H.Q. for the final demob, it seems, but that shouldn't take long.'

Llew sighed. 'It'll be good when they all come back, Edward and all. I just wish young Huw was coming back with them. But there, we've been luckier than most. Some families have lost nearly all their boys. What a damn awful waste of young life!' he growled. Elwyn made his excuses and left before Llew got onto his soap-box!

The next day saw Nell and Elwyn, who had asked for a couple of hours off, meeting the twelve o'clock train from Shrewsbury. When they heard its shrill whistle and saw it steaming round the corner under the Kerry Road bridge, Nell could hardly contain her excitement, and even the phlegmatic Elwyn felt his heart beat a little faster. With a great fuss of noise and steam the train drew up at the platform and their eyes scanned the folks descending from the carriages. There were quite a lot of soldiers, but at last they spotted Gareth, hefting his kitbag onto the platform and looking round to see if anyone was meeting him. His face lit up when he saw his Mam and Dad hurrying towards him and there were no inhibitions when he stooped to kiss his mother and then straightened and gave his father a bear hug. Nell could hardly believe how he had broadened across the shoulders and added enough to his height to appear at least a couple of inches taller than his father. She brushed away her tears of joy and walked proudly between him and Elwyn as they left the station. When they passed Pryce Jones's entrance Rhiannon was waiting on the steps. She had run out of the office when she heard the train steam in and parked herself there to watch for Gareth. He dumped the kitbag on the pavement and ran up the steps to give her a hug, watched from behind the glass doors by some of the sales girls, gazing with envy at the tall, fair-haired boy. They would have loved to have changed places with Rhiannon. She, in her turn, waved him a temporary farewell, and calling 'See you later!' went back into the office. She was pleased to see her brother back, but still she longed for the day when Sean would step off the train and into her arms. She shrugged, sighed and got on with her work again.

Later she joined the other three for dinner and listened while Gareth told them some of his adventures, making light of the bad times in North Africa and fighting their way up Italy, and concentrating on the funny episodes. He told them of the time he had been in a platoon sent to clear a house in an Italian village, where some German troops, left behind during the push, were suspected of hiding. Some of the platoon were sent upstairs, others to the back regions and he was told to search the cellar. He opened the door and peered down the rickety steps, but could see and hear nothing. He didn't think anyone was there, but not fancying carrying his rifle down such an unsafe stairway, he propped it up by the door and descended cautiously. Still there was no sound and very little light, save from a grid which must have opened into the back yard. He was about to turn away and mount the stairs again, when a movement in the corner caught his eye. He peered through the gloom and froze. Four German soldiers crouched in the corner, trying to cover their faces with their caps. It was too late to go back for his rifle. With shaking legs he approached and stood over them. He stuck his hand in his pocket and made the shape of a gun with it. Then trying to sound menacing he croaked 'Hands up, or I shoot!' Whether they understood him or not, or whether they were wearily glad to surrender, they rose to their feet without a word and when he gestured with his head for them to go first up the stairs, they obeyed meekly. When he reached the top he grabbed his rifle with sweating hands and then herded them across the hall. 'Sir!' he shouted up the stairs. 'Down here! They're down here!' The platoon commander clattered down the stairs and when he saw the group of Germans, with Gareth covering them with his rifle, he grinned delightedly. 'Well done, Jones!' he cried, and Gareth gulped and grinned back, weakly.

Elwyn and Rhiannon laughed heartily at the story, but Nell could only think of the narrow squeak her boy had had and got up hurriedly to clear the plates and fetch in the pudding, an apple charlotte made from apples she had bought in the Market Hall. There was a jug of cream which she had ordered from Jack Richards the Milk and she filled four dishes with generous helpings.

Gareth set to with a will, his eyes shining and when he had demolished the first helping, he asked if there were seconds, grinning up at his mother, who was only to pleased to refill his dish. After cups of tea, Rhiannon and Elwyn had to go back to work and Gareth and Nell were left to linger over a second cup. Nell had asked for the day off, and she was glad to sit awhile and bring Gareth up to date with all the news of the family.

'I find Rhiannon changed,' said Gareth, tentatively, looking at Nell over his cup.

Nell nodded. 'Oh, indeed. She's a different girl since she met and married Sean Kerrigan. She seems to think the world of him. And, believe it or not, he's boss!' she chuckled.

Gareth's eyes widened and his eyebrows went up. 'My Lord, he must be some fellow!'

'Well, he is,' said Nell. 'Just what she needed, I suppose. She's certainly a different girl from when she broke up Edward's romance with Ruth.'

Gareth spluttered into his tea. 'She what!' he exclaimed. 'I thought those two were more or less engaged?'

'They were engaged,' Nell said, sighing. 'Ring and all. Poor Edward, it all came to nothing, thanks to our Rhiannon.'

She proceeded to tell him what had happened and he was shocked.

'Perhaps they'll get together again when Edward comes back,' Gareth said.

'Too late for that. Ruth has married somebody else now. I can't help thinking she couldn't have thought all that much of Edward if she could go and marry somebody else so soon. But there, I think Edward was a bit stiff-necked as well, but I know he took it bad when she broke off the engagement without waiting to hear his side of the story.'

Gareth shook his head and whistled. 'And poor old Huw bought it. I liked Huw, too. He was the first of the boys to befriend me when we first came here. He was a good laugh, too.' He paused a little as he thought sadly of his old friend. 'I suppose Edward and Jim will be home soon, too?'

'Jim is home already,' said Nell. 'He's been a prisoner-of-war for the last two years. He's not been very good since he got back, but they hope that he'll come round soon if they're patient.'

'Barbed Wire Blues' I suppose,' said Gareth, grimacing. 'Is that what's wrong with him? I've heard about it. Hits a lot of fellows who've been in prison camps. Pretty nasty, they say. If he's got that, then I'm sorry for him.'

'That's what Llew thinks is wrong with him,' said Nell. 'He read an article about it in the paper, he reckons, and it sounded just like what's wrong with poor Jim.'

'I must go and see him,' said Gareth. 'Maybe he'll talk to me. Somebody whose been in the war, like. There's a lot of folks I want to go and see this leave, anyway. One of the first is old Norman Oliver. Make sure there's a job for me when I get demobbed.'

'Oh, there'll be a job for you all right. He's always telling your uncle Llew that he wants you back. You must go and see Uncle Davy and Auntie Nan too. Tell them you're sorry about Huw. Oh, and meet Roma and little David.'

'Who the heck are Roma and little David?' asked Gareth, with raised eyebrows. 'Am I supposed to know them?'

'Well, Roma was Huw's girl. They must have lived together I suppose. Anyway, Roma was expecting David when Huw was killed. He never knew, poor lad. Roma had nowhere else to go and she came here and Nan and Davy took her in. She's a real nice girl and they love the baby. The image of Huw he is. But I wonder what Edward will think when he gets home? He doesn't know about Roma and David. They were going to get married when the war ended. She was going to tell Huw on the day he was killed. No doubt he would have married her quick enough if he'd lived.' She sighed. 'There now. That's how things happen, isn't it?'

'Whew!' Gareth shook his head. 'Plenty of drama in the Rees family, as usual. I guess I'll meet this Roma character eventually, but she's not one of my priorities. And I've still to meet my new brother-in-law. Has Rhiannon heard when he'll be home, yet?'

Nell shook her head. 'Not yet, but I suppose it won't be long now. Then she'll be off to Ireland to live. To Derry. Sean's got a job in the family firm waiting for him so they sound as if they'll be all right. She's already gone over to the Catholics.'

Gareth laughed. 'What am I going to hear next? Rhiannon a Catholic!'

'Oh she's taken to it like a duck to water. Goes to Mass every Sunday.'

'What do you and Dad think of that?' Gareth asked, curiously. 'I mean the Rees's and the Jones's have always been C.of E.'

'Well, to tell the truth, I don't think our Church ever meant all that much to her. Not like the rest of us. And I'd rather she was a good Catholic than a poor Church of England.'

Gareth shrugged. 'I came across a lot of Catholics in the army. They're no different from us. Only I think they care more for their religion than we do, really. There's no way they'd miss Mass even in the thick of things. There'd always be a priest following them up. Anyway, I've sat around long enough. I'll take my kit up to my room and then have a bit of a wash. I might go out this evening, but right now I'd like to put my feet up for a bit and leave the visiting for later. Haven't had much rest lately. That was a lovely dinner, Mam,' he went on, rising. 'It's a long time since I tasted grub like that. Worth coming back to civvy street just for that alone!' He grinned happily and picking up his kitbag went clumping up the stairs in his army boots.

Nell sighed with happiness. Her lovely boy was back, safe and well, and as pleasant as ever. She said a silent prayer of thanks and then cleared away the cups and saucers and went to tackle the washing up.

After tea and a long chat with his father Gareth decided that he would go up to visit his Uncle Davy and Auntie Nan and leave his visit to Jim until the next afternoon. It was a nice evening in August, cool after the warmth of the day. He strolled along the pavement, past the little fish and chip shop on the corner and turned up Stone Street. The slaughterhouse was closed now and he was glad. He'd hated passing it and hearing the bellowing of the poor animals. It had no place in a little narrow street like Stone Street. There were one or two people he knew, out in their doorways, taking the evening air, and they all greeted him with warmth and came forward to shake his hand. He thought he would call into the little sweet shop and see if the parrot was there, but in the event the sweet shop itself was closed and appeared to have reverted to a dwelling house, which it had no doubt been originally. He felt a vague regret. He didn't like changes. He emerged onto Kerry Road and looked up at the bulk of Pryce Jones's factory. At least it wasn't a factory now. It had been taken over by the War Ag, he'd heard. He sighed and shook his head, then burst out laughing. He was acting like an old man, sighing over changes. A fair-haired girl passed him and looked at him curiously when he laughed. He treated her to his most charming smile and she smiled back, then hurried on up Kerry Road. He looked after her. She looked nice, no raving beauty but really nice. He chuckled to himself, more softly this time. She'd probably thought he was nuts, laughing at nothing in the middle of the road.

He walked on until he came to Plasgwyn. He unhooked the door to the yard and entered, closing it after him, and went round to the back door, entering without knocking as the family always did. 'Anybody in?' he called out, and was startled when the very girl that had passed him on Kerry Road came into the kitchen and in her turn looked quite as startled at the sight of him.

They stared at each other without speaking and it was a relief when at that moment Auntie Nan came into the kitchen. She exclaimed with pleasure when she saw him and drew him into the room. 'I heard you'd come, Gareth, love.' she said. 'How are you? You're looking very well. Here sit down.. Davy'll be here in a minute. He's just sitting in the room listening to the news. Oh it is good to see you. But you're not home for good yet? Just leave, is it?'

251

He nodded. 'Just leave, but I'll be out soon. In a few weeks. It can't come quick enough for me. How are you, Auntie Nan? And Uncle Davy. He all right?' He thought Nan looked a lot older, but remembering Huw could understand why. His eyes strayed to the girl, standing quietly staring down into the fire.

'Oh, look at me,' said Nan. 'Forgetting to introduce you to Roma. Only she's so much a part of the family now that I forget you haven't met her. Anyway, this is Roma.' She faltered for a moment. 'Huw's young lady.'

On that Davy came into the room carrying a little boy, so like Huw that there was no need for explanations. Davy's face lit up when he saw Gareth and he set the toddler down to stumble over and clutch his mother's skirt, Davy put out his hand and shook Gareth's, who had risen when he came into the room.

'Well, Gareth, my boy,' Davy said, taking in the broadened figure and added height. 'You went away a boy and you've come back a man!'

'I hope so, Uncle Davy,' Gareth said, grinning. Then turning to the girl, he held out his hand and she put hers into it. 'We met on the road, didn't we?'

She smiled shyly and nodded. 'I'm Gareth,' he said, 'Nell and Elwyn's son and a brother for Rhiannon. How are you, Roma?'

'I'm very well, thank you,' she said quietly, and disentangled her hand which he was still hanging on to. He blushed like a schoolboy and sat down again, while the little boy hid behind his mother's skirt and peeped out at him from time to time, his thumb in his mouth.

'Have a cup of tea, Gareth.' said Nell, in the time-honoured ritual, and although he was awash with tea provided by his mother, he couldn't refuse, and politely said 'Yes please.' She left the room to get it and Davy sat down opposite him, drawing the little David onto his knee, where he sat contentedly, leaning against Davy's chest. Gareth thought that Davy looked much older, too. The kind grey eyes were tired behind his gold-rimmed glasses and it was clear that the death of Huw had hit him and Nan badly. It must have hit this girl, too, thought Gareth and stole a glance at her, as she sat down on a straight-backed chair in the corner of the room. Her hands were folded on her lap and she gazed down at them with a serene expression on her face. She seemed to be the very opposite of the lively and restless Huw, but then they say that opposites are attracted to each other, he mused. Somehow she fascinated him. She seemed so self-contained and remote, and yet not cold, he thought. Davy was asking him a question and he pulled himself together and answered. Then Nan came back into the room with a tray of tea for them all and a small beaker of milk for the child. They quite obviously loved the little boy, which was quite understandable given that he was all that was left to them of Huw. He took his cup of tea from Nan but shook his head when she offered a biscuit. 'Mam's fed me up until I'm near to bursting,' he said, laughing.

'I'll bet she has.' Nan smiled and took the baby from Davy while he drank his tea, feeding the little one his milk, lovingly.

'I suppose you'll be going back to being a carpenter when you get home for good?' asked Davy. 'Back to old Norman Oliver, yes?'

'Well, yes. If he'll have me.' said Gareth, sipping the strong tea, which was how Nan always made it. One for each person and one for the pot, even if you could stand a spoon in it. He smiled at the thought and looked up to find Roma's eyes on him. He coughed and looked away. 'I expect it'll be all right. Dad says old Norman's always asking when I'm coming back and if I'll still want to be a carpenter. Well, I do. l can't imagine being anything else. I'd like to do some carving too. I saw a lot of beautiful wood-carving over in Europe and I'd like to try my hand at that. I don't know whether Norman can teach me, but if not I'll have a go myself. I used to be pretty good at carving little animals when I could get the right sort of wood. But, anyway, I can't wait to get back and get into harness again.' He was conscious of Roma's eyes on him and it was making him uncomfortable. He thought he was too aware of her and turned slightly in his chair, facing Nan and the baby, and went on talking to them and answering Davy's queries about his demob and so on, until he judged it to be time to go. It was only half-past-seven, and he thought it wasn't too late to make his way up to Crescent Street and beard old Norman Oliver in his den. He made his goodbyes and left, promising to come again. As he told them, he had a full fortnight at home so he had plenty of time to visit round all of the family more than once. He set off down Kerry Road and crossed over Pool Road, making his way alongside the Bridge Wall. He paused and gazed over the parapet at the familiar sight of the River Severn running slowly below. After the dry summer weather the river was shallow, tumbling over the rocks and glistening in the evening sun. As he leaned his elbows on the stone, still warm from the day's sun, he thought how good it was to have a river running through the town. There was always something of interest to watch. It had its moods at different seasons of the year. Now it was tranquil and unthreatening, but before he had gone away he had seen it during the storms of October, when it rushed, swift and dirty, barely keeping within its banks, carrying branches of trees and other detritus along with it. Although he had not seen it in full flow himself, he had heard of the floods and the devastation they caused in the low-lying parts of the town. Now that Newtown was his home, and likely to be for the rest of his life, he hoped, he guessed he would see the full force of the river's fury from time to time in the years to come. He breathed a sigh of contentment. He loved Newtown and really felt it was his home. Canada he had put behind him and felt that his life there had been as much exile as it had for his Mam and Dad.

He tipped his cap to the back of his head and shoved his hands in his pockets. He began to whistle 'Moonlight Serenade' as he walked along. He had loved Glen Miller's band and thought sadly of the bandleader's untimely end over the English Channel, as he was flying into Europe to entertain the troops. The war had had more casualties than just troops. He waved a cheery 'Hello!' to friends he had made before he was called up and here and there stopped to talk and hear them say they were glad to see him back. He thought it was wonderful to live in a small town, where everybody knew everybody, and it warmed his heart to realise how many people he had got to know in the short time he had lived in Newtown. He hoped he never had to leave here again. He really felt this was home and he looked forward to the future and to resuming his life here.

He strolled up Broad Street and looked up at the Town Clock. Nearly a quarter to eight. He quickened his steps and crossed over the Iron Bridge and set off up Crescent Street to the three-storey terraced house where Norman Oliver lived with his unmarried sisters, Winnie and Annie. It was Winnie who opened the door to his brisk knock and exclaimed delightedly at the sight of him. 'Well! If it isn't Gareth. Come in, boy!

Annie! Look who's here!'

Annie came hurrying down the narrow hallway, her wispy grey hair escaping from her bun as it always did. She clasped her hands over her bony chest and her narrow, wrinkled face split into a wide smile. 'Gareth! Well, well! Who'd have thought? Come on in, lad. Don't keep him standing on the steps!' she scolded her sister. Winnie was the opposite of Annie, round and apple-cheeked, her brown hair still thick and straining against a hair-net, her plump figure filling a flowery, wrap-around apron.

'I'm not keeping him on the step!' she said sharply to Annie. 'Come on Gareth. Dessay you want to see Norman. He'll be that pleased to see you. He's in the front room, reading the paper. Annie, move yourself and go and get us all a cup of tea, girl.'

Annie went away, muttering under her breath and Gareth smiled to himself as he remembered how the two women were always bickering at each other and yet, as he knew, it meant nothing. If Norman criticised either of them the other leapt to her defence, but Norman simply shrugged and carried on in his slow, phlegmatic way.

Gareth stayed an hour with his old boss and learned, with no surprise, that his job was waiting for him as soon as he came back. He talked to Norman about the wood-carving he'd seen on his travels and the old man listened attentively and nodded from time to time. After a while he got up and beckoned to Gareth to follow him. Gareth imagined he was leading the way out to the workshop at the back, but instead Norman began to climb the stairs, slowly and stiffly. He paused at the first landing to get his breath, then beckoned Gareth again and began to mount the second flight. When they got to the top he paused again on the landing and indicated a door on the right.

'My bedroom,' he said. 'But never mind that. Come in here.' and he opened the door opposite and led Gareth into a large, light room, bare except for a big, solid wooden table, a kitchen chair drawn up to it, which stood among a sea of wood-shavings. There were shelves around the room and on the shelves stood the most exquisite models of birds that Gareth had ever seen. All kinds of birds, some in flight, some who looked as though they were poised to take off, some crouched as though on the nest. They were carved lovingly from different kinds of wood, carefully chosen to suit the colouring of the species of birds. Gareth stood and gazed, speechless and entranced. He heard the old man give a soft chuckle and he turned to him. 'You?' he asked in awed tones. The old man nodded. 'I never knew.' Gareth said.

'Nobody does.' Norman said. 'Them two down there don't come in here. I don't let them. They know I'm doing something with wood, but then I'm always doing something with wood, so they don't take any notice. If I let 'em in they'd start cleaning up.' He looked down at the carpet of wood shavings with something of pride in his face. 'Nice, innit? Better than an old carpet anyday.' And he laughed until he began to cough.

'Can I pick one up?' Gareth asked, reverently.

'Aye, go on. Nobody's ever handled them birds, but you've got the feel for wood like me. Go on, then. Pick one up.'

He watched as Gareth chose a kestrel in full flight, cradling the bird in his hands, stroking the sheen on the wood of the outstretched wings, noting the lift of the bird's head and the sharpness of the eyes where the wood was darkened. He stared at it for a long time, his heart swelling with joy at the beauty of it and the skill it revealed. At length he placed it carefully back on the shelf, then moved along the walls, gloating over each bird and shaking his head from time to time at the wonder of them.

'Are you coming back to work for me?' asked the old man.

'Oh, yes, please!' Gareth said, eagerly.

'Would you like to learn how to do that?' Norman queried, his arm moving in an arc as he indicated the birds.

'Oh, would I!' Gareth croaked, overcome. 'Would you really teach me?'

'Aye,' The old man nodded. 'But it'll be after working hours, and you'll have to keep your mouth shut, boy! Above all, dunna tell them two down there what we're doin'. You can say you're learnin' to make summat.' He shrugged. 'Chair legs or summat. They wunna know the difference. I canna do with oul' wimmin pokin' round the place. I have enough all day.'

Gareth promised he wouldn't say a word. He noticed that the old man carefully locked the door when they went out and dropped the big key in his pocket, which he tapped and then grinned and winked at Gareth. When they descended the stairs and returned to the front room they were immediately joined by the two women, who must have heard them coming and produced yet another tray of tea. Gareth's insides rebelled, but he forced himself to drink it and to smile pleasantly while he did so.

'Has our Norman taken you into that old room of his up the top?' Asked Annie, glaring at her brother. 'He won't let us in to clean it, so I dessay its thick with dust. He doesn't care, but what will you think of us?'

'Its fine, Annie,' Gareth assured her. 'Just fine.' And he grinned surreptitiously at Norman. They chatted for a while again and at length he left them, his mind full of the wonder of the old man's birds as he looked forward impatiently to the time when he would learn how to create these lovely models. His mood was jubilant as he swung along, across the Iron Bridge, down Broad Street, now quiet as the evening dusk began to fall. He was no drinker, so he passed the pubs on the way, the Elephant and Castle, the Black Boy, the Castle Vaults and as he neared home, the Queen's Head. He surprised his contemporaries when, invited to go drinking, he replied that it seemed daft to him to pay good money to make yourself more stupid than you already were, but laughed so heartily and good naturedly that they couldn't take offence. Alcohol simply didn't appeal to him.

When he went to bed that night his mind was too full of what he'd seen and done during the evening that he found he was unable to get to sleep, so he lay on his back, hearing the branches of the Rectory trees rustle in the night breeze, and the sad hoot of an owl in those same trees, the tall and lovely old chestnuts that stood in the field below the Rectory, where his Dada Rees, his grandfather, worked as coachman gardener. He thought of the old man now. He had mainly only known him as a rheumaticky old figure in the wooden armchair by the fire, but he was a legend in the family, and Gareth wished he'd known him as a younger man. He felt they would have enjoyed each other. He locked his hands behind his head and gazed out at the night sky beyond his window, thinking if he began to count the stars, as he'd done as a child in Canada, he would fall asleep. But it didn't seem to work here in Newtown.

He fell to thinking of Roma. He wondered why he had found her so disturbing when in fact she had been so quiet and serene. He had had little contact with girls, except for Rhiannon, and he wondered if the contrast between her and Roma had accounted for his interest in the latter. He didn't think he could fall in love with Roma, at least he hoped not, but he found his thoughts turned to her again and again. He shook his head and began to think instead of Norman and his beautiful birds. To think he had worked with the old man for all those months before he was called up and never knew about the old man's secret. In his mind he was once again in the room at the top of the house in Crescent Street, treading the soft, sweet-smelling carpet of sawdust and handling the birds, one after another, a rook, fashioned from dark wood, a chaffinch, its rosy breast shining like satin, and so many other lovely species, but above all, that kestrel with the spread wings. It was easy to imagine the kestrel, hovering high in a current of air like a free spirit above the earth.

When he came back for good he would work hard for old Norman, learning from the skilled old carpenter this trade that he loved. And then in his spare time he would go with the old man to the room under the eaves and learn that extra craft, until he, too, could carve and fashion a hovering kestrel like Norman's.

Thus he finally fell asleep, to dream of flying birds with shiny wings.

Homecomings and Shocks

The skies over Newtown were grey and cloud hung over the hills the following afternoon when Gareth set off to Mattie and Llew's house, mainly to enquire after Jim. A fine drizzle hung like mist across the town and Gareth shivered, thinking that it would soon be Autumn. The talk at home was all about Lena and the fact that her baby was overdue. However, Owen had called in to say that he had taken Kathleen up to Plasgwyn, where Nan was going to look after her while Lena went into the hospital. It seemed that at last Lena's pains had started and a woman neighbour was walking to the hospital with her. Owen was now rushing to catch them up. The business of birth was remote from Gareth and he put it from his mind as he huddled under his waterproof cape, which had done good service as a groundsheet and was looking worse for wear, but still rainproof. It was Thursday afternoon and early closing day, so the town was very quiet as he hurried through, the fine rain beading his eyelashes and dripping off the fair hair which his forage cap did little to cover.

He was glad to reach the cottage in Frankwell Street, where a delighted Mattie opened the door to him and drew him inside without ceremony.

'Take that old cape off and hang it behind the door, Gareth love. And your cap. There now, come in to the fire. I'll get you a towel to wipe your face. The old rain isn't heavy but its the wettingest rain there is.' She left the room with a little laugh and came back with a clean, white towel which she handed to Gareth. 'Its good to see you, boy. Sit down, sit down. Llew is working and Jim is in his room.' She lowered her voice. 'He still won't come out of his room except to go to the ty bach, you know. I suppose they've told you about it at Pool Road? Your

Uncle Llew says its because of the prison camp. I think he'll come round, given time,' she added, stoutly. 'He's been through a lot, I dessay, though he won't tell us about it.' She sighed and plucked at her apron. 'But there, I'll make us a cup of tea. Sit you there and dry off by the fire. I won't be a minute.'

Gareth grinned behind the towel as he dried his face and rubbed his hair. The cup of tea was inevitable, he thought, wherever you went. Coffee was still rare here, although more prevalent than tea on the continent. He liked coffee, had acquired a taste for it, but he had little hope of being offered it here at the moment.

Mattie came back with a tray with three cups on it and a plate of scones, thick with butter. Gareth's mouth watered. He'd had a good dinner, but the scones tempted him. Then she fetched in the big old brown pot and poured out the tea. 'Help yourself to milk and sugar, love, while I take a cup up for Jim,' she said.

'When you go up ask him if he'll see me,' Gareth suggested. 'Ask him if I can come up?'

Mattie looked at him doubtfully and drew in her breath sharply. 'Well, I'll ask, love, but I doubt he'll see you. He won't see anybody but me and Llew just now. But I'll take his tea up and I'll ask. You won't be offended if he says no will you?' she said, anxiously.

'Course not!' Gareth replied, sipping the hot tea. 'Just see what he says, right?'

She nodded and left the room, carrying the cup of tea and a plate with two scones on it, and leaving Gareth musing on how many cups of tea he had drunk since he came home. He hoped tea didn't affect your kidneys. The Rees's liked their tea strong. Like bull's blood, his father used to complain.

He could hear murmuring from upstairs and in a moment Mattie appeared looking bemused. 'Well, would you believe!' she said. 'He says he'd like to see you! Go you on up, Gareth. Mind the stairs, now. They're right steep. He's in the room on the right. Well, I'm blessed!' she added with a pleased smile. 'Fancy that!'

Gareth mounted the steep and narrow stairs, his boots noisy on the linoleum treads. He opened the door on the right after tapping lightly and hearing Jim call 'Come in.' It was a pleasant room, light and airy, and the window where Jim was standing looking out faced the river. He turned as Gareth came in and the latter was shocked at the thin and ravaged face that was turned to face him.

'Hello, Jim,' Gareth said softly. 'How're you doing?'

Jim shrugged and pointed to the only chair in the room, 'Sit down,' he said, and sat on the bed, facing Gareth. 'Thanks for coming. I can't face most people.' He was silent for a moment and turned his head to stare out of the window. 'Daresay folks think I'm being awkward. I thought perhaps you'd understand, being through the war and all that.' He was silent again and Gareth nodded. 'I do understand, I think. I know its different for you. Being locked up, like. But its people wanting to know what it was like. How can you tell them what it was like? Unless you've been through it you can't picture what it was like. I know I don't want to talk about it, and all the lads in my mob feel the same. We want to put it behind us now. They don't seem to understand that we've done things we'd never have done normally. I've killed people. People I don't know. People I've had no quarrel with. But it was me or them and what do you do? I never ever thought I'd kill somebody. I never even liked killing spiders. But there, that's war. There's no glory to it. It's a dirty, foul business. Thank God its over.'

Jim turned to face him again. He stared at Gareth in silence for a moment, then he said in a low voice, 'I thought you'd understand and you do, don't you? I'm afraid of people. Afraid they'll keep asking me things and I can't tell them. I want to forget it all. Funny, isn't it? I couldn't wait to get out of that camp, dreamed about it every night. Thought about Newtown and the Bryn Bank and the Crow's Lump, and the River and this little house and my Mam and Dad. When they let us out, the Yanks it was that liberated us. I couldn't believe it. And then, well, it was all too much for me. Fair play, they organised everything, right from the camp on our journey home and I was all right while I was still with the army. But they turned me loose when we got to England, just gave me the train ticket and turned me loose.' He was silent again, plucking at the counterpane with thin, nervous fingers, his face twisted as though in pain.

Gareth reached out and patted his shoulder, feeling the thin bones under the woollen sweater he was wearing. 'Take your time, mate,' he sad, reassuringly. 'It's all right. It's going to be all right.'

Jim nodded but then his face seemed to collapse and he covered it with his hands, his shoulders shaking with deep, agonised sobs. Gareth moved over to sit beside him on the bed and put his arm round the heaving shoulders. He said nothing, just gripped Jim firmly and let him cry.

After a while the sobs died away and Gareth took out his handkerchief and handed it to Jim, who took it shamefacedly, blew his nose and wiped his eyes. Gareth then moved back to his chair. 'Look, don't feel badly about crying,' he said. 'I guess it'll do you good to let go.' He got up and went over to the washstand, where he wet a flannel in the washbasin, wrung it out and took it over to Jim, who wiped his face with it, sighed deeply, and for the first time smiled tentatively at Gareth.

'I do feel better,' Jim said, nodding. 'You see, the journey home was a nightmare. I suppose you'd say I'd lost my confidence. I should have wired Mam to say I was coming, but I just got on to the train and came. I didn't seem to be able to take the freedom and I was frightened to see anybody when I did get home. I couldn't have gone out if you'd paid me. I look out and see the people crossing the Iron Bridge and I have a nightmare. Somehow I see them all crowding me, talking at me, asking questions, questions, questions.' He paused and blew his nose again. 'It's daft, isn't it? Real daft!' He gave a harsh laugh and got up to stand at the window again.

'Look,' Gareth said. 'You've had enough for today. I'll come again tomorrow if you like?'

'Yes, please,' Jim whispered, nodding his head. 'I'd like that. That's if you don't mind. Not much fun for you, is it?' He turned to face Gareth and there was something in his face that touched Gareth to the heart. 'It's all right,' he said. 'I'd like to come. Are you OK now? You haven't drunk your tea and its cold now. Look, I'll take it down and get a fresh cup off your Mam, all right?' and he took the cup of cold tea and carried it down the stairs.

Mattie was sitting at the kitchen table, her teacup cradled in her hands. She looked at him a little apprehensively over the rim. 'Well, how did you find him? Did he talk to you?'

Gareth smiled reassuringly and put the cup of cold tea on the table.

'Yes, we had quite a chat. He'll be all right, you know. He needs a bit of time to adjust, but he'll be all right. I'd like to come again tomorrow, talk a bit more, maybe even coax him to come for a little walk with me. I don't know, we'll see. But he'll be all right. You're doing the right thing, not trying to rush him, not asking too many questions. Don't worry, for his sake.' He laughed. 'Lord, hark at me! Doctor Jones, no less.'

Mattie laughed too. 'Well, lad, you've done him more good than the doctor has, anyway. Come whenever you like. You're the first one he's been willing to see. Oh, I feel better about him now. Thanks, Gareth.'

'Oh, we'll soon have him out and about again, you'll see.' said Gareth. 'Now he could do with a nice hot cup of tea. That one went cold while we were talking. I'll go now anyway. I'll let myself out, you make that tea for Jim.' He put on the cape from behind the door and perched his forage cap on his head. He called 'Cheerio' and went out into the late afternoon, which showed signs of clearing up.

When he got back to No.46, Nell was home from work and Owen was sitting at the table, while Nell prepared the evening meal. Owen was in buoyant mood. 'Congratulate me, Gareth boy. I'm now the proud father of a fine big son!'

Gareth grinned. 'Congratulations! That what you wanted? Mind, there's not a wide choice is there!'

'No,' laughed Owen. 'But we got what we wanted, both of us. He was a real bouncer! Eight pounds, no less. He's to be called Matthew after Lena's Grandad and William after my Grandad. Matthew is what he'll be, anyway.'

'H'm. Very biblical,' said Gareth. 'Anyway, well done you.'

'And that's not the only good news, either,' said Owen. 'I've just been up to Davy's house and they had a letter from Edward today. He'll be home next Monday, for good, too. Nan's like a dog with two tails, and so is Davy. They deserve a bit of good news for a change. Losing Huw knocked them about badly. They've been bricks to take in that Roma. Oh don't get me wrong, she's a nice girl and they've really taken to that little David. But I can't help wondering what Edward will make of it all.' He stood up. 'Oh, well, I must go. Find myself a bit of grub before I go back up to the hospital for the evening visit.'

Nell came in from the back-kitchen just then. 'Indeed you won't go,' she said. 'You'll stay and have a bite with us. There's plenty here. It'll be about half-an-hour yet, so just you sit there and rest yourself. I bet you didn't get much sleep last night.'

'Not a lot,' admitted Owen. 'Well, if you're sure? It'd be better than going back to an empty house. Though I'll have to get used to that for a few days. How long do you think they'll keep her in, Nell?'

'Oh, about ten days, I think. Anyway, you come across for your evening meal with us. Don't forget now. Kathleen will be fine with Nan and Davy, they'll love having her and she can toddle around with little David.'

'Aye, they were good friends already, when I went up there. It'll be a relief if I can come to you for a bit of grub at tea time. I'm not much of a cook. Thanks, Nell, you're a good 'un.'

Nell laughed. 'You'll be taking pot luck, I warn you. I don't have a lot of time for making the meal after I come from work. But I've got some news, as well!' She looked round and winked at Gareth. 'I gave in my notice at the factory today. I always said I'd stop work when you came home, Gareth. Mattie gave her notice in as soon as Jim came home, but she couldn't work out her notice so she had to lose some of her money. But she's not worried. She can always make a bit with her sewing. I've been putting a bit by, so we'll be all right, and you'll be starting back with Norman Oliver in a couple of weeks, so you'll be able to put a bit in for your keep. Oh, yes, we'll be all right.'

When Rhiannon heard that Edward was soon to come home and as yet Sean hadn't been told when he was getting demobbed, she found it hard to contain her impatience. 'Why is it that everyone's getting home before Sean? Its just not fair!' This was the daily refrain and although the family sympathised with her they got a little tired of it.

'Different regiments have different schedules for demob,' explained Gareth. 'After all, I'm not officially out yet, though I think it'll be straight away after I go back to H.Q. Your Sean will be home soon, never fear, and then you'll be flitting off to Ireland. I'm looking forward to meeting this Irishman of yours. He's a brave man to take you on, little sister!'

'Don't you 'little sister' me, boy!' Rhiannon replied, laughing, 'You wait till my Sean comes back. He'll eat you for dinner if you try to bully me.'

Gareth flinched in mock horror. 'I wouldn't dare! I don't fancy taking on a wild Irishman!'

'He's not wild, either!' Rhiannon said, pouting.

'By the way,' Gareth said, curiously. 'How are you getting on with the Catholic Church? D'you go to confession and all that?'

'Of course.' replied Rhiannon, with a toss of her head and Gareth shook his head in wonder. 'Can't imagine it somehow,' and ducked.

Nan and Davy were at the station to meet the twelve o'clock train on Monday. Nan was happy and sad at the same time. Only one of her chicks was coming back to the nest. She knew Davy felt the same. But she was smiling happily when Edward stepped off the train with his kit and she was able to fold him in her arms. At least this one was safe. She stepped back and watched as he gave his father a hug. She took in the tall frame, the mature look in the steady grey eyes and saw the sun glint on the golden hair, the same colour as her hair had been before it had acquired the tinge of silver. She was pleased to see that his frame had filled out and broadened.

Edward looked around him, seeing on one side of the railway the green fields of the Rock farm and on the other the tall, imposing buildings of Pryce Jones's Royal Welsh Warehouse. He sighed and smiled at his mother and father. 'Now I know I'm home,' he said. 'Nothing much changes in Newtown. Thank God!'

'No,' agreed Davy. 'There aren't many changes. The other boys are home, Jim and Gareth.' They were all silent for a moment, thinking of Huw, but Davy hurried on, not wanting to spoil the homecoming. 'Jim's not been so well after the prison camp, but Gareth's been to see him and says he'll be all right.'

They were walking down Station Road and as they turned the corner into Kerry Road, Edward stopped for a moment, looking around him eagerly. 'God, its good to see everything looking the same. I can't wait to get into my own room, sleep in my own bed, after all these years.'

Davy and Nan looked at each other. It was Davy who spoke. 'We've got Roma staying with us at the moment. She was Huw's girl, remember. She came to us after he was killed. She was expecting Huw's baby. She had nowhere to go except to us. Of course we took her in, what else could we do? She's a nice girl and she had a little boy. Toddling now. We couldn't explain it all to you in the bits of letters we were able to get to you. We thought it best to wait until you got home.'

They were still standing on the corner and Edward was listening in silence. Then he said,' You mean she's still there?'

Davy nodded and Nan watched her son apprehensively. He was frowning and it was clear that he didn't like the idea of a strange girl in the house. Especially one who seemed to be taking the place of his brother. He was finding it hard enough to come to terms with the fact that Huw wasn't going to be there. The loss of the lively, vibrant Huw was an agony to him, and he wanted no reminders to make it harder to deal with his memories. He gave a grunt now and turned towards Plasgwyn, some of the happiness of his homecoming dimmed. Nan and Davy followed, glancing at each other. Davy shrugged and shook his head but Nan felt sure that it would be all right when Edward met the nice, quiet Roma and surely he couldn't help loving the little boy who looked so like Huw?

Roma had the dinner ready by the time they came in and was in the middle of laying the table. She had just put David up for his midday nap and now she heard Edward go up the stairs and hoped the child wouldn't wake up. Nan and Davy came in to the kitchen. 'There now, you've got everything ready for us, Roma, good girl,' said Nan, brightly. 'Edward's just gone up to put his kit away and wash his hands. I'm sure he'll be ready for a bite to eat. David gone for his nap, has he?'

Roma nodded and went to check the vegetables and the meaty lamb chops sizzling in the oven. 'I've made a drop of mint sauce to go with the lamb,' she said quietly. 'It's all ready now, I'll just mash the potatoes.' She had been feeling vaguely uncomfortable about the return of this stranger, Huw's brother, fearing he would see her as an interloper. She had asked Nan whether he was like Huw and Nan had laughed and said, 'Not a bit! Not even in looks. Edward's as fair as Huw was dark, and they're not alike in their ways. Edward was always the quiet one, serious, and the right sort to be a lawyer! Now Huw,' she had paused and had blinked away a tear. 'Well, you know what Huw was like. So alive, so bright, so funny.' On that she had turned her back and stared out of the window and Roma was sorry she had asked.

Now that she was about to meet this brother of Huw's there was a fluttering of apprehension in her stomach. She had heard of his broken love affair with Ruth and wondered what effect that had had on him. Did he know that Ruth was married now? Somehow she didn't think that Nan and Davy had told him in their letters. They seemed to think he would have got over it by now. When she heard him come down the stairs she went on straining the vegetables and putting them into dishes, until Nan's voice made her turn round and confront the stranger. 'This is Roma,' said Nan on a cheerful note. 'Roma, this is Edward, our son.'

As Roma held out a tentative hand she saw a tall, grey-eyed man, with corn-coloured hair, high cheekbones and a square jaw. She saw, fleetingly, that he was very like his mother, but his expression was more remote than friendly and when his hand clasped hers it was cool and brief. He nodded to her, said 'How are you?' and turned away to take his place at the table. She felt herself flush a little and glanced towards Nan, but she was carrying the vegetables to the table and seemed unaware of Roma's discomfort. Edward ignored her as she took her place beside him and was coolly polite as he passed vegetables to her, engaging Davy in conversation, meanwhile.

Roma was glad when the meal was finished and she could insist on washing up while Nan and Davy followed Edward to the front room. Edward had turned in the doorway, nodded to Roma and said 'Thank you. The dinner was very nice.' and was gone before she could answer. She felt a little spurt of anger. He had acted as though she was a servant-girl! She leaned over the sink and felt the tears filling her eyes. She had felt so comfortable here, so wanted and Nan and Davy had been so kind, but now? The coming of this unfriendly man, so unlike Huw, looked like making a difference. If he kept this up would she even feel able to stay here?

The rest of the day passed unhappily for Roma. Nan and Davy were so happy and absorbed in the return of their son that they didn't seem to be aware of the frisson of dislike between Edward and Roma. When Roma had fetched David down, she kept him in the kitchen, until Davy came through and snatched him up in his arms, crying, 'David my boy, come and meet your Uncle Edward. Come on through, now, Roma. No need to hide. You mustn't be shy of Edward, you must get to know each other. Come on, show this fine lad off and then we'll have a cup of tea.'

Roma was about to protest that she would stay to make the tea, but Davy ushered her through in front of him and Nan insisted she sat on the settee beside Edward. Then Davy put David down in front of Edward and with a possessive air said 'Now, what do you think of this lad?'

Edward drew in a breath as he stared at the little boy standing in front of him, his thumb in his mouth hiding a tentative smile. What Edward saw was Huw in miniature and for a moment the pain was sharp and he closed his eyes. There was a brief silence and little David gave his mother an uncertain look. She leaned forward and drew him onto her knee, hugging him to her. Then she rose and went to the door carrying the child with her. 'I'll go and make a cup of tea,' she said quietly, and Nan answered, brightly, 'That would be lovely, Roma, dear,' while Davy frowned and looked uncomfortable.

As soon as possible that evening Roma escaped to her room with David, saying she had a slight headache and would have an early night. She sat miserably on the edge of her bed while David fetched his story book from the chair by his little bed and demanded a story. After she had read to him she washed him, undressed him and tucked him in his bed, hugging him convulsively as she kissed him goodnight. Then she returned to sit on her bed and gave herself up to unhappy thoughts. She didn't like Huw's brother, but she had to admit that it must have been a bit of a shock to come home and find her installed here with her child. Maybe it was natural for him to feel a bit resentful. She supposed that he had thought a lot of his brother and it must hurt to be reminded of him. Then perhaps he didn't approve of her unmarried status. She turned onto her stomach and pressed her face into the pillow. 'Oh, Huw!' she whispered. 'Why did you leave me?' and release came in the slow, hot tears that soaked the pillow before she fell asleep.

The next day Edward was a little more relaxed over breakfast and said 'Good morning' to Roma as she carried the big brown tea-pot to the table, while Nan cooked bacon and eggs and fried bread for them all. He watched intently as Roma cut David's bread into 'soldiers' so that he could dip them into the yolk of his fried egg. But when Roma looked up and caught his eye he looked away quickly and began to talk to his father. From time to time he appeared to glance surreptitiously at the little boy with a curious look on his face, but he made no attempt to speak to the child, although he did turn to Roma at one stage and ask her, in what was obviously an effort at politeness, how she liked living in Newtown, but hardly gave her a chance to answer before he turned again to his father.

Later Roma was relieved when Edward went out. He had remembered that it was Market Day on Tuesday and said he would go and look round the stalls. In truth he wanted to see if he could see Ruth, although he was too proud to tell his mother and father so. He had not forgotten her and over the time he had been away he had begun to feel that he should have made more of an attempt to see her again before he went. He thought he might meet her in the town if she was shopping at the market and maybe, just maybe, they could start again. If he could make her listen while he told her what exactly had happened with Rhiannon that night, he was sure they could put it all behind them and make a fresh start. He wanted to go to Martin's office after dinner to see when he could start back. He was eager to resume his career and get his finals and if he could make it up with Ruth it would be a whole new start. His step was jaunty as he made his way down Kerry Road and along Short Bridge street. His mind was full of plans and although he stopped from time to time to greet people he knew, who were glad to see him back, he was eager to look for Ruth, who held the key to those plans.

He felt if he could resolve that quarrel with her, they could get engaged again, for he still had the ring, and then quite quickly they could get married and find a small house somewhere, just big enough so that they could make a start. His gratuity would buy some of the furniture. On the other hand, maybe they could stay at the Bryn where there was plenty of room, until they could afford a decent house. He didn't want to stay at Plasgwyn now, he felt it had been taken over by that quiet girl with the baby, and although he knew that she and the little boy helped to make his father and mother happy, he didn't feel like sharing his home with them.

He was so absorbed in his plans that he had almost bumped into Ruth in the Market Hall before he was aware of her. He stopped and stared at her, his heart turning over. He noticed she had flushed an unbecoming scarlet, but put it down to embarrassment.

'Hello, Ruth,' he said softly. 'How are you? Its good to see you. I was hoping I might run into you.'

She tried to stammer some answer and made as though to walk around him, but he blocked her way. 'Look, Ruth,' he said, pleadingly. 'Can't we forget that quarrel? You must know by now that it was my cousin's fault that night. I know I should have tried harder to explain, but I was so hurt that you had believed her before hearing my side. I've thought a lot about you while I've been away. I'd really like us to try again. Couldn't we?'

He could see she was very agitated, but it was when she put her left hand up to her throat that, with a terrible shock, he saw why. He stared at the gold band on her wedding finger and froze. For a moment neither of them said anything, then Ruth, her eyes wet with tears, whispered 'Sorry, Edward,' and once again made to go past.

Edward put out a hand and grasped her arm. 'Who was it?' he asked hoarsely.

'No one you know,' she said in a low voice. 'An Irish soldier. Jimmy Quinn. We've been married for two years now. He's going to settle in Newtown.'

At first Edward had flushed, but now he was very pale, with a pinched look round his mouth and his eyes bleak. When she winced he realised he had tightened his grip on her arm and was hurting her. For a fleeting moment he was glad she was hurt, but then, being Edward, he slowly released his hold on her arm and stepped back to let her pass. 'Sorry I bothered you,' he said, his voice bitter. 'I hope you're happy.'

Ruth's gaze was troubled as she stood for a moment longer. 'I really am sorry, Edward, please believe me.' She put her hand on his arm in a conciliatory gesture, but he stepped back proudly, his face closed. 'Goodbye, Ruth,' he said, and turned and walked stiffly away. She stared after him sadly but he didn't look round and she went on her way to finish her shopping, soon forgetting him in anticipation of seeing her Jimmy, from whom she had had a letter this morning to say that he would be home at the end of the week.

As for Edward he walked back through the market in a daze. He had been so convinced that she had waited for him as he had for her that he just couldn't take it in that she now belonged to someone else. Over the years he had been away, the vision and idea of Ruth had always been at the back of his mind and one of the reasons why he had so looked forward to getting home was to see her and try to start again where they had left off. He had convinced himself that they could do this, both swallowing their pride and making a fresh start. Now, in one brief moment, all his dreams had crumbled away. He wandered into Broad Street and hardly thinking where he was going, walked down Old Church Street, which led to the small park which had once been the churchyard attached to old St Mary's Church, now a ruin, but with the tower still standing among the prettily laid out park. He sat on a seat there, glad of the solitude, and tried to come to terms with the blow which he had received.

The first thing he realised was that Ruth couldn't have been as much in love with him as he had been with her. That seemed obvious now, but he realised with some bitterness that it should have been obvious at the time of the quarrel. She had been very quick to hand back his ring, and to believe Rhiannon without giving him a chance to explain. He gave a short laugh. How could he really have imagined she would just be waiting here, ready to pick up the threads again. It was different for him, he could see now. He was in another world, so to speak, fighting his way through North Africa and up through Italy, and, he supposed, he had had to have something to cling to, something to fight for, almost. He leaned his head against the back of the seat and stared up at the tower. How long had that been there? Since the thirteenth or fourteenth century, he supposed. It had seen many thousands of men come and go, been remote from their troubles and simply pointed the way to God. He fell to wondering how much faith he still had in God after all that he had seen of horror during the war. He tried saying the Our Father and as the familiar words came to his mind he felt some degree of comfort, realising that at least God didn't alter, He didn't let you down. He sat on a little longer until a cool breeze began to chill him, hinting at the autumn to come. A big magnolia tree grew in the middle of one of the lawns, but its blossom was brown and curled, only its leaves were green and glossy. Whatever happened to humans, nature carried on uncaring. He realised with surprise that he didn't feel nearly as bad as he thought he would. He was coming to accept that he had been dreaming of the idea of Ruth, rather than the reality. He stood up and stretched his legs, walking over to the wall that bordered the river below and leaned on it, watching the river flow by. That was something else that ran on, no matter what happened. He felt vaguely cheered now the rawness of the shock of the sight of that wedding ring was wearing off. He shrugged and left the park, walking along the riverside path and climbing up onto the Iron Bridge, deciding to go to Esther's and say hello to her before returning home for dinner, which he found he was reluctant to do.

He found the little sweetshop at the far end of the bridge was closed, so he had to carry on empty-handed. Anyway, he guessed the children would be in school, having started again at the beginning of September. But Esther had a new baby now, his mother had told him, and so had Owen's Lena. For a moment he wondered sadly if he would ever be in the position of being father to a baby. What was he, thirty? He gave a small chuckle as he climbed the steps of Bay House. Plenty of time yet, if he could ever find the right girl. He knocked and entered and Esther came hurrying from the kitchen to see who it was. She exclaimed delightedly when she saw Edward and threw her arms round him, giving him a hearty kiss on the cheek.

He held her away from him and looked down at her affectionately. 'Well, in spite of all these numerous offspring, you don't look a day older than when I went away!' he said, and meant it.

'Oh go away with you,' said Esther with a pleased laugh. 'I'm not going to say the same to you. You have changed. You look older and wiser and much, much more handsome! How can you walk down Broad Street without being mobbed by females?'

He gave a rueful laugh. 'I should be so lucky, as the Jews say. Funnily enough I was just thinking as I was coming up Bryn Street, that all you lot are married and producing offspring and here am I, without even a female on the horizon.'

'Oh, that'll soon alter,' said Esther, gaily. 'It won't be long before you'll be wondering which one to choose!'

'D'you think so?' he said, his eyebrows raised.

'Oh, come on!' she replied. 'What's wrong with you? You only got back yesterday, didn't you? You haven't had a chance to weigh up the talent yet!' which cheered him up, and made him smile.

9

Walks and Feelings

On Tuesday afternoon Gareth was making his way along by the Bridge
Wall, on his way to see Jim. It was a nice afternoon, with the sharpness
of Autumn in the air, and he noticed that the trees on the Rackfield
were taking on the colours of Autumn. The big chestnut at the entrance
to the Gravel was golden, and there was evidence that the children had
been battering at the branches to bring down the conkers. Sitting on the
Bridge Wall looking morose was Gwilym the Sticks, who looked up at
the approach of Gareth and nodded at him.

'Hey up. You're back home then?' he said. 'Home for good is it?'

'Well, not altogether yet,' Gareth replied. 'Got to go back to H.Q.,
but only for a couple of weeks, for demob, you know.' He leaned his
elbows on the wall beside Gwilym and looked out over the river.

'Oh, aye. Back in civvy street then for you. Goin' back to work for
Norman Oliver, are you?'

Gareth nodded. 'Yes, thank the Lord. I've had enough of army life. I
never wanted to go, anyway, but there you are.' he shrugged. 'There was
no choice. Anyway, its over now and the sooner we get back to normal
the better.'

'I suppose so,' said Gwilym, doubtfully. 'D'you know, I sort of enjoyed
the war. Oh, I know it was different for you young 'uns that had to go
and fight. But for us stayin' at home, well, it was a bit of excitement,
like. Did Owen tell you about the parachutist on the Rackfield. God,
that was somethin'!' His eyes had brightened at the memory.

Gareth laughed. 'Yes, but it wasn't a real parachutist, was it? Just an
old sheet that had blown off the line and covered up Jack Evans, right?'

'Ah but we did'n know that at the time, did we? We went in an' held him at gunpoint!' Gwilym's voice rose in pride. 'If it 'ad been a Jerry we'd 'ave captured 'im. Then we'd 'ave been a right lot of heroes. Dessay we'd 'ave 'ad our photos in the papers an' all.' He sighed and looked wistful. 'Instead of that we 'ad our legs pulled for weeks after. It made me wish I'd 'ave been young enough to go to fight. We 'ad the guns an' the training, d'you see, but no enemies.'

'Never mind, Gwilym,' said Gareth. 'I daresay you wouldn't have liked it. Its not exciting when you're in the thick of it. It frightens you to death. Especially if you're like poor old Jim and get taken prisoner. You know, Llew and Mattie's Jim? I think he's had a pretty rough time of it.'

'Ah, so I heard. Won't come out or anythin'. In pretty bad shape, they say. He hasn't gone round the bend, has he?' Gwilym asked, frowning.

'Good Lord, no!' said Gareth. 'No, no. He'll be all right. Just finding it hard to come to terms with being loose, so to speak.' 'Wish I had a chance to be loose,' Gwilym grumbled. 'I've never been loose since I got married. You think very careful before you go down that road, my boy. It all looks all right from a distance. But once you're hitched, look out. Love 'em and leave 'em is the best way, my lad. You remember that. I loved 'em but I did'n leave 'em quick enough.' he said, with a rueful chuckle.

'I'll bear that it mind,' said Gareth, laughing, and went on his way. When he reached the house in Frankwell, Mattie answered the door and drew him inside eagerly. 'He's been asking about you,' she said. 'Asking what time you were coming. He's eaten better today, too. I think you're doing him good, Gareth, lad. Anyway, go on up and I'll bring you both a cup of tea.'

Gareth mounted the stairs and entered Jim's room. Certainly he looked a little better, there was more life in his face as he smiled and welcomed Gareth in. 'How are you doing now, Jim?' the latter asked, and Jim answered 'I'm a bit better, I think. I enjoyed my dinner today.'

'Your Mam is making us a cup of tea. What about coming downstairs for it? Save your Mam coming up, isn't it? There's only your Mam and me there, anyway.'

For a moment Jim looked like a trapped animal, slowly shaking his head. He was silent for a moment, then he said,' Suppose somebody was to come? I don't think I could face people yet.'

'Well, please yourself,' Gareth said easily. ' I just thought it would be a change of scenery. Tell you what, we could lock the door. Then if anybody did come, you could nip back upstairs if you couldn't face them. How about that?'

Jim looked at him doubtfully, 'I suppose you think I'm being daft. It's just something I can't help. That camp was such a nightmare. I can't put it behind me somehow.'

'Oh well, give it time,' said Gareth, reassuringly. 'We'll just sit here and have a chat.' and he sat on the chair opposite Jim.

'No!' said Jim, suddenly, getting up and clutching Gareth's arm. 'Come on. I'll go down. You go first, will you. Lock the door, right?'

Gareth patted his arm and got up, going towards the door and opening it. Jim hesitated and then followed him slowly as he descended the stairs. Mattie appeared at the bottom with a tray of tea in her hand and stared up at the sight of Jim quietly and carefully coming down towards her. She said nothing, but took the tray into the kitchen and laid the cups out on the table, while Gareth went and locked the door, winking at her as he passed. Jim hesitated at the bottom of the stairs and turned to look back up.

'Come on, love,' said Mattie, encouragingly. 'There's nobody here 'sides me and Gareth. Come and drink your tea, good boy.'

At length Jim came in to the kitchen and sat down. He started to sip his tea, looking round him at the room as though he had never seen it before. But eventually he relaxed and began to talk to Gareth and soon he was chatting quite naturally, while Mattie looked on with a broad smile.

Gareth stayed for an hour or so, but before he went he had persuaded Jim to stay down until Llew came home. Mattie saw him to the door and unlocked it for him. She thanked him with brimming eyes but he brushed away her thanks, gave her a peck on the cheek and set off up the steps to the bridge. He decided to go up to Plasgwyn to see if Edward was in, not admitting to himself that he had a sneaking desire to see Roma again. She had intrigued him, her quietness and remoteness. She was different from girls of his age, although she couldn't have been much older than him. He hurried through the town, exchanging hellos with friends from time to time, until he was letting himself through the green door into the yard at Plasgwyn.

He tapped and entered through the back door and there she was, laying out the tea things while the small boy sat in a tiny chair beside the fire eating a biscuit. Roma smiled and said 'Hello,' shyly and Gareth felt himself blushing like a schoolboy, so he went over and bent down to speak to the child. The little boy, seeing this large man looming over him, set up a wail for his Mama, which brought Roma hurrying to pick him up. 'They're all in the front room,' she said to Gareth. 'Go on through. I'll be bringing some tea in a minute.'

Gareth mumbled something and escaped down the passage to the front room where he found Nan and Davy sitting talking, while Edward was reading the paper. They all greeted him and he went over to sit with Edward on the settee.

'You haven't been down to Pool Road yet,' Gareth said. 'They've been expecting you.'

Edward nodded. 'I know. I'll come down this evening. I only got back yesterday. Anyway, there's plenty of time. I'm demobbed. Are you?'

'No, got to go back next week, but I should be out in about a fortnight. I suppose you'll be going back to Martin's office?'

'Yes. It'll be good to get back to work again. I hope to start back next Monday. Can't be soon enough for me, I must say.'

'Ah, here's the tea,' Davy said. 'Here, let me take that tray, Roma. Have you put a cup for yourself?'

Roma glanced at Edward out of the corner of her eye and shook her head. 'I'm seeing to David just now,' she said in a low voice and went out of the room. Nan looked uncomfortable and Gareth became aware of a slight atmosphere in the room. Edward's mouth had tightened and he hadn't raised his eyes when Roma came in. 'There's something wrong here.' thought Gareth, but he accepted the tea that Nan handed him and carried on talking to Edward about future plans in civvy street.

After he finished his tea Gareth rose to go and Edward got up too. 'If you're going home I'll come down with you. I want to see Auntie Nell and Uncle Elwyn.'

'They'll want to see you, too,' said Gareth. 'And you've nothing to fear from Rhiannon any more! She's only got eyes for her Sean!'

Edward laughed, 'So I hear. I owe her an apology, really. I was a bit hard on her last time we met. But there, maybe she did me a good turn in the end.' Edward ushered Gareth out through the front door and they strolled side by side down Kerry Road.

'Whew!' Edward gave a sigh of relief. 'It's good to get out, to tell the truth. I didn't expect to have a woman and child moved into my home while I was away, and a stranger at that. I know she was Huw's girl and its obvious that the baby is Huw's. No mistaking that. It's just so irresponsible. But that's Huw, all over. He knew better than anybody that a rear-gunner's life wasn't worth tuppence at that time, yet he goes and risks giving a girl a baby. She should have had more sense, if he didn't.' He looked broodingly down at his feet and Gareth coughed uncomfortably.

'Oh hell!' Edward exploded. 'I miss him so much. To come back home and he isn't there. To know he never will come bursting into my bedroom again to borrow a fag, or plague me with some old daftness.' They had reached the bottom of Kerry Road now and drifted over to the Bridge Wall, where they stood side by side, leaning on the parapet.

'It was damn bad luck,' said Gareth. 'A hell of a lot of good blokes copped it in the RAF at that time. It was pretty suicidal, I guess.'

'That's why I'm surprised he got tangled up with this girl. I thought at least he'd got more sense than that. And what's she going to do? She's not going to stay at Plasgwyn for ever, is she?'

'Don't you like her?' Gareth asked, curiously. 'She seems a very quiet girl. Helps your Mam in the house. And Uncle Davy loves the little boy.'

'I know she's quiet, but she's sort of there all the time. Makes me feel uncomfortable. I don't think she likes me, either. I just didn't expect her to be there. Reminding me of Huw. Reminding is too raw yet.' he went on, hoarsely.

'It must be hard for her, thinking she was going to marry Huw, and then being left with the baby. What else was she to do? Mam says her mother wouldn't have anything to do with her. I suppose coming here was the only thing she could do.'

Edward shrugged. 'I suppose so,' he said reluctantly. 'I don't know what I feel about her. I know Mam and Dad like her and they love the little boy. Well, he's so like Huw, isn't he?' He sighed and kicked at the

277

wall with the toe of his shoe. 'Its just - well, she's a constant reminder of Huw. And I keep thinking of her, even when I don't want to.'

'I like her,' said Gareth, softly. 'She's different.'

'Different from what?' Edward gave a hollow laugh.

'Oh, I don't know. Different from the usual run of girls, I suppose. You know what I mean.'

'I'm not sure I do. I'm not much of a judge of girls. Look at Ruth. I come back and find she's married! And there was me thinking I could take up with her again. Huh! It didn't take her long to find somebody else!'

'Well, that was partly our Rhiannon's fault, wasn't it? But didn't anybody tell you that Ruth was married?' Gareth looked at him curiously.

'No. I guess they thought I'd got over her, that I wouldn't be interested any longer.' He looked thoughtful. 'D'you know, after the first shock of finding out, I realised I didn't care. I really wasn't interested! Funny that. I'd thought about coming back to her all through the war and yet now, well, I guess you could say I'm over her. I think so, anyway!'

'It sounds as though you are.' said Gareth. 'Well, now you're free to make a fresh start. Go back to work and find another girl. I'm looking forward to going back to work, too.'

'And find a girl?' teased Edward.

'Don't know about that.' Gareth answered, blushing because a picture of Roma had come into his mind. He realised he was a fool to even think of her. What on earth would he do with a girl who brought somebody else's baby with her! He really ought to get her out of his mind. He turned away. 'Come on, let's get over to No.46. There should be a meal going shortly. You could stay and have some with us. Your Mam and Dad know where you are.'

Edward nodded and followed him across the road. At the moment he was glad to be away from Plasgwyn, at least until he could sort out his feelings about Roma. He knew it hurt his parents to see his unfriendly attitude to her and he couldn't explain it himself. He knew it was out of character for him, but at the moment he couldn't help it. As he mounted the steps to No.46 he put the puzzle from him.

At the end of that week Sean Kerrigan arrived back to claim his bride. Rhiannon could hardly contain herself and declared herself impatient to journey over to Ireland to her new home and to meet her new family. She had been in correspondence with Sean's sister throughout the war and they seemed to have struck up a friendship through their letters. However, she had to work out her notice at Pryce Jones's which would take a week and she would also need some time to get her things together and pack up their wedding presents to send over ahead of them. They reckoned on a fortnight to see them through and booked on the ferry from Heysham to Belfast for the end of the two weeks. From there they would travel up to Derry by train and Sean told them all that he couldn't wait to show off his beautiful bride to his family. Nell and Elwyn liked Sean very much as did Gareth and the rest of the Rees family. They felt that a strong hand like his would do Rhiannon the world of good, especially as she was obviously head over heels in love with him! Edward was especially pleased with Sean for removing the embarrassment of Rhiannon's unwanted attentions. Indeed, at a moment when they happened to be alone in the kitchen of No.46, and Rhiannon had attempted a blushing apology for what she had told Ruth, he was able to brush it aside with a grin and tell her, quite honestly, to forget it, as he had. He was relieved to find that it was true. He was over all that and glad of it.

On the Sunday afternoon Nell and Elwyn decided to take Rhiannon and Sean to Manafon, so that they could make their farewells to Meg and Reini, and let Sean make their acquaintance and that of Henry and his new wife, Olwen. There was no room in the car for Gareth, but he assured them that he wanted to go and see Jim, and perhaps persuade him to come for a little walk, since it was a beautiful, crisp Autumn afternoon. So, after waving the rest of them off he made his way down to Frankwell Street and knocked at the door of the little house. Mattie called: 'Come in!' and he found that the door wasn't locked, which was a good sign. Indeed, Jim was sitting at the table talking to Llew and he looked up at Gareth quite naturally and said 'Hello'. Gareth grinned at the sight and joined them at the table, where they were talking about Newtown's chances against Welshpool in the following Saturday's football match.

'They'll have to play a hell of a sight better than they did yesterday against Caersws!' growled Llew, who had been at the game. 'They were like a load of pensioners! And the Ref! I'll swear he blew up foul-throw for every 'Town throw-in! Somebody shouted, 'What's wrong this time, Ref? Is he holding the ball upside down?' Honestly, he was hopeless. I think Caersws must have hired him special!'

There was animation in Jim's face as he said 'Aw, come on, Dad. You'd have thought he was a great Ref if 'Town had won! Admit it.'

They argued good-humouredly for a while, then Gareth broached the subject of a short walk. 'Its a lovely day,' he said. 'If you wrap up warm it'll do you the world of good. We can go on up Frankwell to Canal Road and then turn up Shoddy's Lane. It'll be nice and quiet there.'

A hunted look came into Jim's eyes as he turned them pleadingly on Llew. 'Oh, I don't know if I'm ready for that yet,' he said, hoarsely. 'I just don't know.' He plucked at the table cloth with trembling fingers and Mattie watched him anxiously.

'It's all right, love,' she whispered, patting his shoulder. 'You don't have to go if you don't feel up to it.'

'No, no,' said Gareth soothingly. 'It was just an idea. You don't have to come. Maybe you and me will go, Llew?' He gave Llew a significant look.

'Aye, why not?' answered Llew. 'It's a nice afternoon. I could do with stretching my legs a bit. God, I haven't been up Shoddy's Lane for years. I hear Joffre Evans has got plans to build all round there. We'd better go and have a look while Shoddy's Lane is still there. I'll just get my coat.'

While he was talking, Jim had fixed agonised eyes on his face. He transferred his stare to Gareth and then his mother. He was breathing quickly and started to drum his fingers on the table. Gareth rose from his chair and stood looking down at him. 'Sure you won't come?' he asked Jim, gently. 'Me and Llew would be one each side of you. We can take it slow. It'll be just a nice stroll.'

Jim rose and went to stare out of the window. It was quiet and there was no-one about. Gareth could see the tension across Jim's shoulders and he went to him and put his arm round him. 'It's all right, Jim lad. You do whatever you want. If you feel it's too soon, that's all right, ok?'

Jim turned as Llew came back into the room. 'Well, who's coming then?' Llew asked in a matter-of-fact way, glancing from Gareth to Jim. The latter braced his shoulders and took a deep, shuddering breath. 'I'll come!' he announced, shakily and Mattie, her face doubtful, went to fetch his coat. She helped him on with it and smoothed the lapels. 'D'you want a muffler?' she asked. 'You mind, you've been in the warm these last few weeks. You'll be nesh.'

Jim gave a little laugh. 'Yeh, I'll have a muffler. I'll be nesh all right. And frit to death.' Tears appeared in the corners of his eyes and he brushed them away angrily. 'What sort of a bloke am I? Frit of my own shadow. Aw, come on then. Let's go before I change my mind!'

They made for the door and Llew opened it and went out first. Jim hesitated on the doorstep and for a second it seemed as though he would have turned and gone back in again, but Gareth was standing behind him and after one panic-stricken look up the Sunday-empty street, he followed Llew, and Gareth brought up the rear. Mattie stood anxiously on the doorstep and watched the men walk slowly, three-abreast, up Frankwell, until they passed out of sight at the far end, having encountered nothing but a cat crossing the street in the Sabbath calm. She sighed and sent up a little prayer of thanksgiving before going in and closing the door.

That evening Owen and his little family decided to stroll up to Plasgwyn to show off the new arrival. They wrapped up warm and with baby Matthew in his pram, carefully saved since Kathleen, and with the latter clutching her father's hand, they made their way up Stone Street and along Cross Street. They encountered Jack Richards, hobbling along painfully, full of rheumatism, the result of working out in all weathers, delivering milk in the mornings and acting as lamp-lighter in the evenings. He propelled his small bent frame slowly over to them and peered into the pram. 'Another little Rees the Parson,' he said with a chuckle as dry and rustling as the blowing Autumn leaves. 'By God, you Rees's is takin' care of the future, in't you? That sister of yourn, that Esther, 'ow many 'as her got now, then?'

Owen laughed. 'A fair few, Jack. Four of her own and two evacuees she adopted.'

Jack shook his head. 'A glutton for punishment, 'er is. But there, if that's what makes 'er 'appy. Nice little gel, 'er allus was. Allus 'ad a word to say to me. People said as 'er was stuck up, but I never found 'er so. Goin' up to your Davy's, are you? Funny set-up there. That gel of Huw's turning up an' ' avin' a baby there. Sure its Huw's, are you?' He leered up at Owen who felt a quick flare of anger, which he quickly suppressed. After all, this was only old Jack Richards the Milk, who picked up gossip from all over the town, even though he was now surely around eighty years old and retired some years. Instead he grinned at Jack and said,' Have you seen the little 'un? You wouldn't ask if you had. The spit'n image of our Huw, he is. Oh, there's no doubt about who fathered that one.'

'Oh, well, that's all right then.' Jack nodded dismissal. 'Ta-ra, now.' And he hobbled slowly towards the door of the house on the corner, where his wife, now dead and gone, had kept a little shop, accompanied by her parrot, who startled all but those used to him, by greeting them with 'What do you want, what do you want!' in a raucous voice. Folks unused to him had found themselves looking nervously round and telling the voice what they wanted, only to be confronted eventually by Mrs Richards, fixing them with her beady eyes and demanding to know what they wanted in a voice that matched the parrot's!

Owen, Lena and the children emerged onto Kerry Road and made their way to Plasgwyn. There they were greeted eagerly by Nan, who exclaimed over the bonny baby and petted little Kathleen. She drew them inside and called to Davy to come and see who the visitors were. Owen thought Davy looked a little tired and strained, but knew that he had never been strong, having a diseased valve of the heart that had kept him out of the first World War, and he was now in his sixties after all. He asked after Edward and was told he was in the front room, 'Head in a book, as usual'. There was no sign of Roma and her child as they were ushered into the front room by Nan, who hurried off to make the usual cup of tea.

Edward laid his book aside when they came in and rose to greet them. He was now in civvies, in sports coat and flannels, a blue sweater lovingly knitted by his mother and a blue and white striped shirt with a dark blue tie. Lena thought he looked very handsome, a wave of blond hair flopping over his forehead beneath which steady grey eyes softened at the sight of them, as though their visit was a relief from something.

She guessed Huw's death would hit him hard. Although they were so different in looks and temperament, they had still been very close, acting as a foil for each other, Edward quiet and steady as against Huw, volatile and impulsive. Although at times Huw had been a sore trial to the quiet Edward, she knew the latter had loved his brother and was very protective of him. She thought she detected pain in the grey eyes as he kissed her cheek in greeting and patted Kathleen's head.

'And where's the new arrival?' he asked and Lena replied, 'He's sleeping in his pram in the hall.'

'Who's he like? You or Owen?' and without thinking she answered, 'Oh, Owen, very much so. Just like you can't question that Huw was young David's father. They're so alike!'

She saw his lips tighten and his eyes grow bleak. He turned away and went back to sit in his chair. Davy glanced at him anxiously but at that moment Nan came in with a tray of tea-cups which she put down on the table under the window. Both Owen and Lena sensed strain in them all and couldn't help feeling that Edward was in some way the cause of it. They found it very puzzling since they knew how much Nan and Davy loved their eldest son, but there was definitely something in the atmosphere,

'Have you heard how young Jim is?' asked Davy, when they had all been served with their cups of tea.

'Getting better, according to Gareth,' replied Owen. 'He's been visiting Jim regularly, I believe, and seems to be doing him some good. Mind, Gareth is going back to H.Q. for demob on Tuesday, but I don't think that's going to take more than a couple of weeks, and then he'll be out for good, and back working for Norman Oliver, I hear.'

'It must be a relief for Llew and Mattie if Jim is improving,' said Nan. 'They were so worried. He wouldn't move out of his room, would he? But last I heard he was coming downstairs, anyway.'

'Yes, well, better than that,' said Owen. 'Gareth came back from there this afternoon full of excitement, when I called in at Pool Road earlier on. Jim had actually been out for a little walk with Gareth and Llew. He was a bit nervous, Gareth said, but only to be expected, first time out. He'll be all right now, surely. Just give him time, isn't it?'

'Well, there now!' exclaimed Nan, with a pleased air. 'D'you know, I think it's down to Gareth. It's since he's been home these past couple of weeks that Jim has shown some signs of getting better. Maybe with Gareth having been through the war as well, he knew how to talk to Jim. Well, I'm that pleased for them. It's been a worry, no doubt.'

They went on talking for a while, exchanging news of various branches of the family: Meg and Reini, Henry and Olwen, Esther and Martin and their family and the arrival of Sean Kerrigan. Regarding the latter Davy said, 'I suppose Sean is ready to whisk Rhiannon over to Ireland?'

'They're off the end of next week, I think,' said Owen. 'Nell says that Rhiannon is taking a trunk full of clothes over. Hoping to impress the Kerrigans, I suppose.'

'Oh, she'll do that all right,' laughed Nan. 'She's really beautiful when she's all dressed up. And when she hasn't got that old pout on her face. Fair play, she looks real happy these days, especially since Sean came back. I think she'll be all right now.'

'Seems like it,' said Davy. 'D'you know what I wish? I just wish that Mama and Dada had lived to see the boys come back.'

'You seem to have forgotten,' said Edward, coldly. 'They haven't all come back! Have you forgotten Huw already?'

Davy turned sharply to his son. 'That was uncalled for, Edward. As if we shall ever forget! I don't know what's got into you since you came home. We've had to come to terms with the loss of Huw. Its been very hard for your mother and me.' He reached out for Nan's hand. 'I don't know how we'd have gone on if it hadn't been for Roma coming and then little David, just like a small Huw. They helped, brought life into the house again. It was bad before, knowing Huw would never come back and worrying every day about you and whether you were safe.'

'I'm sorry,' Edward mumbled, his eyes downcast. 'Its just that it feels as though Roma and her son have taken Huw's place here. As if everybody's forgotten Huw. Well, I haven't forgotten him, if everybody else has.' He looked up and glanced from one face to another, his eyes bleak.

Owen saw that Nan's eyes were filled with tears and he felt angry with Edward. However his voice was quiet as he said, 'Nobody's forgotten Huw, Edward. None of us ever will. But life has to go on and if Roma and David help your Mam and Dad to go on and bring them a bit of cheer, then that's surely to the good?'

Edward shrugged but remained silent. 'Where is Roma?' Lena asked.

'She's in her room,' said Davy quietly, then he looked reproachfully at Edward. 'She obviously knows that Edward doesn't like her and so she keeps out of his way as much as possible. But it's not easy for her. This isn't such a very big house.'

Edward flushed. 'Perhaps I should clear out and leave her to it?' he said, grimly.

Nan gave a little cry and hurried from the room, Davy hurrying after her. Owen got up and closed the door, then turned an angry face to Edward.

'What the hell is wrong with you, Edward? I should have thought you'd have been down on your knees thanking God you got home safely to the best Mam and Dad a chap ever had.' He glared at the younger man and balled his fists. 'You can tell me it's no business of mine, but you're acting like a spoiled kid. After all Nan and Davy have been through, losing Huw and then finding a pregnant Roma on their doorstep, carrying Huw's child. What were they to do? Turn her away and maybe never see their grandchild again? David was all they'd got left of Huw and they were thankful for him. Then you have to come home and spoil that joy by acting like a bear with a sore head. You ought to be ashamed of yourself. I don't understand you. The war must have changed you. You never used to be like this.'

'Look, we'd better go, Owen,' said an embarrassed Lena. 'Mathew'll be waking and wanting a feed soon.' She took Kathleen's hand and moved towards the door. 'Say 'Ta-ta' to your Mam and Dad for us. We'll let ourselves out. And, Edward, think on about what Owen has said. He only said it for your own good. We all think the world of you, you know that, but you're making your Mam and Dad miserable, when they were real happy about you coming home.' As she opened the door and went out, Edward got up and clutched Owen's arm. 'Look, I'm sorry, I really am. Oh hell, I don't know what's wrong with me. I need to talk to somebody about it. I can't talk to Mam and Dad. But you might understand. Can I come and talk to you some time?' He was flushed and distressed-looking and suddenly Owen felt sorry for him. He nodded and said,

'Of course you can. Any time. Sorry I sounded off at you, but I didn't like to see your Mam upset. Believe me they were real thrilled when you came home safe and sound. They needed that after losing Huw. I suppose whatever's wrong it's something to do with Roma and her child. But I don't understand what. She's a real nice girl, very quiet and the little boy's as good as gold, Nan says. I mean, it's not as though she's taken your place in their affections. Nobody could ever do that.'

'I know,' muttered Edward. 'But she might have taken Huw's place.'

'Rubbish!' said Owen sturdily. 'Look, we must go. Come down when you want and we'll talk, ok?' Edward nodded and let them out through the front door.

As they walked down Kerry Road, Owen brooded on the scene they'd just witnessed. 'What the devil has got into Edward?' he said. 'He was always the quiet, sensible one. It's not like him at all. I don't know what can have got into him,' he repeated.

'It's Roma that's got into him,' said Lena, sagely. 'He wouldn't have been like this if she hadn't been here when he got home. Don't get me wrong. I like Roma. I wouldn't like to see him drive her away. But mark my words, she'll go if he keeps making things awkward like he's doing. And that'll break Nan and Davy's hearts.'

10

Peace and Parties

It was Saturday and most of the Rees family had been up to the Station to see Rhiannon and Sean off on the start of their journey to Ireland. When the moment came to say goodbye, Rhiannon had been tearful and Nell's tears had mingled with hers as they hugged each other close. Some of the luggage had gone on in advance, Sean masterfully taking charge of all the arrangements. When the train steamed into the station he shepherded Rhiannon into the carriage and then lowered the window so that she could say her goodbyes to the family. He leaned out and kissed Nell, promising that he would take care of her precious daughter and somehow she knew that he would. Then the engine shrilled a farewell hoot and they were off, Rhiannon leaning out and waving until the train was lost to sight under the Kerry Road bridge. Nell sighed and wiped her eyes with her handkerchief, then, clutching Elwyn's arm, followed the others out of the Station.

Llew and Mattie had come up to see the travellers off, but not Jim, who would only go out if he had Gareth with him. Gareth had already gone up to Wrexham for his demob and they hoped he would be back in another week or so to carry on the good work with Jim. He was certainly much better, eating well and coming downstairs every day now. He had been out with Gareth a few times since the Sunday walk up Shoddy's Lane, but never into the town itself. If they met anyone he would respond to their greetings quietly and Llew and Mattie were confident that he would soon be back to normal.

Edward had gone to the station with Nan and Davy and he and Rhiannon were able to say goodbye without embarrassment. Roma and little David had stayed at home. Roma said she would stay and make the dinner by the time they came back, but truth to tell, given Edward's hostility, she was fearful of intruding into the family circle too much. No-one could understand Edward's attitude to Roma, for they all liked her and knew that she and little David brought a great deal of happiness to Nan and Davy, but this was being spoiled at the moment by Edward's awkwardness.

Roma had been thinking about this a great deal over the last few days. She felt very awkward at Plasgwyn now and had finally made up her mind that she would look for lodgings in the town. She had confided in Lena, who had offered to have David in the day-time if she wanted to go out to work, which she would have to do to supplement the small amount of money she still had. She only hesitated for fear of hurting Nan and Davy who had been so kind to her, but it had to be done. Edward had made it impossible for her to stay. She sighed as she went about checking the vegetables and the home-made faggots in the oven. Why did Edward hate her? Because he did seem to. She brushed a tear off her cheek and looked down at David, playing on the rug before the fire, building a tower with his blocks and then knocking it down with a chuckle. He was so like Huw. At one time the likeness pierced her heart, but for a while now she felt the image of Huw was fading and his memory was more of a sweet dream and not the ache which had brought easy tears. The image that filled her mind now was that of Edward. The stern, remote face filled her waking moments and what pain she had was because of his obvious dislike of her. She tried to dismiss him from her mind but without success. Why was she thinking of him all the time? He gave her no reason to, avoiding her whenever he could and addressing her with cold politeness. She knew that it was upsetting Nan and Davy, and that is why she had made up her mind to leave Plasgwyn. She would manage on her own and perhaps if she no longer saw Edward she could put him out of her mind. After all, why should she be continually thinking of someone who obviously disliked her, and showed it in so many ways.

She would tell Nan and Davy of her decision on Monday while Edward was at work. She could explain to them quietly that it would be better for everyone, and assure them that she would bring David to see them regularly. She was sad, for she had loved it at Plasgwyn and Nan and Davy had made them both so welcome. She had been pleased to repay them a little by helping in the house, cooking and cleaning with a grateful heart and David had come to love his Gran and Granddad. She felt tearful again and scolded herself. At least she had had support while David was born and was small, and that had been a great blessing. She heard the front door open and set about laying the table for dinner as Nan, Davy and Edward returned, exclaiming over the cold day and hoping Sean and Rhiannon would have a good crossing that night.

Owen and Lena, with the two children, walked down from the station with Llew and Mattie. The two women hurried on in front, anxious to get home and make the dinner, while Llew and Owen strolled along discussing the afternoon's football game against Caersws.

"Town need a win today,' said Llew. 'They've been playing like a team of cripples lately. Don't know what's come over them.'

'Well,' said Owen. 'Don't forget a lot of their best players went to the war. Most of them won't play again. In fact some of 'em didn't come back at all. What's left are youngsters from the County School. There's plenty of talent, but they need training and experience, I guess.'

They were approaching the Queen's Head and Llew nodded towards the open door. 'Fancy a quick one? While they get the dinner?'

Owen grinned. 'Why not? It'll have to be a quick one, though, or I'll get shot.'

Llew whistled after the two women, who turned with raised eyebrows. 'Just popping in for a quick one. Catch you up!'

The wives shook their heads at each other resignedly. 'Don't be long, now,' shouted Lena. 'Dinner in half an hour, mind.' and Mattie nodded. 'Yes, you mind now, Llew!' before they went on their way.

The men ducked into the doorway, to be met by the noise and smoky atmosphere of the public bar. As they elbowed their way to the bar and Llew ordered two pints. Owen nudged him and pointed to the small group sitting in the corner. It consisted of Gwilym the Sticks, Owen Neuadd, little Eddie Bowen and Harry Muffin, who lived down The Lot, a small row of tiny cottages off Park Street. Llew and Owen moved nearer to the group, sure of a laugh when these characters got together. Harry Muffin was mumbling that he'd got to go 'to get dinner for 'our kid'. His companions knew that 'our kid' was his brother, now turned eighty. 'Canna he get 'is own dinner yet?' asked Owen Neuadd. Harry Muffin shook his head. ' 'E was never any good in the 'ouse,' he explained. 'Spoiled by our mam, 'e was. An' I promised 'er when 'er was dyin' that I'd look after 'im.' He drained his pint pot and wiped his mouth, but made no attempt to get up.

'But you'm younger than 'im by a bit, aren't you?' asked Gwilym.

'Ah, I'm ten years younger'n 'im,' Harry Muffin nodded assent. 'But I allus 'ad more about me, see.' He looked round the group with watery eyes. 'I wuz allus the sharp 'un.'

The group digested this boast in silence, their minds obviously having difficulty in picturing Harry Muffin as sharp in any way. Owen Neuadd coughed and looked at the ceiling, but Gwilym asked, with a kindly air, 'What you gettin' 'im for dinner, then, Harry?'

'I 'ad a sheep's 'ead from Dodd the Butcher's yesterday an' I made a good pot o' broth with it las' night. I only got to warm it up today,' said Harry, proudly. 'Plenty of veg in it, an' leatils Stand a spoon in it you could. We 'ad the brains for breakfast this morning, fried up an' spread on a bit of fried bread. Hellish good it was!' he said, with relish and pride.

Owen Neuadd grunted. 'If thee't the sharpest, thee dunna need no more brains, Muffin.'

Harry Muffin looked at him suspiciously but all he got from Neuadd was a grin that showed a row of rotten teeth. Harry rose, drawing his tattered dignity round him in the form of a long and ragged overcoat, greasy with wear and obviously meant for a much larger man. 'Thee dussen't know what thee't talkin' about.' he said to Neuadd, contemptuously and with his nose in the air tottered out of the bar.

Gwilym the Sticks shook his head. 'Poor oul' Muffin. Fair play, 'e does a tidy job of lookin' after that brother of his. 'E dunna let 'im out nowadays, not since 'e spent 'is pension on a skinful in the Cross Guns one Tuesday an' fell unconscious in a trench that the Water Board or somebody was diggin' in Park Street. Nearly covered 'im over they did, till somebody saw 'is boots stickin' out. Wonder 'e did'n snuff it! But they pulled 'im out all right. Pretty messy, 'e was, but then you wouldn't tell the difference with 'im. 'E's never been much of an advert for

Sunlight Soap, 'as 'e?'

"Ere, what d'you think,' chirped up little Eddie Bowen. 'You know them new houses the Council is building down by the Smithfield? A builder was tellin' me that they'm building 'em with the closets inside the houses!' He wrinkled his nose in disgust. 'Dirty buggers! I wouldn't like to live in 'em.'

'Oh, they been buildin' houses with the closets inside for a bit now in some places,' said Gwilym knowledgeably. 'I would'n like it meself. I'd rather 'ave 'em down the yard. Bound to smell, mun!'

'Ach y fi!' Eddie Bowen shuddered with distaste. 'What'll they think of next. 'Ave the midden in the kitchen, p'raps.'

They all contemplated the horrors of modern living, shaking their heads. Then, to change a nasty subject, Owen Neuadd turned to Gwilym with a sly air and said, 'So you still got your rifle, Gwilym, I hear?'

Gwilym looked at him suspiciously. 'Course I 'ave. When us Home Guards was disbanded we was told we could keep our uniforms and our rifles. Case we were needed again, I s'pose. Why?'

'Well, I jus' heard as you was threatenin' your missus with it the other day!' said Neuadd, looking innocent.

'Who told you that?' roared Gwilym. 'Dam' lies. What it was, 'er was goin' to lend it to 'er brother, Cyril. Said 'e wanted it to shoot pigeons! Cyril shoot pigeons? Cyril's eyes is that bad 'e couldn't see to shoot a elephant at short range, mun! Good God, could you see Cyril runnin' round loose with a rifle? 'E'd clear Broad Street in two minutes flat, an' leave a few corpses on the way!' He laughed, harshly. 'No, I took it off her, is all, an' chased the oul' fool of a woman inside. 'An' I told 'er Cyril if 'e come round lookin' to borrow me gun again I'd shoot that oul' trilby 'at off 'is 'ead. 'An I could, too!' he added with a confident air.

Whether anyone was likely to dispute this will never be known, as at that moment a large, irate woman appeared in the doorway of the bar, hands on her hips and the light of battle in her small black eyes. She fixed little Eddie Bowen with a glare and he let out a yelp of fear.

'Thought as how I'd find you 'ere, Eddie Bowen!' she cried, eyes snapping and her grey hair escaping in wisps from her screwed-up bun. 'Yer dinner's wastin'. Out!' and she gestured with a thumb towards the door then lumbered through it. Little Eddie scuttled out after her, his

291

face pale and head down.

The rest of the group looked at each other then hastily finished their pints. 'Dessay it's time we was goin' as well,' said Owen Neuadd, shakily. 'My missus said if I'm late for me dinner again 'er's goin' to give up cookin' for me.'

Gwilym sighed and rose. 'Women!' he said, shaking his head sorrowfully. 'We canna do with 'em, an' we canna do without 'em. God 'elp us!'

After dinner on the following Monday, Roma asked Nan if she could have a word with her. She had put David to bed for his afternoon nap after clearing away the dinner dishes and washing up. Davy had gone down to Pool Road to see Nell, so Nan drew Roma into the front room and sat her down in an armchair. 'What is it, love?' she asked.

Roma hardly knew how to start but she knew she had to screw up her courage and say her piece. Twisting her hands together and gazing anxiously at Nan she began to speak. 'You and Mr Rees..Dad.., have been as good as gold to me and made me and David welcome here. I don't want to leave, but I think the time has come for us to go.' As Nan frowned and gave a gasp of protest, she shook her head and went on. 'I really do think it's for the best. We can't stay here in your way for ever. I thought I would get a couple of rooms somewhere in town. I'd like to stay in Newtown. David would miss you both so much if we went anywhere else. Lena says she would have David in the daytime if I want to go out to work, and I'll have to do that soon, anyway. I've thought about it and it seems the sensible thing to do. I can bring David to see you often, or you could even have him here for an hour or two in the day sometimes. I really am thankful for all you've done for me. I don't know where I could have gone or what else I could have done. I'll never forget how kind you've been, really I won't.'

She was flushed and her hands trembled as she plucked at the little apron she wore. She had dropped her eyes to her lap, but now she raised them and looked pleadingly at Nan. There was a prolonged silence, then Nan got up and went over to look out of the window. When at last she spoke, her voice was low and unsteady.

'It's because of Edward, isn't it?' she said.

Roma hesitated before she answered. 'Look, Mam, I think it was a shock for him to come home from the war and find me and David in his home. Strangers to him, you see. He certainly wasn't expecting it, and I think as well that we remind him too much of Huw. I know he must have thought a lot about his brother. Huw talked so much about him that I got to know how close they were, even though they were quite different. Well, whatever the reason,' and she looked down uncomfortably again, 'Edward just doesn't like us here and it's making it awkward for you and his Dad, and that's not fair. So we'll go. It'll be for the best, and we'll still come and see you often. You do understand, don't you?'

Nan turned round and Roma could see the tears in her eyes. 'Oh dear, girl. I did hope it wouldn't come to this. I could see you weren't as happy here as you used to be, and I know that it's Edward's fault. What am I to do? He's my son, and only just back from the war. I know Huw's death has hit him hard. We've had time to learn how to deal with it, although we'll never get over it, but it's too fresh for Edward.'

Roma got up and put her arms round Nan. 'Oh, Mam! I can still call you Mam, and think of you as Mam can't I? But I do think this is the best way. Edward's wishes must come first. As you say, he's only just come back from the war and he needs to settle down in a bit of peace. Maybe he'll feel better about us if he doesn't see so much of us. We're always under feet here.' and she gave a shaky laugh.

Nan sighed deeply. 'You're never under my feet, love,' she said, drawing Roma into her arms. 'You've been like a daughter to me, and to Davy. And we've loved little David, our first grandchild. He's so like Huw that its like having a bit of him left to us.' She caught her breath on a sob and Roma felt her heart break. She loved this woman who had been more of a mother to her than her own mother had shown herself. But she strengthened her resolve. If she stayed all the awkwardness would go on, and then perhaps Nan and Davy would end up asking her to go anyway.

'This will upset Davy, you know,' said Nan. 'You'd settled down so well here and he loves the little one. Don't you think if you were to leave it a bit that Edward would come round and we could all live happy together? He's not a bad man at all. He was always the quiet and thoughtful one. I don't know why he's acting like he is.' She turned back to look out of the window again, while Roma went over to the fireplace and poked at the coals, staring into the flames unhappily. She didn't want to leave, but she knew she must. She felt the tears filling her eyes and hurried from the room to mount the stairs to their bedroom. David was asleep, his face flushed against the white pillow, and his dark Rees curls clustered over his forehead and round his neat little ears. Roma watched him for a while until the closed face of Edward came into her mind and the tears coursed down her face.

She went over to her own bed and threw herself face down, clutching the pillow. Her body heaved with silent sobs The face that haunted her dreams now was not Huw's and this seemed like a betrayal. Why was she thinking of Edward all the time when she knew he hated the sight of her? He'd made that clear from the time he'd come home. He'd no time for David, either, and the little boy sensed it. Well, if she went, at least he'd be happy and then Nan and Davy could be happy, too. He was their son, after all. She sat up and fumbled in her apron pocket for a handkerchief to wipe her eyes and blow her nose. Living away from here she could forget Edward. Get on with making a life for her and David. Suddenly she felt quite exhausted, and lying down again, she drew the eiderdown over her and fell asleep.

Davy meanwhile had returned from Pool Road and found Nan seated in an armchair, clutching a wet handkerchief and with red-rimmed eyes. She looked up at him miserably and he knelt beside her, frowning and anxious. 'Whatever's wrong, love? What's upset you?'

'Roma's going,' she whispered. 'Roma and little David are going.'

'Going where?' asked Davy, puzzled.

'Leaving us. Finding lodgings somewhere. It's Edward, Davy. Oh, I shall miss Roma and the little one so much. But Edward is our son!'

Davy straightened up, shaking his head, his face sad. 'I was afraid something like this would happen. Roma hasn't been happy here ever since Edward came back. I don't pretend to understand the boy. I've tried to think of a reason for him being like he is, because it's not like him, really, is it? Whether it's something to do with being reminded of Huw, I don't know. But what are we to do? This is Edward's home, after all. If anybody goes it can't be him. Oh, Lord, I don't know! I like little Roma, she's a nice quiet girl, and David is our grandson, after all. But

294

there, if she's set on going, we can't stop her. I'm just sorry, that's all. Still, you mustn't vex, love. I suppose we'll still be able to see them. Did she say when she's going?'

Nell shook her head. 'No, she'll have to find somewhere to live first. It seems such a shame, when there's room here.' She shrugged miserably. 'But what can we do?'

'I suppose I could have a talk to Edward,' Davy said doubtfully.

'Oh, no!' Nan grasped his arm. 'No, suppose he thought we wanted him to go? I couldn't bear that.' Davy agreed that that would be worse than anything.

Later, when he came home for his tea, Edward was aware that everyone seemed subdued. He ate his meal and when he and his father went into the front room while Nan and Roma washed up, he asked his father was anything wrong.

Davy stared into the fire in silence for a moment then looked straight at Edward. 'Roma is leaving us,' he said quietly. 'She's staying in Newtown, but she hopes to get somewhere to live in town. Lena has offered to have David while she goes out to work. I daresay we'll still see them pretty often. I hope so, anyway.' He gave a tired smile. 'After all, she's still young and a lovely girl. If she could meet a decent bloke I for one would be glad to see her get married.' Edward had been staring at him while he spoke and now he just said 'Why?'

'Why is she going? Well, I think you know that as well as I do.' Davy answered reasonably.

Edward got up and began pacing about the room with a hunted air. 'No!' he cried, vehemently. 'No! She can't go! Oh, Dad, what have I done? I've made her do this, haven't I? But she mustn't go!'

Davy's face wore a puzzled frown as he stared at his son. 'I don't think you'll be able to stop her, son,' he said quietly. 'Your Mam's tried to persuade her to stay, but while you've got such a dislike of her, she doesn't feel as though she can stay. She thinks she's making us all miserable.'

Edward put two hands up to his head and pressed on his temples. 'You don't understand, Dad. What shall I do? She mustn't go.' He lifted his hands away and stretched them pleadingly towards his father. 'You'll have to stop her, Dad. Please?'

Davy shook his head firmly. 'No, Edward. It has to be you. But I think it's too late. I think she's made up her mind.'

'No!' Edward looked round wildly. 'Where is she? I'll talk to her. I'll explain. God help me. If only she'll listen!' He hurried from the room, leaving his father staring into the fire with raised eyebrows, the dawning of a notion making his eyes widen.

Edward entered the kitchen but only his mother was there, putting away the clean china in a cupboard. She straightened up when he came in, and seeing the expression on his face said, 'What's the matter, love?'

'Where's Roma?' he asked abruptly. Nan looked at him in surprise. 'She's just this minute gone up to her room. Gone to check on David, I expect. Why?'

Edward didn't answer, but wheeled round and she heard him mount the stairs. She frowned and stared after him. She did hope that he wasn't going to upset Roma any more. If only the poor girl could have some peace before she left. Nan shook her head as she hung up the tea towel to dry. She wished..'Oh, what's the good of wishing.' she thought and reached for the baking trays. She'd make some scones for tea. Baking was good for calming you down and occupying your mind.

Edward hesitated at the top of the stairs and stared at the door of Roma's room. With an effort he raised his hand and knocked very quietly. He took a deep breath as he heard soft footsteps approach the door and when Roma opened it and looked at him in surprise he was struck dumb for a moment. 'Can I have a word with you, Roma?' he managed to get out at last. Roma hesitated, blushing hotly, then gasped, 'Do you want to come in?'

Edward nodded. 'I won't disturb David, will I?' he asked, tentatively, but she shook her head. 'Not if you're quiet. He's sleeping.'

He went into the room and sat on a chair with a cane seat, looking round curiously while Roma seated herself on the bed. His eyes came to rest on her and he took in the thick, corn-coloured hair, tied back with a pale blue ribbon, the steady blue eyes looking questioningly now, and the flush on the high cheek-bones. As he continued to stare the flush deepened and she dropped her gaze to her hands, clasped on her lap. He thought, not for the first time, that she was very like his mother, gentle, calm and self-contained, except now she looked up at him a little nervously. He cursed himself inwardly for giving her cause to be nervous of him and he hesitated to speak, afraid that he wouldn't be able to find the words. This increased Roma's anxiety and she wondered what on earth had prompted him to seek her out. At last she could stand the silence no longer and spoke, herself, in a low voice.

'I suppose your Mam and Dad have told you that I've made up my mind to go. I know it will be a relief to you to see the back of us. The family have been very kind to me and I'm grateful for their help but its time now for David and me to move on. I'll try to be gone as quick as I can. It'll depend how soon I can find a couple of rooms for us. I do want to stay in Newtown where I've made friends and Lena is going to have David while I go out to work. So you don't have to worry. We shan't be here much longer.'

Tendrils of golden hair had escaped the ribbon while she slept and softened the contours of her face making her look even more vulnerable than usual. Her hands clasped and unclasped on her lap as she waited for him to speak. His throat was dry and at first he couldn't get the words out. When he did his voice sounded hoarse.

'Don't go!' he said. 'Please, Roma, don't go. I don't want you to go!'

She stared at him with a bewildered air. 'But I must go!' she declared. 'I can't stay here. It's uncomfortable knowing that you don't want me here! And it's making your Mam and Dad uncomfortable. It'll be better all round if we go.' She hung her head and blinked away the tears that threatened. There was no way she was going to let him see her cry. She lifted her chin proudly instead. 'I think I understand why you dislike us being here, but at the time we had nowhere else to go and they made us welcome. Thinking back, I suppose it was a shock when you came home to find a strange woman and child living here. I'm not blaming you, how could I, it's your home. Well, as I say, I'll try to find somewhere else as quickly as possible. Could you please put up with us for a couple more weeks?' Her voice broke at that stage and she rose and went over to the dressing table, picking up and putting down her brush and comb.

'But you don't understand!' he cried. 'I don't want you to go! I couldn't bear it!' He swallowed and went on more quietly. 'I can't expect you to understand. I didn't understand it myself until today. Even now I don't really know why I behaved in such a rotten way to you and the little one. But it was either that or let my true feelings show. The truth is I was attracted to you the very moment I first saw you, but you were almost Huw's wife, almost his widow, and something in me saw it as a betrayal of him if I let myself fall in love with you.' He paused for a moment and they were both silent. 'I was denying my own feelings, but it seemed the right thing to do at the time. It was only when Dad told me you planned to go that I felt I had to make you understand. Or try to. I don't blame you if you hate the sight of me. I know now that I've ruined it. But I was so confused. I still am. But I'm pretty sure that I've fallen in love with you.' He gave a bitter little laugh. 'It's a bit late to discover that, isn't it, after driving you away with my rotten behaviour. Do you think you could forgive me? That you will stay, and at least we could be friends?' He looked at her pleadingly with his head on one side and then he reached for her hand. She let him take it and a shiver of unbearable excitement coursed through her whole body. She was afraid to look up for fear he would read all her feelings in her eyes, so she stared down at the two hands and almost imperceptibly her clasp tightened on his.

'Roma,' he whispered, tightening his grasp on her hand. He was standing by now and he drew her a little closer, reaching for her other hand. For a moment she resisted, afraid for him to read in her eyes what she had tried for so long to conceal, even from herself. Then she sighed, no longer able to hide or dissemble and as she looked up at him, her heart in her eyes, he felt a leap of joy. He put his arms around her and she came into them without hesitation, lifting her mouth for his kiss, which ran through both of them like fire.

They stood thus for an endless moment, lost to the world, until a small sound from David caused them to draw away from each other reluctantly, flushed and laughing shakily. Roma went over to the bed, where David was sitting up, looking doubtfully at Edward. She took him up in her arms and smiled across at Edward, who said 'Hello, David,' very softly, adding 'Hello, Roma!' with a happy grin. Roma kissed her son's cheek and murmured, 'Say hello, Edward?' David stared at Edward but seeing no threat in the smiling face, ducked his head shyly and whispered, ' 'Ello, Edard'.

'Look, we have to talk,' said Edward, gently. 'What about letting Mam take care of David for an hour while we go for a walk? There's so much to say, so much to plan, isn't there? Shall we do that?'

Roma nodded assent and Edward let her take the child downstairs to join Nan in the kitchen and to explain that they were going for a little walk to talk things over. Nan looked a little bewildered, but Roma appeared so happy that she could only speculate and hope, and when she went in to Davy with the news she found that he too was speculating and along the same lines that she was.

And so Edward and Roma, wrapped up in warm clothes against the chill November air, which, truth to tell, they hardly noticed, walked hand in hand up Kerry Road. The trees dripped with cold November mist as they walked below them, talking in low tones and stopping from time to time to time to kiss and to gaze ardently at each other. Edward thought his heart would burst with happiness as he held her in his arms and saw an eagerness in her that matched his own.

'Will you marry me?' he whispered, as they leaned against the gate into Hamer's field, their lips hardly parted from the last kiss. Roma nodded and answered yes with lips and eyes. 'When? Soon?' Edward pressed, eagerly and Roma answered 'As soon as you like!' equally eagerly and with no false modesty.

After another long kiss Edward looked down at her anxiously. 'You're cold, aren't you? Let's go back and tell Mam and Dad that we're engaged! I think they'll be real pleased. We can make our plans in the warm, by the fire, and Mam and Dad can advise on how soon we can marry. There's so much to talk about...where we're going to live and so on. Oh, Roma, I'm so happy!'

'I can't believe it,' Roma murmured. 'Only this morning I was so miserable. And now, well, I'm the happiest girl in the world. I love you, Edward.'

The first Christmas since the end of the war was held as usual at Bay House. All the Rees family were there and Davy looked round the room as they all gathered thinking that apart from the loss of Huw, which was still like a wound in his heart, and the fact that Rhiannon was settled in Ireland now, the family had emerged fairly well from the war. Jim was now whole again, thanks to Gareth and his patience and had taken his place in the group with his old confidence. Gareth himself was back working for Norman Oliver and not only making a very good carpenter, but was learning woodcraft and carving from the old man. This, he insisted, must not be divulged outside the family, in case the Miss Olivers found out! Gareth had been the only member of the family who had not rejoiced at the news that Edward and Roma were to be married, but his disappointment did not last long, since he had his eye on a pretty little clerk at Pryce Jones's who seemed to welcome his tentative and shy attentions.

As for Edward and Roma, after the first shock, the news was welcomed by Nan and Davy and by the rest of the family, who saw it as a happy ending for Roma in particular. Everyone liked Roma and was glad that she had been 'kept in the family', so to speak! Nan and Davy doted on little David and as Mrs Meredith from Merton Terrace on Kerry Road had offered Edward one of the houses in the terrace when she heard the news of the engagement, they would be living quite near, in fact their 'top garden' would be only separated by a wall from Plasgwyn. They were obviously deliriously happy and could hardly wait for the wedding which was scheduled for the first Saturday in January. As Edward said, ' Why wait, when we know our own minds and just want to settle down?'

Davy spotted Meg and Reini at the far end of the long room and thought again what a blessing Reini had been to Meg. He had given her her confidence back and she no longer seemed to be aware of the scar on the side of her face. Although there was ever more silver in the gold of her hair her face was rounded and she retained her trim waist and her curves. From time to time she and Reini looked at each other with eyes still full of love. They had both been through hard times, but now, in the autumn of their days, they were content. They had recently become grandparents, and Olwen sat in a corner, feeding the tiny baby while Henry looked on proudly. 'Dear Lord,' thought Davy with a chuckle, 'The Rees's are spreading like the tribes of Israel!'

Nell, the oldest, was grey-haired now. She sat beside Elwyn, matronly in a burgundy-coloured dress with a white lace collar. Davy remembered how often those long, slim fingers had pinched him if he stepped out of line, and winced at the memory! Elwyn's dark hair had white wings over the temple and in his navy suit Davy thought he still looked like a policeman, straight and stern.

Llew and Mattie were standing by the window, with a glass of sherry each. Llew looked as though he would have been happier with a beer, but he was chuckling at something Jim had been saying and Davy thought that it must be a great relief to Mattie and him that Jim was quite recovered and was now working as a gardener for the Council, refusing to take an indoor job again as he could no longer bear to be 'locked up' as he put it. Llew didn't seem to alter very much. He still propounded his strong socialist views and saw his dream come true when Labour was returned with an overwhelming majority in the July election under the leadership of Clement Attlee. The nation had massive debts after the six-year war and they were warned that they would have to tighten their belts and accept strict rationing for some time to come. But the war was over, and that was something to thank God for.

Owen and Lena and their two children were sitting near the door, talking to Esther. They looked to be a happy family, although Davy knew that Lena's tongue could be quite sharp. He put it down to the fact that she had, in a way, been second-best with Owen, whose first love was the fragile little Mary Ann whose death had seemed a tragedy to Owen at the time. However he had turned to Lena and they had a very good marriage, for he understood Lena's feeling of insecurity, although he had never given her any cause for it since Mary Ann's death and the end of his boyhood dream. They had two lovely children now, Kathleen Eluned and Matthew William, grandchildren for Llew. Sometimes it was hard to remember that Owen was Llew's son by his first marriage and Esther his daughter, since they had both been brought up at 46 Pool Road by Mama with the help of Meg.

His thoughts turned to Mama and Dada then, the rocks which he always thought the family was built on. He thought of Mama's shrewdness and wisdom, the high standards he realised now she had set for her children and the room she had in her heart for Llew's motherless two, and eventually for all her grandchildren and great-grandchildren. He sighed deeply, for he still missed her so much. No.46 Pool Road wasn't the same without her, nor without Dada, rebellious sometimes under her strict rule, but nevertheless more aware than anybody of her goodness and strength and the great kindness behind the sharp tongue.

They had both been great characters, and when they died it seemed the end of an era.

Still, the family were together, ties close as ever, a fact that gave them all security. He watched Esther, commandeering some of the women to help her with the serving of the dinner which she and Edie Davies had spent the morning preparing, and thought, not for the first time, what a wonderful wife and mother she had turned out to be. She had been what Mama had called 'a little Miss Consequence' when she was young, convinced that she was going to marry a rich man and be a 'lady'. Well, he supposed, she had done just that in the end. Martin wasn't rich, but they were comfortably off. Bay House belonged to him and as his parents were now dead, he had inherited a tidy sum from them, plus a good lawyer's office. He still adored Esther, as he had from boyhood, and his love was returned. He tolerated her wish for a large family, but secretly hoped that now they had four of their own, plus the two evacuees that they had formally adopted, she would be satisfied. There was no guarantee of it, though!

Finally Davy turned and smiled at his beloved Nan, who smiled lovingly back at him. He thought with pity of his first wife, the beautiful and wild Elinor, the Rector's daughter. How he had loved her and how she had made him suffer! Her brother Geraint, once his best friend, had rejected him after her death, blaming Davy for the child that killed her, and Davy never told him that it wasn't his child. He had promised Elinor that on her deathbed. He never saw Geraint again from the day of Elinor's funeral. He sighed for that restless and unhappy girl. As for Nan, he had turned to her eventually and found peace, love and tranquillity with her. He reached out and squeezed her hand.

Martin came in with his six children, who had been playing out in the garden under the bare apple tree. At last Esther called to them all to take their places round the big table, with all its leaves pulled out, and the children to the smaller table in the corner. Crackers were pulled and paper hats donned, and they all tucked in to their goose and capon dinners with a will. After the plum pudding was brought in, reeking of brandy, and alight with little blue flames, it was portioned out and covered with white sauce, and after that Llew, as the oldest Rees there, called for a toast. They all lifted their glasses and as Llew looked around and said, quite softly, 'Absent friends!' they thought first of Huw and replied in a murmur, 'Absent friends!' Edward held Roma's hand and they smiled sadly at each other and at Nan and Davy.

After that, they all thought of Mama and Dada and again raised their glasses to 'Absent friends'. Others who had passed on were thought of and toasted, and Rhiannon was remembered with smiles and good wishes.

Thus was the Rees family gathered together on that special Christmas of 1945. The war mecifully over; new generations coming and growing up; older generations inspiring love and the warmest of memories; the one young tragic wartime loss, Huw, so painfully mourned, but leaving a much-loved promise of renewal already made; and all the survivors having found the age-old strength in their family ties, and their ties to the people of their beautiful and eccentric little town of Newtown, new for centuries past, their home nestling among the hills.

The End